Burying the
James Thomas

Copyright © 2024 James Thomas Byrnes

All rights reserved. No part of this book may be reproduced or transmitted in any form or by any means, electronic or mechanical, including photocopying, recording or by any information storage and retrieval system without permission in writing from the publisher.

Stoney Creek Press—Shelby Twp., MI
Paperback ISBN: 979-8-9907602-3-3
Hardcover ISBN: 979-8-9907602-4-0
eBook ISBN: 979-8-9907602-2-6
Title: *Burying the Shadow*
Author: James Thomas Byrnes
Digital distribution | 2024
Paperback | 2024

This is a work of fiction. The characters, names, incidents, places, and dialogue are products of the author's imagination, and are not to be construed as real.

Published in the United States by New Book Authors Publishing

Acknowledgements

To my wife, my foremost pillar of support. Thank you for being part of each novel adventure. You truly keep me grounded and your consistent encouragement does not go unnoticed.

To my developmental editor, Cheryl Bogner. Your input and insights have truly elevated every page of this novel. I am fortunate not only to share in your literary wisdom but also in your friendship.

To my Beta reading team – Jackie Ferranti, Tracy Bonkowski, Janie Filzek, Laura Heid, Renee Jayroe, Diane King, Amy Lomasney, Donna Spicuzzi, and Jody Stafford. Your invaluable feedback has greatly enriched the pages of this book. Thank you for your dedication and support throughout this journey.

Before the Bloodshed

Slovak watched as Tatyana dragged a scalpel across the soft tissue and muscle, forming a pocket within. She had estimated the weight and knew it would take 3mg/L of cyanide to be lethal.

With a teaspoon she scooped from a mound, of what looked like baby powder and packed the cavity. She reached for the needle and suture, then stitched together the edges of the incision. The raw meat was then wrapped in cellophane and placed in the backpack along with the Molotov cocktails.

1:00 a.m.
Farris Family Farm

Slovak watched from afar the lights of the master bedroom turn off. His stare then shifted to Tatyana. She immediately knelt to one knee and removed the tainted meat from the backpack. They had been feeding the dog for the last week and he had really-tempered his barking since their first encounter. She tapped the gate with the barrel of her gun and just like Pavlov's dog, he came running. Fifteen minutes later it was safe for them to proceed.

Slovak stood holding a flashlight as Tatyana manipulated what looked like dental tools into the lock of the front door. She was a master at entry but not all entries went smoothly. They both stood like statues while the rickety door of the farmhouse creaked loudly when opened.

The woman leaned up in bed and listened. Her husband sleeping next to her purred quietly as she strained to hear sounds coming from downstairs.

Surely no one could be in the house, she thought, not with the dog prowling the grounds. Her forehead burrowed into thin lines as she poked her husband in the side of his ribs.

"Hey," she whispered.

"Huh," the man grunted before opening his eyes.

"I think there's someone in the house downstairs!"

The man sat up and lifted the blanket from his waist as he dropped his feet to the floor. His hair was a disheveled mess as he scratched the sides of his temples trying to wake up. He turned to his wife.

"What did you hear?" he asked, a sedated look on his face.

"Not really sure. I thought I heard the door open."

"I don't hear the dog," he said before he stepped to the top of the stairs and listened. The man stood there, head hanging, hands gripping the banister. Hearing nothing, he returned to bed and flopped down.

"Go back to bed. There's nobody down there. If someone was here, the dog would have gone nuts, and we would have heard him."

The woman lay back down and brought the blanket to her chin. She lay wide eyed until eventually falling back to sleep.

Chapter 1

LIVINGSTON COUNTY, MICHIGAN

AUGUST 3

A dark navy van with Lansing Police stenciled on the side idled on the paved driveway about 20 yards from the isolated farmhouse. Inside the kitchen, CSI agents walked carefully around the chalked outlines on the tiled floor. They scraped residue from the walls and counters, putting it in vials and plastic bags to be sent to the state lab for analysis. The scent of charred wood filled the air.

"Hey… Captain?" said Gavin upon entering the kitchen.

Captain Daniels looked up from his phone. "Glad you could finally make the party."

"Sorry, Captain, it's been a long night."

"Tell me about it. I've been here for the past three hours."

Gavin noted the irritation in his Captain's tone. He was still a rookie and showing up late to a crime scene was not a way to impress.

"Whose house is this?" he asked.

"Eugene Farris and his wife Beatrice."

"Farris?!!" Gavin said, startled by the name.

"Yeah. You know 'em?"

"They were headline news a couple years ago. Their nineteen-year-old daughter committed suicide. She was involved in some kind of sex video with some frat boys. It went viral. She claimed she was drugged and made to do it. Story goes that she couldn't handle it and offed herself."

"Isn't she the one who had a nut job older brother that castrated those frat boys?"

"That's the family. Except the older brother didn't chop off their stones. He tormented them to the point to where they thought they were going to be killed and then let 'em go. He was an Army vet and got off on an insanity plea. Last I heard, he was sent to a looney farm."

The Captain stared at the chalked outlines of the bodies. Wrinkles formed on his forehead before he uttered, "For the life of me, I can't figure out why someone would go to this extreme and want this old couple dead. It looks like they almost made it out. As far as we can tell, the fire started in the living room, and they were asleep upstairs. The front door was probably engulfed in flames and the only other door was through the kitchen. The smoke must have gotten the better of 'em before they could get out."

Chapter 2

A dampness filled the air inside the tent like it always did in the temperate rainforest. David heard the rip of the zipper and looked up from what he was reading. Sargent Tim, wearing a head net, quickly re-zipped the tent, then reached for the bug repellent sitting on a makeshift stool.

The black flies were thick, a constant nuisance that engulfed them anywhere they went except when in open water. Tim shook the can and sprayed himself. He was getting tired of this morning ritual.

The tent was well-hidden, covered by cut saplings making it invisible to any search planes above. Logs angled side by side and slanted to the ground made a lean-to dog kennel. Camouflage burlap wrapped the structure keeping the dogs in at night. It had taken Sargent Tim weeks to set up this camp. If someone wanted to get lost and never be found, this part of British Columbia was the place to be.

The US and Canadian authorities were looking for him, but as of yet, had no luck.

Tim had purchased a satellite phone to communicate with his CIA contact. He knew someone could be listening. In his original letter to the agency, he informed them of the date and time when he would make each call. The communication entailed a day of hiking with the dogs. At least five miles in and then the walk back out. A smile always filled Tim's face as he looked to the sky, hearing the search plane flying to the last location where he had made his call.

"Morning, Sarge," David said as Tim walked to the tripod cooking grill set up over an open fire pit. He poured a cup of burnt coffee then went and sat next to David.

"Spirit Bears again, I see," Tim said, noticing ripped pages from a science magazine."

"Check this out, Sarge," David said, as he handed him a page.

"I've seen polar bears before. Plenty of 'em."

"That's just it, Sarge. These bears aren't polar bears. You're looking at a black bear."

3

"An albino?"

"No. Spirit Bears have pigment in their skin and eyes. A single mutant gene causes them to be white."

"So that's a black bear that looks like a white bear?"

"Yes. They're only found here in the Great Bear Rainforest. They estimate there are only four hundred. The natives believe they're sacred."

"Because...," Tim said, his voice trailing off.

"Because in one of the native legends, Raven, the Creator, asked the Spirit Bear to be the Keeper of Dreams. That's his job."

"Dreams!" The Sarge said, then pulled a picture out of his front pocket of a woman surrounded by a group of children. This is all I've been dreaming about ever since I found out she was alive. I can't think of anything else. I gotta get her out."

"What about the aid organization she worked for? Don't they have people to help?"

"You mean CARE?"

"Yeah."

"Not really. They're set up for humanitarian stuff, not a rescue. Remember when that militia group attacked the orphanage, and I went back and found everyone dead?"

"I do, Sarge. I remember how pissed you were. Exactly what you said would happen, did."

"They burned the place down. I just thought Isla was in one of those buildings. Didn't find out she was alive until the militia asked for the ransom."

"Why not send in the military? Hell, we did at least two of those operations."

"She's not American."

"That's right. What about Australia?"

"The Aussies won't tell me a damn thing."

David saw the anguish on Tim's face. He reached over and put his hand on his shoulder. "You're going to get her back, Sarge."

Tim stood and dumped the rest of his coffee to the ground. He then heaved the tin cup towards the tent. "With all I sacrificed for this country. Everything we went through in Iraq. This whole thing about the government not negotiating with terrorists is bullshit. We do it all the time."

Calm returned to Tim's face as he placed the picture back in his shirt pocket and sat back down.

"I'm sorry Farris for getting you into this. Do you ever regret stealing that mithridate for me?"

"Hell, no! You knew the bad guys wanted it to make a dirty bomb and that the CIA would do anything not to let that happen. The mithridate is your bargaining chip. Make the CIA get your girl out of Iraq and then you can give it to them. I'm more concerned about Slovak and what his thugs might do."

David shook his head as he raked his hand through his shaggy hair, remembering what he and Carly went through trying to recover the mithridate her father had hidden.

"Do you find out tomorrow if they made the trade?" David asked.

Tim nodded. "I do. Two hundred and fifty grand in cash for Isla. Once she's out of Iraq and in Australian hands, I'll let the CIA know where I stashed it."

"Why do they trust you? I mean once she's out of Iraq and safe, you could disappear forever."

"At this point, they really don't have much of a choice. The CIA must figure I'm doing this for Isla. They gotta know I want to be with her. I just hope they won't prosecute me once they get it back."

"You mean 'us,'" David said with a smile. "I hope they don't want to prosecute *us,* I'm the one who stole it."

Chapter 3

Four years earlier

Discharged Army Corporal David Farris sat next to his father in the F-350 pickup truck. His hair was short cropped and the chiseled chin he inherited from his father accented his sharp cheekbones. His well-developed pecs and arms could still be seen even though he wore a long-sleeved camouflage sweater. David planned on being a lifer. That all changed with a letter from his sister.

"Dad, has Mom seen anyone since she found Penny?" David asked, as his father drove to the cemetery in Heartland.

"Yeah, she's seen plenty of people.... family, friends. They all came to pay their respects."

"No, I don't mean family. I mean has she seen a doctor or therapist…someone like that?"

"We're not much for that, son. We don't like to air our dirty laundry."

"Dirty laundry! Is that what you think Penny was? Dirty laundry?"

David saw tears trickle down his father's face. He had never seen his dad cry. Ever. Seeing the hurt and pain, David reached over and gently rubbed his father's shoulder.

"Dad, I'm sorry. I didn't mean that. I know how hard this is for you and Mom."

"Your Mom blames herself," his dad replied. "It was her medication Penny used to take her life."

"It's not Mom's fault. It's the fault of those fucking frat boys that I can't get out of my head," David said, striking his fist on the truck's dashboard. "There's got to be someone Mom can talk to."

"I agree she needs to talk to someone. I'll speak with her," he said as he pulled into the parking spot and placed the truck in park. Turning to his son, he said, "I got the biggest grave blanket I could find. Want to keep Baby Girl as warm as we can out here."

Standing by her grave, the dirt still settling, David struggled with what Penny left in her suicide note.

Dear David,

I need you to forgive me for what I'm about to put you, Mom, and Dad through. It is just too hard. Too much whispering, sneering, and taunts. I couldn't take it anymore. Even my best friends deserted me. I did not do those things willingly. I feel so alone, and just want the pain to end. It's too late to call home to try and stop me. I'm already gone. I timed my passing to coincide with you receiving this letter. You take care of yourself, and I will see you on the other side.

Love, Penny

Weeks of meticulous planning had led him to a singular purpose…....revenge. He knew the boys attended Eastern Michigan University. He had borrowed his father's truck several times for the hour trip to campus. Fifty miles away, on the outskirts of EMU, sat the fraternity house.

It was easy to find. Just a few questions to some college kids hanging around the student union quickly gave him the answer. Since there was so much publicity about the case, anyone he talked to knew who they were and the fraternity they belonged to.

Built in the 1850's, the fraternity house was a beautifully restored mansion. Red brick accented by white shutters and tall chimneys screamed of an affluent and privileged lifestyle. Bikes left by their last riders were scattered on the porch and front lawn, covered by a dusting of snow.

David watched young fraternity brothers go in and out of the house, sporting backpacks when they hurried down the steps. He watched, sometimes from the pickup or as a passerby who took a seat on a bench looking over a book. He even mingled among the hordes of students filling the sidewalks—all on their way to class.

Burned in his brain were pictures taken of the two boys from newspapers leaving the courthouse with smirks on their faces.

VERDICT...NOT GUILTY! WILLING PARTICIPANTS IN A SEX VIDEO!

He soon discovered that they often took a short cut to class down a path through a wooded lot. Midterms were the coming week before spring break. David knew most college kids would be heading somewhere warm to bake in the sun and party. The thought of these two *frat punks* slipping a roofie to another unsuspecting girl sickened him. He had made his mind up. He would do it tomorrow.

Before leaving for the campus the following day, David opened the barn door. The smell of baled hay hung heavily in the air. A tractor tire dangled from a rafter, hung years before by his father. Memories of happy times flooded his mind; then he stopped and thought about Penny.

I miss you, Baby Girl. You were so young.

From the corner of the barn, he grabbed a spade and an old bundled blue tarp sitting on a shelf. He reached into his camouflage field jacket and removed his Glock, pulling back the slide making sure a round was chambered. He knelt on one knee and tightened the ankle holster which secured his knife.

Let's get this done, he said to himself, as he did so many times in Iraq.

****

The Frat boys walked down the wood-lined foot path laughing and shoving each other onto the snowy shoulder. Unnoticed, David stepped from behind a row of pines and blocked their path, his pistol raised and pointed at them.

"Hand me your cell phones and don't say a fucking word," David said, keeping the gun level with their heads.

Visibly shaken, the boys fumbled in their pockets and handed over their phones.

A boy with long greasy hair breathed out, "Is it money you want? I have money...take my wallet."

"Keep your fucking wallet. I don't want your money," David spoke, his voice hard and fierce.

"See those footprints heading into the woods? Follow them and keep following them till I tell you to stop, or I'll blow your head off!"

With obvious anxiety, the two looked fixedly at the set of ankle-deep tracks leading away from the path. Reluctantly, they followed the tracks to a very secluded clearing surrounded by thickets of pines and woody shrubs. David, following closely behind, liberally prodded them with the end of his pistol if they slowed down.

A blue plastic tarp was spread out where the tracks ended. The contrast between the blue sheet and white snow created an unearthly, unnatural sight. Laying on the plastic tarp was a dozen or more rubber bands.

"Both of you…Get down on your hands and knees!" David ordered.

The teenagers knelt unmoving on the tarp while David stood off to the side, his eyes appearing unfocused. Seemingly lost in thought, his gaze wandered over the tops of the trees, scanning the branches above.

"Don't move. Don't think you can escape," he threatened. "I see everything, from your fingers twitching to the snot running out of your nose. Both of you-- a fuckin' waste of good air!

"If you're thinking of running, think again. See that squirrel?" he said, pointing with his gun at a branch above their heads. The boys lifted their heads and looked at the branch.

Without notice, David shot, piercing the quiet of the tranquil woods. The bullet severed the branch sending both the squirrel and limb to the ground. The frantic squirrel never lost stride as it hit the snow running, then scurried up another tree. Stunned and in utter shock, both boys looked at David.

"Now, don't think I missed. My bullet went *exactly* where I wanted it to. He then aimed his gun once more, this time taking off the tip of a scrub pine tree. The top of the tree, separated from its body, tumbled to the ground.

"It's not in my nature to kill things that don't deserve some killing. But you guys. You guys are different than that ol'squirrel and that old tree. Those things have a purpose. You boys don't."

David studied the boys kneeling on the tarp, he spat on the snow.

"You repulse me. You shithead bastards! What did you do when you saw my sister crying? Did you feel anything? Any sadness? Any remorse? Any shame? Anything a person who was human might feel?"

David saw the confusion on their faces.

"Penny!" he shouted. "My little sister's name was Penny. Penny Farris."

Panic and dread surged through them as they realized simultaneously that this crazed man was Penny's brother.

"Both of you, stand up! You, Greasy Hair. What's your name?"

The boys stood. Traumatized. Unable to speak.

David asked again. "What's your fucking name, Asshole?"

"Johnny."

"Johnny, what?"

"Peckert" he answered hoarsely.

"Peckert? Pecker? I'll call you Pecker. You're a dick. Suits you fine. Get that shovel and start digging your new home." He pointed with his chin, still holding the revolver. "There, on the other side of that stump.

"Not sure how deep you boys will be able to dig your graves, with this frozen ground and all, but we'll give it a shot," David said. "Sorry, I only have one shovel."

Warily, Peckert walked to the shovel leaning up against a tree and with trembling hands, he grabbed it. David watched as he clumsily held the handle of the shovel and attempted to push the head into the frozen ground.

After a few attempts to dig up the frozen earth, David suddenly said, "Fuck it. Forget it. I can't wait till the thaw for you to be buried. Get over there next to your Bitch. It's time for us to have some fun."

David shouted to them, "Both of you. Take off your boots and pants," he said. "Off with the boxers, too.

David noticed the shorter of the two wearing a Little Caesar tee shirt.

"What's your name?" he asked, taking a step toward him.

"Chaz," he answered.

"Chaz, Chaz...Alcatraz, you half ass piece of shit. Screw it. I'll just call you Pizza Boy, now get down on your knees. Actually, both of you...Get on your hands and knees!"

Keeping the boys at gunpoint, he pulled one of their cell phones from his pocket and tossed it on the tarp. "Whose phone is this?"

"Mine," Chaz answered.

"Come here. Unlock it. If you try to dial 911, you'll be dead before your sorry ass hits the ground!"

Shaking, Chaz stood, stepped forward, and retrieved his phone. He placed his thumb on the fingerprint scanner, then showed David the screen was unlocked.

"Let's try Facebook. You two got a lot of friends, I bet. Wouldn't want them to miss out on this little party. Start Live streaming.

"Hand me your phone," David ordered, "and get back behind your boyfriend. We're going to make a little video just like you two pieces of shit did with my sister."

Chaz did as he was told and stood behind his friend.

"Now, Pizza Boy, kneel behind your greasy-haired girlfriend and doggie style him," David ordered. "Grab that bitch by the hips and start dry humping him. You better make it look real!"

With a backdrop of white and gray, accented by the blue tarp, the two acted out the sodomy. David streamed the entire torment live.

"How does it feel being made to do something you have no control over? You two pukes gutted the spirit of a young girl. I wanted you to experience that before I send you to your graves."

When David felt enough time had gone by to completely humiliate the boys, he stopped live streaming and tossed the phone in the snow.

"Stand up, Fuckers. The fun ain't over."

The boys got up and Peckert crossed his hands over his genitals, waiting for David to speak.

"I was raised on a farm," David explained. "What we did with bulls that were mean or had fucked up genes is castrate them. You know what that means, don't you College Boys? We cut their nuts off."

David slowly lifted his pant leg, revealing his Ka-bar knife strapped in his ankle holster.

"Couldn't let that bull pass those kinds of genes to its offspring. As I see it, you boys have some fucked up genes of your own for what you did to my sister. I'm going to do society a favor by making sure you don't pass those fucked up genes on to anybody.

"How I see it, you have three choices. One, I shoot you here and now. Two, you cut your balls off with my knife, or three, you take those rubber bands and wrap them around your stones until they start to turn blue. Once you band them, I'll let you go. Your choice. What will it be, fellows?"

With shaking hands, the boys moved slowly and made their choice. They each grabbed a rubber band, put it around their testicles, and double twisted it. David observed the strain in the boys' necks as they endured the pain that started in their groin and radiated up their spine.

"Those bands look a bit loose. One more twist around your ball sack, Gentlemen. Don't look like they're turning blue yet."

"Please! I can't…I'm sorry," Peckert cried.

The woods were silent except for the whimpering of the boys. David slumped and he lowered his gun. He didn't feel better. Revenge wasn't as sweet as he thought it would be.

Wiping his eyes, he lifted his head and hollered, "Grab your clothes and get the fuck out of here."

Chapter 4

Carly surveyed the gravestones of the German dead. She knew she shouldn't be there. Her name and past life had been scrubbed by the CIA. She was given the name of Ava Winters and warned by them to blend in. Leave the past behind. It will get you outed.

She followed the headstones and German names like a road map until she reached two unmarked head stones in the midst of hundreds of others. In all of Germany, she was one of only a few that knew the secret. The secret of who rested in those graves.

This was not Carly's first time at the cemetery. She struggled to keep Bo and her mother's wishes to stay safe and let it go. They were able to stay away; she couldn't. Carly bent her head saying a silent prayer.

The sputter and popping of a mini excavator motoring down the road caught her attention. A grave digger drove his machine to the storage shed near the back entrance of the cemetery. A smell of burned oil drifted towards her and she breathed it in, enjoying the smell, a smell she had always liked since she was very young. A smell that brought back fond memories of her grandfather's service station.

The sun had gone down behind the trees and soon, shadows would be swallowed by the night. Carly glanced at her watch. Twenty minutes to make it to the bakery. She hightailed it down the row between the headstones to reach her car which she had parked on the shoulder of the incoming road.

****

The Alte Steinhaus bakery was well known in Dusseldorf. Not only for its wonderful pastries, but also for its legendary past. It was long rumored the bakery was a type of underground railroad that smuggled Jews out of the country during the Nazi regime.

The original brick ovens were still used by the bakers that worked there. Orange-fired bricks separated by quarter inch mortar lines were stacked floor to ceiling. Three large iron oven doors were embedded separately into three of the walls. The fourth wall was lined with four heavy oak counters, each having an industrial mixer mounted to it.

Carly rushed through the brownstone doors of the bakery and looked at the clock. She had made it with a couple minutes to spare. Johann, the pastry chef, noticed the dirt on her knees and asked, "Why your knees dirty?"

Carly put her white apron on and tied the long sashes behind her.

"Had to change a flat. Probably need a new tire," she said.

"You be careful by yourself at night," Chef said. "Young woman should not be out alone at night."

"It's *women*, Chef. The plural of woman is women. You'll need to know that for your test next week."

Carly walked along a long wooden counter and removed a recipe pinned to a corkboard. She stood there silently reading until a smile filled her face, and she turned to Johann.

"Your English translation is coming along. I can read all the ingredients. What are *Nussschneckens*?"

"It's what you Americans call *cinnamon buns*."

Carly went to the side pantry and retrieved flour, sugar, and salt. Following the recipe, she dumped it together in the large bowl of the mixer. She then warmed the milk and butter together before whisking in the yeast. She poured the yeast mixture onto the flour and turned on the mixer to make the dough.

Chef watched Carly make the dough. Then he hung up his apron and traded it for his coat.

"I didn't see any cinnamon. Please don't tell me it's in the dry storage."

"It is. What...? You afraid to go down there?" Johann asked.

"No, it's fine. I don't mind," she said, hiding from him how much she dreaded going to the cellar.

"Okay. I be on my way." Chef lifted his car keys from a hook screwed into the wall.

"No one here tonight. You are on your own. I will make sure door is locked," he said before slipping on his coat and walking down the squeaky floorboard hall. Carly waited until she heard the rattle of the door close and the deadbolt lock before removing a large baking sheet from a rack of ten.

The dry storage was in the belly of *das biest*. That was the nickname given to the bakery by the afternoon shift. Carly felt for the switch at the top of the steps and turned on the one bare light which dimly lit the basement stairs. She held the wooden banister and made her way down.

Even though the cellar was clean and dry, there was still a smell of mold. Carly felt like the spirits of the Jews hidden there long ago had melded into the bricks and that unsettled her whenever she was down there.

Get the cinnamon and get the hell out.

Standing at the bottom of the steps surveying the various spices, she found cinnamon and headed up. Suddenly, a flicker of movement caught her eye-a fleeting shadow that darted across the bakery floor, only to come to an abrupt halt. Her breath hitched, and her heart pounded. She stood frozen, her fingers tightly gripping the bag of cinnamon. The weight of the spices slipped from her grasp, hitting the floor with a muffled thud.

Crouching down and removing a 22-caliber pistol from her ankle holster, Carly continued. Stealthily she ascended the stairs one step at a time until she reached the top. The shadow was still there, waiting, watching, breathing. Carly took a controlled breath and bolted through the door, ready to fire.

Porsche took a quick step to the side and threw her body against a wall.

"It's me!" Porsche blurted. "Jesus!! Put the gun down!"

Carly slowly lowed the gun, her body began to relax. "You scared the hell out of me. How'd you get in here?"

"I jimmied the door. I waited until your boss left and I texted you. I got worried when you never texted back. I snuck in quietly, wasn't sure if you needed help."

Carly looked at her phone and noticed a text from Porsche. "I get no signal when I'm in that cellar."

"You better put that gun away," Porsche said. "You're not in the States…you can't carry that in Germany."

"I'll make sure I say that to Slovak when he comes to pay me a visit!"

Carly lowered to one knee and replaced her gun into her ankle holster.

"I left the cinnamon on the floor. Be right back."

Carly disappeared through the open door to the cellar and reappeared again clutching a large bag of cinnamon.

"I've really built up my muscles working here," Carly said, laying the cinnamon onto the counter beside the mixer.

"You seem a little jumpy. You all right?" Porsche asked.

"I just came from the cemetery. It always eats away at me afterwards."

"You gotta stay away from there. I tell you a million times. It's too dangerous for you to go there!"

"I know, I know," Carly said with a hint of irritation. "Just keep in mind that you have Ahmed's ashes, and you can visit him or touch him anytime. I wasn't given that luxury."

"Look. I still hurt. Even though I have his ashes, I still hurt. I *know* how it feels to lose someone you love. I know *why* you go to those graves, putting yourself in danger to do it. I get it."

Porsche settled on one of the stools in the kitchen.

"Carly, you have been my constant friend, my confidant, and even a kind of savior from our time in the States till now. If you weren't here, I might not be here either!"

What Porsche said jolted Carly.

"Porsche," she said. "You don't mean…"

"Yes," said Porsche. "I caught myself driving down the roadway a few weeks ago… thinking about cranking the wheel sharply to the left, flooring it, and crashing into the river. I thought about it more than once."

Carly stared hard at Porsche.

"Girlfriend, don't you dare leave this planet and leave me behind!" she erupted. "You know what a trainwreck I would be without you here!!!"

"Yeah," said Porsche, flashing a quick smile. "That's why I didn't do it!"

"Besides, we have something new to take care of. Did you get it?" asked Carly.

Porsche handed Carly a manila envelope.

"You know how many Ava Winters there are in Germany? I see why the CIA picked that name. There were hundreds."

"It must be one of the most popular names here. It took me a long time to get used to it, too. People would talk to me and say "Ava" and I would just stand there before it clicked that *I* was *Ava*."

Carly wiped her hands on her apron then took hold of the envelope, pinched the brass clasp together and looked inside.

Her-gaze went from the envelope to Porsche.

"I'll tell him tonight. That is, if he is straight enough to even understand what I tell him."

Porsche searched Carly's face. "What's going on? What do you mean by straight?"

Carly went to the mixer and added the cinnamon. "Bo has changed. He drinks almost every night, and he hates that I am working at this bakery. We have arguments over it."

Carly shut off the mixer and dumped the dough on the floured counter. She started to knead it. "Selling my sketches wasn't bringing in as much money as I hoped for, and the market was only open on the weekends. I was miserable being at home, and then I found this job."

Carly put the dough in a greased bowl and covered it up.

"I have to let this dough rise twice. Would you ever have believed that I would be a baker?"

Porsche burst out laughing. "I picture you more packing a .45 in the kitchen rather than wielding a wooden spoon and a spatula!"

Carly grinned and sat at one of the wooden stools behind the counter.

"Believe me, if I didn't *need* to do this, I wouldn't. I didn't think witness protection would be this hard. My thinking has changed. I wouldn't do it again."

"It is hard getting used to new things" Porsche remarked. "My life isn't as important with Ahmed gone."

Carly nodded, sympathizing with Porsche.

"When something changes in our lives, a part of us dies," she said, thinking of her dad and Artie. "We're never the same."

Chapter 5

An outdoor café on the coast of Bay of Bisca was chosen for the rendezvous. The two men were summoned for a reason, yet to be revealed. As usual, it was a cloudless day in San Sebastian northern Spain. *Kolo* had arranged the meeting.

The CIA, Israeli Mossad, and Australia's ASIS were all aware of this splinter group, known as Kolo, *the "Circle,"* whose tenacles spread throughout the world but mainly in Africa, Europe, the Middle East, and the United States.

Vincenzo using only his first name sat at a round table under an umbrella. He was a large man wearing a white shirt, matching shorts, and wide brim white sun hat. His cotton shirt clung to his body as the sweat rolled down his forehead. Vincenzo sipped espresso from a tiny ceramic cup which looked even smaller held by his enormous hand. His job was to scan the lunch crowd as they made their way in. When all looked secure, he would remove his hat and light a cigar signaling the men to join him.

Borka was the first to arrive.

"May I join you?" he asked.

"By all means," Vincenzo said motioning to a chair across from him.

"Is that espresso you are drinking?" Borka asked, as he lowered himself into a chair knowing that was code to verify himself. Vincenzo nodded.

Borka lifted his hand and raked his hair before removing his sunglasses and placing them on the top of his head. Grego, sitting next to a water fountain fifty feet away, immediately stood and made his way to the table.

"Gentlemen, may I have a seat?"

Vincenzo took another drag of his cigar then laid it into the ashtray as Grego sat down in his seat.

"You really should give those up," Grego said. "Smoking can ruin your health."

After hearing the last verification, Vincenzo signaled for a waiter to come to the table. "We are ready to order," he said. "Please put it on one tab and when we are done, give me the bill."

The waiter brought their food and the three dined on clams mariniere, baby squid in their ink, and baked sea bream. It was now time to discuss why they were here.

"It has come to *Kolo's* attention that there is a vial of mithridate still not accounted for."

"And how can that be?" Borka asked.

"The original operation, shall we say went sideways. The CIA outmaneuvered the person heading the operation."

"You mean outsmarted Slovak?"

Vincenzo paused as his forehead puckered and his brows knitted together.

"How did you know that?"

"I'm supposed to know that. Everyone here at this table probably knows. I'm surprised he and his accomplice Tatyana Nikolaev haven't been taken out already."

"That may come, but for now Alexander and Tatyana are still relevant. They have the most information and remain actively involved. Once we retrieve the mithridate, their futures are uncertain."

"So, this antidote or mithridate as you say. What does it do for you?"

"Pathogens! It's the pathogens that can be reversed engineered and used in the construction of a dirty bomb."

Vincenzo pointed to the operative's phones.

"Get to that email that was sent to you."

Both men picked up their phone and scrolled to an encrypted email that was sent to them.

"We will use this platform to communicate. The password is *InkSpot.* Type in those words and it should bring up some pictures."

The two pecked at their screens. Instantly three pictures appeared… Bo, Carly, and her mother.

"And who are these people?" Grego asked.

"They are a link to the mithridate. The young women is Carly Fletcher. She supposedly was killed in a car crash in the states. *Kolo* believes that was a ruse formulated by the CIA. The male is Bo Harris, and the older woman is the mother of Carly Fletcher."

Borka looked from his phone. "And why do we have these?"

"Our organization has information that they may be in witness protection and could possibly be relocated somewhere in Europe."

"And how would you know this?"

"Let's just say it comes from a credible source within the CIA. That's as much as I can tell you. We need to locate these people."

"And if we find them, what then?"

"That's all you need to know for now," Vincenzo said. "If you locate them, you will be given further instructions from *Kolo.*"

Chapter 6

Bo adjusted the recliner and opened the velvet box. He rubbed his finger over the clear stone before snapping it shut and setting it in the side pouch of the recliner. It wasn't huge, but it was what he could afford on his I.T. job in the city.

Bo waited until Carly's mom had retired to her bedroom before he poured himself another drink. He already had put a sizeable dent in the bottle. He took a sip of his Barenjager bourbon and basked in the familiar warm feeling of alcohol spreading through his body. As he sipped, his fingers traced the faint scar on the side of his face, a lingering reminder of past suffering, even though the physical mark had faded, the memory was all too fresh.

A beam of headlights hit the apartment window. Carly was home. He quickly rose from the recliner and hurried to the makeshift bar on the kitchen counter. Bo refilled his snifter and poured a glass of chilled Rose` for Carly. He lit a single taper candle, adding a soft glow to the counter.

"Hey, Babe," Bo said as Carly walked through the door and handed him a brown paper bag. She placed her purse and the manila envelope Porsche had given her on the kitchen table. Bo brought the bag to his face and opened it, sniffing deeply. "Mmm."

"It's a Nussschnecken. A kind of cinnamon bun," Carly told him. "I've been learning how to make them at the bakery."

Bo crumpled the top of the bag. "I'll save this for the morning," he said setting it next to the toaster. "I don't want to save you, though."

Bo took both her hands and pulled her tightly to him. He rubbed his hands over her back and kissed her forehead and said, "I poured you a wine."

"Wine? For me?" she replied, and seeing the candle asked, "What's the special occasion? It's so late I thought you would be sleeping."

"I couldn't sleep," he murmured. "All I can think about is you coming home and your soft, bare skin."

He slipped his hand under her shirt and fumbled at the hooks on her bra. He nuzzled her neck and while he did, whiskey fumes wafted up to her nose.

"Not tonight," she said, pushing herself away from him.

A dark look shot across Bo's face. "What's *that* supposed to mean?" he snapped.

"Bo," Carly quickly answered. "I didn't mean anything by it. I'm tired and usually when I get home you're already sleeping."

He grabbed his glass and downed it.

"Already sleeping," he mocked her. "Is that what you call it? Why don't you just come out and say it like it is? Just say I *passed out*…like a no-good drunken bastard! All you do lately is bitch about how much I drink."

Carly stared steadily at him. Bo's outbursts, especially after drinking, had become common and mean. She walked into the living room to distance herself. Bo followed her.

"Don't walk away from me. I'm not done talking to you," Bo slurred.

Carly shot back around, her eyes darting at him. "Maybe you should watch how much you drink."

"Why should I? You seem to watch enough for both of us."

"My mom has noticed, too."

"Your mom?" Bo yelled. "You talk about *me* to your mom. Who else do you talk to?!! The Chef?"

"Bo, stop it. Just go to bed."

"Tell me, AAA-vaaah," he said, drawing her name out. "If you aren't giving it to me, then who are you giving it to?"

Carly threw her hands up in the air. "You are such an asshole!! Just shut up!"

Carly and Bo heard the door open from the back hallway. The apartment became silent as her mother wearing a cotton nightgown stepped into the living room.

"What's going on?" she asked rubbing the sleep out of her eyes. "You didn't say 'No', did you, Carly?"

Confused, Carly looked at her mother. "Wait? What are you talking about?"

Bo had already forced himself to calm down. He ran his fingers through his dark hair before looking at Carly's mom. "Never popped the question. I didn't get a chance."

A glimmer of understanding crossed Carly's mother's face.

"I wish I'd never got up," she said, walking back to her bedroom. "I'll leave you two alone."

Bo shrugged. He shuffled unsteadily back to his recliner and dropped into it, head bobbing as soon as he settled in.

Carly stepped into the kitchen and removed the envelope from the table. She grabbed her purse by the straps and brought it with her, setting it on the floor next to the couch.

"Here," she said handing Bo the envelope and nervously watching his reaction.

"Not this shit again!!" Bo barked as he removed a small book with a black eagle emblazoned on a black background. Under the German Coat of Arms was the word *Reisepass*. When he opened the passport, Carly's picture stared back. Under it was the name *Ava Winters*.

"Would you just hear me out?" Carly pleaded, as she sat down on the couch across from him.

"What's to hear?" Bo said, raising his voice. "Looks like your mind is already made up."

He tossed the passport back to Carly.

"Is David the reason you are going?"

Carly bristled. "No! It's not David," she snapped. "How many times do I have to tell you? We were patients at Holy Oaks and became friends. Without him, you probably would not be here. Slovak was about to kill you. Remember!?"

"How can I forget," he said lifting his hand to his cheek and feeling the four-inch scar that started at his ear and curved down to the side of his mouth.

"Then, why in God's name do you have to go?"

"Before I left Michigan, Stacey hinted that Slovak would still be looking for me. She said I could count on that. Word must have gotten out that David kept a vial. Slovak probably thinks we're together."

"I still don't know why David kept it. What could he possibly have wanted with it… to make his own bomb?!! This whole thing probably would be over if he had been honest with you."

"Maybe for you, Bo, but not for me. There has to be a good reason why David did what he did."

"There you go again. Making excuses for him."

"I'm not making excuses!" Carly cried out, louder than she meant to.

"Then why go? Why put yourself in that danger?"

Carly paused for a moment before standing from the couch and walking to a four-shelf bookcase. She removed a hardcover book and opened to a page containing a folded piece of paper. She walked back to Bo and handed it to him.

"Got this little over a week ago."

Bo unfolded the paper and with a confused look began to read.

There was a firebombing at the farmhouse of your friend David Farris. His parents were killed. We believe this to be the work of Slovak. Don't get too comfortable, Ava. Watch your back.

Bo shook his head as his gaze left the note and went back to Carly. He folded it and handed it back. "Who the hell gave you this?"

"I don't know," Carly said taking the note from Bo and dropping it into her purse as she sat back down on the couch. "Found it under my windshield wiper when I left the bakery last week."

"This has to have come from Stacey," Bo said. "Who else would have left it? I bet she had someone put it there. As long as that son of a bitch Slovak lives, this will never be over."

"You're right," Carly added. "He took my family away from me. My dad. Artie. Who is going to be next? *Your* parents? *Your* farm? Anyone I care about could be killed. I can't keep living like this."

Bo said nothing for a while, and they sat in silence.

"It is a war that never ends," he reluctantly agreed. "I wish it weren't true, but I see no end to it."

"And the most God-awful thing," said Carly, "is that if we don't stop it, it will keep going on until all of us are hurt or dead."

Bo grimaced before speaking. "I'm going with you," he said to her. "We'll track him down together...And we will take him out together."

Carly didn't answer him right away. She took a sip and then another.

"You can't," she told him. "I'm going with Porsche."

"Porsche!? You're going with Porsche!" Bo hollered. "Why?"

"Please, Bo, keep your voice down. I don't want my mom coming back out. Can't we talk without you yelling?"

Bo leaned back in his recliner. "Just didn't think this night would end up like this."

"Ahmed meant everything to Porsche. She's had the training and has stayed in touch with some of the people from Deutsche Hochschule."

"Where?"

"Deutsche Hochschule," Carly said. "It's where Porsche did her training and Ahmed was an instructor. Ahmed had a lot of friends in the agency that would like to see Slovak dead."

"Is that how you got the fake passport?"

"Yes."

"Does Stacey know?"

"Not yet. I won't let her know until I'm back in the States. Porsche and I have been planning this since I got that note. I need you here to protect Mom. We're all the family she has left."

Bo reached in the side pouch of the recliner and removed the red velvet box. As he stood he shoved it into the front pocket of his jeans. "I'm heading to bed," he said. "There's a salad in the refrigerator if you're hungry."

Carly heard the bedroom door close, before draining the last bit of Rose`. She walked into the kitchen and rinsed her glass. As she placed the wine back into the fridge, she spotted a silver-wrapped bottle of champagne with purple frilly bows and long curly ribbons streaming down the sides.

She sighed.

Chapter 7

It was a two-hour drive from Dusseldorf to the Frankfort airport. As Bo drove, Porsche quizzed Ava on the many questions US customs could ask before she could get into the States.

"What's your citizenship?"

"German."

"Where is your residence in Germany?"

"Konigsallee 92a 40212 Dusseldorf, Germany"

"Where will you be traveling in the States?"

"I am joining friends, and we are hiking in Michigan's Upper Peninsula."

Porsche smiled. "I like the German accent. Nice touch. Sounds like you lived here your whole life."

"Sort of picked it up with all the hours spent tutoring Chef."

"What is the address of the friends you will be traveling with."

Carly opened her purse and read the address. "54213 Ford St. Detroit Michigan 48223"

"You got this, Ava Winters. Carly Fletcher, rest in peace."

As they pulled into the massive parking lot, Carly could not help but notice the Frankfort Garden Inn. It was a giant hotel built directly above a railway station. The hotel itself looked like a highspeed railway car. Bo lowered his window as he pulled in front of the parking gate. He grabbed the ticket spit out by the machine and drove through the raised arm.

"Tell me your plan again," he said as he drove higher and higher to each level before finding a spot and parking.

"We have to find David," Carly said, fishing through her purse making sure her passport and other documents were in order. "He is the key. He's got the mithridate, and you can bet Slovak wants his hands on it. Once we're in Detroit, I'll let Stacey know."

Bo shook his head. "She is absolutely going to freak out when she finds out what you're doing." Bo paused for a moment then continued. "You know, Carly, Slovak may want you even more than the mithridate. You disfigured him. Your bullet turned him into a monster. He must hate you for that."

"I'm banking on it," Carly said. "This time I will finish the job."

Bo popped the trunk and removed the keys from the ignition.

"Let's get you guys going," he said as he pushed the door open and got out of the Volkswagen. "Don't want you late for your flight."

He removed both bags and slammed the trunk shut. Porsche quickly lifted the retractable arm on her bag. She stepped in and gave Bo a hug.

"I'll leave you guys alone," she said then pulled her bag to the elevator and waited.

Carly leaned in and embraced Bo. "I've got to do this," she whispered in his ear.

Bo hugged her back. "I know."

"My gun is where I always kept it. I think you should start carrying it. You got to protect yourself and mom. Once I kill that son-of-a-bitch, we can move on with our lives."

Bo simply nodded as Carly pulled her suitcase and joined Porsche.

Carly sat in the terminal with her eyes closed as Porsche thumbed through a magazine. She opened her eyes when she heard the flight attendant announce.

"Now boarding flight 4812 Frankfort to Detroit."

****

The pain was excruciating! Carly bent her head toward her knees, squeezed her nose, and blew. Her ears popped then ached, the ear plugs were of little relief. Porsche tapped her friend on the shoulder and held up a pack of gum. Carly took a piece and began to chew, pinching the bridge of her nose as she did. The descent toward Detroit Metro was the same as every descent, PAIN, PAIN, PAIN! It was hard for her to concentrate.

The flight attendant handed Carly three Customs Declaration forms. She took one and passed the other two down, then lowered the hinged tray in front of her. She was happy for the distraction. One by one Carly answered the questions; she was very familiar with the form. *No red flags!!!*

As the plane taxied to the gate, Carly removed her ear plugs, pinched her nostrils one last time, and blew into a Kleenex. Her ears popped but her head felt like she was under water. The people moved slowly as they grabbed their carry-ons from the bins above.

The closer Carly shuffled to the front of the plane, the faster her heart pounded. She knew that customs officials were keen readers of body language and mannerisms. One nervous hesitation or sigh could blow open the whole masquerade. She felt comfortable that her role playing with Porsche would get her through the ordeal. She exited the plane and walked with the herd to the Customs and Border station. *Stay calm.*

Carly entered one line as Porsche entered another. One by one the travelers handed their declaration form and passport to the customs officials. Carly was next in line. An overwhelming sense of calm came over her. She stepped up and handed the official her paperwork.

He was all business as he looked over Ava's documents. He opened her passport and looked at Ava's picture. His eyes then traveled to her. She stared back.

"I see this is your first time in the states. Where are you heading?"

Ava removed the piece of paper with the address on it and read it aloud.

"Reason for your trip?"

"I'm here for a visit. Going to the Upper Peninsula hiking with some friends."

The custom official looked over the paperwork one more time. He then looked back at Ava. "You'll love it up there. The color is great this time of year."

Ava smiled.

"Nothing to declare. Food, jewelry, anything?"

"No, Sir."

The official stamped Carly's passport and handed it back.

"Enjoy your stay."

Porsche was waiting for Carly on the other side of Customs. A small grin was on Porsche's face. They headed to the baggage carousel. There was no need to search the signs for the correct carousel. Stacey was standing next to it, glaring as they approached.

Chapter 8

David lay prone on his cot, his hands crossed over his chest. He listened to Sarge's uneasy sleep, his groans, his mumbling, the rustle of blankets being kicked off, him rolling from one side and then to the other. Almost every night. Like a ritual.

David had plenty of troublesome nights himself. Nights where his mind would not shut down. He couldn't remember his last good night of sleep. At night, it was the worst for him. Always the worst. The pitch black of the forest offered no relief.

He talked to Tim about things that bothered him—things like losing touch with Carly, disappointing his parents, fearing he may have a record and not be able to get a job, not knowing where he was going with his life. He was a drifter, a wanderer, he had no address, no place he could call home.

"Not having a home is a temporary situation," Tim told him. "You are not a drifter, he said matter-of-factly. "You are more a meanderer, Farris. You have a lot of bends and turns to take before you find your place. A place you fit in."

David had fallen back asleep. He didn't even hear Tim get up until the whine of the dogs woke him. Still half asleep, he pushed himself up dropping his legs to the ground. He sat on his cot, and watched as Tim stood outside the tent waving his hands at the mosquitos and blackflies before unzipping the tent and charging in.

"Nightmare again, Farris," he said. "You were moaning in your sleep."

David said nothing at first as he stared at the ground, collecting his thoughts.

"Yeah, it was," he mumbled, then slapped a mosquito from his neck and wiped the dead bug on a knee of his camo pants. "How do those little bastards get in here?"

"When we get back, you need to talk to someone about those dreams," Sargent Tim said. "I'm worried you got PTSD."

"Duh! Really? You think so?!" David said. "You think I have PTSD?? he laughed. "That's why they put me in the mental home, Dumbass."

Tim studied David. "I mean that you may need to see someone again. Seriously. You don't get cured for the rest of your life with a little psychotherapy. You need some maintenance, Man."

You mean a shrink?" David said, shaking his head.

"Maybe."

"Thanks, but no thanks. I've talked enough about my feelings. As far as I am concerned, a couple left jabs and an upper cut is all I need to discuss my feelings. Maybe a gun."

"Yeah, I see how that worked out for you," Tim said. "David, anyone who served needs a little help."

"What I need is a hot shower and a shave," he said scratching the side of his grubby beard. "Let's not talk about this anymore. What time do you make the call?"

Tim looked at his watch. "Thirteen hundred hours. That gives me about two and a half hours."

Scattered across Tim's cot was a canteen, Ka-bar knife, satellite phone, Google Earth map, a pack of beef jerky and head net.

"Don't forget the water for the dogs. They gotta drink."

"Not taking them this time," Tim said. "It's way too hot and it's going to be a pretty steep climb."

David's brows knitted together. "Didn't you say you saw bear tracks and scat not far from the camp?"

"I did," said Tim. "I'll be fine as long as I don't get between a mama bear and her cubs. I'm more worried about the cougars and wolves then I am about your spirit bears."

Tim picked up the Google Earth map from his cot, one of about twenty he had printed before moving into the rainforest.

"We're here," he said pointing to a red circle. "I need to get to some high ground where I can get a signal. Keep your fingers crossed, Farris, that all goes well."

****

The trek to the ridge was arduous. Tim moved with care up the narrow foot path. He walked slowly and deliberately digging his hiking boots into the loose dirt. He had brought additional cleats with him and added them to the bottom of his boots to help him grip the trail.

As he neared the top, the terrain became sparse and more open. In the distance, a river cut through the deep green of the rainforest making its way to the Pacific.

It was 12:45 when Tim found a rock to sit on. He removed his backpack and took a drink from his canteen before switching on his satellite phone and checking the signal. It was strong.

Tim punched the number into his phone and waited. The phone rang once and was immediately picked up.

"We got her," the voice on the other end of the phone said. "She's safe."

Tim raised his open palm to his head and wiped beads of sweat from his brow.

"She was released as part of a six-person swap. Five of the bad guys plus the money for her. This doesn't always work out this well."

Feeling relief, he said, "Let me talk to her."

He kept the phone close to his ear waiting to hear from Isla.

"Tim," Isla said weakly.

"Are you home? Did they hurt you?" Tim immediately said. "Are you ok?"

"Take a breath, Tim. Slow down," she answered. "I'm still in Iraq. I was released a few hours ago, and I'm fine. They just wanted the ransom."

"When do you fly back?"

"Day after tomorrow. Australia doesn't have any presence here anymore, so I have to take a military flight from the Americans. I'll first head to Germany and then to Sydney."

Tim heard the deep voice of his contact speaking to Isla.

"He wants the phone back," Isla said. "Come home to me, Tim."

"I will, I will," Tim said before the gruff voice of CIA Officer Paul Daugherty started.

"We did what you wanted, Tim. Now give us what we want."

"You make sure she's alright until she gets on that plane. Promise me that."

"Have I let you down yet? Where's the mithridate?"

"There's a woodshed next to the barn on my farm."

Daugherty interrupted. "Don't bullshit me. We went through every inch of that shed. We found nothing."

"Would you let me finish? If you look at the shed door you will see where the furring strip boards make the letter X. Remove those planks and in the middle of the X, you'll find a key burrowed into the wood. The key is to a safety deposit box along with the name of the bank where I put the vial of mithridate."

"There's a team on its way as we speak," Daugherty said. "If you've played me, it'll be the end of the road for you."

"So…umm…do you think I'll get prison time?"

"Don't know and don't care. My job is done. Farris might get a break, though, considering what happened to his family and all."

"You mean his sister?"

There was a pause on the phone. Tim heard a muffled conversation between Daugherty and another man.

"What happened to his family!!?" Tim demanded to know, refusing to end the call until he knew what had happened.

"I am not authorized to tell you anything, but Farris should know that his parents are dead. It happened last week. Someone firebombed their farmhouse."

"Firebombed!" Tim cried out. "Someone firebombed his folk's house! Did it burn to the ground?"

"No. Some of it is still standing. We think it could be that Slovak guy and his partner. The ones who put Farris and his girlfriend through all that shit"

"Son of a bitch. Firebombed his parents' house."

Tim set the phone on his knee, and left unbalanced, it tumbled to the rocky ground. He let it lie there, his mind flashing back to the time he visited David at the farm and met Mr. and Mrs. Farris. When Tim called David's mother "Mrs. Farris", she interrupted him and said, "My name is Beatrice. Just call me Bea."

She served him apple pie, kept his coffee cup full, and insisted that he stay for dinner.

Tim's thoughts were broken by the faint yelling of someone on the phone. He scrambled to pick up the receiver and placed it to his ear.

"Hey there! Hello? Hello? Are you still there?" Daugherty was shouting.

"I'm here, I'm here," Tim said in a voice that was both angry and frustrated. "I dropped the phone, for Christ's sakes, and had to pick it up."

"Tim, just to give you a heads up. Don't try to leave Canada and head to Australia. You're better off coming back to the States."

"I wouldn't dream of it," Tim replied sarcastically. "Why would I go to Australia?"

"Don't be cute, Tim. The agency wants you. There are still many questions we have for you and your buddy."

"You just get my girl home safely, then I'll see about answering your questions."

Chapter 9

As Carly and Porsche approached the baggage carousel, they could tell from Stacey's body language it wasn't going to be a pleasant reunion. She stood there stiffly, arms crossed, glaring at the two of them.

"This isn't going to be pretty," Porsche whispered. "She looks pissed."

"Are you freaking kidding me?" Stacey said through gritted teeth. "Do you realize what you've done? You may have blown your cover."

"Stacey, will you just listen?" Carly asked.

"No!" Stacey said. You two get your asses back to Germany before you're both dead."

She held out two boarding passes.

"I'm *not* going back," Carly said, walking past her to the luggage carousel. She watched as bags were jettisoned onto the conveyor belt before removing a suitcase with neon yellow tape wrapped around its handle.

Stacey stood next to Carly, gripping her navy shoulder bag and assessing the crowd in the baggage area.

"What were you two thinking? You know what happened with David's parents. You're playing right into Slovak's hands!!"

Carly turned to Stacey, her face tight and stern. "It's *because* of what happened to David's folks that I *am* here," she said sharply. "Slovak must die. We both know he had something to do with this. I have to get him out of my life. Out of all our lives."

"It was a mistake to tell you about David's parents," Stacey said. "But I thought it was important enough to let you know. No one is happy with you now. And they will not be happy with me either."

"I am surrounded by unhappy people," Carly said, thinking about her mother, Bo, Porsche, and now Stacey. "All because of that bastard."

Carly spotted Porsche snatching her suitcase from the conveyor belt. She had to turn sideways and inch forward to get through the jam-packed crowd that didn't want to move for her.

"C'mon," Carly said as Porsche approached. "We need to get a car and find a place to get some food."

Stacey reached out and took ahold of her arm.

"Can we go somewhere and talk? I have to know what you're planning. I'm not part of the task team anymore, but the Chief updates me with anything that has to do with you."

"How did you know I came back?"

"Even though you went into witness protection, we still monitor you. I was contacted the minute Ava Winters from Dusseldorf boarded that plane."

"You really can't go anywhere these days without someone watching you," Carly said acridly. "I feel like I'm back at Holy Oaks."

"Where are you guys staying?" Stacey asked.

"Not sure. We were thinking someplace close to David's farm."

Stacey was about to speak when she noticed a man wearing a leather biker jacket leave the crowd and walk towards them. She checked him over, looking for a bulge of a concealed weapon. His attention focused on Carly and never left. Stacey felt for her gun. The man smiled and pointed to the ground.

"I think you're going to need those," he said, pointing at the two boarding passes that had fallen from Stacey's coat pocket. Porsche bent down and picked them up.

"Thank you," Porsche said as the man returned to the carousel to grab his luggage.

Stacey took a deep breath and sighed. "You guys are killing me. Let's get something to eat and then we'll head to my place. You can stay the night and tell me what the hell you're planning."

The Honda Civic cruised through the town of Welchester, passing gas stations, gift shops, and businesses with large windows flashing OPEN signs. When the car went by Dublin's restaurant, Carly pictured Ahmed in his long black coat hurrying down the street. And how she jumped up from the restaurant table and chased him, leaving the restaurant without paying the bill.

"Are you thinking about our last visit to Dublin's?" Stacey asked. "How we ran out chasing Ahmed and the police getting involved. I still think about sitting in that police station waiting for Hayes to bail us out and hoping *my* cover wasn't blown."

She glanced at Carly who was biting her bottom lip.

From the back seat, Porsche said, "Ahmed wanted to talk to you, Carly, in the worst way, but his instincts told him it would be the wrong move."

Without hesitation, Carly said, "The biggest wrong move was David taking that last vial of mithridate. That's how all this got started again! I am so pissed off at him for doing that, and I don't understand why he did it."

"The Big Boy restaurant is just up ahead," Stacey replied. "Let's talk more about it when we get there."

Carly stared straight ahead as they drove along, and when she spoke, her voice was deathlike.

"I'm gonna kill Slovak. There is no way around it. The bastard will never stop if I don't." Carly's voice cracked. "He has to die. I swear."

"Carly," Stacey said hoping to soothe her. "I can't let you do that. I understand you feel this way, I really do but I have to get you back to Germany before someone else gets hurt."

"I don't want to hear it," Carly cut in. "Stop talking, just stop talking."

"I can't stop, Carly," Stacey said. "I care about you and getting you back to Germany where you will be safe. It's my job!"

"Is this what I am to you?" she said bitterly. "I'm still a job!"

"That's not what I'm saying. My job was to win your confidence. That's not what it is now! For God's sakes, how long will it take to get past this?!"

Carly turned her head to look out the side window, hiding her face from Stacey. She had forgiven Stacey a long time ago. A long silence hung in the air before a mischievous smile lay over her face. She asked in a low tone, "Did you miss me, Stacey?"

"What?" Stacey said, feeling surprised and glancing at her. "What are you getting at?"

"Did you miss me?" Carly repeated, a little louder.

"I told you. The chief almost took me off the case because he thought I was getting too close to you."

"But, Stacey...did *you* miss me when I was gone?" continued Carly in a teasing voice.

Exasperated, Stacey answered, "Of course, I missed you. How could I not? You became my best friend."

"Then you'll help?"

"I didn't say that!!," Stacey said sharply. "I didn't say that," she kept repeating as she angled the car into the parking space by Big Boy's.

The middle-aged waitress grabbed three menus from the stack on the counter. They followed her to a table in the far corner that was far away from all the others.

"I'll be back for your orders," she said. "In the meantime, someone will bring you your drinks. Specials are listed inside the menu. The Italian Meatloaf has been very popular today."

When the waitress was out of hearing range, Stacey whispered to them.

"There's no more task force," she began. "Once you went into the witness protection program, it was abandoned. I'm now working a case of a suspected serial killer."

"Serial killer," Porsche said raising her brows. "You have a serial killer in the town of Welchester?"

"It's not Welchester," Stacey answered. "The killings are taking place in a couple of states—Michigan and Ohio, that we know of—and the killings have a lot of similarities. That's why the Feds stepped in. It just so happened that a killing took place in Detroit. Some real sick stuff this monster has done. All over the past year."

"Damn," Carly said. "We leave and all hell breaks loose. Sure it's not Slovak?"

Stacey's expression sobered and Carly could see this case was really bothering her.

"I'm sure," she said. "As much of a SOB Slovak is, he doesn't kill for enjoyment. In his warped mind, he thinks he is doing it for a cause. With this guy I can't tell if he kills for a purpose or enjoyment. He leaves clues to toy with the cops."

"What'd he do?" Porsche asked inquisitively.

Stacey shook her head. "Not going there now. I want to know what you two are planning."

Chapter 10

The dogs wagged their tails and darted to Tim as soon as he emerged from the thick undergrowth of shrubs and bushes surrounding the campsite. The light of the sun poked through the towering canopy of western red cedars, western hemlock, and spruce creating a mass of speckles on the patches of dirt.

Tim reached down and patted each dog on its head. He didn't bend over and ruffle their fur like he usually did.

When Tim removed his head net, David noticed the dark, grim look on his face. Tim dropped into one of the camp chairs across from David.

After taking a deep, slow breath, he asked, "Any beer left in the cooler?"

"I think there might be a can left," David answered. "Did something happen with Isla? Is she all right?"

"Yes!! Thank God. She's fine. Heading back to Australia in a couple of days."

"So, then what's up?"

Tim paused then stood from his chair and went to the cooler. He removed the last beer and opened it on his way back, handing it to David. With a puzzled looked, David took the beer and asked, "What the hell is going on, Sarge?"

Tim sat back down, bracing himself against the chair. His chest felt like ice.

"Farris, I'm going to handle this like I did in Iraq…when I had to inform you guys about bad things that happened in the platoon."

He forced himself to look at David who was hunched over in his chair, gripping his beer with a fist.

"There's no easy way to say this, but sometime…sometime in the last week…someone…firebombed your parents' house. Most of the house is still standing. But…your parents did not make it."

****

Stacey pulled into the garage of her townhouse. She popped the trunk and walked to the back of the Honda and lifted the suitcases. "You'll have to share a bed," Stacey said, handing each their suitcase. "Only got one spare bedroom."

Stacey opened the door and stepped aside, letting Carly and Porsche go in first. Porsche noticed a huge Bengal cat jump onto the counter.

"Oh, my God! He looks like a tiger," Porsche said, then proceeded to scratch the cat under his chin before the Bengal mewed and jumped off the counter.

"His name is *Tiger King*," Stacey said, "and, yes, I named him after the show."

Stacey walked through the townhouse flipping on a couple of lights and then the TV. She walked down the wood floor hallway to the guest room. Opening the window, she said, "better then sleeping in a hotel. The only problem you'll have, Carly, is dealing with Porsche's snoring."

"I don't snore!!" Porsche chuckled. "If my memory serves me right, you were the one *sawing logs* when we spent those nights on the road looking for Carly."

Stacey smiled and left the room. "I'm grabbing a beer. You guys want one?"

Carly and Porsche both nodded, lifting their heavy suitcases onto the bed. They each pulled out large tee shirts and sweatpants before heading into the living room.

Stacey sat crossed legged in a large recliner, a Stella Artois in hand. Two open bottles sat on a coffee table in front of the couch. Carly bent and grabbed one and lifted it into the air.

"Here's to Stacey helping us," Carly said as Porsche lifted her bottle and clinked.

"I knew you would come around," Carly said taking another sip. She looked at Stacey whose face was very serious.

"Things are more complicated than what you know," said Stacey. "I didn't tell you everything about David."

"You've lost me," said Carly. "What do you mean that you didn't tell me everything?"

"I knew that if I did, you would have come back here faster, and I wanted you to stay in Germany."

Carly took a throw pillow and cradled it against her belly.

"I've been withholding some information about David, but now that you're back, I guess it doesn't matter. We know why David took that vial of mithridate."

"God! We've been racking our brains forever," Porsche said. She glanced at Carly and then back to Stacey, "We couldn't get our heads around it."

"Did you know that Sargent Tim had a girlfriend in Iraq?"

Carly shook her head. "No. It never came up in the time David and I were with him."

"Her name is Isla Borne. She worked in that orphanage that Tim was so involved in. He adored her. The two fell in love and Tim spent most of his free time working with her."

"Didn't you say Tim lived in foster care?" Porsche asked.

"Yes," said Carly. "According to David, Tim bounced from one family to another. Never able to connect. He was in foster care until the day he enlisted. The Army became his family."

Stacey agreed.

"Oh, that had to be so hard on him," Porsche said.

"David told me that when they were in Iraq, the platoon was ordered to move to a perimeter 30 miles away. Tim pleaded with the upper brass not to do it, that if they did, the entire village including the orphanage could be attacked and killed."

"Was that woman killed?" Porsche asked.

"No, Isla wasn't killed. She was kidnapped and held for ransom. Held for several months. Tim begged the US to negotiate her return. Since she wasn't a U.S. citizen and with the policy of no negotiating with terrorists, they told him to "pound sand". That's when Tim took it into his own hands."

Carly's mouth dropped slightly. "Is that why Tim wanted the mithridate?"

"Yes. It was a crime of opportunity."

"More like a crime of passion," Porsche said.

"About a month after you were in Germany, I got a call from David. First thing out of his mouth was asking if you were alright."

"Really," Carly said, a perturbed look on her face.

"He explained what he and Tim were doing. He wanted middle east contacts in the CIA who could negotiate her release. I got him in touch with Chief Bolton. The Chief tried to get the two to turn themselves in, but Tim wouldn't hear of it. You know how he doesn't trust the government."

"Where's David now?" Carly asked.

"Somewhere in Canada. A place called The Great Bear Rainforest."

"I feel a little better knowing why David did what he did. I just wish he had shared that with me. I felt so betrayed by him. Now I get it, he was helping a friend. Did it work? Did they get this Isla woman out?"

"Not sure? I'm not really in the loop anymore. Been working that serial killer case. It's kept me crazy busy and up at night."

Stacey stood. "I am getting another beer. Who wants one?"

Chapter 11

The boat ride to the rendezvous point was silent. Tim maneuvered the fishing boat through the small islands thick with green vegetation. Mosses, ferns, and festooning tree trunks gave the islands a "jungle-like" feeling.

David sat towards the front of the boat, round shouldered and head hanging. Tim had never seen him look so defeated. As they rounded a corner through a thin cut of water, Tim cut the engine. David lifted his head. Standing on the far side of the shore were two men in fatigues standing next to two camouflaged all-terrain vehicles. As they waved Tim stood and shouted, "Duke, Daisy, Get!"

The dogs immediately jumped into the water and started paddling toward the shore.

"Take care of my kids!" he shouted to the men on the shore. "Plans have changed!"

With that Tim dropped to his seat and yanked the starter rope, starting the engine and speeding off.

"What is going on?" David tried yelling over the whine of the engine.

Tim pointed to his ear with his free hand and shook his head. He gave David a thumbs up all at the same time keeping the throttle floored.

The orange sun was just above the tree line as the two were crossing a large body of water. David noticed something on the far shore that looked metallic in nature. The Sun reflecting off of it gave it the appearance of an offshore light house. As they approached, he quickly realized it was a pontoon float plane. Tim cut the engine and David turned to him.

"Sarge, what the hell is going on?"

"You remember how I planned missions in Iraq?"

"Yeah, I remember. You always had a backup plan. Those second lieutenants fresh out of Officer Training School were gung-ho and wanted to make a name for themselves. If it wasn't for you keeping them in check, more of us would have died. Hell, some of the new recruits thought you could change water into wine."

"Exactly. If we had showed up at the first rendezvous point and no one was there, we would have been screwed. So, I made sure I set up two evacuation points."

"Soooo," David said his voice trailing off.

"Well, I got to thinking. You wouldn't be in this mess and your parents would still be alive if it wasn't for me."

"Sarge," David tried to interrupt before Tim quieted him.

"Let me finish! Just listen! I know you want to kill that SOB and that mother fucker deserves to die. I can't let you do it alone. I know how that hot tempered spirt animal within you can be. This needs to be planned out. We're going to take him out along with that bitch partner of his. It's gotta be planned as a mission like when we took out high valve targets in Iraq."

David shook his head. "I don't know what to say."

"There's something more I gotta tell you, Farris. I haven't been totally honest with you. Or the CIA for that matter."

"What is that sarge?"

"I lied about where I stashed the mithridate. I didn't share this with you because I thought the less you knew, the less trouble you would be in."

David's eyes grew and his brows lifted. "Are you fucking kidding me? You duped the CIA again?"

"You know how I don't trust the government. What if the CIA really did not get Isla out. What would I do then? The woman I spoke to on the phone sounded like Isla, but how could I be sure. The CIA could have set this all up!"

"Oh, they are going to be so pissed."

"I had all intentions of giving the mithridate to the CIA when I turned myself in. That was if they were legit in getting Isla out. But I changed my mind. It's time I help you for a change. I know you want to get Slovak and if you have the mithridate, it may just be the bait to get the rat."

"So, if it's not in the safety deposit box where is it?"

"I have a well on the side of my house. I taped the vial to the underside of the cap of my well head."

David studied Tim's face. He could almost see the gears turning inside his head. He hadn't seen that look since Iraq. A smirk formed on Tim's face. "I love messing with the man. Now let's get in so I can introduce you to Liam, our pilot."

Chapter 12

When Tatyana heard the light rapping on the door, she felt for her sidearm hidden under her loose blouse.

"That must be him," she whispered, then walked to the door and peeked out the peephole. She turned back at Slovak and nodded.

"Open the door," he ordered in a low calm voice.

Slovak watched as Tatyana flipped the U-swing lock and twisted the deadbolt. A man stood there, a big man with an even bigger intimidating aura. She quickly scrutinized his hard eyes and dark hair slicked back.

She stepped aside and allowed him to enter. Markell slowly made his way in, eyes darting around the room, assessing his surroundings. He walked with authority to the empty chair across from Slovak and unbuttoning his jacket, he lowered himself into it which compressed and squeaked as he squirmed to get comfortable. The buttons on his shirt drew tight across his bulging stomach and a black sport jacket barely hid a long stain of some kind.

Tatyana followed him in but did not sit. She remained standing behind him.

Markell turned slightly and looked at Tatyana. "Why do I get this feeling the two of you are a bit on edge."

"When they send an assassin to discuss our plan, I think we have reason to be a little on edge," Slovak came back at him.

"You know, Alexander, I am much more than an assassin," Markell replied with a smug smile. "Of course, I *do* possess those skills, but *that* was when I was a younger man. I proved my loyalty, and my position within *Kolo* has changed."

Markell looked back at Tatyana. "You know, Dear, it is very uncomfortable having someone behind me." Motioning with his head to the couch across from him, he said, "Move over there so I can see you."

Tatyana walked to the couch and took a seat, never taking her eyes off Markell.

"Tell me, Alexander, how did *you* get us into this shitstorm?" Markell asked, his voice reeking with arrogance.

Slovak stared at Markell, hating his haughty attitude. "We had a bit of a problem, but there is a reason for it," Slovak said.

"Bit of a problem!? That's what you're calling it?" Markell ridiculed. "Getting duped by a 21-year-old girl is more than a bit of a problem!"

"She had help!" Slovak retaliated.

"Help?? Who cares if she had help? Your job was to guarantee we wouldn't fail. You know, Alexander, if it was anyone but you, that person would be dead. Along with anyone else involved," he said, fixing his eyes on Tatyana.

"It was too sophisticated!" Slovak retorted, his temper showing. "Someone else was involved. I know it. Nothing else makes sense!"

"Stop making excuses!" Markell spat out. "Remind me to put that on your headstone. 'Here lies Alexander Slovak. A Man of Many Excuses.'"

Markell shook his head and inhaled deeply.

Slovak nodded to Tatyana, and she began speaking.

"We know that all the vials of mithridate were not accounted for. Our source has confirmed that. We think Carly Fletcher's death was a ruse. We believe she and David Farris are very much alive and in hiding or witness protection."

"Witness protection!?" Markell said, raising his voice. "What a nice story! You think that explains everything! Tell me how they are in witness protection if they pilfered some of the mithridate?"

Tatyana paused looking dumbfounded. Her eyes went to Slovak.

"We're trying to figure that out," Slovak answered. "We sent David Farris a message."

"Message!? You know where he is? Why the hell didn't you say that at the beginning?"

"No. I left a message with his parents. I'm sure he'll get it and want to meet with me."

Markell abruptly pushed himself up from his chair and buttoned his suit jacket.

"You talk in circles," he said gruffly. "One thing I know, had it not been discovered that some of the antidote was not recovered, you along with your girlfriend would have walked through the fiery gates long ago. This is your last shot."

Markell reached into his side suit pocket. Tatyana immediately jumped to her feet and pulled her weapon.

"Really?!" Markell said calmly, staring down the barrel of Tatyana's gun. "If I was going to kill you, you'd already be dead."

He pulled out his cell phone, punched in a number, then walked out the door, having dismissed them for now.

Chapter 13

Bo, unshaven and smelling of liquor, stumbled into the kitchen. He reached and opened the cupboard and removed a half empty bourbon bottle and vial of aspirin. *A little hair of the dog* before heading into the office would do the trick. He glanced at the clock and was running late. His boss had warned him, one more late start time and his job at the IT software company would be toast.

Bo was met at the door by his immediate supervisor and someone he did not recognize. The name tag on the stranger indicated she was from Human Resources. Not a good sign.

"Tom, could you please come with us?" his supervisor asked.

Bo, clearly under the influence, staggered for a moment. He momentarily forgot that his witness protection name given to him by the CIA was Thomas Higgins. He tried to compose himself as he walked past the clear cubicles partitioned in the office. All eyes were on him as he walked the walk of shame. This was not his first meeting with HR, but it may well be his last.

"Please, Tom, have a seat," Mike Crane, his supervisor, said as he waved with an open palm to a chair. The two then took a seat at a table with an open file resting on it.

"Tom, this is Fraulein Winkelman from HR. She is here to discuss your performance."

Bo took a deep breath. He knew what was coming.

"Good morning, Mr. Higgins. Like Mr. Crane said, I am Fraulein Winkelman from the Human Resources department. How are you doing today?"

Bo remained silent as the warmth from his flushed chest began to creep up his neck and land on his forehead. Small beads of water formed on his brow.

"Tom?" Mr. Crane said still waiting for a response.

"Could be better. My girlfriend just broke up with me and returned to the States."

"Mr. Higgins," Winkelman asked. "Have you been drinking this morning?"

Bo wiped his forehead with the cuff of his shirt. He was about to deny it like he always did when confronted about his drinking but instead he sheepishly nodded yes.

"Could I get some water?"

Fraulein Winkelman's eyes traveled to Mr. Crane as he stood from his chair and made his way to the water dispenser. He pulled from the tepee of white cups and placed one under the tap. He pulled the lever and heard the gurgle within the translucent blue tank. He walked back and handed Bo the cup.

"Mr. Higgins," Winkelman started again. "I am going to cut to the chase. We want you to enroll in a substance abuse program. I am not sure why you are not being terminated but it came from above that if you complete the program, you can remain at Lufthansa Systems. Your guardian angel is watching out for you. Take advantage of it.

"The program starts Monday. It's a twelve-step program and it lasts three weeks. You will continue to receive compensation during your treatment period. I need an answer right now."

"Can I think about it and get back with you?"

"Absolutely not!"

"Tom! Mr. Crane said firmly. "Get yourself some help. You were a wonderful employee when you first joined Lufthansa. Get yourself cleaned up and maybe just maybe you can get your girl back. I bet your drinking was a factor in her leaving you."

Bo sat, hunched over. The words...*I bet your drinking was a factor in her leaving you...* struck like a bullet in his gut. Bo lifted his head and looked at Mr. Crane, he then looked at Fraulein Winkelman.

"I'm in."

****

Sharon Fletcher glanced up from her embroidery at the distinct metallic click of the deadbolt. Her brows knitted in curiosity as she pondered who might be entering, given that Bo was at work. She was surprised to see it was him. "What brings you home?"

Mrs. Fletcher noticed the scowl on Bo's face. A bad-tempered expression she had gotten to know all too well. She pushed her needle into the fabric of her Cross Stitch and set her project to the side of the couch. Bo said nothing as he staggered to the kitchen and removed a bottle of bourbon from the cupboard.

Standing from the couch, she walked to him. "Bo. What's going on?"

Bo did not make eye contact. He stood, arms stretched and locked at the elbows, steadying himself on the counter. Sharon noticed his shoulders shaking as he was trying to suppress his tears. Mrs. Fletcher moved the bottle away from him and gently placed her hand on his shoulder.

"Bo, what happened? Did you get fired?"

"I'm not fired," he mumbled looking straight into the counter wiping at each eye. "But I have a problem."

"I know you do, Bo. Carly knows, too. Nobody is blaming you. It's a disease, Bo. What you went through when you were kidnapped and your PTSD from the war would put anyone over the edge. You just need some help getting through all of it."

"Lufthansa gave me an ultimatum. Give up the booze and enter a treatment program or lose my job."

"They say until you hit rock bottom, denial seems to win. Have you hit the bottom, Bo?"

Bo looked from the counter, trying to focus. His face was flush, and his eyes were pink. He struggled to keep his composure as he opened up to her.

"I'm the one that is supposed to be strong. I'm the one that Carly should be able to count on. It's not that way though. She's the one that is strong. She's the one that was strong enough to forgive me for cheating on her. It gnaws at me that I am not the man Carly deserves. The booze makes it a little easier to handle."

Mrs. Fletcher walked to Bo and put her arms around him. Bo hugged her back. "You haven't lost Carly yet," she said into his ear. "Get yourself some help and become that man Carly fell in love with."

Bo gently pushed Carly's mother away. He turned to the counter and grabbed the bottle. As he walked to the sink, he opened it and whiskey fumes wafted into the air.

"I want her back. I'll do what it takes," he said pouring the bourbon into the sink.

Chapter 14

Tatyana and Slovak had a clear view of the hotel's portico from their room. Slovak cleared his throat when a black limo with its rear window down pulled up next to Markell who cocked his head forward, leaned in, and listened for a few seconds.

The limo sped away leaving space for a dark sedan to pull up. Markell lifted the handle on the passenger side and climbed in. The sedan headed in the same direction as the limo.

"I knew it," Slovak seethed, and his color turned an ashy gray. "They sent a hit squad."

Tatyana did not speak. She moved from the window and dropped onto the couch.

"Hit squad!! You are talking crazy," Tatyana said, "If they were sending a hit squad, why are the cars speeding away from our hotel?"

"I can't answer that," Slovak said abrasively. "They don't always do things the way you would think."

"And yet we are still alive," Tatyana said. "You must be important to them still."

"I gotta find her."

"Is that what this is about--- getting Carly?" Tatyana asked.

Slovak lifted his hand to his face and felt the thick scar tissue under his right eye.

"It's not just this," he said bitterly. "She did much more, and it changed my life forever."

"You focus on getting the mithridate," Tatyana said, "and I'll handle Markell."

****

The boat puttered up to the side of the float plane. Liam stood on a pontoon and grabbed the rope tossed to him from David. The pilot secured the bow then went and did the same with the stern. David looked at the 1959 DHC-2 Beaver / Float Plane and his heart began to race. He wasn't crazy about flying in big birds let alone in this puddle jumper that was built 30 years before he was born.

"Hey how you doin'?" David said as Liam stuck out his arm and pulled David onto one of the pontoons.

"Watch your step when you get on that dock, eh," Liam said with a Canadian accent. "It's pretty rickety."

Liam turned the latch of the cargo door. Tim could see the strain on his face as he lifted the heavy hatch and locked it in place. "Start with the larger items first, eh" he ordered Tim.

David watched from the dock as the two men loaded the plane. He could not help but notice the hundreds upon hundreds of rivets that kept the tin skin on the plane.

He shouted, "Hey, you sure this thing gets off the ground?!"

Liam stopped loading and looked at David. Tim looked at Liam and laughed. Both of them kept loading the cargo.

When the boat was emptied, Liam offered his arm and helped Tim onto the pontoon.

"God, I was happy to see that plane shining like a light house when we approached."

"Lucky it's a sunny day," Liam said. "It's a great beacon when it's sunny. I've seen that plane reflecting from five miles or more offshore. It sticks out like a sore thumb with all the brush behind it. Let's get you up to the cabin. We can talk from there."

David stepped to the side and let Tim and Liam onto the dock. Liam led the way up a small path through the bush then stopped.

"Let me get us some water. We won't be flying out until morning."

Tim and David waited as Liam walked to a small intake pump. He pulled on the starter rope and the engine kicked in. The pump pulled water from the lake and into a 500-gallon drum supported on stilts. Fifteen feet in the air.

"You guys are actually going to get to take a hot shower," Liam informed them. "The water is fed by gravity to a hot water tank that is heated by propane. At the looks of you two and the smell, I think you can use a shower, eh." Tim and David high fived.

The saltbox trapper's cabin looked like a shack but was highly functional. The roof and sides were plywood covered by tar paper. A tin flue stack stuck through the roof and was covered by a thick layer of tar at its base. There were eight beds in a separate bunkroom separated by a wood partition. A woodburning stove sat in a corner with the door open and the burner plates were stacked on top of each other. It was summer and no need for heat.

A small picnic table was in the kitchen along with a stove and sink. Pots and pans hung from nails. The thing that caught David's and Tim's attention was a prefabbed fiberglass shower.

"How the hell did you get that shower here?" Tim asked.

"The Beaver. That plane is a workhorse. Don't let the looks fool ya. Pound for pound that is the best small bush plane ever built. I had the plane fitted with a turbo prop a few years back, and it is one of the safest planes in the sky. All the materials used to build this cabin I flew in."

"That's how I met Liam," Tim said. "He was at a hunting and fishing show working at a booth. He was booking fly-in fishing trips. I went on at least a half dozen trips with him and I can tell you, this is the first time I have ever been in one of your cabins that had a hot shower."

"It's my only cabin that has one."

Liam stepped to a large chest sitting in the bunkroom. He knelt and opened it removing two large bath towels.

"Who's going first?" he asked tossing each a towel. "Soap and shampoo are already in there. I'm gonna start some chow and we can discuss how I am going to get you two back into the states without Border Protection or US Customs giving you a welcome home party."

Chapter 15

Borka, hailing from Slovakia, and Grego, Hungarian by birth, shared mutual disdain for the other. Neither were born in 1939 when Hungary invaded Slovakia, but both were raised with deep seated hatred, toward each other's countrymen.

Despite their differences, akin to a strained marriage, the two decided to forge an alliance of convenience. Their encounter at the San Sebastian meeting was not their first, and both were aware of each other's reputations. Grego, considerably older than Borka, regarded him as a reckless risk-taker, a novice attempting to carve a name for himself. Conversely, Borka saw Grego as an antiquated figure, dwelling in a bygone era well past his prime.

On a dreary day in Berlin, Grego found himself in a bar overlooking the river Spree, the thick gray clouds threatening a downpour. As Borka walked in with a half-folded umbrella, Grego stood and waved.

"What a lousy day," Borka grumbled as he approached, shedding his rain jacket onto an empty chair. "Have you been here long?"

"Only forty-five minutes to an hour," Grego said, indignation in his tone. "Why is it that you millennials never show up on time or carry cash!?"

Borka smiled. "Did someone get up on the wrong side of the bed and forget to eat his granola this morning?"

"Oh, fuck off and sit down," Grego barked. "Let's get started."

Amidst the ambiance of the bar, Grego presented Borka with something intriguing—an intelligence report from the CIA. With a firm grip, he opened a manila envelope, revealing a two-page report that piqued Borka's interest. Adjusting his chair, Borka delved into the contents, setting the stage for a clandestine collaboration fueled by shared goals and an uneasy camaraderie.

TOP SECRET SPECIAL HANDLING
CLASSIFIED

20 December 2015

Memorandum for Operation Officer for the eastern district of the United States
Subject: Justification for CIA Intervention for missing mithridate. (Slovak Plan)

CIA conducted a 10-month probe into the breach of a clandestine bio lab.

CIA learned that three vials of an antidote referred to as mithridate was taken by a lead researcher, Colonel Arthur D. Fletcher.

Colonel Fletcher harvested and developed deadly pathogens for the US government in the early eighties.

CIA learned Colonel Fletcher suffered a type of mental breakdown where he became convinced that at some point a dirty bomb would be developed and unleashed on the west. He hid three vials of antidote, enough for his family.

CIA learned Colonel Fletcher told his daughter (Carly Fletcher) the whereabouts of the missing vials.

Colonel Fletcher was later found dead in a Detroit Park on April 28, 2015. Cause of death homicide. Alexander Slovak is suspected of being behind the killing.

CIA recovered two vials of mithridate. One is still unaccounted for.

Borka lifted the bottom corner of the page and turned it over. The second page looked like a summary. At the same time a waitress approached the table and the two quit talking. Grego pushed his napkin over the report and both men looked at her. The waitress turned to Borka, "Can I get you something to drink,"

"Guinness stout."

"And another draft for you?" the waitress asked Grego.

"Yes, please."

"Absolutely," the waitress affirmed, flashing Borka a smile before heading back to the bar. Borka stared at her backside watching her hips move from side to side, like a model walking down a runway.

"Mmm, mmm, mmm, that would be nice," he said.

Wrinkles formed on Grego's forehead. "Your dick is going to get you in trouble one of these days. There is no time for that."

"There is always time for that," Borka said grinning. "You're just too old to get it up."

Both men then focused back on the report.

"It indicates that Carly and a certain David Farris departed from a psychiatric facility where they were undergoing treatment, then finding the mithridate concealed by Carly's father. This discovery was integral to the Slovak operation. While three vials were located, only two were successfully recovered. According to my source, the CIA is actively engaged in efforts to secure the third," Grego said.

"What about the whereabouts of our target?" Borka asked.

"This is where it gets interesting," Grego shared. "Their whereabouts is under seal. Very few people know their location. There is mention of a Porsche Berliner. She is somehow tied to our targets. She has family in Dusseldorf."

"So, do we start looking for Americans in Dusseldorf?" Borka asked.

"Might as well. Dusseldorf is about 600 km south of us. It at least gives us a starting point. My contact will ensure we receive updates if any additional information comes to light."

Chapter 16

Tim entered the fishing cabin just as the last of the dishes were drip drying. He had taken the skeletal remains of the walleye and boated them to a deserted island a few hundred yards away. Didn't want bears sniffing around the cabin.

The dinner of fresh caught walleye, Dinty Moore Beef Stew and saltines was one of the best meals the men had had in a while. They had gotten pretty low on supplies.

"I swear I could hear the bears come running when I threw the guts up onto the rocks," Tim said, as he scooped a ladle of water from a pot that had been boiled to kill the parasites.

"They're no dummies, eh," Liam said. "If they don't get to eating fast, the bald eagles will have a field day and they won't get a scrap."

Liam unrolled a map of Canada and the US onto the picnic table. He grabbed the salt and pepper shakers and placed each one in a corner of the map. He did the same with the other two corners using coffee mugs. "Have a seat fellas. Let me share with you the plan to fly you back to the states."

Liam pointed with his index finger to the proximity of the island.

"We are here," he said, then traced the coast of where he was planning on flying. "I'm going to fly the coast all the way down to Vancouver. We won't have any problems flying in Canada. I fly this route dozens of times a year picking up fishermen and hunters and taking them to my cabins. It's going to be dicey when I have to fly low into the states."

David leaned back from the map. Tim noticed David's look and from all the tours in Iraq he knew when something was bothering him.

"Farris, what's up?" Tim said.

David's gaze went to Liam and then back to Tim. "I'm missing something here. Why is he doing this for you? Who would take a chance to fly under the radar and enter the US? If we get caught, all our asses will be in jail, including your Canadian friend.

Liam stood from the table. "I'm getting some fresh air. I'll let you two boys talk."

They both watched as Liam pushed the screen door open with his hand. The heavy spring squeaked as the door settled into place. Sergeant Tim turned to David.

"All right, Farris," Tim said. "I'm going to let you in on a little secret. Liam is my half-brother. Turns out my dad had a wandering eye. He left my mom when I was two and then my mom left me. I grew up in foster care as you know at the same time my dad was starting a new family in Canada. Liam has dual citizenship."

"I thought your parents were dead. Died in some freak hit and run while walking on the shoulder of the road after getting stuck in a snowstorm. That's why you were in foster care."

"Yeah, well…I comforted myself with the image. I got the idea when I was about eight. I was alone again at Christmas. I was watching *It's Wonderful Life*; you know, the one with Jimmy Stewart. I really needed an angel."

David nodded.

"I was always hoping they would come back for me, like when angels get their wings. I would hear that little bell, turn around and there standing would be my mom and dad. Even had an idea of what they would look like. I could see it in the eyes of those orphans in Iraq. Hoping their parents would come for them like angels."

Tim stood from the picnic table and went to a shelf mounted above the sink. Bottles of Canadian liquor sat on the shelf. He grabbed a bottle of Crown Royal and two glasses. He returned and poured himself and David two fingers. They clinked their glasses and downed a belt. Tim then continued with his story.

"Like I said, Liam has dual citizenship."

"How did you find your brother?" David asked.

"I didn't… he found me. I guess on my old man's death bed he told Liam that he had a son in the States. Liam did the research and found me. I had just completed basic training and was stationed in Yuma, Arizona. Found out I got two younger sisters, too."

"Wow, Sarge. I had no idea."

"It's all good, Farris. We can't pick our families. I didn't want to tell you because if we did get caught, I was going to say we took Liam at gun point and forced him into flying us out. The less you knew about the connection the better. That's still going to be our story if we get busted."

David agreed. "Absolutely. I'm with you a hundred percent. You know I wondered how you put this all together. Did he help you set up the camp. Does he know about the mithridate?"

"He knows everything. You really didn't think I alone boated all the supplies out to that island including the dogs, did you?"

"Never really thought about it. Does he know about my parents?"

"Yep. Took the boat out and headed south until I got a signal. Called him on the satellite phone when I made my mind up to help you. He's all in."

Tim lifted the bottle and poured another shot. David took in a deep breath and let out a long sigh. His face looked tired, and his eyes were filled with sadness.

"They're all gone. Penny, my mom, my dad. I have no family anymore."

Tim lifted his glass and held it in the air. David did the same. "You got *me,* Farris. I'm your family now."

They tapped glasses one more time, then downed their shots.

Chapter 17

As Bo walked down the long hallway to his first AA meeting, he made his mind up. He no longer wanted to do what he was told. Thomas Higgins was a phony, an actor, not the man Bo wanted to be.

He entered the meeting room. A dozen or so people mingled about, some sitting, some standing, almost all drinking black coffee and having idle conversation in German. A blond, blue-eyed woman approached.

"You must be Mr. Higgins," Helga Schmidt asked as she pushed out her hand towards him. "I am Fraulein Schmidt, the greeter. My friends call me Helga. Please come in."

Helga removed a typed page from the front of her suit jacket and handed it to Bo.

"These are the topics we are going to discuss tonight. I typed them out in English the best I could."

"Thank you," Bo said lifting the page to study it.

"You're not the first American we have had in our program," Helga said. "This disease does not discriminate on the basis of ethnicity. It can sink its claws into anyone no matter what your nationality is."

Bo looked away from the page and nodded.

"How is your German?" Helga asked inquisitively.

"Oh, it's coming along. I'm using that Babbel app and a couple of others. I wouldn't say I'm fluent by any means, but I can keep a conversation."

"That's fantastic. Can't wait to have a conversation with you in German. I'm your support buddy. Everyone in the program has a support person to call or talk to when they are struggling not to have a drink. I'm the most fluent in English so I usually get the Americans."

Bo smiled. "Great," he said, fixating on her striking sky-blue eyes.

"There is coffee and various kinds of fruit drinks in the back. Help yourself and then take a seat. The meeting should get going in a few minutes."

****

Bo left the meeting feeling strong, better than he had in a long time. The last six weeks had been pretty much a fog. As he walked the streets of Dusseldorf, his mind went to Carly. How was she doing? Was she with David? What did Stacey do when she learned Carly had returned to the states? His mind also wandered to his upcoming date for coffee with Helga.

Part of the program was to meet every other day with your support buddy if you had no family in the country. He was not about to tell Helga about Carly's mom. He said he was alone in Germany. After so many weeks of sobriety, the meetings would become fewer and fewer until eventually they would stop.

Even before Carly decided to leave, Bo was having second thoughts about the witness protection program. When he and Carly had decided to enter the program, both realized it would involve a combination of physical relocation and identity change.

What seemed like the best choice at the time no longer did. Bo had been restless for weeks, struggling with his desire to leave. He never shared that with Carly or her mom. Booze made it easier to handle. Now that he was sober and healing, he was ready to make a change.

Sitting behind a computer in a Dusseldorf public library, Bo stared at the Custom Search Page he created within Google. He could not read German, so he needed the results to come back in English. His fingers deftly danced over the keys typing…**How to get out of witness protection?**

Bo paused and thought to himself, *No one will know it's me*. He then hit Enter.

The search soon brought up various blogs discussing why and how someone may want to leave the program. Before he knew it, he was communicating with someone referring to himself as Rambo.

> *First and foremost,* Rambo typed, *never use your real name or your witness protection name in any correspondence within this blog. Have you done that?*

No. Bo replied.

Good!! You need to give yourself a name. What do you want to call yourself? Never use proper nouns or pronouns that could identify yourself or someone in your party.

Got it. Bo typed. *How about GI Joe?*

Ok, Joe. There are some things you need to know. Will you be leaving by yourself, or will you be doing this with others?

One person has already left. As far as I can tell, she is still in the program.
No pronouns. Remember? Rambo typed.

Sorry!

How many people are in your party, and have you discussed this with them?

Three of us and I have not discussed it with anyone. One of the people in the party is elderly. She is a little frail.

AGAIN! NO PRONOUNS!!

Sorry.

Do the US Marshals know you are planning on leaving?

No.

Without saying where you would like to go, do you want to leave the country you are currently living in?

Yes.

Are the people you are being protected against incarcerated or dead? Are they still a threat?

Living!! YES a threat.

This is going to be the last back and forth we do. From now on we will communicate from this account :
https://myaccount.google.com/u/2/
The password is spearhead4&%   Are you following?
Rambo typed.

Yes. Bo replied.

When you get into the account, you will go to the mailer. There will be a message in the Drafts folder. You will compose a response but never send it. Save it as a draft. I check that site every hour and will respond accordingly. I will compose a response to you and save it as a draft. No one can intercept our correspondence because it will never have been sent. All our drafts will be saved and only seen by me and you. It is not fool proof but it's as safe as we can get. I will then delete the site when you are safe and out of the program. Do you understand?

Yes.

Bo noticed the typing from Rambo had stopped. He typed back…**Rambo???**
There was no response. The connection was terminated. He quickly removed his cellphone from his coat pocket and took a screen shot before leaving the site and deleting its history.

****

Manila Philippines

Rambo was a Harvester, a loose group of Data collectors selling personal information on the dark web. Identity theft was her specialty, selling everything from Social Security numbers to credit card numbers to medical records. Lately, she had branched out and found that outing people in witness protection was very lucrative. Certain individuals and organizations paid big money finding people governments around the world were trying to hide.

Rambo typed furiously as she sat at her computer. She opened the messages between Bo and herself and clicked on > **Show Original** and search for line **"Received from" >.** She was after the IP address which routes Internet traffic to and from computers. IP-based geolocation services like Wolfram Alpha or Spiceworks would do the rest.

The IP would not give an exact location like a home address, but it could give with 75 percent accuracy a user's city. She was pleased to find this IP address originated in Dusseldorf, Germany.

Rambo's questions were designed to be a trap. Like a fly caught in a spider's web, Bo never saw it coming. She needed to create a profile and stay in touch until she could offer up her prey to the highest bidder on the dark web.

<u>Profile of GI Joe</u>
Probably a male and at one time military. (i.e. GI Joe)

Three people in the group. Probably two females. One of the females being elderly.

Definitely Americans. US Marshals involved.

Threat is still active.

Time zone difference of 7 hours. He was on that computer at 7:30 pm which makes it 2:30 am Filipino time.

Best time for him to start checking the email drafts after 6:00 pm German time.

Probably works during the day.

More data needed to complete profile.

Rambo known by her friends as Aurora Fordeliza yawned as she looked at the clock on the wall. She was used to working late hours because she knew most people in witness protection came from the west. The time zones were between 7- and 13-hours difference.

Either that guy doesn't have a clue or I am just getting better and better," Aurora said to her dog *Raspberry Pi* as she shut down her computer and went to bed.

Chapter 18

Borka swung open the door of the Dusseldorf hotel, his disheveled hair mirroring the chaotic state of his appearance, a pungent odor of alcohol trailing him. Grego stood at the door, a manila envelope clutched in his hand. Without a word, he strode past Borka, purposefully brushing his shoulder against him. He caught sight of a nude woman lying in bed through the partially open bedroom door. Without hesitation, he averted his gaze and turned to Borka.

"Tell the whore to get the fuck out of here. I have information to share."

Borka stumbled into the bedroom, the lingering effects of the previous night showing itself in his unsteady gait. After a while, a young woman in her early twenties emerged from the room, followed by Borka. She paused at the doorway, pivoting to face the room.

"When you're done with the old man," she said, "call me. We'll continue where we left off."

As she turned away, her gaze shifted to Grego, a silent acknowledgment, before she gracefully walked out of the room, wearing a smirk.

Grego passed the envelope to Borka before retrieving a water bottle from the mini fridge.

"Here's intel on our guy. Seems like he's attempting to turn things around. Enrolled in a program to kick the drinking habit. Maybe you ought to consider the same," Grego remarked.

"Fuck off! Since when do you give me orders?" Borka retorted.

Borka, clutching the intel, made his way to the bathroom and closed the door behind him. Meanwhile, Grego settled onto the couch, activating the TV with a click. His attention then shifted to the telephone, dialing room service. Time seemed to stretch as he waited, and, growing impatient, he called out to Borka.

"What the hell? Did you fall asleep in there?"

Just as Borka emerged from the bathroom, a sharp knock echoed on the door. Swiftly, Grego opened it, allowing the room service attendant to enter. The aroma wafted through the room as the server poured two cups of coffee and lifted the silver dome, revealing an assortment of fruit and buttery pastries.

"Is there anything else you gentlemen require?" inquired the server.

"That will be all," Grego responded, handing over five Euros.

Borka and Grego sat in a dimly lit room, a small table wedged between them. The air was heavy with an unspoken tension that lingered until the last bite of their breakfast. Grego, finishing his plate, wiped his mouth with a cloth napkin before disdainfully tossing it onto his empty plate, which he then forcefully shoved to the center of the table.

Breaking the silence with a sudden sharpness, Grego declared, "I think you need to join AA."

Borka stiffened, shooting a disdainful scowl in Grego's direction.

Grego clarified, "Not as a member, you idiot! As a way to get close to Mr. Higgins, aka Bo Harris."

Understanding flashed across Borka's face.

"Oh, I see. To befriend him if possible. So, according to the report, he no longer wishes to stay in the witness protection program."

Grego affirmed, "Yes, that's right. He doesn't seem to be the sharpest tool in the shed. He went online, started asking questions on how to get out of being in witness protection. Kolo paid a considerable amount for that information. A Helga Schmidt runs the chapter he belongs to. Her information was in the report."

Borka nodded, recalling the details. "Yes, I saw that."

Grego rose from the table, pushing his chair in with purpose. "I want you to attend the next meeting. Feel out the place and report back to me. We'll then come up with a plan. Let's meet again next week."

As Borka rose to his feet, an unsettling realization dawned on him – he couldn't escape the nagging sense that he was nothing more than a pawn in Grego's game.

"Why do I get this feeling that you're just calling the shots?"

A brief, tense pause hung in the room, Grego turned and left the room without a word.

****

Fog had rolled over the tiny camp and settled over the terrain. Standing on the bluff overlooking the lake, David could not even see the plane. It was early, Tim and Liam were still tossing in their beds. He stood in deep thought, taking in the morning air, staring through a hazy nebulous of a Canadian lake. From offshore he could hear the eerie calls of the loons.

"Won't be flying out anytime soon, eh," Liam said, as he pushed open the screen door, catching it before it slammed so not to wake Tim. He then walked the three steps of the deck and stood next to David.

"You can barely make out the plane," David said. "I don't see how we can take off in this."

"Taking off isn't the hard part. We could fly right through the clouds and get above 'em. It's the landing that would be difficult. This happens all the time. The fog should roll out of here within a couple of hours and we will be on our way before lunch."

"God! I appreciate you doing this for me," David said. "You're taking a big risk."

"No more of a risk than what you boys did in Iraq. I'm sorry for what happened to your family. If I can help get you some closure, I'm all in."

"That's just it. I do want closure but at the same time I think I have had enough. I know the sarge would do anything for me, but I think it is time to turn ourselves in."

Liam rubbed the sleep from his eyes then pushed his glasses up the bridge of his nose. "I've been thinking the same thing. *If* you two turn yourselves in and *if* Tim has a deal with the CIA, hopefully they will live up to it."

David nodded as Liam kept talking.

"If you don't turn yourselves in you'll be fugitives and on the run. Hell, you'd be fugitives now if the CIA wasn't keeping this from getting out. Nothing good can come of this except you getting dead. The sound of the screen door rubbing against the deck caused the two to turn. Tim walked down the few steps and let the door slam behind him.

"I've been listening to what you two have been talking about. I will leave it up to you, Farris. Whatever you choose, you will choose for the two of us. You're the reason Isla is free today. I'll always be grateful. If you want to call it quits, I'll go along with that. If you want to kill that bastard, we can do that, too. It's your call."

****

David sat in the back of the DHC-2 Beaver with wet hands. The strap across his lap was buckled so tightly it almost cut off his circulation. Tim and Liam chatted idly as Liam taxied to the far end of the lake and stopped. David watched the pulleys and steel cables loosen and tighten as Liam turned the plane and angled it into the wind. He then turned to David.

"May be a little bumpy when we first take off, eh," Liam said. "The lake is a little rough."

Liam lifted his arm and gave David a thumbs up, noticing the angst on his face. He then turned and put on his black head set and adjusted various switches and knobs.

The sound of the high pitch Turbo engine began to whine as Liam pushed the throttle forward and the plane began to move. David bounced back and forth as the pontoons struggled to cut through the choppy water. As if falling down the first hill of a roller coaster, David's stomach flipped when the little plane became airborne, and the violent shaking stopped.

Looking out the small window to his right, David's nerves began to calm down. Lakes of all sizes dotted the landscape as far as the eye could see and could be potential landing strips in case of an emergency. He noticed Liam point out the front window showing a cow moose and her calf eating the rich vegetation growing up from a Canadian stream.

Within an hour the Pacific came into view and David knew it would only be a matter of hours before they would fly into Victoria and turn themselves in. Tim had made the phone call.

****

Markell removed the vial of white powder from his suit coat pocket and poured a small amount onto the mirror. The powder spilled in tiny clumps, and he used a razor blade to chop it up into a fine powder.

He had been told that injecting or smoking coke would get him a faster, more intense high, but he rejected that advice. He hated needles, hated them since he was a kid when the doctor gave him those vaccinations. His reaction was severe; the injection site would turn red and swell, his temperature would rise, often followed by vomiting. No injections for him.

Using the razor blade, he divided the powder into three lines. He picked up the rolled twenty-dollar bill, placed it to his nose, and vacuumed in a line. Leaning back, he closed his eyes, waiting for the drug to rush through his system and then did the same with the other nostril.

Within seconds the familiar euphoria flowed over his body followed by increased energy and the urge to bang a hot young thing.

Hearing a knock on the door, he quickly slid the mirror under the couch, stood up, and buttoned his suit jacket.

"You're late," Markell said, groping the buttocks of the blond as she walked past him, her perfume radiating from her body.

"I only have so much time," she said, then slipped off her coat and flung it on the back of a chair, revealing a black sweater dress that was molded to her body. Her blond hair hung loosely over the top of her bare shoulders. A silver triangular locket dangled just above her cleavage.

Markell's eyes raked over her starting with her chest and finishing with her black and silver shoes. She kicked off her high heels and threw her purse to the side before sitting on the couch. Markell sat next to her and removed the mirror from under the couch. He placed it on her lap along with five one hundred-dollar bills.

"Help yourself," he said, as she tucked the cash into her purse then reached for the rolled twenty.

Markell proceeded to slip his hand under her skirt.

"I didn't get your name," he said, looking at her.

"Genieve," she murmured and smiled. "You also may help yourself," she added slyly, moving her knees further apart.

Markell began to stroke her and nibble on her neck. Genieve giggled seeing a bulge pushing through his pants.

"Oh, my," she said flirtatiously, then snorted her line and leaned back.

Markell lifted her skirt and began to remove her panties. She grabbed his hands.

"Let's get somewhere more comfortable," Genieve said.

Markell smiled and stood up from the couch, holding out his hand. "I can't wait to get your clothes off," he said following her into the bedroom.

Genieve stopped by the bed and turned, lifting her sweater dress over her head. He watched as her hair and locket fell back down over her shoulders. Markell pushed her to the bed and removed her panties. Sinking to his knees, he lowered his head between her thighs, and she pulled his head tight. He heard nothing as she unlatched the triangular locket and removed the outer cover exposing a fixed blade. She raked her fingers through the top of Markell's hair and pulled. He enjoyed it when a woman played rough.

Genieve yanked back his head and smiled at him. Markell smiled back, until he felt the cold steel of her blade. He gasped as she slit his throat from ear to ear. Guttural sounds filled the room, and her lap quickly became soaked with his blood. Genieve pushed him to the floor and stood.

"Look what a mess you've made," she said before walking back to the front room and returning with her phone. She snapped a picture and texted it to Tatyana. Under it was the caption…Assassinated the Assassin.

"I really need a hot shower," she said out loud, carefully stepping around Markell's body avoiding any blood still pooling on the carpet.

On her way to the bathroom, droplets of blood from her hips and thighs left a speckled trail.

Chapter 19

Officer Paul Daugherty wearing a black cotton jacket walked into the interrogation room. Emblazoned on the back were the letters CIA. He held two Styrofoam cups of steamy black coffee. He placed one on the laminate table in front of him and handed the other to another officer standing to the side.

A bank of four lights hung above the table and were the only lights in the room.

Daugherty smiled smugly as he pulled off his jacket and draped it over a chair. The jacket that fit his six-foot six-inch frame totally engulfed it. He removed his cowboy hat and set it next to his cup of coffee. Tim fidgeted trying to get comfortable with the shackles that bound his hands and feet.

"Welcome home," he drawled.

Tim immediately recognized the familiar accent. "Your voice doesn't fit your face," Tim said. "I pictured you much older."

"I age well," Daugherty said sarcastically. "Got good genes on my mother's side."

Daugherty lowered himself to the chair seemingly in control of his emotions. In one smooth move he glided across the table grabbing Tim by the collar and sent the folding chair and coffee flying. He pulled Tim to within an inch of his face.

"If that mithridate isn't in that well head, I'm going to beat you myself."

"It's there," Tim assured him, pushing his chin even closer to Daugherty. "Had to make sure my girl was really out. I don't trust the government. When we turned ourselves in, one of your officers let me call Isla. I asked her a few questions only she would know. That's when I told him where I really stashed it."

The door opened and in walked a man holding David by the arm. He wore the same cotton black jacket as Daugherty. "They got it, Sir," the man said. "The mithridate has been recovered."

Chains rattled as David was guided to a seat next to Tim.

Daugherty released Tim, then went and picked up the folding chair. He opened it and sat back down behind the table. He turned to the officer who had just brought David in.

"Mind sending the custodian in. Had an accident and spilled my coffee."

Daugherty sat across from the two and pulled in his chair. "Well, this changes everything."

David studied Daugherty. He had heard a little about him from the conversations he had with Tim.

"I want to thank you for getting Isla out," Tim said.

"Thank me??!!" Daugherty said with a twang. "Didn't have much choice now, did I Tim?"

David said nothing as his eyes moved from one man to the other. He nervously tapped his middle finger on the table. Daugherty looked at him.

"Sorry about your folks," he said. "We think we know who was behind it."

A heavy silence hung in the air.

"Slovak?" David asked.

"Yep. Same person who put you and your girlfriend through hell last year."

Daugherty's gaze went back to Tim.

"You got yourself in a bit of a pickle, Tim. We had to trade some high caliber detainees to get your lady back. A lot of cash too. Not so worried about the cash but the detainees. That was a damn shame. They'll probably be back in the theater within a month."

"You got the mithridate back, didn't ya?"

"Oh, we did. I have to admit not too many men can get the CIA to do their biddin'. Without blowing too much smoke up your ass, I was pretty impressed."

"Should we get a lawyer?" Tim asked.

"A lawyer?" Daugherty said. "Why would you need a lawyer? You haven't been arrested."

"Quit screwing with us," Tim said abruptly. "Just read us our *Miranda rights* and get us a lawyer."

"I think your britches are a little too tight, Tim! Now that you have a bun in the oven and gonna be a daddy, you can't fly off the handle like that. Babies can sense when mommy and daddy are upset."

"What?"

"Isla. I was in Iraq when we did the exchange. I'd say her baby bump was at least four, maybe five months."

Daugherty removed a picture from his front pocket. He slid the picture in front of Tim. David's gaze went to the picture as Tim lifted it to his eyes. "Those mother fuckers," he mumbled.

"Your lady claims she wasn't raped. She was actually treated very well by the women who watched over her. They just wanted her as a bargaining chip. Now, if she was a female US captured soldier than that would have been a different outcome. You're gonna be a daddy, Tim."

Tim sat back in his chair, not saying a word never taking his eyes off the belly bump of a pregnant Isla.

"Why are you doing this?" David asked. "You got the mithridate back."

"Did we!!??" Daugherty asked. "Word on the street is it is still out there and up for grabs."

Daugherty removed another picture from his front pocket and slid it in front of David. You two might not face prison time if you help us get this bad guy."

David studied the picture. His jaw tightened. "Are you sure Slovak is behind my parents' murders?"

A smile grew on Daugherty's face. David studied it, puzzled. His fists clenched and he was about to stand when Tim placed his shackled hand on David's knee.

"What the hell's wrong with you, Man?!!" Tim burst out. "We're talking about his folks."

Daugherty nodded to one of the officers standing by the door.

"Let 'em in, Brooks."

The tension in the room was broken as the back door opened and Mr. and Mrs. Farris walked through the door. David sat, rooted to his chair.

"Mom," he said, just above a whisper.

David's mother immediately ran and threw her arms around him. "They said you were dead," is all David could say.

"It was part of the plan, Son," David's father said as he walked to the two and placed his hand on David's shoulder squeezing slightly.

"I'll be a son of a bitch," Tim mumbled to himself as he looked at Daugherty.

"What plan?" David asked.

Daugherty answered very brusquely. "Why doesn't everyone take a seat? You can catch up later. We don't have a lot of time."

Then, to Officer Brooks he said, "Get these men out of their shackles."

Chapter 20

David's father pulled a chair out for Mrs. Farris before taking a chair himself. "Why don't you start?" Daugherty said, looking at Mr. Farris.

David's father began. "You know how we were remodeling the house, using some of the life insurance money we got for Penny."

"Yeah. I remember," David said. "Penny always wanted the place upgraded. Said living in a house over a century old, made her feel like 'The Walton's.'"

David's mother smiled, remembering how excited Penny would get when talking about how she would design her own room.

"Well," David's father continued. "We got to the point where the plumbing had to be gutted and totally replaced, in the kitchen. The contractors, who happened to be a husband and wife, said it would take a few days and that we needed to find a place where we could stay. We went to the cabin. Didn't tell a soul."

"What's this got to do with the firebombing? Did that really happen?"

"Oh, it did," Mr. Farris said, shaking his head. "The people that got killed were the contractors."

"Contractors?" David asked again puzzled.

"The contractors spent the night. They split the cost of the hotel and took it off the original price. Figured they would get done faster if they could just crash at the house. I let them stay in your room. I saw no problem with it."

Unable to keep his silence, Tim broke in.

"Why did you tell me that David's parents were dead? He went through hell out there."

"I'm sorry about that. It came from higher up," Daugherty said. "We figured this would be one way to get you boys back. We also wanted to protect the Farris's and to keep Slovak thinking that he had killed the parents knowing David would come looking for him."

"Oh, that *bear* wants a piece of Slovak, trust me," Tim said.

"Well, now you may just get the chance."

Daugherty pulled a section of newspaper from a stack of papers that were sitting on the table. "You're just in time," he said as he handed it to David.

"We had this published in the Detroit Free Press to make sure that Slovak would be able to find it."

David looked at the folded newspaper and immediately saw his parents' pictures and names at the top of the page.

Eugene Farris
December 20, 1947 – June 6, 2020
Beatrice Farris
December 23, 1947 – June 6, 2020

Eugene and Beatrice Farris passed away on Friday, June 6, 2020, from a house fire. Lifelong residents of Livingston County, the couple is most well-known for their work with development of the abandoned Farm Street factory into the Heart and Home Soup Kitchen as well as other community projects.

The Farris' are survived by their eldest son David Nathan Farris, a brother William, and a sister-in-law Ginger Westin (Farris). The couple was preceded in death by their daughter Penny Margaret Farris.

Beatrice was a secretary at Howell High for 23 years before retiring. Eugene loved wood crafting and fishing. He enlisted in the Army 1965 to 1969 and served overseas in Vietnam.

A memorial service will be held at the Borek Jennings Funeral Home on Sunday, June 16 from 1:00 to 4:00. Please come and share your stories of remembrance. Following the service, a private burial will be held at the family ancestral cemetery.

David looked critically at Daugherty. "I don't get this. "You faked my parents' deaths and put it in the local newspaper hoping I would see it?"

"Not exactly," Daugherty said. "Hoping Slovak would see it. We're setting a trap for that douche bag."

David leaned back in his chair when the realization of the plan sank in.

"I get it. You think Slovak will stake out the funeral home looking for me to get at the mithridate."

A smile grew on his face. "I still may be able to get my hands on that S.O.B.!"

"Bingo!" Daugherty said. "We want to take him alive. He's risen to the top of the CIA's most wanted list. We finally have a name of the organization he is affiliated with. *Kolo*. They are mainly out of Europe. Slovak probably thinks Carly is with you."

"Carly??" David voice peaked. "Do you know where she is? Is she with her boyfriend?"

"I don't know where she is," Daugherty replied, deciding not to reveal anything he knew.

"When someone goes into witness protection, we don't find out anything about them. However, I am meeting later with Richard Bolton. I believe he was the Chief in charge of the first operation with Carly. Is that right?"

"Yes. He worked with our friend Meghan Conner who was actually Stacey Canter. Agent Stacey Canter of the FBI."

"What?" Daugherty said, faking confusion.

"Meghan Conner was a resident at Holy Oaks," David explained. "Turned out she was an FBI plant placed undercover to befriend Carly. It was a joint operation to get the mithridate back. FBI and the CIA."

"Huh... I'll get more of a lowdown once I speak with Bolton."

"What about me?" Tim asked. "Am I going to be involved?"

Daugherty grinned. "If you don't want to become someone's bitch in Leavenworth, you'll get involved."

"Well, that's not an option! What do you want from me?"

"First, we're going to reunite you with Isla. You got some planning to do. You'll then be headed to Europe. Got some intelligence that the Fletcher's who are under witness protection may be targeted by *Kolo*. We need to get eyes on the ground."

"Is that why you're keeping it quiet that the mithridate was recovered? Trying to take out *Kolo* once and for all?"

"You can never totally take out a terrorist cell. They are like starfish. You can cut off a tentacle and really cripple them but just like the starfish they can grow back. Sometimes worse than the first.

"As far as the CIA is concerned, there is still mithridate that needs to be recovered. We're going to keep that storyline as long as it takes to keep *Kolo* actively searching. We believe it was you, Tim, who put out the word that all the mithridate was not recovered. Are we right?"

"I always have a backup plan. If you were going to play hardball with me, I was going to take it into my own hands. I would have sold to the highest bidder and used that money to pay the ransom to get Isla out."

"That's exactly what you are going to do. Except you will be doing it *our* way. We will send you to Europe to lure the targets in. Only a handful of agents know that we have the mithridate. But you will be given a faux vial that will test positive if needed.

"Not only are we planning to trap the bad guys, but we also want to trap the bad guy in the Bureau."

Daugherty shook his head from side to side in disgust. "We got a "mole" on the inside that needs extermination. So, you will work in the theater of Europe while David works here in the states."

"I'm good with that, but what about Isla?"

"You're heading to The Land Down Under the day after tomorrow. I could only get you five days and two of those are travel time. Things will be happening fast.

"So… you're just going to let us go. No jail time?"

"Let's just say the CIA would hate the story getting out that a former Sargent in the U.S. Army outfoxed the agency," Daugherty replied.

Then he gave a meaningful look to Tim and David.

"Something like that would *never*, and I mean *never* happen, would it, Fellas?", he said, warning them.

Tim quickly caught on. "Nope!! Never!!" he replied.

To which David added, "I don't even know what you're talking about."

Chapter 21

Slovak entered the hotel room carrying a plastic grocery bag. He removed a bunch of four bananas along with a small apple crumb coffee cake. He tossed a local newspaper to Tatyana.

"It's going down tomorrow," he said.

Tatyana looked up from the couch and picked up the newspaper. Her eyes focused on the obituary written for Eugene and Beatrice Farris.

"Do you think he will be there?" Tatyana asked.

"Of course, he will", Slovak said as he peeled back a banana and took a bite. "I had access to all David's medical records at Holy Oaks. I know what makes that boy tick. He'll be there. And if I am really lucky, she will be there, too."

Tatyana lifted her phone from the coffee table and scrolled to the picture of Markell. She handed Slovak her phone.

"This problem has been eliminated."

Slovak tapped the pic and enlarged it. He shook his head slightly. "I can't believe you pulled this off. He was one of the best."

"I told you when men think with their other head, they are vulnerable. Markell was no exception. Sexuality, if used correctly, is a woman's best weapon."

****

Daugherty knew there was a problem, and it was much deeper than what he had previously thought. Intelligence was being leaked about military capabilities and top-secret maneuvers, along with other sensitive topics.

The agency went on high alert and trained IT hackers with high security clearances were tracking the trail of the leaked documents. His superiors were on edge. Slovak was involved so that meant *Kolo* was behind it.

What kept him up at night was *Kolo's* desire to develop a radiological dispersal device or in layman's terms-- a dirty bomb. It was simple, really. Combine a conventional explosive device with some type of toxic or radioactive material. *Kolo* wasn't after a nuclear yield, they were after mass panic. The *threat* of spreading toxic or radioactive contamination would be used as a barging chip. It was a way to even out the playing field.

There was another firestorm brewing, a personal one, and Daugherty never saw it coming. He was gone for extended periods of time, which never raised red flags with Linda Laurice, his wife. She knew what she was marrying into.

They had met while getting their bachelor's degree and both had attended the CST (Clandestine Service Training.) They dreamed of being a husband-and-wife team. Getting the international bad guys and saving the world. That all changed when Linda Laurice found herself pregnant.

They decided she would be a stay-at-home mom. This decision, however, came with a condition. Daugherty consented to ensuring Linda Laurice remained informed and involved. She yearned to continue her work, whether it pertained to domestic matters or had international implications. Midnight phone calls were part of the norm and Linda Laurice never minded them. She stood as his closest ally, a seamless husband-and-wife duo.

But what was up with their intimacy? He had always been so amorous when he returned from long term assignments. She remembered how he would be waiting outside the shower when she stepped out, holding a thick towel to wrap her in. He loved to kiss her when her hair was dripping wet as she ripped off his clothing, piece by piece. The baby seemed to have changed all that. Linda Laurice would watch for more clues. She was nobody's naïve bitch.

Chapter 22

Carly looked from her magazine as she heard the grind of the garage door. "That's gotta be the loudest garage door I've ever heard. You can feel the floor vibrate as it goes all the way down."

Porsche stood up from the couch. "I know what you mean. She really needs to get someone to look at that. If that spring breaks, there's no way to get that door open, even if you pull the track release. It happened to me; I was stuck for hours."

"What do you mean?" Carly asked.

"The garage was separate from the house and the only way out was through the garage door. I started the car and the spring snapped. The door came slamming down and I was stuck inside until Ahmed came to pick me up for a date. I didn't have my cell because I was just letting the car warm up and was heading back into the house. I think I was there for about 6 hours."

Stacey entered the townhouse carrying a cardboard holder with three Starbucks and a folded Detroit Free Press under her arm. "Hope your tastes haven't changed."

"Caramel Macchiato?" Carly said, walking to the kitchen.

"I know you so well," Stacey boasted. "And Porsche, Toasted White Chocolate Mocha."

"I'm impressed. You're all over it," Porsche said.

Stacey removed the drinks from the cardboard caddie and handed each one their cup. She also handed Carly the Free Press.

"Look in the obituaries. David's parents are there."

Carly followed Stacey into the living room. She placed the Macchiato on the coffee table and sat in the armchair where she immediately opened to the obituaries. A few moments passed before she read out loud.

"A memorial service will be held at the Borek Jennings Funeral Home on Sunday, June 16, from 1:00 to 4:00. Please come and share your stories of remembrance."

Carly lifted her eyes from the page. "This is it!!" She burst out. "We have to be at David's parents' funeral!"

"What?" Porsche asked.

"We have to be there. I owe it to David. I'm the one who got him into this. I bet Slovak will be there," Carly went on, "…Hiding under some special rock for degenerate slimeballs."

"Stop being so narcissistic!" Stacey snapped." We're all a part of this…not all the blame falls on *you*."

"I don't think he will be out in the open," Porsche said. "Maybe he'll show in a disguise. Before I was booted from Deutsche Hochschule and Ahmed was fired for fraternizing with a subordinate, he taught a course on deception. Disguise was part of the training. What he did was come in as a guest instructor. Ahmed taught for a full hour before he began taking the disguise off. The class was blown away when we realized it was him. That's when I fell for him which ended up getting him fired and me expelled."

"Like I told you, it takes two to tango," Stacey said. "So, what will you do, Carly, if Slovak does show up?"

"Kill him! I'm going to kill that bastard. I need a gun."

"Carly, you can't just go all vigilante and take him out. I can't just get you a gun. I'm a law enforcement officer for God's sake! Do you want me to lose my job?"

The chime of a text interrupted the conversation. Stacey walked to the kitchen and removed her phone from her suede purse sitting on the counter. Porsche and Carly noticed Stacey's brows knit together.

"I gotta go," Stacey said, fishing for her keys. "Looks like our killer struck again. Promise me you two won't do anything until we talk more."

Carly and Porsche said nothing.

"Promise me," Stacey said again, raising her voice more forcefully.

Carly nodded. "I promise. You ought to get that garage door fixed."

"Yeah, I know. Shakes the whole damn house, but, on the flip side, if anyone tries to get in…I'll be the first one to know."

"Are you going to let the Chief know we're back in town?"

"Oh, he already knows. He's the one who called me when he learned you had left Germany. Wasn't too happy about that."

"Stacey, I'm sorry if I put you in a bad spot. I just want this over with."

"It's a little late for that. Just don't do anything reckless and stay put until I get back."

****

Carly heard her phone ring and grabbed it from the coffee table. Her forehead crinkled.

"It's a 703-area code," she told Porsche. "That's a Washington number."

She raised her shoulders and said, "Hello."

"Ms. Fletcher, this is Richard Bolton, Chief of Station, Central Intelligence."

Carly's eyebrows raised. "Yes," is all she could get out.

"We never met but I headed an operation involving you last year with one of our agents, Agent Canter."

"I know who you are."

"Good. I was wondering if we could meet. Maybe later this afternoon."

"Of course, where?"

"The Detroit area. Agent Canter will know. Will you also extend my invitation to Ms. Berliner."

"Sure."

"Perfect. We'll see you then."

Carly raised her hand as if asking Bolton to stop. She began to pace the room. "Is David with you?"

There was a slight pause. "As a matter of fact, he is."

"Can I speak with him?"

"Make it brief," he said handing David the phone.

"Carly," David said.

"I know why you took the mithridate. Stacey told me."

"I should have let you know. I shouldn't have kept that from you."

"I'm not worried about that now. Is Sargent Tim with you?"

"He is."

"How much trouble are you in?"

"I'm not sure," David answered. "I think the Chief will explain when you get here. Is Bo with you?"

"I came with Porsche."

"They're making me hang up now. I can't wait to see you."

"Me too," Carly said before the phone went dead.

Chapter 23

Sergeant Tim's eyes opened as he heard the mechanical whine of the landing gear pull and release as the huge C-5M military cargo plane began its descent.

The military gear secured tightly under the cargo netting didn't budge as the plane banked slightly, then flattened out preparing to land. The flight to Australia was a little over thirty hours and Tim was pleased the CIA was picking up the tab.

"We'll be landing in Alice Springs within fifteen minutes," the Airman said to the passengers buckled in on long benches mounted to the sides of the plane. "Welcome to the Land Down Under."

There were two US military bases in Australia. *Harold E. Holt* and *Pine Gap*. The base Tim was headed to was *Pine Gap*, operated by the US intelligence community. He noticed over half of the passengers were in plain clothes like him. Made sense being an intelligence base. Tim pulled back his sleeve and checked his watch. His rendezvous with Isla was less than two hours away and he was still in disbelief that he was going to be a dad.

Isla watched as the cab pulled into the driveway and Tim got out. She carefully ran out the door, quite aware of the baby growing in her belly. Tim ran to her and squeezed her tightly. Tears filled his eyes. He spoke into her ear.

"I thought you were dead. I went back looking for you. I never would have left Iraq if I knew you were alive. There was nothing left. Everyone was gone except the dead and burned-out buildings.

Isla squeezed Tim even tighter. So tight he felt the baby kick. Tim looked down at Isla's belly.

"Our baby," he said in disbelief.

"Yes, our baby," she replied with a smile.

Tim's face lit up as he knelt down and placed his hand on her belly.

"Babe," Isla interrupted, pulling Tim up from his knees. "You got to pay the cabbie. Give him a good tip. He has been waiting patiently.

The taxi driver casually leaned against his cab, tapping away on his phone. His attention shifted to Tim as he strolled up.

"I'm sorry, my man. What's the damage?"

"US or Australian?" the cabbie asked.

"US."

"Thirty dollars."

Tim handed the cabbie a fifty.

"Keep it. Appreciated the ride."

He lifted the overstuffed duffle bag lying in the driveway and slung the strap over his shoulder. He followed Isla into her home thinking of how he was going to break the news that he was only there for a few days. The CIA was now calling the shots and Tim would be heading to Europe.

"Throw your bag in my bedroom," Isla said, pointing to a room on her left. "Come out to the kitchen. I'll grab you a beer and make you something to eat."

Tim tossed the duffle bag onto the bed. As he went to leave, something caught his eye. Up on a chest of drawers was a picture in a frame of two women. Two identical women. Two identical Isla's. Tim examined it then placed it back where he found it and then left the room.

"Do you have a twin?" Tim asked as he sat down at the table in front of his beer. "I saw that picture on your dresser. Do you have an identical twin?"

Tim noticed Isla's reaction. She began to speak but then stopped as she fought back tears.

"That was my sister Addison. She died of breast cancer before I left for Iraq. After she passed, I had this void. I just had to get away. That's why I went to work for CARE."

"God, Isla, I had no idea."

"I never told you. I wanted to forget her, and the pain associated with her dying. I know that was wrong but at the time, it helped me cope. I never want that feeling again. I loved my sister."

Tim stood from the table and went to Isla. He brought her in and held her tight. "We will be a family. Me, you, and our baby."

"Tim," Isla started and then stopped.

"What? What's going on?"

"Our baby. We are going to have a girl and I was going to ask you if we could name her Addison, after my sister…If you don't want to, I totally get it."

"A girl? We're going to have a baby girl?"

"We are!"

Tim again placed his hand on her belly.

"I love the name Addison, and I love you. She will have two loving parents that will never abandon her. That is, if you marry me."

"Oh my God…Are you proposing?"

Tim lowered to one knee and removed a small white velvet box from his front jean pocket. He looked up at her and opened it at the same time.

"Ms. Borne, will you do me the honor of marrying me?"

After a pause, a huge smile formed on Isla's face.

"Absolutely!!"

Tim rose to his feet and kissed her. He placed the ring over her finger where it fit loosely.

"I had no idea what ring size to get, so I got it large and thought we could resize it later."

Isla spread her fingers, and the diamond sparkled like fine cut glass. "I will so be your wife, Mr. Holden."

She then threw her arms around Tim's shoulders and pushed him down into his seat.

"You've got to be starving. I'm going to make you something to eat. You got to tell me how you did it. How did you get me out?"

Isla then went to the fridge where she pulled out Vegemite spread and bread. She lifted a steel pan of pea and ham soup and set it on the stove.

"Made this earlier. Hope you like ham and pea."

"I love it. Not sure about the Vegemite?" Tim said, studying the glass jar.

"You'll like it."

"Never had it. I just remember a song from this Australian rock band that mentioned it in one of their songs."

"You're taking about…Men at Work?"

"Yep. That's the band."

Isla dipped a spoon into the jar, then handed it to Tim. "Try it. I'm not going to tell you what's in it, until you try it."

Tim took the spoon of brown goo, opened his mouth, and licked it clean.

"Ummm... Salty with a tad of bitterness. Now what's in this?"

Isla laughed slightly. It's the yeast waste that comes from making beer. It's our version of peanut butter and jelly. We Aussies eat it all the time. Enough with the culinary lessons of Australia. How did you get me out?"

"You tell me first. What happened to the kids?" Tim asked.

"Most of the younger kids went with me. The older boys were recruited by the militia. The kids were assimilated with families. They are young enough that they will adapt. It broke my heart as I watched the village burn."

"Those bastards," Tim said, then took a long slug of his beer.

"So... how did you get me out?"

"I made a deal with the CIA that they couldn't refuse."

"What kind of deal?"

"When I found out you were alive and being ransomed, I tried everything. I was state-side and was getting ready to go back. Then out of the blue, God intervened."

"What do you mean...God intervened?"

"Like this idea to get you out was sent straight from heaven. A friend of mine from Iraq and his girlfriend were running from some really bad guys who thought they had mithridate."

"Mithridate?"

"Yeah. It's an antidote which has small amounts of pathogens. The bad guys wanted to reverse engineer it, to get at the pathogens and make a dirty bomb. David, that is his name, found three vials of the antidote, but he kept one aside for me. The rest went to the CIA.

"Word got out that there was a missing vial. I told the CIA that I would return the vial if they got you out. And, if they refused, I would sell it to the highest bidder and pay your ransom myself. And you know the rest of the story."

Isla brought Tim's plate to the table and placed it in front of him. She leaned in and gave him a kiss, then sat down next to him.

"I knew you would somehow find me. I knew once you found out I was alive, you would figure out what to do. I love you, Timothy Holden."

Chapter 24

It had been over a year since Porsche and Agent Canter had been to Fort Mackinac, the Special Operation Command Center nicknamed by Chief Bolton. Stacey had taken Porsche here the day after Ahmed had been killed.

As they exited on the ramp off I-94 and headed into the industrial area of Detroit, Stacey looked in her rearview mirror and noticed Porsche's eyes swelling with tears.

"Hey, you all right back there?"

Porsche quickly wiped her eyes. "I'm fine," she said. And right after that, she said, "I'm *not* fine. I don't think I ever will be."

Carly turned from the front seat. Her heart sank when she saw her friend fighting back tears. "I'm sorry, Porsche. I'm so sorry. I miss him, too."

Porsche said nothing as she looked out the side window. There were no words spoken all the way to the command center, each one immersed in her own thoughts.

Wanting to break the silence, Carly asked, "How long has David been here?"

"A few days I think," Stacey said. "I believe they were brought here once they turned themselves in."

Agent Canter turned into the drive of the concealed command center. The building with cinder block walls and barbed wire fencing blended perfectly with the other industrial sites. After going through the various security protocols, they entered and headed to the small walled office.

Porsche noticed nothing had changed. There were still coaxial computer cables stretched high overhead which led to rows of tiered Intel data processors. Large TV screens showing aerial shots were mounted on the walls and monitored by military personal wearing microphoned headsets and manipulating yokes. *Still killing the bad guys, I see,* she thought.

From afar, Carly could see David speaking with someone she didn't know. Her heart began to beat faster.

The conversation stopped as they entered the office. Carly and David's eyes met, and he gave her a half smile. Carly softly smiled and looked away. Chief Bolton stood. His look was stern, strong, and extremely aggravated.

"Sit down!" he ordered, staring at Carly and Porsche. They quickly took their seats.

"Nothing," he said. "Nothing pisses me off more than when stupidity puts *my* people in harm's way! And you two are the epitome of that!

"Did you really think *you* were going to march back and catch these friggin' assholes when the entire CIA has been looking for them for months?!!!" he thundered.

His face tightened and he shook his head.

"What the hell possessed you to come out of witness protection? Do you have any idea what it takes to get people into that? Our agents risk their lives. The time, the effort, and you two pissed it away."

Heavy silence fell on the room. No one looked at anyone else. David stared at his hands, Porsche clasped her hands in her lap, and Carly stared at the floor.

Blindsided by Bolton, Porsche tried to answer. Her lips moved, but nothing came out.

Carly saw Porsche struggling to speak.

"It was me," Carly interrupted. "I talked Porsche into leaving Germany and…"

"Oh, bullshit!!" Bolton said, as he glared at both of them. "You both are idiots!! You have as much sense as a nit's ass! Ms. Berliner's a big girl. You think you have that much influence over her?"

Carly looked at David. "I lost it when I heard David's parents were killed. I could think of nothing else. David would not be in this situation if it weren't for me."

David's eyes widened. Bolton's eyes narrowed.

"How did *you* know that David's parents were killed?" he shouted out.

"There was a note on my windshield…one night when I was working at the bakery."

With his temper still high, Bolton's eyes burned into Stacey.

"What??? You think I did it?!" Stacey said. "I…I had nothing to do with it."

Stacey rubbed both palms on her legs and Bolton saw a slight tremble in her hands.

"I wouldn't do that!" Stacey said, realizing what a mistake it was letting Carly know. "I know better. When you called and told me she was on her way back from Germany, I was as surprised as you."

"My parents aren't dead!!" David blurted out. "It was a lie to get me back."

Carly squinted and her brow knitted "What the hell are you talking about?" Her eyes immediately went to Stacey. "Who isn't dead?"

"I have no clue," Stacey said baffled. "It's the first I heard this!"

"What's going on??? More lies???" Carly fumed. "Get me out of here. I can't stand this anymore."

All eyes traveled to Bolton and then to David.

"Don't look at me!" David hollered while slamming both hands on the table. "I had no idea about any of this… I about went crazy in the woods when I heard Mom and Dad were dead. I wanted to kill someone. I even thought about killing myself."

"Killing yourself? You considered ending your own life? While I took a risk coming here for you! I don't believe any of this!!"

Bolton raised his arms, attempting to tamp down the barrage of emotions in the room. It did not work.

The commotion was too much for Porsche. She stood, face flaring, took hold of her personal alarm lanyard and yanked, releasing the pin. A sudden high-pitched 130-decibel squeal caused everyone to stop and cover their ears.

Two men, guns drawn and wearing military fatigues barged into the room. Porsche reinserted the pin and calmly said, "Now that I have everyone's attention, can we please stop yelling and continue?" She sat back into her chair.

The military men slowly lowered their weapons as they scanned the room. Confused, they looked toward the Chief for explanation.

"Sorry, Gentlemen. We're all good here," he assured them. "The conversation just got a little heated."

Bolton's gaze went to Porsche.

"Ms. Berliner. Where did you have your agency training again?"

"Deutsche Hochschule, Germany," she said.

"They should have never let you go."

Chief Bolton suddenly recognized that he had neglected to introduce the unfamiliar figure standing off to the side. Raising his hand, he redirected his focus to the man who had been silently observing.

"My apologies, Officer Wells, please sit down" he began. "Ms. Berlinger and Ms. Fletcher share a common past with me. It at times gets a little heated."

Officer Wells approached the table and took a seat.

Chief Bolton once again addressed the group.

"This is Officer Aleister Wells from the Detroit Forensic Science Division. He is the lead investigator brought in not only to identify the bodies of the victims, but also to determine what materials were used in the firebombing. He will be working with Agent Canter as we move forward."

Stacey's gaze met Aleister's, and a subtle nod passed between them. In response, Aleister offered a warm smile.

"Let's take a break and regroup in 10. Can I interest anyone one in a cup of coffee?"

"Officer Wells, care to join me?" Stacey invited. "Might as well bring you up to speed on what transpired over the past year."

Aleister stood. "Sounds good to me."

"Coffee sounds excellent, Chief. Mind if I tag along?" Porsche asked.

"The pleasure will be mine."

The room was quiet with just Carly and David in there. An uneasy calm crushed the air between them. David stood and shut the door, then returned to the table. He sat next to Carly.

"I hated you at first," Carly said. "For the longest time, I couldn't get my head around why you took the mithridate and why you betrayed me."

"I wanted to protect you. I didn't want you involved."

"I don't need your protection."

David scooted his chair a little closer.

"Look, Carly, Tim needed to get his girl back. He was getting nowhere with the government."

Carly placed her hand on David's knee. "I know the whole story. Stacey told me."

David stopped and leaned back, a puzzled look on his face. "Are you still pissed?"

"Yes. A little," she answered. "But, David, what saves you is that you put other people before yourself. I get that."

"That's what you do when you care about someone."

David looked into Carly's eyes. "What about Bo? Are you two together?"

A knock on the door ended the conversation and the door flew open. David immediately headed back to his chair.

"Anyone seen Canter?" The Chief asked.

"I'm here, Chief," Stacey said walking in with Officer Wells in tow.

The ever-confident Bolton was pressed to find the right words to begin. He hated working with civilians. They didn't have to follow orders like the enlisted. And they could ask questions. The enlisted could not.

Brushing these concerns aside, Bolton decided to start from the beginning.

"*Everyone* was kept in the dark. No one knew, *not* David. ...*not* Canter. The two persons dead were contractors, a man and his wife, not the Farris'.

"We needed David to turn himself in and when the opportunity arose, we went for it. David's parents wanted him back and we wanted the mithridate. They agreed to go along with the plan if their son was not prosecuted. As far as the community is concerned, the fire at the farmhouse was a tragic accident brought about by the home renovation. From Officer Wells's investigation, we knew this was no accident. All indications led to Slovak, from the poisoning of the dog to the sheer brutality of the attack. So, we decided to up the stakes and set a trap."

"What kind of trap?" Agent Canter asked.

"You and Officer Wells will stand in for Ms. Fletcher and Mr. Farris when we conduct the sting. You're a bit taller than her, but I think you can pull it off. Mr. Farris and Officer Wells have similar physiques."

"What about me?" Porsche asked.

"If you agree, you will be returning to Germany. We have intelligence that there is a cell working in Europe. You'll meet Timothy Holden, better known as Sergeant Tim. Your job is to keep an eye on Mrs. Fletcher and Bo Harris, while at the same time trying to flush out the cell."

"Are they in danger?" Porsche asked.

Chief Bolton paused for a moment. He looked at Carly with furrowed brows.

"Unfortunately, until Slovak is taken out, no one in Carly's circle is safe."

Chief Bolton swept his gaze across the assembled group. "Any other matters to address?" The room stayed hushed, prompting Bolton to press on.

"Excellent. The sting, if all goes as planned, is happening the day after tomorrow. It will take place at the mock funeral of David's parents. We hope Slovak will pay us a visit."

Chapter 25

The day was perfect for a mock funeral. Grey skies with hints of rain shrouded the mourners at the funeral home. They clutched their umbrellas at their sides making sure they were prepared if the heavens opened up. The priest, wearing a black robe, stood in back of the chapel and greeted mourners as they took their seats.

There were two viewings that day: Eli Taylor and the Farris's. An elderly woman gripping her walker caught Carly's attention. She looked around the chapel through bifocals, seemingly confused, until a director came and asked if he could help. After a brief conversation, he pointed her in the direction of the adjoining viewing room. She trudged down the carpeted hallway pushing her walker in front of her.

Carly shook hands with David's family and friends as they came to pay their respects. The service lasted a little over an hour and it was time to leave. A slight mist began to fall as David and Carly led the crowd leaving the funeral home. Carly noticed an abandoned walker left next to an empty parking space.

"David," she whispered grabbing ahold of his arm as the crowd gathered around two hearses.

He leaned his head toward her.

"Look at that walker," she said pointing.

"What?" he said, looking where she pointed. "Some old person left it. I'm sure they'll be back to get it."

Carly left David's side to get a closer look. She tilted the walker slightly and examined the rubber feet and wheels. *No scuff marks.*

Returning to David's side, Carly spoke quietly. "An old lady with a walker came into the chapel before the service. We were talking to your Aunt GiGi and Uncle Bill at the time. Your aunt was telling us that they had to go back to their farm, that there was something she wanted to place on the graves—some family thing. She said they would only be gone a few minutes…fifteen at the most."

"Are you talking about that old lady who was at the back of the chapel?"

"Yes. The one wearing that blue dress that nearly dragged on the floor. There was something about that old lady," Carly continued. "Could that old lady have been Slovak?"

David looked questionably at her. "You think Slovak was already here? Why?"

"That walker looks brand new, like it was never used. Plus, it's on the other side of the parking blocks. Whoever left it there had to step over those blocks before getting into their car. There's no way that frail old lady could have done that. She had a hard-enough time getting down the hall."

"You might be right. Let's just keep everything going as planned and we'll let an agent know when we can."

Carly nodded and took hold of David's arm.

Agents dressed in black huddled with the others as two sets of pallbearers carried the empty coffins to the waiting vehicles. The priest recited one last prayer as the mourners dabbed their eyes and blew their noses.

"The family invites you to a luncheon at *The Lady of Faith* recreational hall at 2:00 p.m. They hope you can join them," Father Carl announced. "The burial is private and only for immediate family. This concludes our service."

The caskets were loaded, and Carly and David walked to the limo and climbed in. Agent Canter and Officer Wells were there, disguised as David and Carly.

"I think Slovak was here!!" Carly burst out as she sat down across from them. "I saw him! He was using a walker and dressed like an old woman."

"How can you be sure?" Agent Canter asked.

"Someone left a walker and I think it was used as a prop," Carly said, pointing out the window.

"Let's hope so," Stacey said. "That's what this is all about. Trying to flush Slovak out."

The small procession left the funeral home and headed to the family cemetery. Six cars with orange magnetic flags followed the limo. The two hearses led the way. The trap was set.

Chapter 26

Jeremy Boike and Mark Loman waited for the funeral procession to pass. They waited at the end of the long gravel driveway leading to Josh's house. They steadied their bikes, using the kickstand to keep them upright. It was a small town, and the boys knew that the bodies in those two hearses were the Farris's. They stood silently, straining to see the passengers through the dark windows of the limousines.

"You know how that fire started, don't you?" Jeremy asked Mark.

"I don't know…I heard my dad tell my mom something about renovating the house."

"That's what they want you to believe, but it ain't so."

"What aint so?"

"Josh told me it was Penny, their daughter."

"Penny!!? How could it be her? She's dead."

"That's just it. They say if you kill yourself, you go straight to hell. Penny killed herself in that house. Josh told me she came back and wanted to take her folks back to hell with her."

"Why would she do that?"

"I don't know. Ask Josh when he gets here."

There was no way the boys would go up to the run-down green and white-sided mobile home which had stood there since the first Slindy family member moved into the area. Josh's dad, well-known to the Livingston County police, was ornery and belligerent when he was drunk, which was more often than not.

The last time they knocked on the trailer door, Bill Slindy stormed out of the trailer wearing only stained undershorts and a dirty t-shirt. His drunken voice cussing at them as they peeled away.

"Get out of here, ya little bastards," he yelled while raising his fist in the air and shaking it at them. "Get your trespassing asses out of here before I call the cops!"

That happened early in the Spring and from then on, they waited for Josh on the road that passed their home.

"Ya think he's comin'?" Mark asked. "What if he is grounded for another week."

"He's probably just waiting until his old man passes out. He'll be here."

Five turkey vultures circled high over the field by the trailer. Their wings tilted up and down as they glided in the thermal updrafts.

"Something's dead over there," Jeremy said. "Probably a rabbit."

"Yeah," Mark replied. "Or maybe it's Josh's old man. Laying out in the field while Josh digs his grave."

Both boys crossed their arms over their stomachs and bent over laughing, then picked up stones and threw them, aiming at a rusty sign on one of the fence posts.

"Here he comes," Mark said seeing Josh pedaling his bike full speed. Josh skidded just in front of them, causing pebbles to fly and a dust cloud to linger in the air.

"You got 'em?" asked Mark, waving his hand not wanting to breath in the dust.

A sly smile crossed Josh's face. "Every time Pa passed out, I snuck a cigarette out of his pack. I got three."

"Let me see 'em," Mark insisted.

Josh reached into the pocket of his jacket and pulled out three wrinkled cigarettes. "This should be enough to get us through our meeting."

"You got the lighter?" Mark asked looking towards Jeremy.

Jeremy pulled it out of his front jean pocket and gave it a flick. "Ready to go."

****

Tatyana sat in a black sedan waiting in the Magnuson Hotel parking lot. She was getting nervous, hadn't heard from Slovak in over three hours. Finally, a gray-haired lady pulled in and parked next to her.

"Morons!" Slovak barked as he opened the car door and got in. He ripped off the gray wig and tossed it in the backseat. He lowered the passenger sun visor and looked in the mirror, removing the makeup as he spoke.

"The place was crawling with Feds!!" he shouted. "I knew someone, or some agency helped her last year. I can spot a Fed a mile away and they had no *clue* I was there."

"Settle down before you have to eat a nitro," Tatyana calmly said. "We planned for this. I actually like this better. A shootout would have been such a bitch…Fun, maybe, but such a bitch!"

****

It was easy to find them. A Google and White Page search turned up William and Ginger Farris. Their address was there, and Slovak and Tatyana had surveilled the house for the past couple days. From the start, the plan was to kidnap the couple, but abruptly changed when Slovak insisted on abducting Carly from the funeral home. The blue dress that hung to the floor concealed an 8mm Glock pistol along with a can of military grade pepper spray.

It was a stroke of luck that they found William and GiGi coming out of their house carrying a grave ornament. Slovak and Tatyana thought they would have to wait until the couple returned from the funeral service. Aunt GiGi and Uncle Bill were accosted in seconds. Their hands were tied, and their heads hooded before being thrown in the back seat of the car and driven to the grain elevator.

The couple was marched into the ramshackle building. An overwhelming odor of gasoline and chemicals penetrated the air. They were zip-tied into two decrepit armchairs before their hoods were removed. Instantly, acrid fumes assaulted their senses, making their eyes water. The two looked on in horror.

"You'll get used to the smell," Tatyana said, inhaling deeply. Chemicals sat on the table where they had constructed the Molotov cocktails used to firebomb David's farmhouse.

Aunt GiGi broke down. "Who are you?" she said between gasps for air.

"I will slit your throats if you don't tell us what we want to know," Slovak said, his voice cold. "We're after David and his girlfriend. Where have they been living?"

Aunt GiGi looked confused; her hair hung in disheveled curls around her face.

"I don't understand," she barely got out.

"As far as I know, he was somewhere in Canada," Uncle Bill choked out. "Some rainforest, something like that. I don't think my brother really knew."

"Please don't hurt us," Aunt GiGi pleaded. "Today at the funeral home was the first time we've seen David in five years. He was in the Army and then when Penny died, he…" Aunt GiGi faltered.

"He tortured some boys and got sent to the nuthouse!" Slovak finished up for her.

Aunt GiGi nodded.

He walked toward her, deliberately, one step at a time. Withdrawing a wooden handled knife from his pocket, he pressed the button causing a swoosh as the blade was released. He sliced through the ties binding her wrists and let her rub the deep imprints caused by the tight restraints. Then, he held out her phone.

"Take your phone," he instructed her. "Do exactly what I say."

She squirmed and her eyes grew wide with the switchblade resting against her throat.

"Call a family member or your closest neighbor," Slovak continued. "Tell them that you have been kidnapped and to call your phone to get in contact with your kidnappers."

Aunt GiGi's hand trembled as she took her phone and called.

Slovak took the blade away from her neck and stood in front of her, arms crossed, watching her.

"Kate," Aunt GiGi urgently spoke into the phone. "I need you to call the police. This is no joke. Bill and I have been kidnapped. Tell them to dial this number, the one that appeared on your phone. I'm supposed to tell you that we are being held for some kind of ransom." Her gaze then shifted to Slovak.

Slovak snapped his switchblade shut and took the phone hanging it up.

"Tie her back up," he ordered Tatyana.

He slipped the phone into his side pocket on the way to a picnic table littered with jugs of chlorine bleach, turpentine, and diesel fuel. He brushed the containers aside to make a spot to sit.

"I need to catch my breath," he wheezed. He removed a small bottle of pills from his shirt pocket and allowed one to dissolve under his tongue. In a few minutes, he felt his chest relax and he felt better.

"Once the Fed's, or whoever they are, realize these two are missing, they're going to try and contact them. I'll get at least five miles from this place and wait for them to call. Once I give them our demands, I'll ditch the phones."

"What's the plan?" Tatyana asked.

"Same as last time. The mithridate for the hostages."

"And if David doesn't have it?"

Slovak felt at the scar tissue just under his right eye. He ran his fingers over his sunken cheekbones. He mused, the expression on his face shifting from cruel to hateful.

"The mithridate...ah, yes, the mithridate," he brooded. "If he has it, that will be a bonus," he finally said.

Tatyana stared hard at him; unsure she understood him.

"A bonus?" she said cautiously. "You... don't... really care about the mithridate, do you?"

"Ah, Tatyana...... finally you got it," he said, sardonically. "It's about time."

His words disturbed her, chipped away at that hard surface she protected herself with.

"*I. Want. Her*," he added, saying each word deliberately. "She *is* mine."

"And me?" Tatyana said. "What about me?"

"You're a big girl... you'll figure it out," he said calmly as he headed out the door.

Chapter 27

The funeral procession passed the partially charred farmhouse. Dumpsters half-filled with debris sat idle, left exactly how they were before the attack. The cars and limo followed the dual hearses as they passed an apple orchard before ascending a hill. Agent Canter felt for her gun.

At the crest of the hill was a small half-acre cemetery completely enclosed with a wrought iron fence. A huge capital letter F sat atop the iron arch gate. Mounds piled from two newly dug graves lay covered by green synthetic turf.

"Hang tight," Agent Canter said as she opened the door to the limo and she and Officer Wells got out. "It could get crazy out there."

Carly's gaze went to the small graveyard. "So, Penny your sister is buried here?"

David shook his head. "Penny is in Heartland. My mom always said this place creeped her out and there was no way she would ever be buried in my dad's family cemetery. We have plots on my mother's side in Heartland."

The mourners exited their cars and congregated around the hearses as the coffins were lifted by the pallbearers and carried to the graves. The team waited patiently, but no one was there except for the spirits of the Farris dead.

Father Carl said his last prayer. Not bad for an agent who was actually an atheist. The team walked slowly through the iron arch gate and got into their waiting vehicles. They felt dejected, demoralized. Agent Canter and Officer Wells got back into the limo.

"The son-of-a-bitch is a no show," Canter said as she pulled off her wig. "Somehow he knew." She turned her attention to Carly.

"I think you could be right, Carly. As much as we prepared, we didn't prepare for him showing up like that."

"I didn't either. It was only later when we were leaving the chapel and I saw that walker…left behind in the parking lot."

"You don't get to be his age in this business without being crafty," Stacey said.

The conversation was broken when Stacey's phone rang. David and Carly watched as she struggled to keep her facial expression free from any emotion.

"Yes, Sir. I will."

Agent Canter placed her phone into her front inside pocket of her coat. She looked at David. Her expression was somber.

"The police are investigating a missing person report. It has to do with your aunt and uncle."

"Uncle Bill and Aunt GiGi?" David asked, alarmed.

"Yes. A police report was made by a neighbor. The FBI got an update because the last name was Farris."

"I just saw them a couple of hours ago. They were at the funeral home. Do my parents know?"

"I'm not sure at this point. The Chief will fill us in once we get back."

"It has to be Slovak," Carly worried out loud, her eyes narrowing. "I bet that was part of his plan all along."

Carly watched as David looked out the window, avoiding anyone's gaze. Her heart sank, realizing once again it was, she that brought this to him.

****

Tatyana paced back and forth in the dilapidated grain elevator. There were too many unknowns and she hated it. She didn't know what was taking Slovak so long. She didn't know what the outcome of this kidnapping would be. And she definitely didn't know there were three teenage boys hiding in a storage loft on the second floor. Neither she nor Slovak had noticed the almost fully hidden bicycles in the scraggly bushes outside the building.

The boys watched in horror as the old couple was marched into the grain elevator wearing hoods over their heads. They heard the man with the scarred face and menacing voice threatening GiGi, a neighbor they knew from church suppers held at the Lutheran church in town.

"We got to do something," Mark whispered.

Jeremy, the oldest in the group, pulled out his cell phone from his back pocket. He had silenced it before entering the elevator. Peering through the slats of the wooden floor, his heart pounded rapidly. With his index finger and thumb, he brought Tatyana into view and began snapping pictures.

He then turned to his friends. "I'm sending these to my dad," he whispered. "I'm going to let him know we're at the silos. He's working the desk today at the police station. He'll know what to do."

"We are going to be in so much trouble," Josh said.

"Trouble!" Mark said, "Trouble? If they find us, we're dead."

****

"Let me see those photos," Agent McGuire said to Greg Johnson, Jeremy's father. The police station was filled with FBI and local police, all scurrying about, anxiety at a high level. Johnson handed McGuire his phone. "Swipe to the right," he said.

"It's my kid," Officer Johnson continued. "He's at the old grain elevator which is set to be demolished any day. He's hiding with some of his buds. You can tell these pictures were taken from above. They must be in a loft. Who is that person with Bill and Ginger?"

"She's connected to an international terrorist ring that we have been trying to apprehend for the last couple of years," he said matter-of-factly, then handed Johnson back his phone.

"What the hell is she doing in Livingston?" Johnson said, angst in his voice.

"It's a long story. Let's concentrate on getting the hostages and the kids back. At this point, she doesn't know the kids are there. We have to separate her from the hostages. You said it's a grain elevator?"

"Yes. It's set to be demolished any day. The place is almost falling down on its own."

"How can we separate her from the hostages?" Agent McGuire said more to himself than aloud. "I've got an idea."

The diesel truck was loud as it belched and heaved, turning into the parking lot. A couple of hours had passed since GiGi called her neighbor. Tatyana heard the squeal then hiss of the air brakes.

Uncle Bill glanced at Aunt GiGi and then to Tatyana. Instantly, she leaped to her feet and placed the hoods back over their heads.

"You make a fuckin' sound and the last thing you'll hear is my gun!"

Aunt GiGi began to cry.

Tatyana headed to a broken window and cautiously peered out.

Controlled Demolition Inc read the sign on the big rig. One man jumped out wearing a yellow hard hat. *Fuck*, she thought.

Tatyana waited. She could execute the two men one at a time as they entered the building. *She had trained for this*, she convinced herself.

"Come on! Come on!" the man was yelling, over the annoying beep of the truck being driven in reverse.

"A little more," he shouted, waving his arms helping the driver position the truck close to the building.

There was an eerie silence as the driver turned off the truck and jumped down from the big rig. Diesel fumes filled the air. Tatyana watched as one of the men lifted a steel cover exposing a control panel. She could hear the mechanical whine of hydraulic stabilizing feet being lowered to anchor the 110-foot boom. The men looked up as the eight-thousand-pound forged steel wrecking ball rose into the air. They would have the first silo leveled within an hour.

Tatyana's palms began to sweat as she placed her hand around her gun and the other on the handle of the door. She would kill them where they stood, no time for talk. She would then drag their bodies into the plant. She knew what she needed to do.

Tatyana pushed her shoulder into the steel door and rushed out to the men, gun raised. The crosshairs of the FBI sniper rifle were on her in seconds. It only took one shot to take her out.

Chapter 28

The limo drove Carly, David, Agent Canter and Officer Wells, directly to Fort Mackinac. Chief Bolton was waiting as they went through their last security protocol and walked into the compound.

"Your Aunt and Uncle are safe," Bolton announced. "They're with your parents."

David stopped, a puzzled look on his face. "What? I thought they were kidnapped."

"They're alive and well, I assure you."

David released a protracted sigh, battling to keep his eyes from welling up. He looked at Carly and opened his arms. Without hesitation, she immediately walked into them.

The Chief wasted no time as Carly, David, Stacey, and Aleister, took their seats around the table.

"Your aunt and uncle were kidnapped. They were rescued, but we did have a casualty."

"Slovak!?" Carly blurted.

The Chief shook his head. "Tatyana Nikolaev."

David's gaze jumped right to Carly. He remembered how much heartache Tatyana had brought her. Carly had shared everything with him when they had escaped Holy Oaks and driven to Sergeant Tim's for a safe place to hide.

"How did the bitch die?" Carly asked.

"We had a little luck. Three local boys were hiding in the loft of the same elevator where Slovak constructed the Molotov Cocktails used to firebomb David's house. This is also where he took your aunt and uncle. One of the boys contacted his father who was an officer in the Livingston PD. That was our big break.

"Slovak had left Tatyana alone with the hostages. The kid was texting and updating us by the minute. We needed to separate Tatyana from the hostages and get her out of that building. A couple of agents drove a demolition truck up to the building and raised the boom. Tatyana thought the building was about to be leveled on top of her. When she ran out to confront the workers, our sharpshooter took her out."

Chief Bolton turned to Carly.

"Ms. Fletcher, would you refresh us on your relationship with Tatyana Nikolaev?"

Carly's face tightened before she began telling her story.

"I met her when Bo and I returned to Michigan. Bo had just been discharged from Walter Reed and was doing outpatient therapy for his PTSD. We were both going to Wayne State. She was an adjunct professor and offered Bo a computer science internship for returning vets. From the first time I met her, I didn't trust her. It was something about the way she looked at Bo. Anyway, I later found out she was working with Slovak and part of the effort to get the mithridate my father had hidden."

Chief Bolton nodded in agreement. "Please continue."

"She seduced Bo, won his trust, and held him as a hostage. She and Slovak sent me a video of Bo being tortured. They said if I didn't give them the mithridate, the same thing that happened to my little brother Artie would happen to Bo. My little brother was murdered. So was my father."

"Son of bitch," Officer Wells murmured, shaking his head.

"With the help of the Agency, we tricked them. We got Bo released and they got fake mithridate."

Carly paused, gazing into the distance before continuing. "I shot Slovak. It was my bullet that disfigured him. I blocked it out of my life and only realized it when I was at Tim's farm. The Agency faked both mine and Bo's death and placed us in Federal Witness protection. That's about it."

Chapter 29

Isla sat at the kitchen table, her fingers gently caressing the golden circle that surrounded her finger. The weight of her wedding band was nothing compared to the weight on her heart as she lost herself in her thoughts. The room was thick with emotion, as Tim entered, his eyes keenly attuned to Isla's demeanor.

"That doesn't look like the face of a blushing bride," he said.

Isla looked up, her eyes met Tim's with a mixture of happiness and anguish.

"Just tell the Americans to fuck off. You already sacrificed enough for that country," she implored.

Tim, moved by her plea, pulled out a chair and took a seat beside her. His hand found hers, Isla traced the contours of his gold band, a silent plea for him not to leave.

"That's not the way the CIA works," Tim explained. "I made them do what needed to be done to get you back. They don't forget. I gotta keep up my end of the bargain or I'll end up in Leavenworth."

"Our baby needs her daddy," Isla uttered.

"That's why I am doing this. We need closure. As long as that Slovak guy is alive, this won't be over."

"Can't they do it without you?"

"Hold on," Tim said, rising from the table. He disappeared into Isla's bedroom, returning with documents from his duffle bag, that held secrets meant only for him. He handed them to Isla.

"I'm not supposed to share this, but I will," Tim admitted, "There is a mole within the CIA. They purposedly leaked within the organization that all the mithridate was not recovered. That information ended up in the hands of a terrorist cell in Europe. That's why I am heading there."

"So, they're using you as bait," Isla whispered.

In that moment, passion intertwined with sacrifice and love clashed with reality. This was hard for Isla, and even harder for Sergeant Tim.

****

Porsche noticed Sergeant Tim exit his plane at the Düsseldorf Airport. She removed her scarf from around her neck, signaling everything was a go. She had surveyed her surroundings, making sure she was not being tailed. Both had received a thorough briefing from the CIA regarding their mission upon arrival in Germany. They had engaged in several secure video conferences through a link established by the CIA.

They exercised caution, refraining from any overt acknowledgments. With a leak within the Bureau, uncertainty loomed over whether information about Porsche's and Tim's mission had been compromised.

Tim strolled toward the carousel, anticipating the arrival of his duffel bag. Meanwhile, Porsche exited the terminal and made her way to her Volkswagen. The coordination for these actions was arranged during the video conference both had participated in with the agency. Tim met Porshe in the parking garage. She popped the trunk and Tim tossed his bag in and got into her car. The two were headed to Porsche's grandparent's house.

"Well, it is nice to meet you in person." Porsche said.

"Is it?" Tim said abruptly.

Porsche, feeling the tension in the air, casually retrieved her pack of cigarettes. Lowering the window, she nonchalantly lit one. While her usual practice was to inquire about others' preferences regarding smoking, his gruff attitude led her to think, *screw it.*

After driving for several minutes with no conversation, Porsche finally broke the silence.

"Look, I don't know your story, but we have to work together to get this done. Can you tell me why you're doing this?"

Tim looked at Porsche. His expression was dark, torn.

"I have no damn choice. I left my five-month pregnant wife, even though I swore to myself that I wouldn't lift a finger ever again to assist the U.S. government."

"Why no choice?"

"Because I am trying to keep my skinny ass out of Leavenworth! Why are you doing this? You some kind of mercenary? Sucking on the US cash titty."

A pause filled the air. Porsche could feel the blood rushing to her head, her grip on the steering wheel tightening involuntarily. The urge to scream clawed at her, yet she managed to maintain a facade of composure. Her eyes briefly met Tim's before returning to the road ahead. She calmly said, "They murdered my fiancé."

At that very moment the pieces of the puzzle came together. Tim remembered David and Carly explaining her attempted kidnapping and that someone was killed. That someone was Ahmed Osman. Called upon by Carly's father for help.

"Well, aren't I the asshole!" Tim said, wishing he could take it back.

"It's all good. Don't worry about it. How would you know who I am?"

"That being said, I am truly sorry. My mouth gets me into trouble at times."

Porsche navigated down a quaint street that resembled a village, choosing a spot along the roadside to park her car. She turned and faced Tim.

"Let's start over. I heard you're the guy who put one over on the CIA."

Tim nodded, a smile breaking out on his face. "You could say that. They're getting their payback with me and this operation. I am sorry about your fiancé."

"I am too. He was a great guy. Carly's father sent for him when he was in trouble. He died helping Carly. I want to get those bastards!"

Tim nodded. "What's our next step?"

Porsche discreetly retrieved a pistol from beneath her seat and passed it to Sergeant Tim, her expression serious.

"Be careful…This isn't the States. You get caught with that here and you are in a world of shit," she cautioned.

"Appreciate the advice. I'll keep this under wraps."

"Bo and Carly's mom live ten minutes from here. I figured we can get you a hotel room and I'll stay at my grandparents. Shouldn't raise any red flags. I lived with my grandparents before I left with Carly. We can start tomorrow."

Chapter 30

Borka stepped into the AA meeting room and was promptly greeted by Helga. Across the room, he spotted Bo seated in the semicircle of chairs.

"You must be Mr. Radovic," Helga remarked, extending her hand toward Borka.

A faint smile played on Borka's lips as he observed her captivating blue eyes.

"Please…call me Borka. Mr. Radovic makes me feel so old."

Borka clung onto Helga's hand for an uncomfortably prolonged moment, his touch feeling intrusive. Helga, feeling uncomfortable, struggled to retrieve her hand.

"Glad you could make it, Borka. Please, take a seat with the group. Help yourself to some coffee; the meeting will commence shortly."

"Of course," he replied.

Borka casually strolled up to Bo, sipping the customary strong brew from his white Styrofoam cup. Bo acknowledged him with a nod, as Borka sat.

"I'm Borka, Borka Radovic," he stated.

"Tommy, Tommy Higgins," Bo replied.

As the meeting concluded and attendees began gathering chairs to return them to the rack, Borka turned towards Bo.

"Any plans? How about a drink?"

Bo initially remained silent, but then a smile gradually appeared on his face. Judging by the expression on Borka's face, it seemed like a casual attempt to break the ice.

"What did you say your name was?"

"Borka."

"Are you a standup?"

"My ex thinks so. Actually, she never quite grasped my sense of humor. That's one of the reasons I'm here – too much humor and booze in our relationship."

"I feel you. My issue was the opposite, too much booze and not enough humor. My ex would certainly vouch for that."

"You sound American. Definitely not a European. What brings you to Dusseldorf?" Borka inquired.

Bo focused before responding, a feat he couldn't have accomplished when he was still on the bottle.

"I work for Lufthansa. I'm an IT software developer. Got transferred from the States. Been here for a little over a year."

Borka nodded. He pulled out his phone and asked…

"Could I have your number? According to the guidelines of our meeting, I'm supposed to have a buddy that I can contact in case I am looking for a drink. Would you mind being that buddy?"

Bo hesitated at first and then pulled out his phone.

"Of course," he agreed. "My number is… +49 156 /8856-2216."

"Why don't you send me a text and then I'll have yours," Bo suggested.

"Great idea," Borka said.

****

As Bo trudged home from the meeting, a breeze blew through the air, causing him to turn up his collar to ward off the dusting of snow and chill. The dimly lit streets cast long shadows as he made his way to the local restaurant. He had ordered take-out for him and Sharon. As he stood in line waiting for his time to pay, he looked across the street to the entrance of a dimly lit bar. Bo's brows furrowed.

Is that Borka?

Bo settled his bill for the meal and stepped out into the chilly night. Originally, he had planned to head straight home, but now things didn't add up. Carrying his bag of take-out, Bo made his way to the bar.

"Sir, can't bring food in here," the heavy-set bouncer croaked.

"I won't be staying. Just looking for a friend."

Bo surveyed the bar, and his eyes fell upon Borka, who was raising a shot glass while seated in front of a beer. An elderly man signaled with his shot glass, and the two of them swiftly downed their drinks, followed by a hearty gulp of beer.

"I'll be damned," Bo muttered under his breath, then turned and exited the bar.

****

Mrs. Fletcher stood in the kitchen, loading the dirty plates and silverware into the dishwasher when she heard the distinct sound of a text arriving on Bo's phone. Hoping it was Carly, she put down her dish towel and walked to Bo. He sat in the recliner; his face betrayed a shadow of concern.

Hey, Buddy, the text read. *It was nice meeting you today. This sobriety thing is really making me feel good! Give me a buzz any time and maybe we can do coffee before our next meeting. Regards, Borka.*

"Is that Carly?" asked Mrs. Fletcher, her curiosity aroused.

Bo, momentarily lost in his thoughts didn't respond immediately.

"Bo," Mrs. Fletcher called out again, gently pulling him from his thoughts.

"Sorry," Bo said. "It's not Carly. It's my boss, Mr. Crane, extending his congratulations for my month of sobriety and being part of the program."

"That's truly wonderful, Dear. I'm happy for you. Carly will be, too."

"I hope so," Bo explained while at the same time texting back to Borka.

Bo texted back, *Here if you need me.*

As Mrs. Fletcher returned to the kitchen, Bo discreetly removed a book from the shelf, securing Carly's concealed 22-caliber pistol and sliding it into his pocket.

****

Borka tossed the phone onto the chair before dropping down to the bed in the hotel room. His lady friend giggled as he pulled her close and began to caress her backside.

"Now, where did we leave off?" Borka whispered.

Chapter 31

Slovak sat at the counter of the podunk diner sipping his morning coffee. Double cream and three sugars. He knew it was just a matter of time before another assassin team would be sent to finish the job Markell had started. Slovak had failed at his mission and when you fail the *Circle,* the *Circle* is unforgiving.

This international group of terrorists will stop at nothing. They tie up loose ends and Slovak was a loose end. They would pursue him for years if that were what it took.

As Slovak waited for his sausage and gravy biscuits with a side of bacon, something did not feel right. He had chills and his heart felt like it was gripped and twisted by a steel hand. He reached into his pocket for his vial of nitro and popped one under his tongue. It would only take a minute. His head ached and vision in one eye was blurred.

"Will there be anything else?" the waitress asked as she set his breakfast down in front of him.

He shook his head. "All set."

Slovak mixed the thick gravy into the buttermilk biscuits with his fork then took a large bite. It didn't taste good, so he reached for the salt and shook a generous amount on to the gravy. That didn't help. Then he added some pepper. Nothing tasted good. His appetite was gone. He pushed his plate away and leaned back in his chair. In seconds, he lost consciousness and collapsed on to the floor.

The loud chatter in the diner died down, becoming almost silent as customers stared at the huge man lying on the floor.

"Call 911," someone shouted.

"Oh, my God!!" the waitress named Kelly yelled as she set her coffee pot on the closest table. She wiped her hands on her apron and ran to the man that had just fallen. Dropping to her knees, she knelt next to him, clueless as to what to do next.

"I need some help here!" Kelly yelled. "Does anyone know CPR?"

A woman dressed in royal blue scrubs knelt next to Kelly. "I'm an ER nurse. Let me see if he's choking."

The young lady placed her hands on Slovak's chin and just below his nose and opened his mouth. "There's nothing there," she said. "I'm going to start chest compressions."

****

Slovak was in and out of consciousness as the ambulance rushed him to the hospital. Dream like images that made no sense flashed and then were gone in a split second. The EMT worked the oxygen bag, pushing air into his lungs, keeping him breathing.

"You get any ID on him," he asked his partner, as the two EMT's removed the stretcher from the ambulance, kicking out the wheeled legs.

"All I found was a wallet with credit cards—all different names and lots of cash."

The two partners rushed him into the ER as the nurses came running.

"He's coding," the emergency nurse heavily draped in PPE gear said, as they wheeled the ashy, gray-skinned man into a glass-enclosed isolation room. A team of three nurses gowned, gloved, and masked frantically took vitals, waiting for the doctor to join them.

"His blood pressure is low, and he has a 102 temp," a nurse said as the doctor approached.

"What are his oxygen levels," she asked before taking her stethoscope and checking his heart.

The nurse immediately slipped the pulse oximeter over his index finger and measured.

"55mm Hg," the nurse shot back.

"Wow! That's low! We've got to vent him."

Lying in a hospital bed, John Doe never regained consciousness. He lasted five days on the ventilator before his heart gave out. Cause of death... heart failure with complications due to COVID 19.

His body was sent to the county coroner and, as with all John Doe's, the police worked together with Forensics. The coroner worked the scientific side—fingerprints, dental records, DNA, while the police took pictures and went about town asking questions as to who this unidentified person was.

It did not take the CIA long to identify Slovak's body. Attempts were made to locate the next of kin, but with no success. The funeral home eventually cremated his body, and the CIA removed his name from their terrorist watchlist.

****

In the clandestine realm of espionage, the departed frequently find themselves resurrected. Officer Daugherty stood by the hospital bed, observing the man awakening from unconsciousness, his eyes attempting to focus. Despite the CIA's efforts to veil the identities of their top personnel, Slovak recognized Paul Daugherty, acknowledging the presence of a formidable figure in the room.

"Have I died and descended into hell?" Slovak inquired, barely able to speak and attempting to find a more comfortable position in bed, only to discover his movements restricted by shackles.

"You may wish you had gone to the fiery gates, by the time I get done with ya." Daugherty retorted with a twang in his voice.

Slovak grunted, desperately requesting, "Water. I need water."

Daugherty stepped to the hospital bed and removed the leg and arm shackles. He grabbed the white Styrofoam cup and placed the straw in Slovak's mouth. Slovak sucked with urgency…

"Easy does it, Chief," Daugherty said sarcastically, pulling the straw from his mouth. "They just yanked out your vent, you don't want to push it too hard."

Slovak pushed himself higher in the bed. Daugherty positioned a chair alongside and took a seat, fixing a silent, intense stare on Slovak. No words were exchanged between them, until Slovak finally broke.

"What happened to me? Do I have COVID?"

"Well, Alexander…You don't mind if I call you Al, do ya?"

Slovak looked at Daugherty with distain. He knew when he was being played.

"I prefer Alexander."

"Well, Alexander, you don't make the rules here---I do! Tell you what…I'll split the difference and give you the nickname Raccoon. How's that sound?" Daugherty remarked.

"Why the fuck would you call me 'Raccoon?'"

"You look like one chief. You got a couple black eyes. Looks like the Doc's vented you through the nose. Had to put in a couple of stents to keep you breathing. May be a little tender for the next few weeks."

"Fuck off," Slovak said, turning his head away from Daugherty.

Smirking, Daugherty rose from his chair and seized the Styrofoam cup. He removed the plastic cover with the protruding straw and slowly poured the water over Slovak's head.

"I've water boarded over a hundred people, not all men," Daugherty remarked. "You gotta ditch that attitude before that cup becomes a bucket."

Daugherty tossed the cup onto the bed and went into the bathroom returning with a towel. He dabbed the excess water from Slovak's face and sat back in the chair.

Smugly, he asked, "Are we good now?"

"I hope I give you COVID and you die," Slovak spewed, as he once again turned his head away from Daugherty.

"There you go again with the attitude. You never had COVID. We made it seem like you did. It was the only way we could keep you alive and safe from *Kolo*. As far as they know, you're dead!"

A look of bewilderment crossed Slovak's face. He still would not face Daugherty. He couldn't understand why the CIA would stage his death. After years of actively seeking to kill him, why now would they do this? They wanted something.

"Are you aware your colleague Ms. Nikolaev passed?"

Slovak's head snapped around. "Tatyana!? Was it *Kolo*?"

"Not *Kolo*. Despite their desire to see you and your girlfriend dead, you owe your life to me. A sharpshooter eliminated her when we rescued Farris's aunt and uncle."

"Cut to the chase. What's your game here?"

Daugherty reclined in his chair, extending and crossing his legs while placing his hands behind his head.

"The CIA has a bit of a problem. There's a leak within the agency that we need to patch up. Our intel points to your nephew, Borka Radovic, as somehow linked to this information breach. We need a name of who is supplying this information."

"And why should I help?"

"You're living on borrowed time. The CIA is your lifeline. Assist us, and you'll avoid a one-way ticket to Leavenworth. Or we could leak that you're not as dead as they believe. How long do you think it will take before *Kolo* pays you a visit?"

Daugherty scratched the side of his scruffy beard before he continued.

"What would you say if, for once, we turn a blind eye to Ms. Fletcher?"

"Carly?? I don't know what you mean."

"Cut the crap, Alex. We're not dancing around this any longer. You crave revenge. The humiliation of being played by her, coupled with the grotesque mask she slapped onto your face – it's eating at you every damn second, twenty-four-seven."

There was a long pause in the room before Slovak spoke.

"So, if I supply a name, I am free to operate as I please?"

Daugherty stood from his chair and handed Slovak a burner phone, fake passport, and an airline ticket.

"We've gathered intelligence indicating that your nephew, Borka Radovic, has been in contact with Bo Harris. He is actively searching for the mithridate he believes still exists. Borka is collaborating with Grego Szabo, the individual receiving the leaked information."

"How do you know such a thing?"

"We're the CIA. We know everything," Daugherty declared with confidence.

"Of course," Slovak acknowledged with a hint of sarcasm. "Because, naturally, the CIA knows everything."

"I have made arrangements for you to head to Germany. You will need to conceal your identity, both Ms. Fletcher and David Farris will be on that flight."

Chapter 32

Carly stood in the dimly lit kitchen; her mind fixed on the chalked outlines that marred the floor where the horror had unfolded. The air hung heavy with the acrid scent of charred wood and damp plaster, a reminder of the fire that had ravaged the space.

"So, this is where that couple died," Carly remarked.

Officer Wells nodded solemnly. "It is. As far as we can tell, they first poisoned the dog."

Carly's eyes shifted towards David. "I am so sorry...Sorry for getting you involved with all this. That's why I'm going to kill that son of a bitch."

A shiver coursed down David's spine as the harsh reality sank in; these brutal killings were targeted at his parents. The kitchen, once a witness to shared meals and laughter, now bore witness to a malicious scheme brought about by people David wanted to kill.

The conversation stopped as Agent Canter's cell phone suddenly rang. Her hand reached for the device, and she glanced at the caller ID.

"It's the Chief," she announced. Taking a few steps away, creating a physical distance from the group. As she engaged in the conversation, her expression shifted. The hushed tones of Agent Canter's conversation with the Chief remained a mystery to the onlookers, leaving them to speculate about the unfolding development.

The group observed in suspense as Agent Canter lowered her phone and casually strolled back and joined them. Her expression bore a blend of shock and relief, leaving the group anxious for an explanation.

"What's going on? You look like you've seen a ghost," Officer Wells inquired, his tone a mix of curiosity and concern. Stacey took a moment, her eyes still reflecting the unexpected news.

"He's dead."

"Whose dead!?" Carly asked unable to contain herself.

"Slovak!!" she said, her words in disbelief. "The son of a bitch is dead."

"How did he die? Was it the CIA?" Carly asked, her voice cold, bitter. "I hope it was a painful death!"

"Not the CIA. According to the Chief it was COVID. He was an unidentified John Doe. They ran forensics and DNA and it hit on Slovak."

"So, this is over," David uttered, his voice tinged with disbelief.

"I'm not so sure," Agent Canter countered. "You heard what the Chief said. *Kolo* is alive and well in Europe."

The room, once heavy with the revelation of Slovak's demise, was now cast in a shadow of uncertainty.

****

Chief Bolton strode into the rear office at Fort Mackinaw, a determined expression etched on his face. Cradled in his hands was a folder, a repository of Alexander Slovak's medical records. Seated around the table were Carly, David, Officer Wells and Agent Canter, their attention captured as the chief nonchalantly tossed the folder onto the table.

"I still can't wrap my head around the fact that the S.O.B. is dead," Bolton remarked, his voice a mix of disbelief and contempt. "If anyone's curious, here are the details, straight from CIA Officer Paul Daugherty." No one bothered to glance into the folder.

Agent Canter, breaking the silence, inquired about the next steps. "So, what's next, Chief?"

"Well, your services aren't required in Europe. Porsche and Sergeant Tim can manage that theater of operation. I'm considering freeing up your time to focus on the serial killer case, I heard he struck again."

"And me?" Officer Wells inquired.

"I figured you could stay on and work with Canter. You could team up on this case. God knows we could use it. And we could use your forensic skill."

"I'm good with that. You'll clear it with the Division?"

Chief Bolton gave a firm nod. "Consider it done." He then shifted his attention to David and Carly.

"Both of you are free to go. Carly, if you choose to go back to Germany, exercise caution."

Carly's attention shifted towards David as his phone buzzed with a new text message. With a curious expression, she watched as he raised his phone to read the message.

"Well, I'll be…" he exclaimed, a smile playing on his lips. "Looks like the Sarge went and tied the knot down under in Australia."

"That's incredible!" Carly exclaimed. "With Slovak out of the picture, I feel much safer about heading to Europe. There's a lot to discuss with Bo and my mom."

"You mean, 'we' are headed to Europe. I've stuck by your side this far; I hate to miss out on the rest of the excitement. Besides, it'll give me a chance to help the Sarge reunite with his family."

Chief Bolten raised Slovak's file from the table, directing his attention to the assembled team.

"I'll organize your return to Germany. For the time being, I strongly recommend staying in the witness protection program until we give you further notice."

He zeroed in on Agent Canter.

"Agent Canter, your task starts today. Unfortunately, the killer has struck again. Before you depart, I'll provide you with the details of the crime scene. Officer Wells can join you later pending approval from his division head."

Chapter 33

Agent Canter noticed the sea of blue and white squad cars parked in front of the tiny house. Yellow police tape encompassed the entire yard. Down the street tall antennas were raised into the air transmitting the devasting news to the general public. Another murder…another dead female found.

Canter presented her identification to the officers stationed outside the house, holding back the persistent news crews. As she stepped inside, she quickly recognized Captain Vitamer from the Detroit Forensic Science Division. Their previous collaboration on a case had left her impressed with his exceptional skill set.

"Hey, Canter," Captain Vitamer greeted her, glancing up from his computer stationed on the kitchen table. "Heard you're teaming up with Officer Wells."

"Yeah, the Chief is sorting out the details."

"It's all set. He's in the back with the victim."

"Well, that was quick. Glad to have him on board," Canter responded.

"The sick bastard struck again. He left his calling card. Same as last time."

He motioned with his head to the empty chair sitting across the table. "Have a seat," he said. "Just got sent the latest profile of our boy. We're still taking pictures and collecting evidence. Let's give them a minute and then I'll take you back where we found her."

Agent Canter placed her purse on the table, pulled out a chair and sat. She looked around the tiny kitchen and couldn't help but feel what this victim had gone through. An open juice container sat on the counter next to a toppled bottle of Tylenol.

A broken glass lay on the floor, identified with a small evidence triangle marker. Small droplets of blood dotted the kitchen floor and led in the direction of the hallway. Canter knew this is where the attack had begun.

"Who found the body?" Stacey asked.

"Her mother. She walked in on this mess. I guess she had watched her dog and was returning it. Just like before, we found a bloody axe and some bloody clothes on the side of the house. He wants us to find them. It's a game to him. Forensics will check for a match."

Captain Vitamer deftly maneuvered the mouse, bringing up the profile. He angled the computer so Stacey could see.

"Let's dive into the mind of this crazy son of a bitch," he remarked.

Agent Canter scooted her chair closer, keen to get a better look. Vitamer then began to paraphrase the report.

"The FBI has a complete DNA sequence for our guy. He's leaving his mark on the victims with his semen. Seems like he wants full credit for his kills."

"Can't we crosscheck his DNA with one of those ancestry genealogy sites like we did for the Golden State Killer?" Stacey asked.

"We caught a lot of shit for that. It's heading to the courts. I guess there's a lot of people who don't want those sites used for law enforcement."

"Really? Bet those bleeding hearts would feel differently if the killer struck someone in their family."

"I'm sure you're right," Vitamer said and continued reading the report.

"BAU (Behavioral Analysis Unit) believes the perpetrator has been in and out of mental institutions from a young age. He is an avid reader and most likely has a high IQ. From evidence recovered from the crime scenes, his genre of choice is demonic in nature with a fascination of Jazz in the early 1920's."

"Is this one dressed in a flapper outfit?" Canter asked.

"She sure is. Straight out of the Roaring Twenties."

"As he became of age, he most likely began using drugs and drinking alcohol. The subject likely has taken medication to control schizophrenia or bipolar disorder."

"Is that all?" Canter questioned, shifting her gaze from the computer to Vitamer. "That narrows it down to thousands of people just in the Detroit area!"

"I know, but that's what we've got. Demons, Jazz, and the 1920's."

Officer Wells stepped into the kitchen, his eyes first meeting Stacey's. "It's official, we're a team."

"Yeah, I heard. Great," Stacey replied.

"We're all set in the back, Captain. Ready for you to wrap up. The photographer is waiting for you."

"Perfect," he said, rising from his chair.

Agent Canter was careful not to step on any of the blood evidence smeared on the floor as she followed Vitamer down the narrow hallway. Pictures knocked sideways and strewn to the floor showed that Dominique had put up a hell of a fight. They entered a bedroom where the body was staged. Dominique sat in a folding chair in the far corner of the room.

"Jesus," Stacey said, turning her head away, swallowing hard to keep the bile from creeping up her throat.

"You all right, Canter?" Vitamer asked.

"Just give me minute."

Dominique Hutcheson wore a red short one-piece dance dress with fringy tassels just above the knee. A matching red headband with a red feather was placed around her head. Black and gold high heel shoes matched a vintage black and gold cigarette holder placed between the victim's index and middle fingers. Her throat was slit, and she suffered severe head wounds. Whitish-gray semen lay in a clump, ejaculated on her chest.

"Another flapper," Canter said as the two approached the body.

"What's this? The third victim?" Vitamer asked. "Every crime scene has something to do with the Twenties. Look at this place. It looks like a slaughterhouse in here and yet her body's clean, very little blood on it."

"He must have bathed her." Canter said. "He cleaned her up, dressed her and then masturbated over her. I bet she wasn't raped just like the others. What a sick bastard."

"We think he left a note again," Officer Wells said, walking up behind the two. "It's in the end of her cigarette holder. Looks like a tiny rolled up note. Thought it was a cigarette until we took a closer look."

Vitamer walked close to the victim and studied the cigarette holder. "Did you dust this for prints?" he asked never taking his gaze from the note.

"Yessir. It was clean," Aleister said, then handed the captain a pair of blue latex gloves.

Vitamer donned the gloves and carefully removed the cigarette holder from the fingers of the victim. Rigor mortis had set in and it took a few seconds to separate the fingers. He detached the note from the cigarette holder and placed the holder in an evidence bag. As he unrolled the paper, he said, "This sonofabitch loves the cat and mouse chase."

"Detroit Public Library. Louis Armstrong Biography, pg. 48."

"What!??" Agent Canter asked, a little taken aback.

"That's all it says," Vitamer repeated. "Detroit Public Library. Louis Armstrong Biography, pg. 48."

"Should we head to the library?" Officer Wells asked.

"Yes... absolutely," Vitamer said soberly. "Look at every book that says anything about Armstrong. Probably a ton of them. If they're closed, call the mayor and get someone to open it. Also, I want all the surveillance footage of who was in that area of the library in the last week. I'm going to finish up here and get this poor girl to the coroner."

Chapter 34

The suitcases stood ready, and boarding passes printed, as David waited by the minivan. Stacey and Carly stood on the porch of the townhouse.

"You are and always will be my little sister," Stacey said, standing close to Carly. "I know you don't always believe that, but you really are."

Touched, Carly closed the distance between them, holding Stacey in a tight embrace. Tears welled in Carly's eyes as they held onto each other, a silent acknowledgment of all they had been through.

"You listen to me, Carly Fletcher," said Stacey. "You're part of my life and that will never change, even if you are an ocean away. When you get everything in order in Germany, you promise to let me know what your plans are."

"I will. I promise."

David yelled from the minivan. "We gotta go, we're gonna miss the flight."

"One second," Carly shouted back as she moved in and hugged Stacey one more time.

"Thank you. Thank you for everything. I'll stay in touch and keep you updated once I get settled in."

****

Porsche entered the hotel room, a steaming cup of coffee cradled in her hand. She passed it to Sergeant Tim, who had just swung the door open. His duffel bag sat sprawled across an unoccupied bed, clothes spilling out in disarray.

"What's going on?" Tim inquired, noting Porsche's evident anxiety. "You sounded pretty anxious on the phone."

"Slovak's dead!" Porsche explained.

"Dead? The CIA got the son of a bitch?"

"No. You're not going to believe this. It was COVID. He died of complications from COVID."

Tim raised the cup to his lips, blowing on it before taking a sip. Lingering shock still etched across his face.

"I can't believe a tiny virus got him. Serves the bastard right. Sort of wish it was a little bit more violent for all the hell he put Carly and David through," Tim remarked, the bitterness in his tone reflecting the resentment.

"You and me both."

Shifting the conversation, Porsche handed Tim a photograph of Bo and Mrs. Farris.

"Bo goes by the name of Thomas Higgins and Mrs. Farris goes by the last name of Winters, same as Carly."

Tim set his coffee down, attentively studying both pictures. He then looked to Porsche.

"How about I start following Bo? See where he works and where he plays. I want to get a feel as to his daily routine."

"Good idea. I should let you know both Carly and David are heading back to Dusseldorf. They fly in tonight," Porsche revealed.

"Tonight? Does Bo or Carly's mom know?" Tim inquired.

"No…I am going to get them from the airport. Carly is still going to be in witness protection and as far as David is concerned, *Kolo* probably thinks David is still in Canada with you."

"That Agent Canter. Isn't she the one that was undercover and befriended Carly when they were at Holy Oaks?" Tim questioned recalling what David had told him in Canada.

"Yes. I got to know her pretty well when we were looking for Carly. She's the one that called me to let me know they were flying in."

"Alright. I'll take a quick shower and then we can head out."

"Sounds like a plan," Porsche agreed.

Chapter 35

Stacey and Officer Wells sat in an unmarked car in front of the Detroit Public Library. A police cruiser with two officers pulled up beside them and lowered the passenger window.

"Agent Canter?" the officer asked, leaning forward to see past his partner.

"I'm Canter," Stacey said.

"We're waiting on the Head Librarian to open the place. He should be here anytime."

"Great. Can someone get surveillance footage of the outside area?"

"Absolutely. We'll get you footage of a 3-block area. Is that enough?"

"Should be. We'll compare it with footage from the library."

A black sedan pulled up and parked behind Agent Canter. Stacey looked in her rearview mirror.

"This has to be our guy," she said to Officer Wells.

A tall man wearing jeans, tee-shirt and sandals walked to the squad car. Canter watched as the pedestrian leaned in and talked to the officer through the driver's open window. After a short conversation, the librarian headed to the two flights of concrete steps that led to a beautiful white marble building. He waited at the top for Canter and Wells

"Wait here," the librarian said, indignation in his tone. "I have to unlock the building and disarm the alarm."

Officer Wells waited until the librarian was in the building. "Must have gotten up on the wrong side of the bed. Doesn't seem very happy."

"Given the way he's dressed, this might have been his day off."

"Ok," the librarian said as he returned. "My name is D'andre McNeil and I apologize for being snippy. Only get four days off a month and this was one of them. You need some kind of book?"

"Yes," Canter said. "Biographies about Armstrong... Louis Armstrong."

D'andre nodded. "Follow me."

Stacey entered the building and was struck by its beauty. Huge stained-glass windows allowed sunlight to shine through. The dome ceiling raised sixty feet into the air and was adorned with artwork. Many paintings depicted the early industrial days of Detroit. After entering an elevator, the librarian pushed the second-floor button.

"So, what's this all about?" D'andre asked.

"We're investigating a case," Stacey said.

"What kind of case?"

"We're not at liberty to discuss that," Officer Wells said.

The door to the elevator opened to a huge lobby with rows upon rows of books. The librarian slid into a narrow cubby and bent over a computer. He shook the mouse and mumbled to himself. "Biography, Louis Armstrong."

D'andre typed the descriptors into the book classification system. Canter heard the printer spit out a page.

"Got it," D'andre said grabbing the printout and pointing to the large sign that hung from the ceiling and read, Biographies.

"Looks like all our books are here," he said reading from the printout. "They're in alphabetical order by last name. Anything else?" D'andre asked handing Canter the printout.

"Can you get us security footage, say for the last week?" she asked.

"Let me call our head of security. He should be able to get that for you."

Canter and Wells made their way to the Biography section. Wells snapped on a pair of latex gloves and started combing the books.

"That's all of them," he said placing the last of the books that had anything to do with Armstrong on top of the bookshelf.

"This reminds me of that creep Dennis Rader," Stacey said.

"Who?" Aleister asked.

"Dennis Rader. He was the serial killer BTK and left a note for the cops in a book at a library."

"Oh, that's right. Bind, Torture, Kill…He was one sick bastard."

"This could be some type of copycat," Stacey suggested. Her attention then going to the printout.

"It says that there are five autobiographies. If we don't find what we are looking for, we may have to go through all of these."

Stacey put on her own gloves and began screening the books, stacking them to the side as she went.

"Let's see if we get lucky," Aleister said then proceeded to start opening books to page 48. On his third one he stopped. "I've got something," he said as he carefully removed a folded piece of paper wedged tightly into the crease of the binding. He handed it to Stacey.

Stacey unfolded the yellowed rice paper. It crackled as she pressed the sheet flat. At first glance, she knew the offset type was done on a manual typewriter.

"Whoever left this typed it with as much attention to detail as he gave to the presentation of his victims," Stacey concluded. She then read the letter aloud.

Hottest Hell, March 13, 1919
Esteemed Mortal of New Orleans: The Axeman
They have never caught me and they never will. They have never seen me, for I am invisible, even as the <u>ether</u> that surrounds your earth. I am not a human being, but a spirit and a demon from the hottest hell. I am what you Orleanians and your foolish police call the Axeman.

When I see fit, I shall come and claim other victims. I alone know whom they shall be. I shall leave no clue except my bloody axe, besmeared with blood and brains of she whom I have sent below to keep me company.

If you wish you may tell the police to be careful not to rile me. Of course, I am a reasonable spirit. I take no offense at the way they have conducted their investigations in the past. In fact, they have been so utterly stupid as to not only amuse me, but His Satanic Majesty, Francis Josef, etc. But tell them to beware. Let them not try to discover what I am, for it were better that they were never born than to incur the wrath of the Axeman. I don't think there is any need of such a warning, for I feel sure the police will always dodge me, as they have in the past. They are wise and know how to keep away from all harm.

Undoubtedly, you Orleanians think of me as a most horrible murderer, which I am, but I could be much worse if I wanted to. If I wished, I could pay a visit to your city every night. At will I could slay thousands of your best citizens (and the worst), for I am in close relationship with the Angel of Death.

Now, to be exact, at 12:15 (earthly time) on next Tuesday night, I am going to pass over New Orleans. In my infinite mercy, I am going to make a little proposition to you people. Here it is: I am very fond of jazz music, and I swear by all the devils in the nether regions that every person shall be spared in whose home a jazz band is in full swing at the time I have just mentioned. If everyone has a jazz band going, well, then, so much the better for you people. One thing is certain and that is that some of your people who do not jazz it out on that specific Tuesday night (if there be any) will get the axe.

Well, as I am cold and crave the warmth of my native Tartarus, and it is about time I leave your earthly home, I will cease my discourse. Hoping that thou wilt publish this, that it may go well with thee, I have been, am and will be the worst spirit that ever existed either in fact or realm of fancy.

--The Axeman

Canter's gaze left the letter and went to Wells. She was speechless. The letter ended with a handwritten sentence and a signature.

*You Midwesterners beware. What my **brother-in-death** did to the good people of New Orleans over a century ago will seem like child's play. Let the dancin' begin! --**The Jazzman***

Chapter 36

Bo wound the scarf snugly around his neck and emerged from his apartment, greeted by the crisp morning chill. A layer of snow lay on the ground, painting the world in a sea of white. Sleep had eluded him, burdened by the unsettling thoughts he had unearthed during the AA meeting with his newfound acquaintance. As he navigated through the fresh snow, a nagging suspicion gnawed at him—perhaps, just perhaps, it was someone or something entwined with Slovak. He ran his finger down the scar that Slovak had given him, from the center of his cheek to the corner of his mouth.

As he entered the public library, he went directly to a computer station, unbuttoned his long trench coat, placing it to the back of the chair. He undid his scarf and let it drape over his shoulders, before pulling out the chair and sitting. He looked at his phone and brought up the image of the web address Rambo his handler had given him.

Bo immediately typed the web address into his browser.
https://myaccount.google.com/u/2/

Once there, he entered the password spearhead4&% and went directly to the drafts folder. There was a message waiting for him.

GI Joe,

Your disguises have been purchased as you requested. They are at the shop we discussed in Dusseldorf. I would grow a slight beard to cover your scar. You can never be too cautious.
   Rambo

Bo swiftly closed the site, erasing any traces of the search from his history.

Scar! **Scar!** The word exploded in his mind. The harsh reality hit him—he had been compromised. The acquaintance from the AA meeting may have been a setup.

Am I just being paranoid? A sense of urgency gripped him; he needed to turn the page swiftly. Whether true or not, he felt both he and Mrs. Fletcher were now in imminent danger.

****

Bo ascended his apartment stairs with urgency, taking two steps at a time. Swinging open the door, he called out for Mrs. Fletcher. Hearing nothing, he rushed to her bedroom, finding her lying on the bed, resting.

"Bo," she said startled. "What are you doing home from work?"

Bo went to the closet, grabbing a suitcase as Mrs. Fletcher sat up.

"Bo, have you been drinking? What's going on?" she asked.

"No…I haven't been drinking. We can't talk now. I need you to pack some clothes. Pack enough clothes to last a couple of weeks. I will explain everything once we're out of here."

"But where are we going.?"

"There's no time now. Please, just trust me. Pack as fast as you can and meet me in the front room. We're running out of time."

Mrs. Fletcher met Bo in the front room. He tossed his cell phone on the counter and reached out toward Carly's mom.

"Give me your phone. We are going to leave them here. We might be being tracked."

Carly's mom handed over the phone.

****

As Tim and Porsche maneuvered through the expansive parking lot of Lufthansa Systems, an unsettling tension gripped them. The CIA had provided them with the make, model, and license plate of Bo's car. Yet, as they scoured the rows of vehicles, the car was not there.

"Well, this isn't good," Porsche said, her expression creased in concern.

"Think I should go in and ask? Maybe he called in sick?" Tim asked.

"What happens if he is there? What are you going to say if they go get him?"

"Good point."

Observing an employee, briefcase in hand, emerging from the building, Porsche drove towards him. Lowering the window.

"Excuse me please," The man halted, offering a slight smile. "Yes."

"Have you seen Tom Higgins today?"

"No," the man replied, shaking his head. Porsche nodded thoughtfully, driving away, leaving the man standing there.

"Something's up. When we got briefed, we were told Bo was doing great! He was making all his AA meetings and never missing work. Let's go check out the apartment. This is making me a little nervous."

"Sounds good."

****

Bo navigated his car into Helga Schmidt's driveway with a sense of purpose. Though he hadn't divulged the complete truth to Carly's mother, he believed the opportune moment would reveal itself in due time. That time was now. Unbeknownst to her, there was an additional driving force behind Bo's success in Alcoholics Anonymous – a force named Helga.

Their connection was more than friendship; it was a bond forged through shared battles with alcoholism. Bo and Helga's relationship went beyond the surface. It was an understanding only those wrestling with the same compulsive disorder could truly comprehend.

Throughout the six weeks Bo spent in AA, he engaged in daily conversations with Helga. They had many conversations over strong German coffee. Conversations during group meetings, and conversations walking in the park. He was developing feelings for her, and he wanted to know where that might lead. He would explain his complicated relationship with Carly but at the same time making sure he was keeping the secret of their past. That past was about to get shared.

Helga was older than Bo by two years. Her first and only marriage was to an airline pilot. According to Helga, he had a lady in every city. Vodka made being alone for days more bearable and she simply drank those other women away. They had no children and were married young.

"What if I had tried harder?" she told Bo. "If I had been a better wife, maybe he wouldn't have left me."

"You can't do the *what if's*," Bo consoled her. "It will eat at your soul. You were young and you made a mistake. He's the big loser if you ask me."

"Maybe you're right," Helga reasoned. "The SOB cheated on me, not the other way around."

Helga rushed from the house at the sight of the car pulling into the driveway. Bo cut the engine and directed his attention to Mrs. Fletcher.

"I'll explain everything once we get inside. Just had to make sure you were safe first."

Mrs. Fletcher said nothing as they both left the car.

"Thomas, what is going on?" Helga asked. "Your phone call sounded frantic."

"Let's get in and I'll explain," Bo reassured her.

Helga opened the door and showed Mrs. Fletcher to the couch before sitting in a recliner next to her. Bo retrieved the luggage and joined them inside, placing the bags on the carpet before closing the door with a purposeful click. He then drew the drapes closed. The room became eerily dark until Helga stood and turned on a lamp.

"Tell me what the hell is going on," Mrs. Fletcher demanded.

Bo settled into the seat beside Mrs. Fletcher, gently grasping her hand.

"I think we might be compromised," he stated.

"Compromised?? What are you talking about?" Mrs. Fletcher responded, her confusion evident.

"Ever since I quit drinking my thinking has become clearer. I've been feeling the urge to leave witness protection."

"Witness protection!??" Helga said, her disbelief audible.

Bo's gaze shifted to Helga.

"I haven't been totally honest with you. My name is not Tom Higgins. I am Bo Harris. I used to live in Michigan."

"I don't understand. Are you in trouble?" Helga asked.

"Why do you think we are compromised?" Mrs. Fletcher interrupted.

Bo rose from the couch, a restless energy pushing him into a measured pace across the room. His fingers ran through his hair in a gesture of anxiety as he grappled with finding the right words.

"I was working with what I thought was a handler that helps people who want to get out of witness protection," regret in his voice.

"Oh, Bo," Mrs. Fletcher sighed. "What have you done?"

"I was corresponding secretly over the internet. Using an alias. I would supply information to Rambo, my handler, and he would tell me the next steps to do. But he said one thing that got me suspicious."

"What was that?" Helga asked.

Bo unconsciously felt at the scar on the side of his face. "He knew that I had a scar on my face. I never had made that known. We were discussing concealment strategies, and he suggested growing a short crop beard to hide my scar. I realized he was doing research on me! And then, that Borka guy shows up."

"He seems like such a creep," Helga added. "There is something about him I don't trust."

"You know, after our first meetings, I saw him drinking at a local pub. He texted me that night and lied about the last time he had a drink."

"So, do we let the right people know? FBI, CIA?" asked Mrs. Fletcher.

"Not just yet," Bo suggested. "Let me do a little more digging. As far as Borka is concerned, he most likely thinks he has totally duped me and is in control. I think we need to turn the tables on him."

Chapter 37

Canter handed the letter to Alister. "Put this in a separate evidence bag," she said. "It's paper thin and I don't want it to tear." She then looked around the library.

"What are you looking for?" Aleister asked.

"A computer. There's something I got to check," she said pointing to a bank of computers in the far-left corner of the library and then heading toward them.

"Right now? Can't we check when we get back to the station?" Aleister asked following close behind her.

"I don't want to wait. I want to check it now," she replied.

"Hey…stop!" he said. "Talk to me. What's going on?"

Stacey turned and fully faced Aleister.

"When I was a trainee at the FBI academy in Quantico, there was this evidence room, more like a vault filled with files of unsolved murder cases. One of the cases stood out to me because of the savage nature of the killings. These killings happened in New Orleans in the early 1920's."

"Why'd the case stick out?"

They continued moving toward the computers.

"I saw pictures of murder victims. There was this baby, like two years old. The picture I saw was of a mother, face covered in blood, holding her two-year-old daughter. Both were battered with an axe… the mother lived, but the little girl didn't. I mean… who could do that?"

Aleister shook his head in disbelief. "Someone without a soul! That's who."

He pulled a chair from a neatly stacked chair caddie and handed it to Stacey. He then removed one for himself. Stacey shook the mouse as they sat behind a computer and doubled clicked on Google. She typed in the descriptors, "Murders of the 1920's New Orleans" and immediately sites appeared showing press reports of a killer dubbed 'The Axeman of New Orleans'.

Aleister tilted the monitor so that he could read along with her.

From May 1918 to October 1919, the city of New Orleans, Louisiana was in a panic over a serial killer nicknamed "The Axeman." The first to succumb to his murderous ways was an Italian grocer named Joseph Maggio and his wife Catherine. As they lay sleeping in their apartment, their throats were cut with a straight razor and their heads were bashed with a hand axe. A little more than a month later, another couple, both grocers were brutally murdered in the same fashion. The murders continued for over a year. Final tally, six dead, six injured.

Stacey scrolled down the site. "I'm almost positive this is the guy who killed that baby." She then found another chilling account.

Rosie had awakened to find her husband struggling with a large man wielding an axe. When her husband fell to the floor, the assailant turned on her as she held her daughter and begged for their lives. Undaunted, the killer slammed the axe down, first on the daughter and then to the mother.

Near the bottom of the site was a link entitled *"Letter from the Axeman"*. Stacey double-clicked and instantly the letter appeared.

"Oh, my God!! This is the same letter we found in the book," Stacey said, unnerved.

"I'll be a son-of-a-bitch!" Aleister softly exclaimed. "It is."

Stacey placed both hands to her temples and rested her elbows on the computer desk.

"The killings stopped after the papers published the letter from the Axeman, and the majority of the townspeople did exactly what they were told. They danced to jazz that entire Tuesday night. Many of the townspeople believed the killer wasn't human, more of a dark spirit."

"So, our killer is mimicking the Axeman," Aleister reasoned.

"I think so. It's been almost 100 years to the day that the Axeman struck. Of course, he isn't alive now. I have a feeling this is only the beginning. Our killer wants to be famous. He's calling himself the Jazzman."

"So, he kills in the most gruesome, grisly way to capture our attention."

"Yes!! And we in law enforcement and media are his enablers. We're in the game with him."

"This guy's gotta be really demented…deranged…a real lunatic."

"You would think he is, but not all are. Look at the BTK killer from Kansas, Dennis Rader. He was the guy who also left a note in a book years ago. He was a case study at Quantico. He had a normal upbringing. No traumatic childhood events that would explain anything. He was evil and he knew it. Rader's thing was control. He would bind his victims then talk with them for hours all while letting them know that when the conversation ended, so did their life."

"So, what's the difference with our boy?"

"Our boy may *really* think he's an angel of death doing the work of his dark Majesty. I think he has some type of psychosis."

"God!" Aleister said shaking his head. "I've worked a lot of cases, but this son of a bitch can keep you up at night."

"He already has," Canter said quietly.

D'andre returned to the deserted Biography section where he had left Wells and Canter.

"Where'd they go?" he said to himself before spotting them over in the computer area.

"Security is here," he said walking up to them. "They should be able to get you the footage you want."

****

He lay there, eyes closed, fully aroused. Memories of his last kill were euphoric, bathing him in that sexual high he so desired.

He heard a pound on his locked bedroom door.

Frustrated, he stopped...removing his hands from the middle of his body.

"What!?" he snapped.

"Open the door," a crotchety voice shot back between hacks of a smoker's cough.

He pulled his sweatpants up from his knees.

"Just a minute," he yelled.

Charlie jumped to his feet and cracked the dead bolt opening the door an inch. An older man, deep lines etched in his face and a cigarette jutting from the corner of his mouth stared back. In one hand was a glass of water. In the other, two green pills.

The old man lifted both arms slightly, "Here."

Charlie took the pills and water from his grandfather and closed the door with his foot. Cupping the pills in his hand he relocked the dead bolt and placed the water on his nightstand. He then opened the little drawer on the cabinet. He tossed the Latuda onto the growing mound of other meds—pale green ovals, round yellows, and blue capsules that he couldn't remember the name of. That crazy doctor giving him those pills… didn't he check out the side effects before prescribing them?

He removed a cigarette from the pack on his dresser and lit one. Inhaling deeply, he fell to his bed, letting the smoke fill his lungs before exhaling and blowing it toward the ceiling.

"You're a *Dick*, Jazzman, and you'll always be a *Dick*," the voice in his head taunted.

Charlie's eyes darted to the corner of the room and fixed on his guinea pig standing on its hind legs looking through the glass of his cage. The guinea pig nervously twitched and turned its head smelling the air before dropping down to all fours.

"Quit calling me a *Dick*," he shot back, raw anger pouring through him. "I told you that's what my daddy called me. I hate it."

"Having a bad day, Jazzman?" the voice in his head said sarcastically. "I thought you liked doing *it* with Daddy."

"What do you know, Asshole?" Charlie said to Pugs. "That's a big lie! It never happened!"

Charlie ignored Pugs and finished his cigarette. Butting the smoke in the ashtray lying next to his bed, he walked to the glass terrarium and swooped up Pugs in one hand. He kissed the rodent on the nose and brought him to eye level.

"Why ya been such a prick to me lately?" Charlie whined.

"Because you haven't been listening. You gotta Jazz it up. No one knows about the Jazzman. They know about the Axeman, but you're not him. As far as I am concerned, you're nothing but a big pussy. Do you hear what I'm saying? The Jazzman's a big pussy!!"

Rage gripped Charlie and he began to squeeze. The guinea pig squeaked and squirmed before chomping down and gnawing his hand.

"Mother Fucker!" Charlie yelled before flinging Pugs back down to his cage landing on the soft sawdust floor.

"Hey, Pal, take it easy," a tranquil voice in Charlie's head said. "We're a team. I'm just trying to help."

Charlie lifted his hand to his mouth and caressed the wound with his tongue. He didn't mind the taste of blood. He dropped to his bed and scrolled down his playlist. Within seconds King Oliver's Creole

Jazz Band played in the background over his portable Bluetooth speakers.

Chapter 38

The unassuming figure in a black suit and fedora went unnoticed in the economy class, a sea of passengers wearing facial masks as the remnants of the Covid pandemic gradually faded away. The prevalence of mask-wearing provided the ideal cover for the man, who concealed a facial deformity beneath his disguise.

Slovak's eyes remained fixed on Carly as she and David retrieved their carry-ons, preparing to exit from the plane. His eyes followed her every move, a silent observer in the bustling moments before they stepped off the aircraft.

Porsche stared at the huge screen showing the arrival times and flight numbers of the inbound planes. Flight 844 Detroit to Frankfort. *Awesome!* She thought. *Their flight is on time. Gate Seventy-five.*

****

Alone by the luggage carousel, Porsche stood vigilant, her eyes continuously scanning for potential threats. Carly and David were taking longer than anticipated to clear customs, leaving Porsche feeling a growing sense of unease. At last, she spotted them and greeted them with a wave as they approached. A feeling of relief washed over her.

David stood by the carousel to retrieve the luggage, as Carly walked directly to Porsche. They hugged seamlessly, blending in with the crowd of travelers.

"Let's not talk here," Porsche said, smiling as if she had just reunited with a relative. "Tim is waiting in the car."

****

As casual as the three of them appeared, no one paid attention to the man in the fedora walking leisurely behind, dragging a suitcase. His training allowed him to remain concealed while at the same time never losing sight. He blended perfectly with the masses walking to the parking structure.

Carly jumped in the front seat while David got in the back. The two men shook hands while Carly waved to Tim. Slovak lowered to his knee, seemingly to tie his shoe, giving him time to snap a picture of Porche's license plate. As they pulled away, Slovak nonchalantly turned his head, the group was oblivious to his actions.

Porsche slipped her credit card into the card access gate and punched a few numbers on the keypad. The arm lifted and she pulled out, heading to the apartment.

"What do you mean, they're gone," Carly voiced concern.

"Just what I said," Porsche replied. "I know the make and model of the car you've been driving, and it wasn't at the apartment or at Bo's work."

"Did you try and call?" David asked from the back.

"Of course. No one picked up," Porsche said, looking into her review mirror. She then turned to Carly. "Do you still have your key?"

"Yes," Carly said, lifting it from her purse.

The car barely stopped as Carly darted from it, followed by David.

"Wait for us," Porsche yelled! "We're armed!"

****

The four stood just outside the apartment as Sergeant Tim and Porsche drew their weapons. Carly inserted her key into the lock, swinging the door open. She stepped back, alongside David as Sergeant Tim and Porsche rushed through door. Porsche nodded toward the two bedrooms at the rear, signaling Tim to follow suit. Once the apartment was secured, Porsche announced, "All clear!"

Carly entered the apartment followed by David. The apartment was exactly the way it was when she left. A feeling of dread overtook her when she thought about what Bo will say with David in tow. As she looked around, her stomach turned, she noticed the two phones sitting on the counter.

"That's why no one answered," Carly said picking up the phones. "Something's not right, why would they leave without their phones?"

Carly walked to the bookcase and removed the novel where she kept her twenty-two-caliber pistol hidden.

"My gun's not here. Bo must have taken it. That makes me feel better, but at the same time worse."

Chapter 39

Agent Canter stood just outside the Patrick V. McNamara Federal Building on Michigan Ave. in Detroit. An American flag mounted to the white stone and glass building barely swayed in the mist. She opened and closed her umbrella rapidly before entering the building, shaking as much rain off as she could.

Stacey wiped her shoes on the rain-soaked rug and nodded at the security guard on the way to the fourth floor. She by-passed the crowd hovered around the elevator and went directly to the stairwell where she climbed the sixty-eight steps. As she entered the hallway, agents, secretaries, and other support personal scurried in and out of offices. She met Special Agent Gideon at the door of the office, and they walked in together.

"Morning, Margaret," Stacey said to Gideon. "How have ya been?"

"Good...you?"

"Little tired today. Nothing this double shot espresso can't cure," Stacey said holding up her cup.

"Double espresso won't cure my problem, not even a double scotch," Gideon said quietly so only Stacey could hear. "I wanted to turn this case down...refuse it altogether, but...when the Deputy Director said, 'Take it,' I had to. Discussion over!"

Vitamer and Wells along with three other agents stood up from chairs in the office waiting room.

"Morning," Agent Gideon said. "Looks like we are all here."

The seven proceeded down a hall to a separate conference room. Gideon, who was in charge of the case, unlocked the door and turned on a light. Clipped to a whiteboard were pictures of the three victims. Their names were printed in all caps just below their faces.

In the room was an office table with eight chairs around it. Clear plastic bags containing evidence from the last crime scene sat in the middle of it. In front of each chair was a yellow legal note pad, beige manila envelope, and a pen. A screen for a PowerPoint presentation was set up to the side.

"Have a seat," Gideon said, pointing to the empty chairs.

As they settled in, Gideon went to Officer Wells and reached out her hand. "I heard you're the new detective on the beat."

"Yes, this is the first time I worked a case with help from the FBI."

"You're a lucky guy to be working under Captain Vitamer. He's the best in the biz."

"Gideon, stop," the captain said. "You're going to make this old boy blush."

The team took their seats around the table. Agent Gideon sat at the head.

"I'd like you to meet Captain Vitamer and Officer Wells from the Detroit Forensic Science Division. We've partnered with the division for this operation." The men exchanged nods and Gideon continued.

"You know why we're here. We have at least three victims and the killer's making it perfectly clear that these killings are connected. That's why this task force has been put together. The mayor is going to go public regarding these homicides and there's going to be a firestorm once that happens."

Gideon picked up the manila envelope and squeezed the clips, pulling out its contents.

"These photos and documents follow with the PowerPoint presentation Agent Canter is about to share. She looked at Stacey and nodded. "Ready."

Canter stepped from the table to the podium where a laptop sat. She showed the first slide as Gideon dimmed the lights. The slide read *Operation Roaring Twenties.*

"I'm going to start with our latest victim and work backwards." She then pressed the clicker to advance the next slide.

"Dominique Hutcheson's body was staged like the other two crime scenes. Though there was plenty of blood in the hallway and in the bedroom, Dominique had no blood on her. She was clean and, we presume, bathed before being dressed in a fringy, red flapper dress out of the Roaring 20's. She had a feathered headband around her forehead. Lots of huge rhinestones on it.

"A cigarette holder was placed into her hand and at the end of it was a rolled note, resembling a cigarette."

Agent Canter held up the cigarette holder in the clear evidence bag and passed it around the table. She then continued.

"The note had instructions directing us to the Detroit Public Library. There we would find a message on page 48 of an Autobiography of Louis Armstrong."

She moved forward to the next slide revealing the letter from the Axeman. "The message was a letter written by someone calling himself the Axeman. It's in your packet. I'll give you some time to read it."

Stacey went to the bottled water dispenser and got a drink. She checked a couple of texts then returned and continued.

"Looks like our boy is mimicking a killer from the twenties that was never caught. Everything has to do with jazz. The letter is verbatim of a letter written to the people of New Orleans in 1919."

Agent Canter pointed to the slide showing the letter.

"This letter was typed on a manual typewriter. An *Antique Early 1920's Standard German typeface.*

"The letters uppercase M and T are distinct. You can see where the keys have been worn and the top of the letters are barely visible. We're checking pawn shops and flea markets as well as eBay to see if we can get lucky. It's a long shot, but we don't have a whole lot to go on."

Canter held up another evidence bag that had both the razor and hatchet in it. "We found these two items along with bloody clothes tossed on the side of the house. We assume that he changes clothes after he commits the murder.

"The axes and razors used in all three murders are from the same era 1920-1930. I think a good place to start would be to look into collectable clubs. See if there are any organizations who collect and trade these. Maybe even some of those axe throwing bars."

"An axe throwing bar," Vitamer repeated, obviously amused. "I always wondered who the first person was that thought drinking alcohol and throwing axes was a good idea."

"I've done it," Aleister blurted out, then was embarrassed when the older agents looked at him and chuckled.

The meeting lasted a little over an hour when Agent Gideon rose from her chair. "I don't know about you, but I need a break. Let's take fifteen and regroup. We'll go over the next two cases when we come back."

Everyone but Agent Canter left the room, murmuring about the case.

"This killer reminds me of Lucas," Captain Vitamer said to Aleister as they stood in the hallway.

"Who?" Aleister asked.

"Lucas. Henry Lee Lucas. He was a killer out of Chicago. One sick bastard. He started with prostitutes and then moved on from there. He confessed to over a hundred murders but recanted most of them."

"Why does he remind you of our boy?"

"Because of the way he messed with the cops. He seemed to really enjoy trying to outsmart them. Sort of like what's going on with this guy. Using murders to play his own mind game."

"And we are part of it," Officer Wells agreed.

Captain Vitamer shook his head. "Don't have much of a choice. He's written us into his play. I just hope we catch the bastard before *he* is confessing to over a hundred murders."

The team reassembled and chatted idly until Agent Canter put up a new slide. They sat and she continued. A picture of Josie Davis, the first victim, who was quite young and looked a lot like Rihanna, appeared on the screen.

"Josie Davis was 22 and born in Lima, Ohio. Her body was staged like the others. Sitting in a kitchen chair, like she was at a 1920's Speakeasy. Black dress with a matching headband. Black gloves rose to her elbows. She was wearing black stockings rolled down to just-below-the-knee. Her body was washed, and she was not raped. Semen was left on her chest. Looks like the creep masturbates on them once he stages the scene.

"Josie was an Ohio State grad and landed her first job at a tech startup in Toledo, *Velocity Technologies.*

"Didn't the other victims work in tech?" one of the agents asked.

"Our latest victim, Dominique Hutcheson, did," Canter said.

"What about Eleanor Wickens?" Gideon asked. "Was she a professional woman?"

"No. I was hoping there was a tech connection too, but there isn't. This woman seems to be the total opposite of the other two. She was from Toledo. All three killings have been within a 75-mile radius across state lines. Ms. Wickens was unemployed and had two young children. According to Social Services, she lost custody from time to time while doing stints in rehab. She was also arrested for domestic abuse against the father of one of her kids.

"She was dressed like the others. The killer left his calling card, semen on her chest, no sexual intercourse. Same M.O....a straight razor and a hand axe. As far as the clothes are concerned, they're costumes. We can check out local costume shops and see if we get lucky."

Agent Canter placed the clicker on the table. "That's it from me."

Gideon pulled the last sheet from the envelope. She held it up, signaling to the agents to do the same.

"Just was made aware of this yesterday. We have a profile of the killer's DNA. Problem is we may have a team of killers. Maybe some type of *satanic cult* if you will. The semen is from three different men. None of our victims have been raped. We've profiled the DNA through our data system, but there's nothing as of yet."

Gideon scanned the table. "Any questions…anything we missed?"

The agents looked to one another and shook their heads as they gathered the documents and placed them back into the manila envelope. "Any leads… anything you find goes through Canter. I'll be busy putting out fires and dealing with the media.

"Captain, you and Wells… check out pawn shops and thrift shops. Any place you see that would sell these types of things."

Vitamer pushed his chair back and said, "I say we do pawn shops first and then we can lunch at one of those axe throwing bars. Maybe Wells can impress me with his throwing skills."

"Very funny, Captain. Can you give me a minute? I'll meet you in the lobby."

"Sure," the captain said waving to Gideon on his way out of the door.

Stacey was placing the last of the evidence bags in what looked like a suitcase with wheels as Aleister approached. "Need a hand?" he asked.

"I'm good… but thanks."

"I was wondering. Umm… would you like to get dinner this Friday?"

Stacey looked at him.

"I mean we could discuss the case. You know a working dinner. Professional."

"I would love to," Stacey said. "Only if you promise that we don't discuss the case. No shop talk."

"Deal!" Aleister said. "You'll text me your address? Any particular restaurant you like."

"I love Mediterranean and Italian and Chinese…I *even* love a good pizza and a mug of beer. Any of those places have axes?" she said mischievously.

Aleister smiled slightly then said, "I've got a place in mind. No axes allowed."

Chapter 40

Slovak entered the hotel room and Borka and Grego were already there. Empty white Styrofoam containers overflowed from a tiny trash container, sitting next to the mini fridge. A half empty cognac bottle and two shot glasses sat on a small table in the corner. The unmistakable aroma of raw minced pork and onions lingered in the air. Slovak cast a discerning gaze across the room before removing his fedora, draping it casually on the lampshade.

"Well, you haven't changed at all nephew," Slovak said. "Once a pig, always a pig."

"Nice to see you too, Uncle." Borka retorted.

"Let me see the intelligence and I will be out of here before you can say pigsty."

Grego looked on from a recliner. He had a briefcase draped across his lap. He stared at Slovak, saying nothing. Finally, he spoke.

"I still don't understand why I should share my intelligence with you. What is in it for me?" Grego questioned, his tone skeptical.

Slovak's gaze shifted from Borka to Grego and back again.

"Why look to him?" Grego asserted, his eyes locking onto Slovak. "It's me you have to convince."

A wry smile slowly crept across Slovak's face.

"I don't know you, my friend, but I assume my nephew has filled you in. If you give me what I need, you will be handsomely rewarded."

"And if I refuse?" Grego shot back.

Slovak eyes looked shark like, they seared into Grego.

"Then, it will be out of my hands."

After a slight pause, Grego manipulated the combination on his briefcase, extracting the intelligence report secured from his confidential source. Standing with purpose, he handed the document to Slovak. Slovak, in turn, opened the report and scrutinized its contents. A shock registered on his face as he discovered that the report delved into the disastrous operation he orchestrated in the United States.

Slovak looked from the report to Grego.

"Where did you get this? Who is your contact?"

"That my friend does not concern you. This is the caliber of intelligence I can provide. Is this information sought by *Kolo*?"

"No. I have a Chinese group that will buy every bit of information they can get their hands on. How much for the report?"

"Twenty thousand."

"Done," Slovak said with authority. "I understand you also are looking for the missing mithridate," Slovak lied, aware that the missing mithridate was a fabrication.

"It is progressing well, Uncle," Borka interjected. "We have established contact with Bo Harris and are proceeding as planned."

Slovak's brows furrowed in surprise as he asked, "Bo Harris?"

"You know him?"

Slovak's heart quickened.

"I am intimately familiar with Mr. Harris. What are your intentions regarding him?" Slovak inquired.

"We haven't reached that stage yet, Uncle," Borka reported. "I'm currently building a rapport with him, and once the time is right, we'll find that mithridate and according to *Kolo*, we'll have everything we could ever want."

"Keep me informed of your progress."

Slovak directed his attention to Grego.

"I require additional intelligence from your source. I will have your money day after tomorrow."

"Look forward to working with you," Grego assured him.

As Slovak left the building, he was relieved tha*t Kolo* still believed he was dead, and that his nephew and Grego still believed there was a missing vial of mithridate. That information had not leaked yet and he prayed that it never would. Slovak slipped his hand into the side pocket of his coat removing a burner phone. He dialed and waited for Daugherty to pick up.

"Yes," came Daugherty's curt response.

"I've made contact with my nephew. I anticipate obtaining the information shortly. I need you to wire twenty thousand in U.S. currency, to the bank you set up in Dusseldorf. Also, you need to disseminate some false information so that it gets leaked to my source. Keep track on who you share this information with."

"I know how to do my job," Daugherty shot back, irritation in his voice.

****

Helga strolled from the kitchen carrying a tin of cookies. She opened it and sat it on a small table in the middle of the room. Bo, with restless energy, continued to pace with a sense of urgency.

"Sorry. I need to go shopping," Helga announced casually, plucking a cookie from the tin and offering it to the room. "Help yourself."

"Should we set a trap for Borka?" Bo abruptly asked. "Try to find out who he works for."

"I think we should tell the CIA," Carly's mother said.

"Bo, she might have a point," Helga remarked. "This entire situation is bizarre. I find myself questioning who you really are."

Bo stopped pacing and approached Helga. He gently grasped her shoulders and drew her in. A peculiar expression crossed Mrs. Fletcher's face as their embrace revealed a connection that surpassed mere friendship.

"You've been a constant support, and I genuinely value that. I wasn't completely honest with you, but circumstances left me with no choice. I owe my recovery to you, and I trust you."

There was a pause before Helga responded. "Then you need to trust me now!" she said urgently. "Bring in someone who can help. You can't handle this alone."

Helga gently disengaged from Bo's embrace and settled into a chair, prompting Bo to reluctantly follow suit.

"I don't know who to trust." Bo admitted. "The CIA could be involved? Whoever I was communicating with, seemed to have some intelligence training."

"Well, then, Thomas, or dare I say Bo, what's your plan?" Helga inquired.

Chapter 41

Stacey and Aleister stood outside the Detroit Renaissance Tower. They marveled at the glass and steel cylindrical structure reaching seventy-three stories into the sky. The sun had set, and the silo was aglow. The elevator, entirely made of glass, traveled on the outside of the building. Stacey's stomach turned slightly; she wasn't crazy about heights. The doorman, standing just outside the elevator, greeted them and asked if they were celebrating anything special.

"It's our first date," Aleister said. "I guess that could count as special."

"Enjoy your ride" the doorman said sending the couple up the side of the tower to the seventy-first floor. Below, Detroit sparkled like stars in a galaxy. As the elevator rose, so did Stacey's grip on Aleister's arm, squeezing harder and harder the higher and higher they went.

"You all right?" Aleister asked, noticing Stacey looking at her feet and not out the glass.

"Not really," she said. "I've always had a problem with heights."

The elevator stopped with a slight jerk and the door opened to the Highlands Restaurant. Stacey immediately exited the elevator and felt better once she was inside.

"Do we have to sit right by a window?" Stacey asked, "Could we sit a couple tables in?"

"Absolutely," Aleister said. "We don't need to eat here if this isn't working for you."

"No!! No!! All good. Nothing a glass of wine won't cure."

Wearing a tuxedo, the tall dignified maitre'd, stood beside an oak service podium in the foyer and greeted them.

"You are Mr. Wells and Ms. Canter…reservations at 8:00?" he said, his voice smooth, low, and professional.

Aleister nodded.

"Could we have a table away from a window?" Aleister asked. "Maybe one a little further in." The maitre'd studied the seating arrangements charted on the podium.

"Of course, Sir," he assured him. "Please follow me."

As they followed him, Stacey realized the restaurant was slowly turning. She marveled at the Canadian shore, lit up like an amusement park on the far side of the Detroit River. The maitre'd helped Stacey with her chair and placed menus in front of them.

"May I let your server know what you would like to drink?"

"Glass of Malbec, please."

"And you," he asked Aleister.

"I'll have a bourbon *Old Fashion*, light on the bitters."

"And your bourbon sir?"

"Maker's Mark."

The maitre'd nodded. "Enjoy your meal."

"So, are you packing?" Stacey asked noticing he ordered a drink.

"Wouldn't come to the Big D without it."

"Are you ever worried about having alcohol in your system if you had to use your weapon."

"I am, but the way I see it, better tried by twelve than carried by six."

"Good point," Stacey said.

"You can order whatever you like even if it's not on the menu. The website said the chef will make special requests."

Stacey smiled, "I'm not that high maintenance. I can order from the menu."

Aleister laughed. "I've only been here once. It was for my grandma's eighty-fifth birthday. I always wanted to come back."

"I can see why," Stacey said, surveying the dining room and other couples who were there.

A cell phone vibrated, and Aleister reached into his suit pocket. He looked at the Caller ID.

"I'm sorry, Stacey," Aleister said. "I have to take this."

Stacey smiled knowingly. "Yeah... Sure. Go ahead."

She watched Aleister holding his cell phone to his ear, walking surely and confidently around the dining room, disappearing behind the bar which sat in the center.

The waiter placed the Old Fashion on Aleister's side and the glass of wine in front of Stacey. He looked quizzically at Stacey.

"We aren't ready to order yet" she told him. "Come back when my friend returns."

Stacey took the liberty of taking a few sips of her wine and studied the crowd more carefully. A very thin blonde matron with tired eyes sat across from a middle-aged man with an expensive suit, probably an Armani. Both of them barely looked at each other and hardly spoke.

At a table a few feet away, the maitre'd seated two ladies, about the same age. They were laughing as they took their seats. One wore a tailored black jumpsuit, low-cut with long sleeves. The sparkling earrings that shone through her spiky red hair were most likely diamonds.

The other one was dressed in a short silver dress which stretched tightly over her chest and hugged her entire body. Her eyes were heavily rimmed with black eyeliner and the long golden hair which spiraled down to her waist was probably a wig. The sleeveless dress revealed well-toned arms with scatterings of orange and blue butterfly tattoos down to her elbow. Stacey guessed they were in their early thirties.

Aleister reappeared, coming from behind her, and took his seat across from her.

Stacey, holding her wine glass, looked at him and said, "Well, Sam Spade...are we safe?"

He smiled and gazed ruefully at his drink. "You knew?"

"Once a cop, always a cop," she said. "I took your absence for an opportunity to do a little recon of my own on this dining room. We appear to be free of swindlers, scoundrels, and low lives...at the moment."

"So, you didn't think I ran out on you??" he teased.

"You forget, Wells...I know where you work," she said, flashing him her best flirtatious look.

The server returned and took their order. The two lifted their glasses and toasted.

"To our health, wealth, and all that jazz," Stacey said dryly

Aleister nodded. "I get your meaning."

"I want to hear more about your grandma. Eighty-five!...I bet she is some awesome lady."

"*Was* an awesome lady. She died a few months back."

"Oh, I'm sorry."

"Don't be. She loved her life. She was one of the first female cops to join the Detroit PD."

"That's amazing. Like Rosie the Riveter, she paved the way for women like me."

"Never thought about it that way, but yeah… pretty much."

The server brought their dinner. Both of them ordered the New York Strip, his rare and hers well done. Midway through the meal, Stacey asked, "Could we talk a little shop? I got a question about the case."

"I thought we weren't going to talk shop."

"I know, but this case is really bothering me."

"Secretly, I was hoping you would bring it up. What's on your mind?"

"What do you think about genetics?"

"What do you mean?"

"We have the killer or killers' DNA. Our data bases are coming up empty. Since they are leaving their calling card at every crime scene, they don't fear getting caught. It leads me to believe they have never been arrested and we have nothing on them."

"Good point, but how does this fit with genetics?"

"We could send one sample of DNA to one of those ancestry sites."

"Don't those sites fight that at every turn?"

"They do. They're all about privacy. If we get a valid search warrant, they have to comply. They don't have a choice. Orrrrr…."

"Or what?" Aleister asked.

"Or maybe I won't even get a warrant. Just go it alone."

Aleister nodded. "What do we have to lose? We're dead in the water right now."

"It's not that simple," Stacey said. "We could end up with family trees that contain thousands of relatives. Uncles to Grandparents to Great Grandparents. We could end up spending a lot of time together. Tracking down those family trees could require evening hours and probably weekends."

"All the better," Aleister said, lifting his drink.

Chapter 42

Carly emerged from a rear bedroom and entered the main room where Porsche, David, and Sergeant Tim were gathered.

"They've packed their suitcases. It seems like wherever they've gone, they intend to stay for a while," she informed the group.

As everyone's focus shifted, the distinct ringtone of a text message echoed through the room, it was coming from one of the two phones sitting on the counter.

"That's gotta be Bo's phone; my mom never texts," Carly remarked as she approached the counter, retrieving Bo's phone. Simultaneously, she entered the password, explaining...

"Bo and I know each other's passwords. We set it up as a safety measure, just in case something happened to one of us, and we needed to use each other's phones."

A furrow formed between Carly's brows as the group observed her. She focused on the message and then conveyed it to the others.

"This is a text from a guy named Borka. It seems Bo's involved in some AA program here in Dusseldorf. Borka wants to meet for coffee before the meeting tonight," Carly explained, shifting her gaze from the phone to the group.

"Do you know who this Borka is?" David asked.

Carly shook her head and, returning her attention to the phone, replied, "I haven't a clue. In all the time I've been here, I've never heard of a Borka."

"Well, that's a starting point," Porsche suggested. "I think you should reply and ask where he wants to meet. We could have Tim surveil the location and see if he can gather information about this guy."

"Maybe tail him to the AA meeting," David chimed in.

"I like that idea," Carly agreed. "Once Tim identifies this guy, I could text back, saying I'm skipping the meeting due to not feeling well. Tim can then follow him to the meeting and back to his place."

"It's worth a shot," Tim added.

Carly swiftly composed a message…
Hey, Borka. Sounds good. Where would you like to meet?
Almost instantly, a response popped up…
How about we meet at Coffee Bar Dusseldorf on Flustra St. It's just down the street from our meeting.
Carly typed back, *Sounds good. What time?*
Borka's reply came promptly, *How about 5:30?*
Carly responded. *See you then.*

As Carly lifted her gaze from the phone, Porsche proposed, "How about Tim and I head to the Coffee Bar, since I know where it is, and you and David can stay here, just in case Bo and your mom return."

"Okay, I'm good with that," Carly agreed.

****

At three thirty in the afternoon, Porsche and Sergeant Tim stepped into the Coffee House on Flustra St. The air was filled with the enticing scent of robust coffee and cinnamon Nussschneckens. The bustling atmosphere greeted them, with customers forming long lines awaiting their turn to place orders for coffee and pastries.

Amidst the scene, men and women sat engrossed behind open laptops, typing away at their keyboards, seemingly detached from the outside world.

"Why don't you take that table in the back?" Tim suggested, gesturing toward the last available spot in the place. "I'll get us some coffee."

"Sounds good. Double cream, double sugar."

"My kind of girl," Tim remarked with a grin.

Porsche sat at the table, surveying her surroundings, seeking the best location for Tim's surveillance. Her training emphasized the importance of appearing natural and blending in. She knew Tim was a decorated war veteran, but as far as she knew, he had no training in clandestine surveillance.

She also entertained the notion that Borka might be entirely legitimate, and her apprehensions could be baseless. Nevertheless, Tim had to remain vigilant and prepared for any situation.

Tim approached the table carrying the two cups of coffee. Pulling a chair beside her, Porsche positioned it to offer a perfect view of the shop. She patted the chair next to her, inviting Tim to sit.

"I don't feel comfortable with you doing this alone," Porsche said, as Sergeant Tim lowered to the seat and scooted in.

"It's better and safer with two."

Tim nodded. "I've got no problem with that. Worked many details with women warriors."

Tim surveyed the coffee shop, searching for the best seat to observe everyone who entered. He gestured with his chin towards a centrally located table by the window.

"What about over there?" he said. "I can see anyone who enters, and I will be able to see which way they go."

Porsche nodded while continuing to survey the shop.

"I think you're right," she agreed. "It would be better if we present ourselves as a couple. We can put our heads together and make sure he is our guy. It will also be a lot easier to tail him, once we split up."

Tim nodded approvingly. "That's a solid plan. Let's get back and discuss it with David and Carly."

"Agreed. I will drop you off and you can fill them in. I'll swing by my grandparents' place and grab a couple of firearms for David and Carly. I hope this is all for naught, but we can't take any chances."

****

Helga remained patient, awaiting Bo's attempt to explain.

"Like I said, my real name is Bo Harris, not Thomas Higgens. Tom is my witness protection name provided by the CIA. I was abducted by a terrorist group and held for ransom."

"Ransom!?" Helga exclaimed, taken aback. "Someone tried to extort money from your family?"

"It wasn't money they were after; it was a substance called mithridate."

Lines etched between Helga's brows as she rubbed her temples, trying to stop the migraine she could feel coming on.

"Mithridate!?"

"Yes mithridate," Mrs. Fletcher interjected. "My husband was a CIA operative. He served on a bioweapon taskforce, working on developing antidotes to biological weapons. Mithridate was the antidote he had created. The terrorists were after it to reverse engineer into a dirty bomb."

Helga shook her head in disbelief, shifting her attention from Mrs. Fletcher to Bo.

"All our conversations. All the things I opened up to you about. Were all lies?" Helga asked, a mix of hurt and confusion in her eyes.

"No! I really had a girlfriend who left me. It was my fault. I didn't realize until I got sober, and I have you to thank for that."

"These people are ruthless," Mrs. Fletcher continued, her voice heavy with grief. "They killed my eight-year-old son in an attempt to extort my husband. In the end, they murdered him, too. Carly just got caught in the middle of everything."

Bo stood once more, his restless pacing adding to the tension in the room. He continued.

"Word leaked that Carly's father hid some of the mithridate. He was worried about a potential attack and wanted to safeguard his family. Before he was killed, he gave clues to its whereabouts to Carly. They wanted to ransom me for the mithridate."

"Did she give it to them? Is that why you're still alive?" Helga inquired.

"The CIA synthesized a harmless mithridate and she used that to trade for me. They then arranged for our deaths in a fake car accident. That's when we went into witness protection."

Bo settled back in his chair; an uneasy silence fell upon the room until Helga broke it.

"So, what do you think we should do?" she asked.

"Nothing for now, let's just keep everything the same. During the meeting tonight, see if there is anything off with that Borka character. Maybe this is all in my head and I am just paranoid. I can only hope to be so lucky."

Helga inhaled deeply, exhaling with a long sigh.

"I can do that."

Chapter 43

Agent Canter opened Outlook and smiled. Forensics had sent her the *markers* or STR's (short sequences of genes within the DNA) of the serial killer. She quickly opened it and downloaded the file to her desktop. Her plan was to upload it to a website called *GEDmatch*.

GEDmatch was an online service where users could find close matches to their DNA sample. The samples could come from any testing company such as AncestryDNA, 23andMe or a forensics lab in Michigan. These matches would be distance relatives of the killer.

The internal FBI data banks had produced no results. Canter had several variables to consider. Are the killer's closest relatives still alive? Do those relatives have living family members? Can those relatives be found?

Stacey logged onto the site and uploaded the file. She glanced from her computer to see Officer Wells walking into her office holding a paper bag. 'Oasis Lebanese Grill' the bag read, and he lifted it into the air.

"You brought lunch," she said with a grin as she moved items on her table to make room for the food.

"I texted you but never heard back so I winged it…Hummus, grape leaves, and beef tenderloin tips."

"I never saw your text. I have been here since 5:30 a.m. I just uploaded his DNA file and I'm waiting to see what comes back."

"Perfect timing," Aleister said. "Let's eat and you tell me how this stuff works."

The two sat around a small table. In between bites, Stacey explained how DNA genetic profiling could work.

"I'm by no means an expert, but I'll give it my best shot. We are going to create family trees of the killer by finding his relatives. There could be hundreds of relatives down to the present day."

"Couldn't that take forever?"

"It could, but we'll focus on the ten closest relatives. I went to one of the criminal justice profs at Wayne State and asked if any of his students needed to do an internship. We're getting two students to help with the research."

"You're brilliant, Agent Canter."

"I know... right," Stacey agreed with a laugh, then continued.

"So, we have to build out these family trees name by name. We'll look at census records which could lead to birth records which could lead to obituaries. We may have to travel to cemeteries to get names and dates. Hopefully, we will find a fork that can lead us to him."

"I'm in," Office Wells said as he took a bite of steaks tips.

****

Charlie had done his reconnaissance. The Jazzman needed to change it up. A restaurant manager had caught his eye. She looked professional compared to the other servers in their ballcaps and matching polos. Her uniform was neatly pressed. A dark blue blazer, white blouse and blue skirt radiated confidence. She was a strongminded bitch alright and stood out from the rest of the employees in the Crab Shack franchise.

Charlie hated authority... the teachers, the principal and strong-minded managers who treated their employees like dirt. He considered himself more of a nonconformist, unconventional in his thinking while others considered him a lunatic whose crazy ass ought to be locked up!

The manager's name was Amber...such a pretty name. He had followed her home several times when her shift ended. He knew her route and he knew how he was going to do it. On the day the Angel of Death would come for her, he went for one last meal.

For a Friday night the Crab Shack had just started to get busy. Charlie waited only a minute to get a table. Robert, his server, took his order quickly and disappeared into the kitchen.

While Charlie waited, he watched Amber seating customers and chatting with them. She was not aware of him, but his gaze never left her. When his food arrived, Charlie began with the French fries. He dipped each fry in ketchup and then Ranch dressing, a habit he developed after reading about it on the internet.

The fried shrimp was especially good that night. Knowing how tomorrow morning would end made each bite of food better. As more and more patrons filled the establishment, it was clear that the restaurant was not prepared for such a crowd.

Amber barked orders with military precision. Servers and bartenders scrambled to please their customers.

At the table next to Charlie, a broad-shouldered man with whiskers waved his arm and called out to get Amber's attention. She rushed to his table.

"Is there a problem?" she asked.

"I cannot find my waitress. She disappeared and has not been back to the table. My food is cold, and I can't eat it this way. That's the way she brought it."

Amber snatched the plate and went back to the kitchen. In a few minutes, the waitress returned carrying the plate. She set it down in front of him and apologized.

"Your order was remade. I am new here, and I am sorry I did not get back to you sooner."

Charlie noted that her eyes were red and watery.

"That's okay," the man said, noticing how distressed the waitress was. "Everything's okay now."

Charlie looked across the dining room and noticed Amber glaring at the waitress. He also noticed that she said something to each person coming out of the kitchen, and how some of them grimaced as soon as they were past her.

Robert approached Charlie's table and asked, "Is there anything else I can get for you?"

"No…just my bill," Charlie answered. "But, if you don't mind telling me, is the waitress okay who waited on the table next to me. I think her name is Terrie."

"Yeah, she's okay," Robert answered in a low voice. "The kitchen is going crazy now. Lots of yelling going on."

Without Robert saying it, Charlie knew that Amber had laid into the waitress enough to make her cry. *That's the way it always is…people who have authority know how to embarrass and humiliate those beneath them.* Charlie silently fumed.

Amber was standing at the podium when he was leaving the restaurant. He smiled when she said, "Have a nice day. We hope to see you again."

"You have a nice day, too, Amber," he said to her. "You'll definitely see me again."

****

Amber and her husband lived in a Northern Oakland County subdivision carved out of what was once a cornfield. Five thousand square foot mini mansions dotted the hills on half acre lots.

Many of the farmers in the area had long since passed and the grandkids were chomping at the bit to sell. Developers were paying exorbitant prices. Farms that were in families for generations were subdivided and sold to the highest bidder.

Amber loved animals and she owned a horse. She kept Rex at a barn about a mile and a half from her home. The farm was one of the last properties not bought up. Probably a holdout for more money she figured. Rex was the only horse on the property.

Charlie had been in the barn plenty of times and noticed a framed picture of the horse with the name Rex engraved on its glass. The barn, Charlie thought, would be the perfect place for the killing. It was secluded and would be ideal for staging.

He had determined that Amber must be leasing the place. When he broke into the farmhouse, axe in hand, no one lived there. The house smelled musty, and the appliances were unplugged. He did not like to kill during the day, but he would make an exception for Amber. She was worth the special effort.

While scouting the farm, Charlie discovered an old, overgrown two-track road that entered the property from the back forty. A chain with a rusty "No Trespassing" sign hung across the trail. The weeds were high and the track barely visible. A perfect place to enter the property.

He watched through binoculars as Amber rode the narrow trails that cut deeply into the woods. He became excited as his plan formulated in his head. He knew Amber never worked weekends. That time was spent with Rex.

Charlie knew everything about Amber. Five foot seven, brunette hair, weight looked to be a hundred and twenty pounds. Very slender. Perfect figure for a 1920's flapper. He had a fleeting thought, *Should I kill Rex?* How utterly amazing it would be to look into Amber's eyes and watch her expression as she walked into the barn and noticed Rex. The fantasy subsided. *Gotta stick to the plan.*

It was 6:00 a.m. Sunday morning and most of Amber's neighbors were sleeping as she pulled out of the driveway heading to the barn. Amber's plan was to take Rex for a short ride, then be back home by

10:00. Mass was at noon and she and her husband were planning on attending. Amber walked into the barn. Recognizing her, Rex's ears pricked forward. He nickered, whinnied, and waited for her to come. He loved seeing his Amber.

"Well... aren't you the sassy one this morning," Amber said as she rubbed the top of his muzzle. Rex pranced in place anticipating the ride as she threw the saddle pad on him followed by the saddle. She cinched his girth and Rex lowered his head pushing his nose into the bridle and taking the bit. He knew what was about to happen. He couldn't wait for the ride.

Just when Amber was buckling the throat latch, Rex's head lifted, and he pinned his ears flat back. Snorting and tossing his head, he pulled against her hold on the bridle. Startled, Amber turned and saw a hooded figure holding an axe pull the barn door closed. Adrenalin rushed and her blood pressure soared as she tried to gather her thoughts.

"What do you want? This is private property," Amber choked out.

"I want you," he said.

Amber stepped back as Charlie cautiously crept toward her, axe raised in his hand.

"Don't resist me, Amber. There's someone who wants to meet you."

"Not today, Fucker!!," Amber yelled as she reached into her jacket and pulled the small caliber handgun her husband insisted, she carry when going to the barn. Charlie stopped.

"Have you ever killed anyone?" Charlie asked just above a whisper, moving ever so slowly toward her. "Put the gun down, Amber."

Amber said nothing and squeezed the trigger. Instantly, Charlie fell back against a stall rail still clutching the axe. Using his elbows, he pushed himself upright and hurtled toward the barn door. She shot again but missed. He felt the bullet blow by his head and lodge into a plank in the door.

Charlie lifted the heavy handle, letting out a moan as he did. He bolted from the barn as Amber reached for her phone and dialed 911.

Chapter 44

Daugherty found himself longing for a restful night's sleep, a luxury that seemed to elude him entirely. He never slept, he just dreamed.

While Ambien provided some relief, it required a couple bourbons to extend its potency. The unintentional shedding of over fifty pounds had become apparent, catching the attention of his wife, Linda Laurice. The intimacy that once defined their relationship had now become a distant memory, leaving Linda Laurice wondering, *is that SOB cheating on me?*

Daugherty WAS indeed CHEATING! He had gotten into bed with the devil, himself. Few people within the agency knew about the Slovak operation. Leaks coming from the agency got officers outed and worse, killed. Daugherty would go to extraordinary lengths to find out where and who was leaking.

Aware that the source of the leak originated within his division, consisting of twenty-four individuals bound by an oath, Daugherty devised a plan. He decided to split the team into two groups of twelve officers each. Each group would be provided with distinct sensitive information. Through careful observation, Daugherty intended to identify the leaked information by noting the divergence between the two groups. Subsequently, he planned to halve the team responsible for the leaked data and repeat the process, narrowing down the pool of suspects. Slovak was his point man in Europe, and Daugherty hated it. The sedatives and alcohol made that easier to handle.

****

Carly glanced through the peephole upon hearing a knock at the apartment door. Recognizing Tim, she swiftly opened it, and he entered carrying a bag from the coffee shop.

"Thought you might be hungry," Tim remarked, handing the bag to Carly.

David rose from the couch. "Don't know about Carly, but I'm starved."

"Where's Porsche?" Carly asked, handing David the bag.

"She went to get you guys a weapon from her grandparent's house. When she found out you two were coming, she connected with some of her sources and secured them."

"That's good," Carly said. "Even though Slovak is dead, I will feel better armed."

David pulled out a muffin from the bag and offered it to Carly. She waved it off. "No thanks, not hungry." Her gaze went to Tim. "Did you come up with a plan?"

"Yeah," Tim said. "Let's sit and I'll fill you in."

David and Carly took seats on the couch, while Sergeant Tim settled into the recliner.

"Porsche wants to do it together. She feels she has had more of the training and is a little worried that this guy might pick me off, especially if he has had training in counter-surveillance."

"That makes sense," Carly replied. "Continue."

"Porsche and I thought we would get there thirty to forty-five minutes early. Just before 5:30 you would call him and hang up. That will identify who he is."

"I like it," David added.

"You'll then immediately text him and let him know you are sick and won't be making the meeting. We will take it from there."

"I like it. Hopefully we can find out what the hell's going on," Carly said.

The abrupt knock at the door, silenced the three mid-conversations. Sergeant Tim retrieved his pistol from beneath his shirt. Carly approached, gazing through the peephole. She turned to Tim…

"It's Porsche."

Porsche walked into the apartment, a duffle bag in hand. Placing it on the kitchen table, she unzipped it and spoke to the group.

"Come and get it."

Porsche removed two small caliber pistols and placed them on the table, along with a box of bullets. David immediately grabbed the box of rounds and loaded a gun, handing it to Carly, before loading the other.

"Remember, you're not in the States. There aren't any open carry laws. Keep these well-hidden."

"I appreciate you, Porsche," Carly expressed. "I don't know what I would do without you. Do you think Stacey would approve."

The two shared a light-hearted laugh. "Arming you and David. I don't think so." Porsche replied.

"I got a text from her earlier today," Carly told the group. "She wanted to know how things were going. I didn't mention about mom and Bo. I think I'll keep that to myself until we know more. She's already dealing with that serial killer case, and the last thing she needs is another worry."

"Probably a good idea," Tim added. "I told them the plan and they're all in."

"Great!" Carly replied.

Porsche glanced at her watch.

"Hey, we got to get going. I want to be there at least a half hour early."

****

Porsche and Tim reached the coffee house later than anticipated due to heavy traffic and construction delays, leaving them with only minutes to spare. At the counter, three men sat individually, while two more occupied tables, engrossed in their work on computers. The rest of the seating was taken up by couples and solo women.

Porsche joined the line, while Tim secured a table at the back—perhaps not ideal for surveillance but the best option available. Checking her watch, Porsche sensed it was time, and she suspected he was already here.

A ringing phone drew her attention, and she turned to observe a man with dark hair, olive skin, and high cheekbones glancing at his phone.

Following a brief pause, he shook his head, retrieved some euros from his back pocket, and placed them on the counter. Porsche's gaze shifted to Tim as the man retrieved his coat from the back of his chair and left, with Tim swiftly following suit.

As Tim exited the door and disappeared from view, Porsche abandoned the line, making her way outside. The chill in the air caused her breath to rise, as she saw Tim a half block or so ahead.

The streets were light with foot traffic, making it challenging for Tim to maintain a low profile. Borka paused at a redlight, allowing Porsche to catch up.

As the traffic signal shifted to green, Tim advanced, forging ahead of Borka and leaving Porsche to maintain the surveillance. Turning down a nearby street, Borka proceeded for a few more blocks until he reached his destination, a municipal building located at 36 Oberlanderstrae Street in Dusseldorf. The sign taped to the door read, "Your new life awaits…Dusseldorf AA Beginner Meeting".

Porsche bided her time, patiently observing as a few more individuals entered the building before stepping inside for a closer look. Spotting Borka seated within the circle of brown chairs, she decided to leave. Dialing Tim, she relayed her location, strategizing for a prompt rendezvous.

Chapter 45

Agent Canter was excited as Aleister walked into her office. She looked up from her desk, barely able to contain her enthusiasm.

"I just got a text from Ancestry. Our boy's DNA is in processing. We should get results back in 2-4 weeks."

"So, what happens in processing?" Aleister asked.

"They've given me a timeline to show the progress. When they first get the sample, the lab checks to make sure there is enough of it to test and that it is free of *particulate matter*."

"Hang on, Dr. Canter," Aleister said. "You need to dummy this down. What's *particulate matter*?"

"I guess there's these microscopic particles like dust that we can't see. They separate them from the liquid. Now don't quote me on this. I'm just learning as we go along."

"No... continue. This stuff is fascinating," he said, placing his hand over his mouth and faking a yawn.

Stacey chuckled. "So, they take the clean sample and extract the DNA from the semen. They then incubate it with magnetic beads."

"And that means????"

"What I can make of it is the DNA sticks to these magnetic beads and then they wash the beads and what's left is the raw DNA."

Aleister raked his hand through his hair. "Damn! There are some smart people out there."

"I know... right. We'll be getting back the ethnicity estimate of our suspect and any DNA matches within a couple of weeks."

****

Two weeks had passed, and the DNA ethnicity report was sent to Agent Canter's email. This was the first lead that the two could run with. The killer's ancestors came from England and Northwestern Europe and settled in the thumb of Michigan.

Aleister and Stacey reasoned that made sense since the killings took part in the proximity of Michigan. The report also stated that the family members linked through shared ancestors could possibly still live in the area. Their first task was to whittle down the population of the various towns in the thumb. Stacey and Aleister along with the two interns focused on cities with a 2000+ population. There were twelve such cities.

The team focused on three DNA matches that shared common DNA segments with the killer. All three matches were third cousins. The family trees ranged from just under a hundred members to over a thousand.

Some of the trees dated back to the late 1600's. The team quickly realized that this would be a painstaking endeavor and they needed help. They elicited the help of a former Detroit district attorney Mark Casandra. Mark had recently founded a company that worked in the burgeoning industry of genetic genealogy.

Interconnections Inc. took the raw DNA data given to them by Agent Canter and developed a profile. As the potential pool of suspects was narrowed down, the genetic sleuths used public records and other means such as travel documents, credit card records, and ATM interactions to determine which possible suspects could have been in area at the time of offense. The data pointed to a possibility of sixteen suspects in the Detroit area and the leads were given to Agent Canter.

****

They had a name, a face, and a distant match. Keith Joseph Kesler was by all appearances a law-abiding citizen. A few traffic tickets from his late teens and a solicitation of a prostitute charge were the only blemishes on his record.

Wells and Canter needed his DNA so it could be compared to the killer's. Kesler was a Union official and held a powerful position within the Teamsters. He had recently filed for divorce and was living in a Detroit motel not far from the union hall.

Canter and Wells sat in an unmarked car making small talk on a side street off Woodward in Detroit. They watched as hookers walked to their John's car, adjusted their tight, painted on skirts and leaned into the passenger side window. After a brief financial negotiation, the John would pull around the corner where the lady would catch up with him.

"How many of those pervs do you think are married?" Stacey asked.

"I bet most," Aleister said. "But if you're getting it at home, there's no reason to stray."

"What's that supposed to mean?" Stacey said, indignation in her tone. "So, if a wife doesn't want to have sex with her husband, it gives him the right to hook up with a prostitute and bring home a disease."

"Easy, Agent Canter," Aleister said trying to defuse the conversation he had gotten himself into. "I know you are armed and you're making me a little nervous."

"No...I'm serious. Why would you think that?"

"Well, for one thing, men need sex more than woman. It's a proven fact. You can see it in all species of animals and humans are no different. When women realize that a man's sex drive is so much more than a female's, the world will be a better place. It's not totally your fault. We haven't done the best job educating you ladies on how you should submit."

"Oh, I'm going shoot your chauvinistic ass and leave you on 8 Mile."

Aleister bit his lower lip trying to hide the smile that was growing by the second. No longer able to hold it, he burst out laughing.

"What's so funny?"

"I just *mansplained* you!!"

"*Mansplained?*"

"Yeah. It's where a man talks condescendingly to a woman on a subject that he really knows nothing about and tries to wing it. Figures he can pull one over on the little lady."

"I am no one's little lady, Little Man!" she declared.

Stacey gave Aleister a half punch in the arm followed by a grin.

"I'm starting to get this picture of you as a prankster," she said. "You know...on a stage...in front of an audience... Maybe you missed your calling Officer Wells. Maybe you should have gone into standup comedy."

Aleister cut the conversation off. "Here's our boy," he said pointing to their suspect leaving the motel. Wells immediately picked up his camera and started taking shots as Canter started the sedan. The two followed closely until he went to a bus stop and waited with another dozen people.

"Drop me off at the corner. I'll take the bus with him," Wells said.

Agent Canter passed the bus stop and turned the corner. She barely parked before Aleister jumped out of the car. "I'll keep you posted," he said before slamming the door and jogging to the bus stop.

By the time Wells had made it to the bus, people were already loading. He entered the back of the line and shuffled in along with the other passengers. He paid the fare, spotted his target and then took a seat.

The bus stopped at three locations before Kesler stood and exited on the fourth. They were now downtown, and Wells was worried that when he exited, Kesler would realize he was being tailed. He needed Kesler to eat, drink, or smoke. Anything recovered that Kesler discarded could and would be used to extract his DNA. No warrant was necessary for discarded property.

Officer Wells strolled behind his target until Kesler stepped onto a porch of a townhouse. He pressed the buzzer and waited before a woman came to the door and let him in.

Aleister had to do something to bide some time. He walked to a vendor on the street with a view of the townhouse. He bought a coffee and called Agent Canter.

"What's up? Any luck?" Canter asked.

"Not yet. I followed him to a townhouse, and he's inside."

"Where are you? Can I park so you can at least sit in the car?"

"No. I'm on a side street with vendors set up on both sides. I'm good. There's a bench and I can keep an eye on the townhouse. Hopefully, he won't be in there long."

"Ok. I'll just be waiting for your call." Agent Canter said. "Let me know when you need to be picked up."

"Will do. Thanks," Aleister said.

Wells sat on the bench, coffee in hand, hoping Kesler's visit would not take up the entire day. He surfed the web and played a couple games he had downloaded during the boring hours of his last stakeout. He looked up from his phone and saw Kesler exit the house. He became excited when he noticed Kesler was smoking a cigarette.

Aleister stepped from the bench as Kesler walked back toward the bus stop. He kept his distance as the target took the last drag of his smoke and tossed the butt to the ground.

Wells waited until Kesler was out of view before stepping up to the boulevard to collect the evidence. He removed a latex glove from his pocket and put it on his right hand. He pinched the cotton filter and took a long look before placing it into a small evidence bag. Feeling elated, he placed the evidence in his jacket pocket and dialed Canter.

****

The forensic lab technician unlocked the door of the sterile room. He pushed his arms through a white coat that was hanging in his locker and buttoned up. On his lab bench in a plastic bag was the cigarette butt Officer Wells had retrieved from the suspect.

The tech snapped on the white latex gloves lying next to the sample. All equipment used in the extraction had been irradiated with UV for five minutes. The technician reached into his side coat pocket and put on his glasses. He then opened the evidence baggie and dumped the butt onto a petri dish. Using sterile scissors and forceps, he removed a 1 cm piece of the cigarette paper.

He proceeded to cut the paper into quarters and each quarter was then cut again. The Tech placed two samples into separate 0.2 ml PCR tubes. The samples were now ready for DNA extraction. The results would be compared to the semen found on the body of Dominique Hutcheson and emailed to Agent Canter when ready.

****

"How long did forensics say it would take?" Aleister asked Stacey as they walked into the office and turned the lights on.

"Two days," Stacey said, walking to her computer workstation and shaking the mouse. "I'll check my email in a second. Today is day two."

Agent Canter placed her cloth lunch bag in the refrigerator.

"I'm making coffee… want some?" she asked.

"I got it," Aleister said then grabbed the glass pot from the coffeemaker and walked to the sink.

"Where do you keep the coffee?" he asked as he poured the water into the top of the coffee maker?"

"Third shelf on the right," she said pointing.

Maxwell House Morning Blend. Aleister read, as he took a brown filter and placed it in the maker. "How many scoops?"

"Three."

Stacey sat behind her workstation and opened her email. As she searched the subject lines one in bold letters stood out. **FORENSIC PROFILE COMPLETE**

"It's here!!" Stacey said, moving her mouse and clicking on the email. Aleister turned on the coffee maker then stood behind Stacey. They both read the findings together.

FBI Forensics conducted a DNA extraction and analysis using 13 core STR loci to determine identity from a discarded cigarette butt, and a semen sample recovered from a crime scene. The following is the analysis:

As its name implies, an STR contains repeating units of a short (typically three- to four-nucleotide) DNA sequence. The number of repeats within an STR is referred...

Aleister shook his head. "Can't they say if this is our guy without all this scientific bullshit?"

Stacey scrolled down to the bottom of the page.

CONCLUSION:

FBI Forensics determined the allele profile of the 13 core STR's for both the evidence sample (semen recovered from the body of the victim) and the suspect's sample. (Discarded cigarette butt) statistically **MATCHED.**

Stacey swiveled in her office chair and raised her hand to high five Aleister.

"We got the son of a bitch!!" she said excitedly.

Chapter 46

As the AA meeting concluded, Porsche and Tim observed the departing attendees from their concealed vantage point in the alley that separated the buildings. A well-thought-out plan was in place. Tim would continue surveilling Borka while Porsche entered the building and spoke with the director.

Porsche approached, patiently waiting for a man to conclude his conversation with Helga. As he left, Helga's look shifted to Porsche. "May I help you?"

"Um, yes, hi. I'm looking for a friend who I believe attends your meetings. His name is Thomas Higgins."

Helga's heart quickened, and Porsche noticed a subtle shift in her expression.

"Um, yes. Tom does come to our meetings. Not sure what happened, but this is the first meeting that he has missed since he started. May I ask your name?"

"Porsche. Porsche Berliner. I just returned from the States and wanted to surprise him. Our families go way back. Could I leave you my name and number, and if he shows up next week, ask him to give me a buzz."

"Absolutely," Helga replied, retrieving a pen and note card from her briefcase before handing them to Porsche.

****

Helga's abrupt entrance echoed with a resounding "OH MY GOD!!" as she dropped her briefcase to the floor, then quickly turned and locked the door. Startled, Bo sprang from the couch, his heart racing and brows furrowed.

"They're onto us, someone is aware," Helga rambled, moments before Bo approached and firmly grasped her shoulders.

"Helga," Bo demanded, his tone unwavering, "what the hell happened!?"

"Someone is looking for you, Bo. They know you go to my meetings."

"Was it Borka?"

"No. It was a woman."

"A woman!?" Bo questioned.

Helga slipped out of Bo's grasp and retrieved her briefcase. Placing it on the coffee table, she opened it and removed the note card containing Porsche's contact information. Returning to Bo, she handed it to him.

"She said her name was Porsche." Helga revealed.

"Porsche!? Porsche Berliner!? Mrs. Fletcher asked, her surprise evident in her tone.

Helga's head snapped towards Mrs. Fletcher. "You know her!?" she asked, stunned.

"She's with my daughter. They're supposed to be in the United States."

Helga shook her head, then continued. "She told me she just got back from the States. That's what she said."

Mrs. Fletcher turned to Bo. "Do you think Carly is back!?"

A perplexed expression crossed Bo's face as he scrutinized the note card.

"This is Porsche's number, but how could she know I'm in AA?" Bo mumbled to himself.

He then looked to Mrs. Fletcher.

"Did you let Carly know? I really wanted to surprise her. I asked you not to."

"Bo, I swear. I never said anything to anyone," Mrs. Fletcher responded with conviction.

Turning to Helga, Bo asked, "What did she look like?"

"Definitely European. I could tell by her accent. About five six, maybe five seven, athletic build. She had short-cropped blond hair that framed her face, tucked behind her ears with bangs. All businesslike."

Bo took a deep breath and let out a long sigh before reaching out his hand to Helga.

"There's one way to find out. Can I borrow your phone?"

****

Tim trailed Borka for more than ten city blocks, shadowing him until he entered what appeared to be a nondescript bar. The area looked seedy, somewhat run-down, a stark contrast to the more polished cityscape just ten blocks away.

He positioned himself and watched as a growing number of patrons entered the speakeasy. A bouncer stood at the door, scrutinizing those seeking entry. Tim's inability to speak German prevented him from progressing any further.

He swiftly texted Porsche, disclosing his location. Within fifteen minutes, she arrived, slightly out of breath but ready for action.

"Got here as fast as I could," Porsche remarked. "Where's our boy?"

Tim pointed across the alley to a black brick building with an A-frame style roof.

"See that building? The guy went in there. Looks like some kind of club."

Porsche glanced at the surroundings. "Yeah, this isn't the best side of town. It might be an afterhours club."

"It would be great if we could get in there," Tim suggested, "Maybe get a pic of our boy. Not speaking German, I didn't think I'd get past the front door."

"Probably not," Porsche said. "Given the location I'd bet it's a gambling joint with some men's entertainment, if you catch my drift."

"Men's entertainment? I've noticed women going in there," Tim remarked.

Porsche chuckled. "You Americans can be a bit prudish. This is Germany; women here occasionally enjoy a taste of the wild side. I can get into that bar," she assured him confidently.

"Is it safe?"

"Safe or not, we need a picture of this guy." Porsche said. "Watch my smoke. This was my favorite part of my clandestine training."

Sergeant Tim watched as Porsche stepped out of the alley and approached a stranger who seemed on his way to the bar. Extending a cigarette, she appeared to be asking for a light. Without hesitation, the man fumbled in his pocket, produced a lighter, and lit both Porsche's cigarette and one of his own. After a few minutes of casual conversation, Tim noticed Porsche taking the man's arm, and together they entered the bar.

****

As Porsche stepped into the dimly lit afterhours club, a haze of smoke hung in the air, revealing scantily clad young women gracefully moving on stripper poles. A mix of men and women occupied the surrounding seats, eagerly awaiting a dancer to strut by and pause just long enough to have her G-string stuffed with euros.

"What are you drinking?" Hans inquired, invading her personal space and crudely grabbing her backside.

"Riesling," Porsche replied with a forced smile, even though she wanted to break Hans's arm.

"Riesling it is," Hans affirmed, then turned and headed for the bar.

Porsche surveyed the crowded dance floor, a mosaic of men dancing with men, women twirling with women, and the occasional heterosexual couple. In the far corner, a trio of men sat huddled around a table, engrossed in their conversation, oblivious to the pulsating energy around them. Striving for a closer look, Porsche was abruptly halted when Hans reappeared, bearing the drinks.

"For you," Hans said, offering Porsche her wine, but not before his gaze traced a path up and down her body.

"Well, thank you," Porsche responded, in a sultry voice.

The glasses chimed together in a toast, and both indulged in a sip. Porsche seized Hans's hand, guiding him towards a secluded side bar. Placing her glass on the counter, she did the same with his. Leaning in, she closed the distance between them, pressing her body against his.

"Let's dance. I adore this song," she whispered.

Porsche guided Hans to the far end of the dance floor, situating themselves as close to the trio's table as she could. They danced intimately, bodies pressed together, lingering for an extra song. As they prepared to leave, Porsche retrieved her cellphone from her back jean pocket, drawing Hans closer to her side.

"I want to take a selfie," Porsche declared, extending her phone as far as she could, ensuring the trio at the table became the backdrop of the photo.

Upon returning to the bar, Porsche took a sip of her wine, then shifted towards Hans.

"I need to pee," she informed him and proceeded on her way.

With not enough light to view the pic, Porsche decided to exit the ladies' room. Hans was there to greet her. He placed his arms around her waist and pulled her in tightly. She could feel his manhood bulging through his pants.

"Woe, Big Guy," Porsche said, playfully trying to push him away. "There will be plenty of time for that later."

"Now is the time!" declared Hans, forcefully ushering Porsche into a secluded room and locking the door behind them. As he turned to face her, his expression transformed, revealing an unsettling anger and hatred.

"I know women like you," he spewed, creeping towards her. "You're a dick tease, playing games for free drinks, never intending to follow through. But tonight, Porsche, things are going to change."

As Hans closed in, Porsche retreated until he lunged, attempting to forcibly tear open her shirt. Porsche countered by delivering a well-aimed knee to Hans's groin, sending him sprawling to the floor. With practiced ease, she dropped to one knee, retrieving her pistol from the ankle holster. She then approached, gun drawn at his head.

"Get up, you piece of shit," Porsche commanded.

Hans gradually stood; hands raised in surrender.

"Please don't. I have a family," he pleaded.

"They might fare better without you. Get in that corner," Porsche ordered, gesturing with her gun.

Hans complied, walking to the far corner, and standing there.

"Undo your pants and drop them to your ankles," Porsche ordered in a stern tone.

Hans, with a peculiar expression, complied, unbuttoning his pants. As they dropped to his ankles, Porsche, motioning with her gun, adding, "Drop the boxers too."

Hans hesitated. "Do it! Or I'll blow your damn head off!" Porsche threatened.

Reluctantly, Hans dropped his boxers to his ankles.

"Why is it that guys with a little dick are always the biggest assholes?" Porsche chuckled. "Turn around and face the corner, put your hands behind your back."

Hans turned and placed his hands behind his back.

"Interlock your fingers," Porsche ordered.

Porsche pressed her shoulder into Han's back. She leaned close to his ear and firmly cupped his genitals. Giving them a twist, Hans let out a groan.

"Think about it the next time you try to rape a woman," Porsche whispered as she twisted a little more. "The next time you may not be so lucky."

Porsche turned and left, as Hans dropped to his knees, whimpering in pain.

As Porsche emerged from the speakeasy, Tim hurried towards her.

"Damn, Girl! What took you so long? I was about to bust in!" he exclaimed.

"Let's just say I had to get a firm grip on a couple of things before I ended it with a twist," Porsche replied with a mischievous smile.

Sergeant Tim looked confused. "What?"

Porsche chuckled. "I got the pic. How about I head back, and you wait for our reformed alcoholic to leave."

"I can do that. I'll follow him and see where he's staying," Tim replied.

"Might be awhile. He was really throwing them back," Porsche informed him as she walked away.

Chapter 47

Agent Canter stood from her workstation and went to the table where Officer Wells had opened the latest file on the killer. He had just received it. It was the police report of Amber Carlson taken by the police officers who had responded to the attack. Officer Wells began to thumb through it.

"So, this has to be our boy," Wells said, flipping the yellow sheets of his legal pad and uncapping a ballpoint pen. "Something doesn't add up."

"What?" Stacey asked.

"It says the blood taken from the last crime scene is female."

"Say that again," Stacey asked, her forehead forming into lines.

"According to Forensics, the blood from the attacker of Amber Carlson was female."

"Female!! How is that possible? We collect semen at every site."

Aleister flipped back a couple of yellow pages. "There's more. According to the report the police recovered a backpack. It had a blue fringed dress, long stockings, duct tape and get this… used condoms with semen."

"Are you freaking kidding me?" Stacey said stunned. "Our serial killer could be a woman?"

"That or a copycat," Aleister reasoned. "Maybe our killer isn't working alone. Maybe the Jazzman is really a jazz duo?"

****

With the DNA match to Keith Joseph Kesler, a warrant was secured, and an arrest team was assembled. Captain Evans of the Detroit PD headed the briefing. Three plain-clothed officers along with Wells and Canter sat in a row of brown folding chairs waiting for the meeting to begin.

Captain Evans stepped from the podium and handed each officer a sheet containing information about Mr. Kesler.

"This is our suspect," the captain stated. "Keith Joseph Kesler."

The officers browsed the rap sheet then one asked, "Is this our serial killer? There's not much on our boy. A couple of traffic tickets and solicitation of a prostitute charge."

"I'm gonna to turn this over to Agent Canter of the FBI. She'll fill in the details."

Agent Canter stepped to the podium.

"The answer is Yes. We think this is our killer. We have a match of his DNA to a semen sample taken from one of the crime scenes. We're not sure if he will be armed. His preferred method to kill is with an axe, and I would not put it past him to be armed in some way. He is into the cat & mouse chase. He's left clues to taunt the police."

A voice from the back called out. "So, he thinks he is smarter than us. How is this arrest going down?"

"This morning at 10:00 a.m. We would like to take him into custody with a routine traffic stop, but he uses public transportation to get around. He is separated from his wife and staying at the Rivertown Inn on Jefferson. He is a Teamster's official and takes the bus to the Union Hall downtown."

Agent Canter motioned to Officer Wells to get the Teamster jackets.

"Our plan is to wait for him in front of the Union Hall on Trumbull. You can mill around the building and blend in with the other Teamsters. We've got these Teamster jackets for you."

Officer Wells lifted one of the jackets out of the box and held it up. "Welcome to the brotherhood of the Teamsters, Gentlemen. Hope you all take an XL."

"I almost became a Teamster," one of the men said. "But instead, I became a cop."

"Officer Wells will be riding the bus with the suspect," Canter continued. "He has taken the bus before when we were doing surveillance and shouldn't be a red flag."

Canter looked at the clock mounted to the wall above a whiteboard in the room. "It's 8:30. We have plenty of time to get into position. Any questions?"

No questions were asked, and the team put on their jackets. The arrest was set for ten o'clock.

Chapter 48

Aleister placed his debit card on the contactless reader and paid for his bus ticket. He then placed the card back into his wallet as he shuffled down the aisle and sat three seats behind Mr. Kesler. The bus was sparsely filled, and Wells had hoped for more riders.

A mother and young daughter sat all the way in the back. The toddler stood on the back seat waving to people as they passed on the busy thoroughfare. An elderly African American couple with salt and pepper hair sat at the first seat behind the driver. Before the bus pulled away, another dozen or so riders with brief cases and wearing back packs loaded onto the bus.

Wells leaned back and tried to stretch out his legs. It wasn't easy for his lean 6-foot 3-inch frame. He removed his phone then texted the team that everything was a go. There would be four stops and on the fifth they would hit Trumbull Ave. Estimated time of arrival...9:55 a.m.

It was an overcast morning, but no rain. A perfect day for what he believed would be the biggest collar of his career. City Hall was pressuring, especially with the gaffe Special Agent Gideon made during her first news conference. She explained that the three murders were indeed related and that women needed to take precaution and, in some cases, arm themselves."

The comment of arming oneself went too far. The mayor demanded clarification, and the Feds were not happy. Appearing at a second news conference with her was Dana Nessel, Michigan's 54th Attorney General.

"What I meant by arm yourself," Gideon clarified, "is the use of non-lethal means such as mace or bear spray. I strongly recommend NOT purchasing and carrying a firearm without the proper training and licensing. If you want to take it further, PLEASE take the training for a concealed weapons permit." Agent Gideon then turned to the Attorney General and asked if she would like to say anything.

Nessel stepped to the podium. "I agree with Special Agent Gideon. Women need to take precaution. Added locks and security systems to your home is a good idea. We will catch this person. In the meantime, be smart and take precautions."

****

Wells stared out the window, running through scenario after scenario, preparing for the impending arrest. This pre-arrest ritual was normal for him, making sure he had all his bases covered.

The squeal of the airbrakes brought Wells back into focus. This was the last stop before Trumbull. Kesler along with a half dozen others stood and exited the bus.

Damn, Damn, Damn!! He thought as he too left his seat and exited the bus. The team had not anticipated Kesler taking an earlier exit. Wells tailed from afar and called Agent Canter.

To make the bust, Agent Canter dressed like a sex worker, blending in perfectly with the other girls working the street.

Canter leaned up against the Teamster building, a cigarette jutting from her mouth. Her four-inch heels would be tossed aside if she was the one to make the arrest. Stacey heard her phone ring from the silver sequin purse that hung around her neck and barely fit her phone. When she saw it was Aleister, she became alarmed.

"What's going on?" she asked.

"He got off at MLK Blvd."

"Martin Luther King?"

"Yep."

"Damn!!" Stacey moaned. "Let me tell the team and we will head over."

"There's no time. If I can make the arrest, I will."

"Be careful. We'll get there as quick as we can."

"Will do," he said before the phone went dead.

Officer Wells watched as the suspect along with the rest of the pedestrians stopped for a light on MLK Blvd. Kesler pulled a pack of cigarettes from the side pocket of his sport jacket.

He tapped the pack and placed a cigarette between his lips, then lit it. He inhaled deeply as the light turned green and the crowd began to move. Wells was close behind. There were too many people to make an arrest by himself. He needed to get Kesler away from the crowd so if things went sideways, no one would get hurt. He was looking for his team and his team was rushing toward him.

Aleister was chameleon-like, moving with the crowd as they made their way to their destinations. The first of the team he noticed walking towards him was Stacey. Everyone noticed Stacey. Her hair was ratted, and her lips were the darkest red he had ever seen. Her skirt wasn't much more than a belt and her sweater hugged her like a glove. Agent Canter, walking toward Kesler, stepped in front of him and abruptly stopped.

"Hey, got time for some fun?" she asked.

Kesler looked Stacey up and down, casually tossing his cigarette to the ground.

"Um…um…um," he stammered. "How much?"

Officer Wells drew his firearm from the leather holster under his suit jacket. "Keith Joseph Kesler," he shouted. "Put your hands in the air. Detroit PD!"

Kesler's arms shot into the air as Aleister grabbed him by the back of his shirt collar. "Get to your knees," he said, holding his service revolver to his head. Kesler fell to his knees.

"Lay flat on your stomach and put your hands behind your back," Wells ordered then removed his handcuffs attached to the side of his belt and cuffed each wrist.

"You have the right to remain silent," Wells stated as he lifted Kesler to his feet.

"What the fuck's going on!!? Who the fuck are you!!?" Kesler erupted.

"You have the right to an attorney. Anything you say can and will be used in a court of law."

"Why do I need an attorney?" Kesler shouted.

Aleister felt around Kesler's waist before patting down each leg searching for a weapon.

"He's clean," he said to Stacey.

Kesler, realizing the two knew each other, again asked, "Who *are* you people??? What the fuck's going on?!!"

Agent Canter got close to Kesler, so close he could smell the perfume Stacey had lathered on.

"You know how much work it was to find you? I have had nightmares about you. How does it feel to have had your last jazz fest?"

Kesler looked dumbfounded as his brows knitted into thick lines. "I don't know who you think I am, but you got the wrong guy. Just to set the record straight, I hate jazz."

Stacey focused on the tall lanky balding man wearing a Teamsters jacket. A feeling came over her. A feeling that made her doubt herself.

This has to be our guy. His semen was left at the scene, for God's sake. A blue and white was called and Kesler was taken into custody. Canter and Wells would interrogate the suspect at a later date.

Chapter 49

Helga and Mrs. Fletcher watched as Bo sat on the edge of the couch, dialing Porsche's number. Raising the phone to his ear, his attention shifted to the two women.

"I'll make sure it's really her before I share anything," Bo said.

Porsche stopped mid stride when she heard her phone ring. Retrieving her phone from her pocket, she glanced at the screen.

"Hello," Porsche answered.

"Um...Porsche?"

"Yes, this Porsche. Who am I speaking with?"

"Um...I need to first make sure this is you. Your dog--Bear. How do you get him to come into your grandparents' house when he is chasing squirrels?"

Porsche, taken aback by the question, asked, "Who is this?"

"First answer my question, then I'll tell you."

"Is this Bo?"

"Answer the question."

"Um...I lure him with a peanut butter-covered cracker. He can't resist, even when he's treed a squirrel."

Bo nodded toward Helga and Mrs. Fletcher, a sense of relief washing over their faces as they eased back into their chairs.

"Porsche, it's me, Bo."

"Now it's my turn," Porsche responded. "What's the password Carly's father had her memorize growing up?"

"Mr. Etadirhtim."

Porsche began to pace, a worried expression crossing her face.

"Bo, where are you?"

"I'm staying at a friend's house. I think I've been outed," Bo admitted.

Porsche eyes widened. "Outed! Oh my God, how could that have happened?"

"It's a long story. I'll tell ya when we meet. Is Carly with you?"

"Yes. She's back at the apartment and just to let you know, Slovak's dead."

"Dead!" Bo exclaimed shocked. "Was it Carly?"

"No. Believe it or not, the SOB died of Covid. Please tell me Carly's mom is with you."

"She is, and she's safe."

"You know Bo, you may not be out of the woods just yet. Some bad guys are still looking for you, or should I say the mithridate."

"I figured as much."

"And there is something else you need to know," Porsche said, trying to find the words.

"What's that?" Bo asked.

"Um…I'm just going to tell you. David came back with Carly."

"Farris! His ass should be in jail! Did he say why he stole the mithridate!?" Bo exclaimed, his voice getting stronger and louder.

"Bo, take it easy. I'm not far from the apartment. I should be there in ten. I'll have Carly call you back at this number?"

"Ok,"

"Give me ten or so and I'll be back in touch."

****

Borka stumbled out of the speakeasy accompanied by two men. Sergeant Tim discreetly trailed him as the men parted ways. The journey took fifteen minutes, slightly extended by Borka's detour into an alley to relieve himself. Tim took note of the hotel Borka entered before making his way back.

****

The silence of Carly's apartment was broken by a sudden knock at the door, jolting Carly and David awake. Jetlag weighed heavily on them, evident in their drowsy state. Peering through the peephole, Carly identified Porsche and opened it. Anxious to hear the results of the surveillance, David sprang from the couch.

Porsche entered the living room with a sense of urgency, placing her pistol on the coffee table. "You won't believe what just happened to me," she exclaimed. "Call Bo immediately. I promised him you would the moment I returned."

Lines etched in Carly's forehead. "How did you hear from Bo?"

"I gave my phone number to the director of the AA meetings that Bo attends. Her name is Helga. Tim and I followed that Borka guy to the building where the meetings take place. I bet she's the friend he said he was staying at."

"And my mom is with him?"

"Yes. Bo said he thinks he's been outed. That's why they left and didn't take their phones. He was worried that the phones may be tracked."

"Outed!? How the hell did that happen?"

"He didn't explain. We'll find out when we meet. I saved the number of the phone he is using."

"Where's Sarge?" David inquired.

"He stayed behind to continue to tail Borka. Get this, the guy left the AA meeting and went directly to a bar. Something doesn't add up."

Porsche looked at her most recent calls and then at Carly. "You ready for the number?"

Carly nodded.

As the phone rang, it unnerved Helga. She glanced at her screen, then back at Bo.

"I don't recognize the number," she remarked.

"Answer it," Bo instructed.

Helga swiped the incoming call. She paused briefly, then raised the phone to her ear, "Hello."

"Hi," Carly said. "I'm looking for Bo. I mean Tom. Tom Higgins. Is he available?"

Helga's attention shifted to Bo. "He's right here," she said, handing him the phone.

Bo took the phone and immediately began pacing the living room. "Carly," he said.

"Bo. What's happening? Porsche said you think you're outed," Carly said with a sense of urgency. She listened as Bo sighed before starting to share the details.

"Carly, before you say anything I want you to know that I'm sober and haven't had a drink since you left."

"That's great Bo, but it sounds like you're in trouble?"

"I might be. We might be."

"How did this happen?"

Bo sensed Carly's terse response echoing in the air. Running his fingers through his hair, he continued to pace, tension filling the space around him.

"I was tired of being in witness protection and started to do research on how to leave."

"What kind of research?"

"I found a source online that was helping. At least I thought he was helping. Come to find out, it might have been a scam, and he was playing me. He knew stuff about me that I never shared. That's when I realized, I might have been duped."

"So, how long have you been communicating with this guy?"

"A few weeks. It all came tumbling down, just a couple of days ago. That's when I packed up your mom and headed to Helga's. There's this guy who appeared out of nowhere, and I can't shake off this feeling of distrust towards him," Bo revealed, a tinge of uncertainty in his voice.

"Is his name Borka?" Carly inquired.

"How did you know that?" Bo said surprised.

"He left you a text message. He wanted to meet for coffee before your AA meeting. I texted back pretending to be you. Porsche and Sergeant Tim staked out the coffee shop and followed him. That's how we found Helga."

"Sergeant Tim?" Isn't that the guy that worked with David to steal the mithridate? And speaking of David, Porsche told me he came back with you."

Carly's eyes widened, and she shot Porsche a stern look. Overhearing Bo, Porsche raised her arms in an apologetic gesture, mouthing the word, "Sorry."

"Yes, he did. He's played a crucial role in all of this. We really need to meet. There's so much you don't know. Can we arrange a meeting at your friend's house?"

"Let me see what she thinks. I will text you the address if she is down with it."

"Ok, sounds good. Can I talk to my mom?"

"Absolutely," Bo said, then handed Mrs. Fletcher the phone. "Carly wants to talk to you."

"Hi, Honey," Mrs. Fletcher said. "I can't believe you're back, and Slovak's dead."

"Yes, Mom. The SOB died of covid. I wanted to kill the bastard myself for what he did to Dad and Artie, but never got the chance. More importantly though, how are you? Are you ok?"

"Oh, yes, Dear. Bo has been taking good care of me."

"Ok, mom. I will see you soon. Tell Bo we need to meet as soon as possible."

Carly ended the call and set her phone down on the coffee table. Porsche lifted her phone, swiftly tapping through her photos. "I think I got a picture of the guy!" Porsche exclaimed with excitement.

"Borka?" Carly asked.

"Yeah, it was dark," Porsche replied, "I hope we can make out his face."

With a pinch of her thumb and forefinger, she expanded the picture on her screen. "It's pretty dark, I gotta brighten it up," Porsche said.

She tapped the Edit button and navigated through the editing tools, eventually finding the brightness dial. With a slide to the right, the picture gradually illuminated, revealing its hidden details.

A look of utter shock filled Porsche's face. She said nothing and handed the phone to Carly. David leaned in, peering over Carly's shoulder.

As Carly scrutinized the image, her heart sank. Seated at the table were Borka, Grego, and Alexander Slovak!

Chapter 50

Amber Carlson walked into the Michigan Federal Bureau of Investigation with her husband. She was wearing black slacks, and a red sweater. Her husband was freshly shaven and also wore black pants and a red sweater. Wells had heard that when people get married and live together, they end up turning into each other. He wondered if they had planned to dress like twins or if it had just happened.

Wells and Canter had been there since 8:00 am. Their plan was to concentrate on the female blood found in the barn and the pictures Mr. Carlson would provide.

"Good morning," Stacey said. "My name is Agent Canter, and this is Officer Wells. She motioned to the four empty chairs around the table.

"Please have a seat. Can I get either of you something to drink?"

"I'm all set," Dan, her husband, said as he set his cell phone on the table and scooted in.

"I'm fine, too," Amber said.

Once the four had taken their seats, Aleister began.

"Mr. and Mrs. Carlson, I would like to tape our conversation today. Do either of you have a problem with that?"

Both shook their head no.

Officer Wells flipped through a yellow legal pad and clicked a pen. He then tapped his cell phone and set it in the middle of the table.

"Mr. and Mrs. Carlson, you are both aware that our conversation is being taped."

"Yes," they said in unison.

"Mrs. Carlson, would you start from the time you left your house to when you had the encounter with the intruder?"

Amber nodded. "Every Sunday I get up and head to the barn around 6:00 a.m. I like to ride early because we usually go to Mass at noon. The barn is just a couple of miles away, so it only takes me a few minutes to get there. I pulled into the driveway of the farm and parked. I grabbed the barn keys and the 32-auto pistol from the glove compartment."

"Good thing she had that gun," Amber's husband interrupted. "She didn't want to carry it, but with these killings we've been hearing about, I insisted on it."

"He has pictures of the guy," Amber shared.

"I did read that in the police report," Aleister continued. "You gave those pictures to forensics?"

"I did."

"Tell me about it."

"Well…the detectives asked if there were any security cameras on the property. Since no one has lived in the farmhouse for years, there weren't any cameras. It got me thinking about my trail cams. I damn near had a heart attack when I looked at the sim cards."

"Brilliant," Aleister said.

"Since Amber leases the barn, I have permission to hunt the property. I have three trail cams set up to monitor the deer. I caught him on various cameras throughout the woods. I think he enters from the far side of the property, never coming in from the road. The timestamps on the pics are always after midnight early morning."

"Do you have those pictures with you?" Aleister asked. "Forensics hasn't finished with them yet."

"Sure do," Dan said as he lifted his cell phone and opened up his pictures. I have six of them. They're not the greatest, the camera is pretty cheap. He then handed his phone to Aleister.

"You can see the timestamp on the lower left-hand corner of each picture," he said.

Agent Canter slid her chair closer to Officer Wells. The two scrolled the grainy pictures, studying the features, zooming in on head shots. In every picture the individual wore a baseball cap and a hoodie. Most of the pictures were grainy.

"Would you text us those pictures?" Aleister asked, as he handed Mr. Carlson back his phone.

"Of course."

"So, would you continue Mrs. Carlson?"

"Absolutely. I opened the barn and walked in. The police said he had jimmied a back window and that it wasn't his first time in the barn. It still gives me the creeps that he might have been in there a few times with me. I started getting Rex ready for a ride when my horse jerked back. That's when I turned and saw him. He very nonchalantly walked to the barn door and shut it. I told him this was private property and said he was trespassing."

"Did you recognize him?" Stacey asked. "Anything stand out?"

"He was the guy in those pictures. He knew my name. He called me Amber and started walking toward me carrying an axe. I had only shot the pistol a few times. I really don't think he thought I was going to pull the trigger. When I did, he fell back and almost collapsed, but he caught himself on one of the stall rails. I fired again but missed. He stumbled to the door and opened it and then ran out. I stood there for a few seconds wondering what just happened and then I called the police."

"So, you are sure he was alone. He didn't have an accomplice?" Agent Canter asked.

"I'm positive. He was alone. I told the police that."

Amber noticed Officer Wells glance toward Stacey.

"What?" Amber asked. "What am I missing?"

"The blood evidence retrieved from the barn was female."

"FEMALE!" Amber's husband said in a raised voice. "You're saying the attacker is a woman?"

"We can't rule that out," Agent Canter said. "It surprised us too when we got the forensic report. If you had to describe him, what would you say? Tall, short, thin?"

Amber paused for a moment collecting her thoughts. "Now that I think of it, I remember him being a little short for a man, maybe 5 foot 6 or 5 foot 7. Not tall like Dan. He was pretty stocky with broad shoulders. It might have been the hoodie that made him look so muscular on top."

"When he spoke, was their anything unique in his voice?" Stacey asked.

"Like I said, he knew my name. He spoke more in a whisper then actually talking."

At that moment, her husband placed his hand on top of hers.

"I used to love going to that barn. I haven't been back since this happened. My husband goes and feeds Rex and our goat, Billy. He then takes Rex for a ride. Until this man or woman, for that matter, is caught, I don't think I can go back there."

"I assure you, Mrs. Carlson," Aleister said, "we are going to apprehend this person and put him away. You have my word on that."

"Does this have something to do with the killings we have been hearing about on the news? This is freaking out our neighborhood and community. I have reporters camped outside my home."

"We can't really talk about an ongoing investigation," Agent Canter said.

"I'll take that as a yes," Mr. Carlson said. "Please catch this person. The sooner, the better."

Aleister wrote a couple more notes and turned the page of his legal pad. He wrote both the names of the Carlson's down, then removed two of his business cards from his wallet and handed one to each.

"What is the best number to call if I need to get back in touch?"

Both separately recited their numbers before Aleister turned the recording app off. "If you could, Mr. Carlson, would you text me those photos to the number on that card?"

Mr. Carlson picked up his phone. "I'll do it now."

****

Agent Canter and Officer Wells had discussed how they would go about interrogating Mr. Kesler. He sat at a table with his attorney as the two walked into the interrogation room at Detroit PD. Stacey carried a manila folder in her hand.

"Jon Fennell," the attorney said as he stood and handed Stacey one of his business cards. She placed the card in the manila folder before pulling out a chair and sitting across from them.

"I'm sure your attorney let you know this is being video recorded," Stacey started.

"I see the camera up in the corner," Kesler said.

"Can you state for the record your full name?"

"Keith Joseph Kesler."

"Mr. Kesler, can you tell us what you do for a living?"

"I am a Teamster Official. I have been part of the Union for over 35 years. The Union is what made this country great! Now these young punks think they can go it alone without the Union. They weren't even born when we had to fight our way to a decent contract."

"I'm sure you're right, Mr. Kesler, but I only want you answering questions related to this investigation."

Kesler leaned back in his chair and crossed his arms. "Fine."

Stacey removed a picture of Dominique Hutcheson from the folder she had brought to the interrogation. She placed it in front of Kesler.

"Can you identify the person in this picture?"

Kesler lifted the picture and studied it. He placed it back on the table. "She looks familiar. Is she a Teamster?"

"No. Why would you say she looks familiar?"

"I don't know. I meet with lots of people every month. I'm a Union Rep. When management is hassling one of our members, I'm called in to straighten things out. Over the years, I have met with hundreds of people. Maybe I met with her."

"What would you say if I told you she was murdered, and your semen was recovered from the crime scene. We have a match to your DNA."

Kesler's brow crinkled, and he turned to his attorney with a bewildered look. "This is freaking crazy. I didn't kill anyone and how do they have my DNA?"

"You don't have to say a word about that," Mr. Fennell advised.

Kesler shifted his look to Stacey. "I don't have a thing to hide. I'll answer any goddam questions you have. I'll give you as much DNA as you want. Do you want me to rub one off in a cup?"

"That won't be necessary, Mr. Kesler," Agent Canter replied casually, not wanting to give him the satisfaction that his last comment was crude.

"How do you think your semen was left at the crime scene?"

"I don't know. Was she a working girl?"

"You mean a prostitute?"

"Yeah. I've been separated from my wife for months. We haven't been close in years. Men have needs. I'm no different."

"I'll be a son of a bitch," Officer Wells mumbled to himself just loud enough for everyone at the table to hear. "Agent Canter, would you mind if I asked a few questions?"

Stacey's eyebrows raised. They had not planned on Aleister asking any of the questions. "Of course," Agent Canter said, with a confused look on her face.

"I see you have had an arrest for solicitation. I take it she was not the only girl you ever paid for sex."

"Like I said, I have needs and these girls fill those needs. I'm not proud of that, but it is what it is. I have been with dozens of ladies."

"So do you have sex in your car, or do you go to a hotel?"

"Both."

"Officer Wells, I don't see where you are going with this?" Mr. Fennell interrupted.

"I am trying to figure out how your client's semen could be left at a crime scene if he wasn't there. May I continue?"

Mr. Fennell again nodded.

"Mr. Kesler, do you always use protection when you have sex with these prostitutes?"

"God, yes! Don't want any diseases."

"After you have ejaculated, what do you do with the condom?"

"I don't do anything with it. The lady usually grabs it and tosses it out the window when I zip up. What does that have to do with anything?"

Aleister suddenly stopped. "Would you excuse us for a minute. Agent Canter could I talk to you in the hall please?"

The two stood and walked out of the interrogation room. Once outside, Stacey quickly turned to Aleister.

"What's going on???" she asked.

"I'm not sure we have the right guy."

"What!!??" Stacey said, with a look of confusion.

"You're not going to believe this story I heard last week."

Chapter 51

One Week Earlier

It was the second Friday of the month and payday. The designated day that cops from the 12th precinct met at Buddy's Rendezvous Pizzeria for a few beers and several pieces of square Detroit style pizza.

Axel Shepherd, nicknamed "Dog", drove through the parking lot of the iconic pizza place and snagged himself a parking spot—right in front of the huge "Voted 1" blue ribbon painted on the gray brick wall.

He scanned the parking lot for familiar cars and saw a white Blazer belonging to Kaede Ong or K.O. as he was called-- Axel's best friend and one of only two Asian police officers on the force. The back end of K.O.'s car was smashed, a casualty of a rear end collision on Mt. Elliot.

He entered through a back door and saw Aleister, Gaines, and K.O. already seated with long neck bottles of beer in front of them and a half-eaten basket of chicken wings in the center of the table.

"You guys couldn't have waited for me," Dog kidded. "Some of you boys should pass on the fried food or you'll be needing a new uniform by Christmas."

Aleister tossed a crumpled napkin which hit Dog in the chest.

"Couldn't tear yourself away from that new lady, eh?" said Gaines, the most senior officer of them all.

Dog chuckled. "That's where I'm going after we are finished here," he said. "She just loves having me around! I *fix* things for her."

"I bet you fix her things for her," Gaines added. "If *booty calls* qualify for fixing things."

Loud laughter erupted from the table. Jennie, their usual waitress, plopped a bottle of Modelo in front of Dog.

"Thanks, Love," he said to her, and she responded with a smile and a nod of her head.

"Pizza should be out in 15 minutes," she said in a low, raspy voice. "They got a little backed up in the kitchen."

Her hips swayed under her short black skirt as she walked away, heading for the kitchen.

"I think they should put an apron on that back end of hers," Axel remarked. "That's some tempting real estate."

"I heard she already has some cop boyfriend...some guy out of Poletown," Aleister said. "Don't laugh now, but I think his last name is Kowalski!"

Laughter.

"Everyone loves Kowalski Sausage. Where you been, Aleister?" quipped Gaines. "The wife won't have any other kind of hot dogs at our cookouts. I brought home some Oscar Mayer franks, and she threw them out!!!!"

Jennie wove her way through the narrow aisle of tables carrying their large pizza on a silver tray. She was aware that every fellow's eyes in the place followed her, and they were not checking out the food. She pushed the wings to the side and set the pizza in the center of the red checked tablecloth on the table.

"Another round?" she asked.

"Yeah," said K.O., "and bring me a shot of Jameson."

Aleister gave K.O. a quick look.

"Dude, take it easy on the shots. You gotta get out there and drive."

"I'm only having one," K.O. answered. "I'm good."

"Is there a full moon out?" asked Dog. "The riffraff and lunatics are out in full force."

He pulled two pieces of square pizza onto his plate.

"You're not going to believe the dumbass I met today. I was parked outside the precinct and a guy drove up beside me, rolled down his window, and asked for directions to Mexican Town. I told him where to go and as he was driving away, I decided to run his license plate, and get this… the idiot was driving a stolen car!"

"No freaking way!!" Aleister said as Jennie returned with their beers and handed each a bottle.

"I'm not kidding, and I had to go after the jerk, just when I was ending my shift. I called for back-up, and we went after him. Caught him on State Fair. I flipped on the lights, called out on the speaker for him to pull over, and he did!! Good, I thought. But then he jumped out of the car and started running. Damn, he was fast. The sucker could really move. We chased him for a few blocks and then he gave us the slip running behind some houses. We'll get him, just not today."

Gaines looked at Dog for a few moments before saying, "Yup, you'll get him. Maybe he will turn himself in like those kids who spray painted the Dutch Boy bakery."

"Not a chance in Hell," Dog replied. "When's the last time you had a car thief turn himself in?"

Momentary silence fell at the table, and they became surrounded by the low buzz and murmurs of people at nearby tables.

Gaines finished his pizza and took a long drink of beer.

"I got one for ya," he said. "You know I got a call for a robbery in progress at the Dollar Store on Riopelle. We got there in just 3 minutes, but as soon as we pulled up, the manager of the store came running out swinging a baseball bat.

"He get away…he run away…he go down street that way," and he pointed in the opposite direction.

"He grab cash drawer. Get 87 dollar. He wear hoodie over his head and run away hanging on to drawer."

"Careful with your Asian dialect," K.O. said with a grin. "Those are my people."

"So, we drove down the street looking for the guy. About four blocks down we found the cash drawer, and no one was in sight except a couple of young women pushing strollers followed by a couple teenagers playing with their phones. We asked them if they saw anyone wearing a hoodie running down the sidewalk and they just shook their heads. We had to go back and get a report written. We picked up the cash drawer on the way. The manager was happy to get the drawer back but grumbled and sputtered the whole time about losing the money."

"So that's how you ended your day… writing a robbery report?" Aleister asked.

"Hardly!!" Gaines spouted.

"As we left the Dollar Store, we're driving on Riopelle and a couple of women waved their arms to signal us to stop. We pulled over and one of these women wearing a flowered grandma dress asked if we could do anything to stop 'the hoes' from tricking in front of their houses. She said, 'Mr. Officer. Look at all this...' and she pointed to a trail of used rubbers littering the street. She was really worked up! I looked and sure enough, there were plenty of them scattered around the street. Some needles, too. I didn't know what to say to her. Then the other woman started talking. She said, 'I got little kids and when we come out here in the morning to go to school, they say 'Mommy, what's those things on the sidewalk? I told them to stay away from them and that they are ugly trash stupid fools throw on the street.'

"All I could tell them was that I would write up a report and would send a patrol car to check things out. Then she said for us to tell the city to send out more people to pick up the trash. According to them, sometimes a guy comes around and picks up the condoms, puts them into a trash bag, but doesn't pick up all of them. And he doesn't pick up the needles."

"The city is sending someone to clean up used condoms?" Dog asked, laughing. "Who the hell would want that job?"

"I don't know," Gaines said.

****

The following day, Stacey finished the last sip of her morning coffee as the waitress brought the check. She nodded to the waitress who was dressed in a green plaid kilt, black knee-high boots, and a white shoulder less top. Aleister's eyes briefly scanned her cleavage busting out of her shirt as he tried his best not to notice.

"So, you really think our killer is collecting semen to throw us off the track?" Stacey asked.

"Why not?" Aleister said. "It all makes sense. We have female blood at the Carlson's barn and three used condoms stowed in a baggie within that backpack. Our killer could be female and brilliant. Whoever it is, loves this cat and mouse game. I think it is a real possibility."

"I think I need to get out and talk with some of the ladies who work the street."

"You thinking about going undercover?"

"Yeah. If what you're suggesting is true, then I need to check it out. Who would know better than the ladies working the street."

Chapter 52

Daugherty poured four fingers of bourbon over a few ice cubes, relishing in the pop as the liquid met the ice. He took a heavy sip before refilling and capping the bottle. Satisfaction filled him as he reflected on the success of his sting operation.

From an initial pool of twenty-four suspects, he had effectively narrowed it down to twelve. The information he leaked was sensitive yet not lethal. What haunted him during sleepless nights was the fear of one of his officers being exposed due to his own negligence.

A discreet knock on the hotel room door jolted Daugherty back to reality. Whether you call it a hunch or a woman's intuition, Linda Laurice had been right. Daugherty was having an affair. As he opened the door, a stunning redhead smiled back.

"Hey," she murmured, walking in with her overnight bag in tow. Daugherty hung the "Do Not Disturb" sign on the door and closed it, securing it with the chain and deadbolt. He turned and entered, drawing her in for a lingering kiss. She responded in kind, until playfully pushing him back and with a mischievous grin grabbed his crotch...

"Glad you're happy to see me," she quipped.

****

The family house on the Rhine that Helga had inherited had been in the family since the early 1940's. Her grandfather, newly married, had purchased the home right before he left to fight the British. He never returned.

"Is there a place where I can unpack my suitcase?" inquired Mrs. Fletcher.

Without hesitation, Helga rose from her chair.

"Of course," Helga replied, then retrieved Mrs. Fletcher's luggage sitting in the corner. "You can have my room; I will sleep on the couch."

"I've got the couch," Bo said, as the two strolled down the narrow hallway. The aging wooden floors emitted creaks and groans, bearing witness to the eighty-four-year-old home's history.

After showing Mrs. Fletcher to her room, Helga returned and settled beside Bo. Reflecting on the day's revelations, Bo acknowledged, "I can imagine this has been overwhelming for you, considering all you've discovered."

Helga, taking Bo's hand, locked eyes with him and asked, "What's truly astonishing to me are your feelings. Was it all just an act?"

"No, absolutely not," Bo replied emphatically. "Maybe, in the beginning, when I was still grappling with my struggles, it might have seemed that way. But as time passed, and I became a better person because of you, my emotions became genuine. Carly returning doesn't change that."

"Do you still have feelings for her?" Helga asked, her eyes searching for answers. Bo hesitated, prompting Helga to rise from the couch and turn away. Sensing her emotional withdrawal, Bo stood and gently turned her around by the shoulders.

"Helga, don't. Please don't shut me out," he pleaded. "Of course, I still have feelings for Carly; we've been through a lot together. But those feelings have changed. Now that I'm sober, I recognize that. I will always love her. She saved my life."

Helga leaned in with affection, initiating a kiss. The two embraced just as the squeak in the floor announced Mrs. Fletcher was back in the room. An uneasy tension permeated the air.

"Um... I," Bo stammered, his words faltering in the aftermath of their interrupted moment.

"Bo," Mrs. Fletcher spoke with a reassuring tone. "I'm not here to pass judgment. Carly is the one who chose to leave. Feelings change, and it's no one's fault. If you are married, you try to work through those changes. If you're not, you can leave. That's just the way life unfolds."

The tranquility of the moment was abruptly disrupted by the ringing of Helga's phone. Bending down to the coffee table, she retrieved it and glanced at the screen. "I think it's Carly," she remarked, handing the phone to Bo.

Accepting the phone, Bo tapped the speaker and responded, "I haven't discussed it with Helga yet."

"Bo! We've got a problem," Carly's urgency echoed through the line. "I think Slovak is alive!"

Bo, now pacing anxiously, held the phone as Mrs. Fletcher and Helga listened. "What do you mean he's alive?" concern etched on his face.

"Bo, we need to meet," Carly insisted desperately. Bo's eyes sought Helga's, and she nodded in agreement.

"Carly, we can meet here."

Chapter 53

Agent Canter pulled down on her mini skirt when she got out of the unmarked car then swung the door shut. She was in a high crime area of Detroit.

"Test. Test," she said, then looked at Agent Wells who gave her a thumbs up. Aleister lowered the passenger side window. The sun was just setting behind the tall, dilapidated buildings and the ladies of the night were beginning to gather. Stacey added some bright, red lipstick to her mouth and crouched down by the passenger window.

"God... I love it when you fix yourself up for me," Aleister said. "I want you to wear that exact outfit on our next date."

"Who said there was going to be a next date?" Stacey shot back.

"Good one, Canter. All kidding aside, you be careful out there. How long do you think you will be able to talk to the ladies before a pimp comes up and tells you to get the hell off his turf?"

"I hope long enough to find out if any of them have seen someone picking up used condoms. When I drove by 8 Mile, there had to have been dozens thrown on the street. I think we are on to something here. How else could you explain why Kesler's semen was left at the crime scene."

Aleister watched as Agent Canter's 4-inch heels clicked down the sidewalk and turned the corner. He listened intently as a man with a pockmarked face and cigarette jutting out of the corner of his mouth pulled up to her.

He lowered the passenger window and tossed the butt toward Stacey.

"How much for a blow job?" he shouted through a haze of smoke. "I only got ten minutes."

"Not tonight, Honey," Stacey yelled back never losing her stride.

Aleister knew Stacey was armed and could handle herself, but this part of town made him nervous. The ladies eyed her suspiciously as she walked towards them. This was their working part of the street and an unfamiliar face meant only one thing-- dumb or cop.

"You a cop?" one of the three girls asked, eyeing Agent Canter from head to toe.

"Hardly," Stacey said.

"Are you one of Angelo's new bitches?" the same girl asked.

"I am."

"You better be because here he comes."

Stacey saw a man walking towards her wearing a bright turquoise suit and matching wide rim felt fedora. Three gold chains were draped around his neck and dangled on his open chest. A gold cross hung just above his navel.

"Who the fuck are you? You a cop?" Angelo asked, lifting his head and looking down at her. If you're a cop and don't tell us, that's entrapment and that will be tossed in court."

"I'm not a cop," Stacey told him.

"What are you doing on my corner, Bitch? This is my territory, and you best get your skinny white ass off of it. Unless you lookin' for a new *'Daddy'* and in that case, that would be me."

Stacey noticed Aleister in the unmarked car speed around the corner. The others noticed it, too.

"I am a Federal Agent," Stacey said, as Aleister pulled next to them. "I'm not here to bust you. I just have some questions."

She then pulled out her ID from the little purse across her shoulder and yelled to Aleister. "Stay in the fucking car."

The ladies stood nervously staring at the broken concrete walk not wanting to make eye contact. This was not the first time they were harassed by Vice. Angelo did all the talking.

"You said you weren't a cop, and you are. That's illegal."

"I told you, I'm not here to bust you. I am a Federal agent working a homicide case. You answer my questions and I get in that car and drive away."

"Damn it!!" Angelo said, nervously looking around for more cops to come pouncing at any second. "I ain't no snitch. Why should I answer any questions you got?"

Stacey nodded toward Aleister who now had the window down. "He's a cop. If you don't work with me, I can't say that he won't bust you and your ladies."

Aleister produced his badge and stuck it out the window.

Angelo looked at it and then back to Stacey. He shook his head from side to side, then figured his odds were better if he cooperated. "What do you want to know?"

"Have you or any of your girls ever noticed anyone picking up used condoms from the street?"

"What kind of nasty-ass question is that? Who would want used condoms?"

"I just need to know."

"Tish…Reno…Geri," Angelo said. "Answer that nasty-ass question."

All three of them shook their heads and sheepishly said, "No."

"Never. None of you ever remember anyone picking up used condoms."

"We are in the service industry, "Geri said, "We ain't nobody's maids."

Stacey reached in her purse and pulled one of her cards. She handed it to Angelo.

"This is your "Get out of Jail" free card. If you put the word out and get back to me with any information, next time you get in trouble call me and not your attorney. I can be a really good friend in times like that."

Angelo took her card and read it before sticking it in his pocket.

****

The following morning Wells entered Agent Canter's office carrying two Tim Horton cups of coffee. She waved her hand motioning for him to come in and sit. She mouthed the words "Thank you" when she noticed the drinks.

"Yes, ma'am. I will," Stacey said before ending the call.

"Triple cream, triple sugar?" Stacey asked as she gently tossed the phone on her desk and strolled around to sit at the table where Aleister was already seated.

"Yes, ma'am, I remembered."

"Thank you."

"Listen, if I ask you something, you promise not to laugh?"

"Depends on what it is."

"Have you ever heard of remote viewing?"

"Remote viewing?" Stacey scoffed. "It's not reliable. The Pentagon stopped funding it in the 90's."

"I got this call from a Kate Bender who is a remote viewer and says she can help."

"Are you kidding me? You want us to talk to some clairvoyant. You should have brought me vodka instead of coffee before laying this on me!"

"Would you just hear me out?"

Stacey leaned back in her chair crossing her arms in front of her chest.

"Go ahead."

"This lady knew things about this case that have never been made public."

"Like what?"

"Like she knew the killer set the whole knife block outside the window of Dominique Hutcheson's home, before entering her house."

Stacey sat up in her chair, suddenly seeming to be interested.

"What else did she say?"

"She knew there was a letter from someone called the '*Jazzman,*' and that he carries an axe."

Stacey interrupted. "Anyone could know that with a little research on Google. When Gideon had the news conference, she stated that the killings are taking place with an axe."

"But would they know that the clue that sent us to the Detroit Library came from the fingers of Dominique Hutcheson."

"Damn!! The cigarette holder. She knew about that?"

"Not totally. She never specifically said cigarette holder, but she knew the clue came from the fingers of the victim."

"Did she specifically say knife block?"

"Pretty close. She knew the killer set knives from the counter out onto the back deck before crawling through the window."

Stacey paused for a moment. "She sure knows a lot about this case. When is she coming?"

"Tomorrow at 10:00. Are you in?"

"Why not? Sort of dead in the water. What do we got to lose?"

Chapter 54

The seven-hundred-mile trek from Kansas to Michigan took little over fourteen hours. Kate Bender knocked on the open door of Agent Canter's office. She was nothing like the gypsy Stacey had envisioned. Instead of a woman wearing a long flowing multicolored dress with matching scarf tied around her head, she was dressed in a loose baby blue sweater and pair of faded jeans.

Kate was beautiful, actually stunning. She had high cheek bones, flawless skin, and deep green catlike eyes. Her chestnut hair hung to her shoulders. She held what looked like a large artist sketch pad under her arm and a purse with a long strap hung down over her shoulder.

"You must be Kate Bender," Stacey said holding out her hand. "Please come and have a seat. Officer Wells just stepped out. He should be back shortly."

"Perfect," Kate said. "This will give you time to cross examine me."

Stacey was surprised and said nothing as she followed Kate to the table where they both sat. Kate smiled slightly and scooted in her chair, placing her elbows on the table and resting her chin on her clasped hands.

"So, what would you like to know?" Kate casually asked.

"Officer Wells tells me you are a remote viewer. That's some impressive stuff you told him about our case. Those details were never made public. How do you do that?" she asked with some suspicion.

"It's an ability I have. I was born with it. I use my gift for the good. Well, most of the time for the good anyway."

Officer Wells entered and saw Kate and Stacey sitting at the office table. He pulled out a chair and joined them.

"Mrs. Bender, I take it?"

"Ms. Bender," she said. "I'm not married. I tend to scare off my suitors when they get to know the real me."

Aleister paused momentarily, not really sure how to respond.

"Um...I'm glad you agreed to meet with us. You lead the way. Just tell us what you need."

"The first thing I need is for both of you to take me seriously."

Kate opened her artist pad to a blank white page. She removed a set of colored pens from her purse. "I need you both to step out of the office and discuss details of another crime scene that were never made public. I don't want you to discuss Dominique. Talk about one of the other three murders."

Aleister looked at Stacey and then back to Kate. "You mean the other two murders. There was a total of three."

A half smile formed on Kate's face and her green eyes locked onto Aleister.

"I assure you there were four. You just don't know it yet. Hopefully, after today, you will."

Stacey saw the mesmerized look on Aleister's face. She playfully snapped her fingers in front of him.

"Focus, Wells," she said.

Aleister looked away and shook his head. "That was weird," he muttered.

"I want you to discuss as much detail as you can. Once you are done, come back to me and I will have sketches and information that the two of you discussed about the crime scene."

Stacey stood up from the table and walked to a three-drawer filing cabinet in the corner of her office. She removed the file on Josie Davis.

"Shall we?" she said to Aleister and headed out the door.

The two went into the vestibule where the vending machines were located. The place was empty. They sat at a round lunch table where Stacey removed pictures of the gruesome crime scene and spread them on the table.

They studied each picture. Stacey tried to imagine the abundance of fear the victim must have been experiencing as the crime unfolded. She then began to read from her notes.

"Josie Davis was 22 and born in Lima, Ohio." She looked up. "Wasn't she the first victim found? We didn't at that point know what we were dealing with."

"Yes, she was. She was found sitting in a kitchen chair, like she was at a 1920's Speakeasy. She wore a black dress with a glittering headband. I remember she had black gloves up to her elbows and she was wearing black stockings rolled down to just below-the-knee."

"Wasn't her body washed?" Stacey asked. "And she wasn't raped. Semen was left on her chest, so we just assumed that he masturbated over her. With what we now know about Kesler, I'm not sure if the semen actually came from the killer."

"And that's when we thought it might be two men committing the murders because the semen found on Eleanor Wickens our second victim didn't match what was found on Josie," Aleister added.

Stacey nodded in agreement. "And then the female blood from the barn threw us for a loop. If I remember right, the killer didn't start playing his *Whodunit?* game until the third murder."

"Yeah, you're right. It was Dominque Hutcheson where he actually left a note. Do you think that's why he crossed state lines? He knew the FBI would be called in and he wanted more people in the game."

"It's possible," Aleister remarked.

Stacey removed a map of the surrounding states where the murders had taken place, from the file. She unfolded it and spread it out over the pictures. She circled with her index finger the three cities in two states where the murders had happened.

"Two in Ohio and one in Michigan," she said. "He's not going to stop until we stop him. That's all I got. Can you think of anything else?"

Aleister shook his head. "Nope. I think we covered it. Let's go see if our girl can fill in the blanks."

Officer Wells and Agent Canter folded the map, gathered the pictures, and placed everything back in the file. They walked into the office where they found Kate Bender leaning back in the chair with her eyes closed. She was holding a pen.

There were at least a half dozen drawings sketched on separate sheets of paper lying on top of each other. The top sketch and the only one visible was a map showing the states of Indiana, Michigan, and Ohio.

Chapter 55

Helga felt a surge of uneasiness as Porsche's car entered the driveway, her stomach churning with nerves. She watched as Carly, David, Porsche, and Sergeant Tim stepped out of the car. It was easy to spot Carly based on Bo's description. Despite Helga's attempt to resist the green-eyed monster, it overwhelmed her. She forced a half smile as they entered and kept her composure. Bo had retrieved additional folding chairs from the cellar, ensuring everyone could be accommodated in the front room.

Carly swiftly approached her mother, and the two shared a heartfelt embrace. "I've been freaking out since I got here," Carly confided in her mother. "You can't believe what's been going through my head with both of you gone." Turning to Bo, she enveloped him in a warm hug, and he reciprocated.

"I'm so happy for you, Bo," Carly expressed. "Sobriety isn't an easy thing."

Bo nodded appreciatively. "Well, I had help." He turned to Helga. "Everyone, meet Helga Schmidt. She pulled me out of the depths of alcoholism and despair. Now there are two ladies to whom I owe my life."

Bo shifted his attention to David. "How could you steal from Carly!? I thought you were her friend!"

Sergeant Tim interjected, "He did it for me. I asked him to."

A perplexed expression swept across Bo's face. "You're that Sergeant Tim who helped them save me. I don't know if I should thank you or punch you in the face. What the hell did you need mithridate for?"

"I had a lady friend who was kidnaped and held hostage in Iraq. The government wouldn't help because she was Australian. Having the vial of mithridate got the government to listen. They assisted, and that Aussie is now my bride."

Bo's eyes shifted between Carly and David. "Maybe there is more to this then I first thought. Let's continue this conversation later."

"Well, if everyone's settled, we need to get down to business," Porsche declared. "Why don't we sit and discuss what we found."

The room hushed as everyone took their seats. Porsche initiated by retrieving her phone and handing it to Bo. "Take a look; Slovak is alive and thriving. Can you confirm if the person seated beside him is Borka?"

"Indeed, that's him," Bo affirmed. "And as for Slovak, you can't overlook his unmistakable face."

"I think we should contact Agent Canter and let her know what's going on," David suggested.

"I'm not so sure," Sergeant Tim said. "The CIA told us Slovak was dead and now we find out he's not! That smells of an inside job to me. Remember what the Chief said, it came straight from CIA Officer Paul Daugherty."

"Do you think the Chief is involved?" Carly asked skeptically.

"No, absolutely not," Tim assured. "He seems like a straight shooter. It's Daugherty whom I don't trust."

"But why would the CIA tell us he's dead when he's not?" Bo asked. "And now there's a possibility that my cover may have been compromised. Could that too be CIA!? This is my fault."

"That's in the past," Carly reassured. "Don't beat yourself up. Look what I did, going back to the states, facing the risk of exposure, Slovak was relentless in his pursuit. I just can't get my mind around why the CIA would be helping?"

"I am not totally convinced they are," Porsche shared. "I mean, why would they?"

"Is it possible that Slovak has turned into a double agent?" mused David aloud.

"Doubling as an agent for the US? I find that hard to believe," Carly remarked. "I'm inclined to agree with Tim. If Slovak is involved, it's likely in some covert operation for the CIA—something clandestine known to only a select few."

Porsche stood from her chair. She strolled to the window, drawing back the drape, she looked outside before turning her attention back to the group.

"Ok, agreed. We'll keep this among ourselves until we have concrete confirmation. It's time to take action. I'll reach out to some of my former colleagues at the agency. I'll find a suitable site for the operation."

Porsche's attention shifted towards Bo. "We need you to re-establish contact with Borka. He's our connection to Slovak. Arrange a coffee meeting with him. Apologize for having to cancel yesterday's coffee date. Tim, David, and I will take care of the rest."

"Set it up for tomorrow, early evening. That'll give me enough time to find a place."

Porsche turned her attention to Carly. "You should return to the apartment with your mom and Bo. If our suspicions hold true, we need everything to appear normal. If Slovak is involved in a CIA operation, he likely knows you're here."

****

Carly, and Bo drew their firearms as Mrs. Fletcher inserted the key, unlocking the door. With swift coordination, they burst through the entrance while Mrs. Fletcher remained in the hallway. Once the apartment was secured, Carly called for her mom.

Bo headed straight to the counter where he had left his phone, swiftly composing a message to Borka. Almost instantly, a reply appeared, confirming Borka's acceptance.

"Carly," Bo asked, "Would you like something to drink? Don't have any booze, but I have seltzer water or tea." His attention then turned to Mrs. Fletcher. "How about you, Mom?"

"No, it's been a crazy, hectic day. I think I'm heading to bed," Mrs. Fletcher replied as she headed down the hall.

Carly entered the kitchen and filled the tea kettle with water. "Do you want a seltzer?" she asked, bending down into the fridge and pulling one out.

"Thank you," Bo replied, taking the bottle from Carly. "Let's talk."

Carly prepared her tea and joined Bo in the living room, taking a seat across from him. The radio played softly in the background.

"Where are we at, Bo? I mean, you're doing great. You look great, and you seem healthy," Carly remarked.

Bo nodded, agreeing with Carly's assessment. "I do feel good, Carly. Better than I have in the last month or so."

A long pause ensued, and tension hung in the air. Carly avoided Bo's eyes, dunking her tea bag into her cup. She then looked up from her cup.

"I'll cut to the chase. I've noticed the way Helga looks at you and how you try to conceal it. Is there something going on?"

Bo began, stumbling over his words.

"Um…This past year has been hard on you. It's been hard on both of us. My drinking made it all the worse. Since I quit the booze, my thoughts are clearer now. I came to realize that maybe it just wasn't meant to be."

Bo's reaction caught Carly off guard. "What do you mean?"

"I believe we are soulmates, I really do, but not the kind that are destined for an entire life together. We fell in love but, over time, our love changed. It's not like we don't love each other. It's just a different kind of love."

Bo remained motionless and only his even breathing could be heard.

"You have to be honest with me, Carly," Bo said. "Do you have feelings for David?"

"The short answer is yes. Now that I've learned why he took the mithridate, my resentment has gone away, and I've realized just how much I care for him."

A feeling of relief washed over Bo's face.

"I think you and I should give these new relationships a chance," Bo said. "If we are meant to be, then in the end, we'll be together."

Bo stood up, pulling Carly close to him. He bent forward and touched his forehead to hers. They stood like that, unmoving, holding hands. A familiar *Coldplay* song, faintly played from the kitchen.

When you try your best, but you don't succeed,
  When you get what you want but not what you need,
  When you feel so tired, but you can't sleep
  Stuck in reverse

Carly whispered, "That won't be us, Bo. We're not stuck, we're moving on."

****

It was a bitterly cold night, even by Dusseldorf standards. The wet snow blew sideways as Tim and David stood poised, just outside The Dusseldorf hotel. In her car, Porsche waited, anticipating the awaited text. Her contacts had delivered a black site. Sergeant Tim, holding a syringe containing a quarter dose of Etorphine hydrochloride, prepared for action.

Borka Radovic emerged from his hotel, flicked up his collar, and unfurled his umbrella. Bo had orchestrated a rendezvous, and the plan was for them to grab coffee once again at the Coffee House on Flustra St.

Unaware of the impending events, Borka strolled, retracing his steps through the alley –the same shortcut he had taken the night before when Tim had discreetly followed him. Executing their well-laid plan, David emerged suddenly from behind the dumpster as Borka walked past.

In a swift move, Borka's umbrella went flying as David tackled him from behind, rendering him defenseless and unable to reach for his gun. Tim dropped to his knees beside Borka's head, administering the Etorphine hydrochloride into his neck. Without hesitation, Tim sent a text to Porsche. Within seconds she sped around a corner and David and Tim hustled into the back, pulling Borka with them.

Chapter 56

Back at the Bureau in Michigan, Kate Bender opened her eyes when Stacey and Aleister walked back into the office. She looked drained, her face was drawn, greenish white in color.

"Are you all right?!!" Stacey asked. "Would you like some water?"

Kate pinched the bridge of her nose and closed her eyes again. In a low muffled voice she said, "Migraines, I get these migraines when I do a viewing. A bottle of water would be great."

Aleister quickly walked to the fridge and removed a bottle of water as Kate fished through her purse looking for her migraine medication. "Thank you," she said grabbing the bottle that Aleister had opened and swallowing two pills.

"These viewings sometimes kick my ass when they get intense. This one was off the charts. Just give me a minute. Would you mind turning off the lights and shutting the blinds. I do my viewing by candlelight."

Kate reached into her bag and removed two round candles and set them in front of her. She wiped the sweat from her forehead with the sleeve of her shirt as Aleister lowered the blinds and turned off the lights.

"I haven't had a séance since high school," Aleister said returning to the table and sitting next to Stacey.

"This is not a séance, I assure you," Kate said.

The color in the room had vanished and only grays and shadows could be seen. The candlelight flickered on her face as she moved the two candles to the top of the table.

"This is where we'll start," Kate said as she placed the drawing of the three states in front of them.

"Evil has taken place here," pointing to the state of Indiana. "Someone died that has to do with these other three killings. It happened years ago but not for the reasons associated with the latest killings. When and if you get this person, you will find a connection to a killing in Indiana."

Kate turned the picture over and grabbed another from the pile. Stacey and Aleister stared at what looked like icons designating the men's and ladies' room. They were no more than stick figures with the female having a triangle for a body.

"There are two personalities at the crime scenes," Kate began.

"I knew it!!" Stacey said excitedly. "That explains the female blood. It's a male and female team."

"I didn't say two people. I said the presence of two personalities. People can have more than one personality. With this, there is an evil personality and a moral personality. There is a battle raging between the two. The personalities both hate and love each other."

Kate moved the drawing to the side and placed a sketch of the Yin and Yang symbol next to it. She traced around each figure with her index finger. First, she traced the Yang or white of the swirl and then went to the black. When she lifted her head, she looked frightened.

"There are opposite forces here that may actually be complementary and interconnected."

Stacey reached out her hand. "Can I see that picture?" she asked Kate.

Stacey brought the drawing close to her. She studied the curves. "What's this symbol stand for again?"

"It's an ancient Chinese philosophy. The Yin is dark, negative and female. The Yang is light, positive and male."

"Oh, geez," Stacey moaned. "Here's another dig on women written by a man. Just like Eve and the apple. It's always the woman's fault."

There was an uncomfortable silence at the table. Stacey wished she could take the words back the minute they left her mouth. Kate's reaction was subdued, restrained. She simply reached into her bag and set two tarot cards on the table between the candles. One card depicted the Grim Reaper; the other card was the Tower. Kate then continued.

"Humans possess these qualities, and one keeps the other in check. These seem to be reversed. It's the Yang or male that is dark and evil not the Yin. It is causing great conflict and confusion. Death is a byproduct of this conflict."

"So, what causes the Yin and Yang to get messed up?" Aleister asked.

"It can be many things but mostly consistent trauma starting at a young age. During the years of development. The philosophy believes we all possess these traits, but one keeps the other in line. That's why humans can, for the most part, live in harmony with each other."

Stacey shook her head. "We knew we were looking for a whack job, but this person seems over the top."

Kate took the tarot cards and set them in the middle of the table. She then placed the last three sketches around them forming a type of cross. Each page had a letter scrawled on it. There was a capital X, a capital R, and capital E. Dark red lines cut through the middle of each one.

"These make no sense to me," Kate said. "When I do a viewing, I don't always know what I am seeing. One thing I can tell you there is hatred and death associated with these letters. Something to do with revenge. If you figure out their meaning, you're going to catch the killer."

Kate glanced at Stacey's troubled face and felt some sympathy for her. She tapped the two tarot cards.

"I don't know if this will brighten your spirits, Stacey, but you *are* going to get your man."

****

Charlotte knelt on the kneeler in the confessional of Old Saint Mary's. She heard the screen of the confessional window slide open. She along with Father Jovani made the sign of the cross. This was not her first time to confession.

"Bless me Father, for I have sinned," Charlotte spoke into the screen of the confessional hiding Father Jovani. "My last confession was three months ago."

Through the worn mesh of the window screen, Charlotte could see the shadow of a figure straighten up and lean in. Father Jovani recognized the voice, and his heart began to pound.

He cleared his throat before he started. "And why are you here, my child? Is it your brother again?"

"It is, Father. I am worried that Charlie is planning something terrible again."

"And why do you think that?"

"Because he told me. I can always tell when he is in *that* mood. He uses foul language and is off in his little world. What worries me is when he becomes silent. That's when things happen. He has been getting pretty quiet these days."

"Is it time for you to go to the police? How many other killings are you going to let happen?"

"I have thought about that. There have been plenty of times where I want to turn him in. I always change my mind at the last minute. Deep down, Charlie is good.

"It's just the bad things that have happened to him over the years that made him this way. Let me think about it, Father. As always, I appreciate the talks you have with me. I am looking forward to seeing you at Sunday Mass next week."

"I, as well, my child. God bless, and may God bless your brother."

Chapter 57

Agent Canter stepped to the podium next to Special Agent Gideon. She hated the spotlight and here she was, smack in the middle of it. It was tight as the two stood shoulder-to-shoulder on the small stage. The sign language interpreter watched and waited patiently as the press conference was about to begin.

Word had gotten out that Kate Bender had done a remote viewing and multiple TV networks were attempting to interview her. The state public affairs office was packed, and the press was about to pounce.

Gideon sipped from a cup of water, before clearing her throat and beginning.

"I am Special Agent Gideon. I am in charge of this investigation." Gideon tilted her head toward Stacey.

"This is FBI Agent Stacey Canter. She is my lead investigator on the series of killings that have taken place in our state and others. She is here to update you and share where we are with this case."

Gideon stepped back from the podium and gave center stage to Stacey. She scanned the room and saw Aleister standing to the side of the reporters who had gathered. He flashed her a quick wink and subtle nod. She gave him a faint smile, adjusted the papers on her podium, and began.

"Thank you, Agent Gideon. As you probably know, we have had three killings, all of them women in their early twenties. We do believe these killings are related and that they are being committed by the same perpetrator. The killings have taken place in southern Michigan and northern Ohio. I am here because we need the public's help."

A reporter stood from her chair and shouted, "Is it true that you hired a psychic because you have no leads in this case?"

"Is it true that all the murders have been done with an axe?" another reporter yelled from the back of the crowd.

Stacey lifted her hand. "STOP!! PLEASE" she said. "I don't want this turning into a "free for all". You read the press advisory. Please, let me finish my address and then I will answer any questions you may have."

The room became silent as Agent Canter read from her typed brief.

"In an effort to solve this case and to apprehend who is responsible for these senseless killings, the families of the victims have agreed to help in any way and to release the names of their loved ones. With this in mind, we hope the media will respect their privacy and direct all questions and any information to the FBI.

"Our victims' names are the following: Josie Davis of Lima, Ohio. She was 22 years of age and as far as we know she was the first victim.

"Eleanor Wickens of Toledo Ohio. She was 24 years old, and she was our second victim."

"Our third and final victim as we know it was Dominique Hutcheson. She also was in her early 20's and lived in the Detroit Metro area.

"There is a common thread in all three murders that has never been released to the public. We are releasing this information now to see if the public may help. At all three crime scenes the victims were dressed in a 1920's flapper outfit. The person committing these killings is calling himself *The Jazzman*."

Instantly the room filled with chatter. A reporter's arm shot up and Agent Canter recognized him.

"Would you elaborate? What do you mean a flapper outfit?"

"It's just what I said. Once the victims have been killed, they are bathed and dressed in a 1920's flapper outfit complete with stockings and feather boa." The reporter then asked a follow up question.

"So, is it true the killings have been done with an axe?"

Canter paused for a moment and took a deep breath, letting it out slowly.

"Yes, that is true. The weapons of choice on all three murders is a straight razor and hand axe."

Another reporter stood and Stacey recognized him. "Is it true you have made an arrest in the case?"

"Yes," Agent Canter began and then stopped before starting over. "Yes. It is true we did make an arrest…but certain things have come to light and now we don't believe he is our guy."

"Could you give us a name? What makes you think he may not be your man?"

"That I cannot comment on. Those details are not being released at this time."

A woman in the middle row raised her hand. Canter recognized her and she stood. The reporter flipped a spiral note pad until she stopped and read from it.

"This Kate Bender. Is the case so weak that you had to consult a fortuneteller?"

Stacey shook her head briefly before she answered. "Ms. Bender is not a fortuneteller. She is what's called a *'Remote Viewer'*. She contacted our office and had information about a case that was never released to the public. We had a conversation with her. That was the extent of it."

Stacey noticed Aleister nodding his head and flashing her a smile.

"Jazzman???" another reporter said. "Have you talked with this person? How do you know he calls himself the Jazzman?"

"No, we have not talked with him. He has left written clues and signed them "The Jazzman." Agent Canter stared into the cameras. Her following statement was developed with the help of the behavioral science team.

"This person is a fake. A phony! He is mimicking a killer from the early 1920's called the Axeman. Our killer is trying to resurrect what had taken place in New Orleans almost a century ago. There is nothing original about this killer. He is a coward. He stalks women and kills them when they are alone.

"We think he is a narcissistic psychopath with little self-esteem. This is why he preys on women. This is why we are looking to the public for help. If you have any information, even if it's just the slightest of a connection, the FBI would like to hear from you."

****

Charlie pointed the remote and clicked off the news before fishing out a cigarette from a pack resting on the nightstand. He lit it and his pace increased as he walked back and forth hotboxing his smoke.

"Easy, Big Boy," Pugs, his guinea pig, said with a sarcastic tone. "You're going to hyper ventilate. I think she is right. You're nothing but a phony."

"Fuck-off!!," Charlie yelled as his stride continued to increase.

"You gotta do something with that bitch. She's making you look bad."

"She's a fucking FBI agent. What the hell can I do with her?"

"Oh, I get it," Pugs said derisively. "You can handle weak vulnerable women but when it comes to strong women, you wimp out."

"I'm not a fucking wimp!"

"Then prove it. Take the bitch out! But not before you take out the preacher."

Charlie stopped in his tracks as Pug's beady red eyes looked at him. "Why are you bringing that up again? Quit messing with me."

"If your sister keeps talking to that priest, your goose is cooked, sizzled, crisped."

Charlie butted the cigarette and pulled a chair next to the glass terrarium. He raked his hand through his hair and sighed. "I know you are right, but Charlotte really likes Father Jovani. She said he can't go to the police."

"Bullshit!" Pugs said. "I wouldn't take a chance. The Jazzman needs to silence that fucker before your ass is back at a mental institution and you will be locked up for life. Remember how many years you were there when you set that guy on fire."

"He had it coming. He was doing bad things to Charlotte."

"Of course, he had it coming, but they still locked *you* up."

Charlie sat in silence. He knew Pugs was right. Charlotte had gotten really close with Father Jovani and that could be a problem. He couldn't give a rat's ass about the Padre. The Jazzman could take him out in a heartbeat. But Charlotte would never forgive him.

What if Father Jovani had an accident? he speculated. A smile grew on Charlie's face as he leaned back in the chair, crossed his arms in front of him and closed his eyes.

Chapter 58

Upon awakening from sedation, Borka found himself immersed in what initially felt like a dream. The figures around him, outfitted with masks, seemed too surreal to be genuine. However, as the fog of confusion lifted, the harsh reality took hold—this was no dream.

Borka sat in a dimly lit cellar, the air heavy with the damp odor of mold and mildew. He was securely bound to a chair, each ankle restrained, one arm fastened to the chair's arm, and the other secured behind him. Wire-cutting-pilers rested on a table next to him. The ominous realization settled in – his constrained position hinted of torture.

Borka's attention gravitated towards the masked figure who spoke, unmistakably discerning it as a female voice.

"You can make this difficult for yourself if you prefer," she remarked, lifting the pliers from the table. Borka nervously squirmed in his chair as the figure approached with deliberate steps.

"Wait!" he pleaded. "You got the wrong guy! I have no clue what you're talking about!"

The concealed figure shook her head while placing her hand on top of Borka's, gripping the fingernail of his pinky with the pliers. Borka sat frozen, eyes widened with fear, until the room echoed with a shrill scream.

Stepping back, she opened the pliers, letting the bloody fingernail fall to the floor. Borka's head hung low, hyperventilating. She stepped forward once more, placing her hand on top of his.

"Wait!" Borka's scream pierced the air. "What do you want to know?"

The masked figure walked over to the table and placed the pliers down. Retrieving a notepad, she studied its contents before lifting her gaze to meet Borka's.

"Mr. Radovic," she began, her tone measured. "I'll afford you an opportunity. Answer my questions truthfully, and for every falsehood, I'll take a nail. Clear?"

Borka nodded, his breaths shallow and ragged.

"Good. I'm pleased we have an understanding. I'll be concise. Why are you in Dusseldorf, and what's the purpose of your meeting with Alexander Slovak? Remember, honesty is crucial. Each falsehood costs you a nail."

Borka's mind raced, his stare fixed on his finger, now throbbing and bloody. He inhaled deeply, gathering his thoughts, and began to speak.

"I'm on a mission with Grego Szabo. Our objective is to locate a product our handler is eager to acquire."

"What product?"

"Something called mithridate."

The figure flipped another page of her notebook. "So far, so good. Don't blow it now. Who is your handler?"

Borka hesitated briefly. He understood the consequences if word got out that he had divulged information. "Well," she said.

"Kolo," he muttered.

"You are doing well," the figure assured. "Is Slovak running this operation?"

Borka's expression changed into one of astonishment, a wave of shock sweeping across his face. Thoughts raced through his mind, questioning how they could be aware of Slovak. Immersed in thought, Borka remained silent.

The figure released a deep sigh, allowing the notebook to fall with a thud onto the table. With purpose, she seized the pliers.

"Wait!" Borka pleaded. "He's not part of our operation. He is here to acquire sensitive information from my partner."

"What kind of information?"

"Information leaked to him by a source within the CIA."

"Who is his source?"

"I have no idea."

Once again, the figure stepped in, pressing her hand on top of Borka's and reaching for the pliers.

"Wait," a male voice said from behind his mask.

Porsche stopped and stepped away, letting Tim continue.

"So, if Slovak is not part of your operation. Why did he hook up with you?"

"As I mentioned, he appeared unexpectedly. Somehow, he was already aware of the information Grego was gathering. He paid for it and wanted more. Slovak is my uncle."

Tim's focus shifted from Borka to the other two. "Follow me."

Porsche, David, and Tim left Borka alone and went into the adjacent room. Each removed their mask.

"This whole thing reeks of a counterintelligence," Tim began. "The CIA did shit like this all the time in Iraq. Why else would we be told Slovak is dead and he just happens to show up in Dusseldorf?"

"I agree," Porsche said. "Someone had to share intelligence with Slovak within the Agency. This just can't be coincidence."

"But why?" David questioned. "What's the benefit to the CIA?"

"It must be significant," Tim suggested. "Something substantial enough for the Agency to collaborate with Slovak."

Porsche's forehead furrowed as she spoke, her tone weighed down by the gravity of her words. "During my time in the academy, they instilled in us the belief that the absolute worst thing that could happen is the outing of officers."

"So, are you saying," David mused. "Are you saying, if Slovak is indeed collaborating with the CIA to get sensitive information here, it raises the question, could there be a leak within the Agency?"

"That would explain why Daugherty put out the word that Slovak died of covid," Porsche suggested. "It could be part of a sting to trap the leaker."

David expressed concern, "So, if what you say is true, sending Carly back to Germany with me was indeed part of the plan, it meant that there was full awareness of the potential risk to Carly's life, considering her as possible 'collateral damage'."

Sergeant Tim shook his head in dismay. "After everything she's been through, the CIA pulls something like this."

"It revolves around the integrity of the Agency," Porsche emphasized. "Like I said, the confidentiality of information is sacrosanct. But the CIA may not be aware of what's going on."

"How so?" David asked.

"Daugherty may be going rogue, trying to handle this himself," Porsche suggested.

"Regardless of who is behind this, Slovak is and always will be a threat as long as he is alive. I say we 'TAKE OUT' the SOB!" David asserted.

"I'm with you, my brother," Tim agreed.

"You had me at 'TAKE OUT'," Porsche said.

The trio donned their masks with an eerie sense of purpose, reentering the room where Borka awaited. Their intent was clear, ensure his survival momentarily, using him as bait to craft a trap for Slovak. Beyond that point, Borka's existence became dispensable, a stark reality dictated by the unforgiving nature of the business he chose to be in.

Chapter 59

Agent Canter's look shifted from her computer to the phone resting on her desk, drawn by the chime of an incoming text message. The unfamiliar number sparked an interest in her. As she read the message from Angelo, her eyes widened, never really believing she would hear from him.

"*I got some information about that nasty ass who has been collecting used rubbers. Meet me at the Stonehouse Bar off Woodward next to the State Fairgrounds. Don't bring your cop boyfriend. I will be there 7:00 tonight.*"

Stacey texted back the 'thumbs up' emoji.

****

The air was thick as Charlie strolled the grounds of Old Saint Mary's Catholic Church in Detroit. He wore a hoodie, sweatpants, and sneakers. He stopped in front of the gothic style church and focused on the heavy stone. The cathedral seemed to defy the laws of gravity. It would topple, of course, if it wasn't for its pointed arches, flying buttresses, and ribbed vaults.

Those architects were brilliant back in the day, he thought, *when churches were built with bare hands. Back in the day when women knew their places. And back in the day before bitches got the right to vote. The Catholics got it right,* he pondered. *You won't see a bitch ever becoming a priest.*

He needed to get in and see the place, but he didn't want to run into Father Jovani. Charlie looked from side to side before stepping under the rounded stone archway. A dim light accented the stoop and made visible the iron handles of the wooden doors. He grabbed the handle and pulled before cursing in his head when he realized the door was locked.

This is a goddam church...Thought they were open twenty-four seven.

Charlie leaped from the porch and onto the grass of the church grounds. He walked to an oval window long ago encased with iron bars. He cupped his hands to the side of his eyes and looked in. The building was dark, except for a light shining up to a huge crucifix with a figure of Jesus Christ on it. The plan of getting into the church would have to wait.

****

Agent Canter pulled into the parking lot of the two-story Stonehouse Bar. The Stonehouse was the oldest continuously licensed bar in the city of Detroit. She parked next to a black Ford Escalade with the windows down. The pungent smell of "skunk" filled the air as she exited her car. *Why not?* she thought. *It's legal now in Michigan, just not with the feds.*

Stacey made her way to the front of the bar passing two young lovers fooling around in the backseat of a Chevy. She pushed open the door and the place was packed. Men and women sat at the bar, sipping craft beers such as Purple Gang Pilsner and Lavender Jam. She scanned the place and spotted Angelo sitting under a neon blue sign that read Ralston Street Grill.

"I hafta tell you, I never thought I would hear from you," Agent Canter said as she pulled out a seat and sat at the table with Angelo. "I really appreciate it."

"This ain't no good deed out of the kindness of my heart. This is a strategic move, just in case I need a favor, *Stacey*."

Stacey focused on Angelo's face. She smiled slightly when she realized Angelo had done his own research on her. He was playing her. He knew her first name. Probably had her followed and knew where she lived, too. This was not the first time she dealt with organized crime, and she was not about to let this two-bit pimp put her on the defense.

"Cut the crap, Angelo...I'm not one of your girls that you can mind-fuck and then beat their ass if they don't listen to you. You'll refer to me as Agent Canter or I will be up your ass more than your boyfriend is!"

Angelo puffed up his chest and scooted in his chair. He clearly wasn't used to people talking to him like that, especially a woman. The waitress sauntered to the table and interrupted.

"What can I get you, Sweetie?"

"Nothing," Agent Canter said. "I won't be staying long."

"Another one, AA?" the waitress asked.

Angelo shook his head. "I'm all set."

"So, why am I here?" Agent Canter asked. "What do ya got for me?"

Before Angelo could start, a burly man looking like Mr. T. complete with a mohawk approached the table. A white button-down shirt covered his V-shaped upper body and fit tightly over his well-defined pecs. The first three buttons of his shirt were open, and a gold cross dangled from his neck. He groped Stacey with his eyes starting with her head and working his way down.

"Mmm, mmm, mmm!!! What do we have here, Angelo?"

"She not for sale, Marcus. Get the fuck out of here."

"Keeping her for yourself, Angelo? After you break her in, give 'Big Daddy' a call."

Angelo shook his head. "You'll be the first. Now, get the fuck out of here."

Angelo reached into his pants pocket and removed a round pendant with what looked like a brown leather shoelace attached to it and slid it to Stacey. "This came off your nasty ass dude."

Stacey lifted the pendant and read what was inscribed on its surface…

He that soweth the good seed
is the Son of man
Matthew 13:36-40

On the back of the pendant was the name Old Saint Mary's Catholic Church, Detroit.

Stacey's brows drew together.

"Where did you get this?"

Angelo snapped his fingers into the air towards a girl sitting on the other side of the bar at a lone table. He motioned with his hand for her to join them. The woman got up from the table and pulled her gold mini skirt down towards her knees. She grabbed her gold purse.

Men turned and stared as the stunning tall black woman walked across the wooden floor. Her heels clicking with the rhythm of her pace. She took a seat next to Agent Canter, set her purse on the table, and pulled in her chair. Stacey noticed an Adam's apple protruding from her table guest's throat.

"Tell her what happened, Orchid," Angelo ordered.

Orchid turned over his arm and showed Agent Canter a long scar that started just below his wrist and stopped just above his elbow.

"I was working my territory when I noticed this guy walking the street. I've seen him before. He picks up used rubbers. Just thought he had a kinky fetish. To each his own you know what I mean? I figured I would see if he wanted a little fun. When I approached him, he went absolutely crazy on me."

"What did he look like?" Agent Canter asked.

"He really wasn't that big. He obviously didn't know who he was messing with. Anyway, out of the blue, he whips out this straight razor and cuts me with it. I grabbed ahold of his hoodie and yanked it off his head. When I did that, I ripped off that church necklace or whatever that is," pointing to the pendant on the table.

"Tell her what he had shoved in his belt," Angelo interrupted.

"A hammer or something. It had a wooden handle. The weird thing was when I yanked down this guy's hoodie, he screamed like a girl."

"What do you mean, he screamed like a girl?" Agent Canter asked.

"Just like I said, he had a real high voice. Like a girl dressed like a man. I should know if you know what I mean. He cussed me out and ran away. Lucky for him, I was going to kick his ass."

"Did he have long hair or short hair?"

"It could have been long, I think. It was dark and hard to tell. It was all tied up on his head like a man bun."

"Man bun?"

"Yeah. It's like a knotted-up ponytail. The lady, if that is what she is, definitely wanted to come across as a dude. I should know… right? Anyway, when Angelo sent the text asking if any of us had seen this cat, I remembered seeing him. I kept that church necklace as a souvenir. Never seen this dude since."

"Thank you, Orchid. This could be very helpful. Could I keep the pendant?"

"Fine with me," Orchid said, then looked at Angelo for approval. He nodded his head then asked Agent Canter if she needed anything else.

Stacey scooped up the pendant and placed it in her side suit pocket. "Nope."

"You can go, Orchid. Go make me some money."

Orchid opened her gold purse and removed her lipstick and facial powder. She flipped opened the mirror and placed a thick layer of red lipstick on both lips checking in the mirror for any smears. After dabbing her face with powder, she stood. Orchid knew all eyes were on her. She loved the attention. Angelo grinned as a man followed her out of the bar.

Chapter 60

Special Agent Gideon walked into her office and placed her brief case next to her desk. Agent Canter and Officer Wells were already there sitting in chairs in front of her desk.

"So, why am I here again on a Sunday morning?" Gideon asked, as she pulled out her overstuffed brown office chair and took a seat.

Stacey handed Gideon the pendant Orchid had given her.

"This might have come from the neck of our serial killer."

Gideon's eyes grew wide as she read the verse on the back of the pendant. "Do tell, Agent Canter," Gideon replied.

"I got this from a pimp who owed me a favor. One of his ladies got into a scuffle with a guy who carried an axe in his belt. She ripped this from his neck in the scuffle. The pendant is from Saint Mary's church."

"An axe?" Gideon asked.

"Yes, I'm heading there this afternoon. I have a meeting with the priest from the parish, Father Jovani. Maybe he can lead me to the person who owns that pendant."

"Definitely a great lead," Gideon said. "Great sleuthing, you two. Keep up the good work and keep me posted."

****

The heavy oak doors of Old Saint Mary's swung open with ease. Stacey immediately smelled incense as she entered the church. It had been eight years since she lost her faith, and she vowed not to return. Images of that day immediately flooded her mind. The casket draped in an American flag. Her mother's tear-soaked eyes. A lone bugle playing taps.

Stacey stopped in front of the crucifix and made the sign of the cross. The entire front pew was empty, and she took a seat by the aisle. She was there for one reason, and it wasn't to cleanse her soul. She had a lead, and she was following up on it. The meeting she had set up with Father Jovani would take place after Mass.

Father Jovani stepped to the altar. His gold and red robe draped over his shoulders and almost touched the floor. Stacey hoped the killer was here. In the midst of all these believers. A devil in disguise.

Stacey purposely sat at the front of the church. She had a perfect view to scrutinize each worshiper as they filed past her one by one to receive their *Holy Communion*, their *Body of Christ*.

Charlotte stood and entered the long line that snaked down the center of the church. Her knees buckled when she noticed Agent Canter sitting in the pew watching every celebrant receive communion. The pounding of her heart matched the pounding in her temples as she moved closer and closer to Agent Canter.

"Keep your shit together," Charlie whispered into Charlotte's head. *"She doesn't know who you are."*

"I can't do this, Charlie. There's a reason she's here. I'm going to run."

"Listen, Charlotte!! If you run, we are dead. Just keep yourself together and play it cool. She has no idea."

Charlotte slowly kept pace with the other celebrants moving step by step towards Father Jovani. Her eyes met Agent Canter's and she quickly looked away. Her stomach was spinning, and her head seemed in a fog as she stood face to face with Father Jovani.

"The body of Christ," Father said, as he held the bread wafer into the air.

Charlotte did not speak. She held out her hands.

"Say it...Say it, Charlie instructed. *"Don't bring attention to yourself!! Say the goddam word!!"*

"Amen," Charlotte said just above a whisper as Father Jovani placed the host into her cupped hands. Charlotte placed the wafer into her mouth and made the sign of the cross and then made her way back to her pew. Agent Canter paid no attention to her as she knelt on the kneeler.

Mass ended, and several members of the congregation filed out of the church. A few, however, stayed to clean and dust the sanctuary and prepare the vessels for the next Mass. Charlotte left the church and waited outside by the aged statue of Mary, whose pale blue garments were faded from the sun.

Charlotte held her hands together in prayer and bowed her head in front of the statue. She didn't care about praying. What she wanted to see was where Stacey went when she came out of church.

Agent Canter walked through the vestibule doors holding a manila envelope under her arm and headed directly to the rectory.

Charlotte watched as Stacey pressed the brass doorbell beside the six-panel door. Father Jovani answered the door wearing his cassock. The long black sleeved garment fit tightly to his body. He was thin with a slight paunch; gray had invaded his temples. His white, stiff collar kept his head upright, his posture slouched a little.

"Father Jovani?" Stacey asked with a slight smile holding up her credentials. "I am Agent Canter. I am the one who called you asking for an appointment. I appreciate you seeing me."

"Yes, yes. Please come in," Father said, motioning with his hands. "I was just making a cup of coffee. Could I interest you in one?"

"That would be wonderful. Triple sugar, triple cream."

"Wow!! A girl after my own heart. Good to know I'm not the only sugar fiend in this congregation."

"I'm not in your congregation. I'm just here to talk to you."

"Please have a seat," he said, pointing to the couch. "I'll grab the coffee and we can talk."

Stacey placed the manila envelope she was holding on a coffee table as she lowered herself to the couch. A Jack Russell puppy bolted from the bedroom and scampered next to her leg. She reached down and petted him. The little pup pushed and wiggled up against her.

"Buddy," Father Jovani said, returning with the coffee and setting the cups on the small table next to the envelope. "Leave her be. Get over here and sit with me in my chair."

Buddy stopped immediately and leaped onto Father Jovani's lap just as he was settling into the chair. "Take it easy, Buddy...I don't want to crush you."

Father Jovani caressed the little pup and got him to calm down in his lap.

"My apologies, Agent Canter. He's just shy of a year old and has not learned proper manners yet. I'm working on it."

Stacey laughed as she lifted the mug and took a drink then set it back on the table. She lifted the envelope and squeezed the brass fasteners, removing the pendant she had received from Orchid. She handed it to Father Jovani.

"What can you tell me about this?"

Father Jovani took the pendant by the leather shoelace and brought it close to his eyes.

"Matthew 13:36-40," he said before flipping it over and seeing that it came from his church.

"What do you need to know?"

"How do you get one of these?" Stacey asked. "Do you have a record of who may have bought this?"

Father Jovani shook his head. "I'm sorry but the church has given out so many of these over the years. We have fundraisers and pendants like this are very popular. There really is no way to know. Why are you asking?"

"We believe this pendant might have belonged to a killer we are trying to apprehend."

Father Jovani blinked his eyes, looking confused.

"You believe a killer had this pendant?"

"It's possible. Did you see the news conference I gave last week about a serial killer? We are asking for the public's help. This was a lead given to me."

Stacey once again reached into the beige envelope and removed 6 photos that were enhanced from the field camera of Dan Carlson. She handed them to Father Jovani.

"I have not shared these photos with the public yet. They were taken at a farm in Oakland County. We believe the person in these could be our killer. Would you take a look and see if this person looks familiar?"

Father Jovani set the pendant on the coffee table and took hold of the photos. Stacey watched as the expression on his faced changed, after pausing on the third picture. His forehead burrowed into ridges as he continued through the stack.

"I know they are a little grainy, but we could not get them any clearer. From the surrounding trees, we guess this person is maybe ...five-six, five-seven and weighs about a 150 pounds or so.

"His head is covered by a hood and his face is blurred," Father Jovani said. "I'm sorry, Agent Canter," handing the photos back to her. "I'm afraid I can't help you. This person doesn't look familiar."

"I understand," Stacey said, taking the photos back and placing them in the envelope. "Can you hand me the pendant."

Father Jovani grasped the pendant from the table and handed it to Stacey. "I wish I could be of more help," he said.

Agent Canter placed the pendant back in the envelope then reached into her side coat pocket and removed a business card.

"If you think of anything or someone comes to mind, could you give me a call?" she said, handing him the card.

Father Jovani took the business card. He glanced at it and sat it on the table next to his cup.

"Of course. I will help in any way I can. But on another note, you never told me what church you belong to."

"That's because I no longer go to church. I don't believe in going to a brick-and-mortar church or belonging to a specific religion. I pray in my own way and that works for me. I'm sure my dad is looking down and not real pleased with me."

Stacey paused for a moment and took another sip of her coffee. She was trying to figure out how she got herself into this awkward moment. She hadn't prepared herself for this.

The years of ministering had made Father Jovani wise. He nodded and didn't press the issue.

"Well… if you ever find yourself looking to join a church…I would love for you to join mine."

"I'll keep that in mind, Father," Stacey said standing from the couch and shaking Father Jovani's hand.

****

Father Jovani couldn't wait for Canter to leave. He pressed his hands together before pacing to the liquor cabinet. He opened the door, and then quickly closed it. No liquor. No good.

Those photos……they weren't clear, yet there was something very familiar about the way the figure on the trail stood. He couldn't be sure. Even if he was sure, he couldn't tell anyone.

Father Jovani stood at a crossroad, and he didn't know which way to go.

****

Officer Wells looked up from his computer as Agent Canter walked into the office carrying a bag and two bottles of spring water from a local deli called 'Lettuce'. She set them on the table where Aleister joined her.

"I'm freaking starved," he said, pulling out a chair and scooting in. "What are we eating?"

"Avocado turkey wraps and kale chips."

"What?"

"An avocado turkey wrap and kale chips. Give it a chance. It is delicious. It was my turn to pick, so I decided to get us something healthy."

Aleister picked up the wrap and studied it.

"Look, Canter. I agreed to eat healthier, but I am suspicious of anything that looks like a vegetable."

"Come on. Try it. I guarantee you'll love it. Besides, I didn't complain when it was your turn to pick, and we ate sliders, French fries, and washed them down with Bud Lights."

"So true," Aleister agreed, tearing the paper from the wrap and taking a big bite. His face lit up.

"This is really good," he said through a full mouth. He then cracked open his water and took a big gulp. After setting it down, he asked, "How was your meeting with the priest?"

Stacey took a bite of her wrap and wiped the corner of her mouth with a napkin. "Not so good," she said, opening her water. "It turns out the church has given out many of those pendants over the years. There's really no record of who got what when. As for the pictures, he said our boy doesn't look familiar."

"Damn, I was so hoping that could lead us somewhere."

Stacey got a peculiar look on her face. She opened her bag of kale chips and ate a couple before continuing.

"There was something with Father Jovani."

"What do you mean?"

"I really can't narrow it down but when I showed him the photos from the Carlson's farm his demeanor changed."

"How so?"

"I got a feeling he wasn't telling me everything. Again, it's just a hunch but something didn't seem right. I'm going to do some more digging with that church."

****

Charlotte lay awake in bed, her eyes wide staring at the nicotine-stained ceiling. Her mind spun to the sound of Pugs on his wheel.

"You gotta do something, Charlotte," Charlie pleaded. "That agent is getting close to Father Jovani. You saw her go into his office."

Spinning, Spinning.

"How many times do I have to tell you, Charlie… he won't go to the police."

Spinning, Spinning.

"Charlotte, how can you be so sure? I know he's not supposed to…but I just don't trust him. He's got to be dealt with!!!"

Spinning, Spinning, Spinning!!!

Charlotte placed both hands over her ears as she closed her eyes and her face contorted.

"Shut up, Charlie!! Just shut up!!," she yelled. "I can't take your nagging anymore. I made up my mind. Nothing is going to happen to Father Jovani. I am going to stay away from church until all this blows over. I want you to stay away, too. Is that clear, Charlie?"

The spinning in Charlotte's head slowed. She closed her eyes and fell asleep.

Chapter 61

Sergeant Tim remained with Borka, as Porsche dropped David at Helga's residence. Their strategy hinged on maintaining the status quo. Bo would continue in his daily routine, while Carly and her mother carried on with their regular lives.

****

Daugherty found himself caught in a whirlwind of conflicting emotions—relief and perplexity intertwined. All his officers emerged clean, unscathed from the scrutiny. Yet, the puzzle lingered, the higher-ups had demonstrated that the leaked information was linked to his division.

Now, he braced himself for the impending barrage of questions, poised at the entrance of a daunting gauntlet.

What was he missing? How could this confidential information come from within his own ranks? The focus now zeroed in on him. Was he a pawn in an elaborate setup?

Maybe there was a Judas that lurked among his ranks? It became evident that someone wanted to bring him down. Stepping into the building and making his way to the interrogation room, his heartbeat raced in tandem with anticipation.

The forthcoming answers to their questions held the potential of landing his ass in Leavenworth, or worse yet, dead. As Daugherty stepped into the room, he discovered himself on the opposing side of the table. A solitary chair awaited him, positioned before three stern-faced men seated behind it. He recognized only one, a Texan, and longtime friend, who he nicknamed, Bronco. Now, it was his moment in the hot seat.

The CIA has its own internal investigative unit called the Office of Inspector General (OIG). The OIG was responsible for conducting investigations and audits within the CIA. They investigate allegations of misconduct, fraud, or other issues involving CIA personnel and operations.

"Please, Officer Daugherty, have a seat," one of the investigators gestured, waving towards the chair before him.

Daugherty pulled out the chair and sat down. He had frequented this room many times, just not on this side of the table. He was well-acquainted with their interrogation tactics; good cop, bad cop, and the sympathetic one in between. Paul was ready for the shit-show to begin.

"Officer Daugherty," the lead investigator asked, as he handed him a picture. "Could you tell us who this woman is?"

Paul looked at the photograph and swallowed hard, determined to keep his composure. The image before him revealed his redheaded mistress. In that moment, the harsh reality crashed into his awareness — he was the focal point of an internal investigation.

Daugherty casually tossed the photograph onto the table, reclining in his chair. He rested his hands behind his head, crossing his ankles with a nonchalant twist.

"Let's cut the crap, Gentlemen. You know who she is and how she's tied to me. Hell, you probably know if she is a natural red-head and what position she likes best. Have you boys been putting cameras in my hotel room?"

Daugherty scrutinized the expressions etched on the faces of his interrogators; not a hint of amusement lingered.

"Paul! For God's sake," Bronco interjected urgently. "You don't want to find yourself in Leavenworth or, God forbid, something worse."

Daugherty acknowledged the gravity of his old friend's words.

"Officer Daugherty," another investigator probed. "Have you been confiding in your friend, Ms. Schafer? Perhaps under the influence of a bit too much bourbon?"

"Kelly Ann? Oh, hell no! Absolutely not," Paul twanged back. "I'm sure you've vetted Kelly, and you know she's clean. Otherwise, she would be here."

"Paul," Bronco stated, "I've known you and Linda Laurice for, what, twenty years? Is someone blackmailing you? Maybe saying they're going to Linda Laurice?"

Daugherty firmly shook his head. "There is no way!" he declared.

"So, Ms. Schafer would never go to your wife?"

"Never."

There was a pause in the room. Awkward glances were exchanged among the men until Bronco continued. He handed Daugherty what looked like a bank statement.

Daugherty leaned forward, retrieving the statement. His brow furrowed in concentration as he scrutinized the sheet, realizing its origin came from his bank.

"Paul," Bronco inquired, "can you elaborate on the source of income of those three deposits? The ones highlighted in yellow…It's nearly fifty grand!"

"I have no fucken idea!" he said. "Someone is trying to set me up!" He handed Bronco back the statement.

"Office Daugherty, an interrogator asserted, "we've traced some of the leaked intelligence, and it originated from your home. Given your bank accounts, it's not looking good."

A look of shock swept across Daugherty's face. "I've got a lot of enemies. It could be any one of them."

"Paul," Bronco declared with a serious yet sympathetic tone, "you are hereby on notice that you are under investigation. As of now, you are to cease your duties until further notice."

Daughtery sprang from his chair, the sudden movement causing it to tumble to the ground.

"Paul! Take it easy," Bronco said, attempting to calm him. "We're just following protocol."

Daugherty reached on his side and removed his clip-on holster along with his pistol and placed it on the table. He reclaimed his fallen chair and seated himself.

"So, what now, Gentlemen?" he asked.

"Paul," Bronco implored, "go home to Linda Laurice and your kid. Think about how you are going to explain this. You know how this works, there's no way to contain rumors."

****

On his journey home, Daugherty took the scenic route, contemplating the best way to confront Linda Laurice. The undeniable evidence pointed to the fact that sensitive information was both originating and leaking from within the confines of his own home.

A more thorough investigation by the OIG would undoubtedly reveal more information leading straight to him. Linda Laurice had the training, the access, and was the only person in the world who could have pulled this off.

Paul understood the root cause, his infidelity. It was the powerful force that drove individuals to actions they never thought themselves capable of. Linda Laurice, once a devoted wife and exemplary mother, now faced the grim prospect of serving time in a federal prison. Her desire to destroy him, made her do the unthinkable, leak sensitive material and pin it on him.

Daugherty couldn't let that happen to the mother of his child. As he sat high upon the bluff in Northern Oakland, County, he made his decision. He hoped his friend, Bronco would close the investigation, once he was gone, allowing Linda Laurice to retain her survivor benefits. "Dead Man's Curve" as the locals called it, was an eighth of a mile up. Through the years, that stretch of road had claimed numerous lives, and the next victim in its tragic narrative would be CIA Officer Paul Ramon Daugherty.

Chapter 62

It had been several days since Father Jovani had last seen Charlotte and he was getting concerned. This was not like her. She was always at church at least every other day.

Father Jovani scanned the church directory and found Charlotte's address. It was not the first time he made a house call. He had done plenty over the years. He knew she lived with her grandparents in a suburb north of Detroit. It was a forty-five-minute ride by bus and a ten-minute walk from where he would be dropped off.

****

People stood from benches and gathered in a makeshift line as the bus squeaked and squealed to a stop. The accordion door swung open and Father Jovani, along with the other riders, shuffled onto the bus and found a seat. As the airbrakes released and the bus began to move, he closed his eyes and went over his plan one more time. He had made house calls before, mainly to administer communion to the elderly and attend to the sick. The seminary hadn't prepared him for this house call, nevertheless, it had to be done.

As he disembarked from the bus, a subtle wave of acknowledgment rippled through the crowd, drawn to the crisp white collar of his shirt. With a nod, he acknowledged their silent greetings, knowing it would be another ten to fifteen minutes before he reached Charlotte's neighborhood.

Father Jovani read the addresses as he walked on the sidewalk. He came to a stop when he found what must be Charlotte's home. There was no address anywhere to be found.

The house, much older than the others on the block, did not fit the newer styles of housing in the subdivision. Father Jovani figured it might have been the original farmhouse before the land was sold and subdivided.

The grass lay untended, while the maple trees lining the boulevard had grown unruly, their roots buckling the sidewalk. Grass had grown through the pavers leading to the house and Father Jovani was careful not to trip on the uneven bricks. As he made his way to the front door, he noticed someone looking out an upper window and quickly disappearing behind a curtain.

****

Father Jovani stepped onto the porch and pressed the doorbell. Not hearing a ring, he knocked. He stood waiting, waiting for what seemed like an eternity. He knocked again, this time with more force.

"I'm coming," shouted a voice from the other side of the door.

"Hold your goddam horses. I can only move so fast."

The door squeaked open a crack and two brown eyes under bushy eyebrows peered out. An older man with gray whiskers and long braids looked suspiciously at Father Jovani.

"Good afternoon," Father Jovani said. "Is there any chance I could speak to Charlotte?" He paused. "I'm Father Jovani, the priest at Saint Mary's."

"I know who you are," the old man said, as he tied his terry cloth robe covering faded, blue sweatpants and stained wife beater T-shirt. "When I saw you were a priest, I figured you were the one she talks about." The old man turned and walked away, with Father Jovani in tow.

"Charlotte speaks quite highly of you. Sorry for swearing. Thought you might be a salesman. Do you get those salesmen coming to the church? Trying to sell you magazines and such. Damn nuisances they are!"

"Not really," Father Jovani answered, following close behind him.

"Come have a seat," he said, pointing to the sofa in the living room. "I'll go get Charlie."

"Charlie???" Father Jovani asked surprised. "Your grandson?"

Charlotte's grandfather stopped. Father Jovani noticed a peculiar look on his face. He gave a half grin.

"Just our little nickname for Charlotte."

He then turned and shuffled away.

In the bedroom, Charlie had faded away and Charlotte frantically started ripping off her clothes. She threw her ballcap to the ground and undid her bun before shaking her head and letting her hair fall loosely to her shoulders. She pulled the hoodie over her head and tossed it to the bed. Her faded pair of jeans followed.

Charlotte grabbed a summer dress from her closet and slipped it on. She ran to the bathroom and applied some lipstick, before brushing her hair. She heard her grandfather calling from the bottom of the stairs.

"Charlotte, you have a visitor."

"I hear you, Grandpa. I'll be down in a minute."

"That priest friend of yours is here."

"I know. Saw him from the window," she answered. "Let him know I will be down in a minute."

Charlotte paused giving herself one more look in the mirror. She took a deep breath and headed down the stairs. As she walked into the living room, Father Jovani stood.

"What a nice surprise," Charlotte said with a bright face. "I didn't know you knew where I lived."

"I had an idea but to be honest with you, I used Google maps. I love that app. For someone like me that is directionally impaired, it's a life saver."

"Please sit down. Can I get you something to drink?"

"No. I won't take much of your time. I haven't seen you for a couple of weeks and I wanted to make sure you were okay."

"I'm fine. I was exposed to someone that might have had Covid. I took the rapid test, and it came back negative. I'm staying away just to be safe."

Father Jovani nodded his approval. "Some bad stuff that Covid is. Glad you tested negative. On a different note, I was wondering if you would like to help run the fall fundraiser. I have been meaning to ask you, but I haven't seen you lately."

"I would be more than happy to work on a committee if that helps," she answered. "I can't do a lot because I am starting a new job," Charlotte lied.

Father Jovani paused for a moment. Lines formed in his forehead, and he pushed his glasses closer to the bridge of his nose. Thank you. I'll keep that in mind. Where's the new job?"

Charlotte hesitated. "Umm…Amazon. They're always looking for drivers or warehouse people. They have great benefits."

"That's what I heard."

An awkward silence filled the room before Father Jovani continued.

"There's another reason I came here today," Father Jovani said. "I had a visit from an FBI agent. She is investigating the serial killer we've all been hearing about on the news.

"She showed me some pictures of a suspect. Taken in a woody area by a trail cam she said. The pictures were grainy, but I could still see a likeness to you. Is it possible this could be your brother?"

The old man crept up from behind. He had been listening to the conversation.

Charlotte looked distant, unresponsive. She had sunk into herself. It was if the lighting in the room had changed. Father Jovani noticed dark circles form under Charlotte's eyes and the color left her face.

"I really wish you hadn't seen those pictures," she said, her voice detached and emotionless. "It's going to make it very difficult now."

With one powerful blow from Grandpa's cane, Father Jovani was knocked out cold.

****

Father Jovani heard the squeak of the steps and noticed the sliver of light that appeared from the bottom of the door. He waited as the shadow appeared from the other side. He never knew if it would be Charlotte or Charlie.

He had come to know both over the past week. The room was dark, and the only sound that could be heard was the metal clink of the chains that bound him.

The back of his head still ached but the white gauze had far less blood than the days before. He lifted the arm of the recliner and sat up. His stomach ached; he was hoping whoever was on the other side of the door brought him something to eat.

Charlotte balanced the breakfast tray with one hand and picked up the keys sitting on the orange five-gallon bucket next to the door. As she entered and flipped on the light, Father Jovani squinted, temporarily blinded from the bright, ambient light. He lifted his hand to shield his eyes and was relieved to see that it was Charlotte.

"Charlotte," he said in a low whisper. "Thank God, it's you."

"I brought you something to eat," she said. "I also want to change the dressing on your head."

"Is it morning?" Father Jovani asked. "Did you bring what we discussed."

Charlotte set the tray on his lap, then took the key from her robe and unlocked the chains that bound his hands. She removed an old *Timex* watch from her wrist and handed it to him. He stretched the band over his left hand, then tore off a piece of bread and jammed it into his mouth.

"I can't tell you how terrible it is when you lose all track of time," he mumbled as he chewed his food and swallowed a sip of his coffee.

"I'm sure it is. Just don't let Charlie know I gave that to you."

Charlotte walked to a far dresser in the corner of the room. She pulled open a drawer and removed white gauze, rubbing alcohol, adhesive tape, and scissors. She placed the scissors in her side robe pocket and carried the rest of the items, placing them on a small table next to the recliner. This was not the first time Charlotte had cleaned the wound.

Charlotte cut a strip of gauze and dropped the scissors back into her robe. She lifted the rubbing alcohol and soaked it.

"This is looking much better," Charlotte said as she removed the blood-stained gauze.

Father Jovani winced as Charlotte dabbed the gash with rubbing alcohol.

"Your grandfather still has a hell of a punch. What did he hit me with?"

"His walking cane."

Abruptly Father Jovani threw his hot coffee over the back of his head and into the face of Charlotte. Before she could react, he reached back and grabbed a fist of hair and brought her head to his shoulder. With his free hand he took hold and flipped her, landing Charlotte in his lap and sending the tray flying. The two wrestled to the floor. Father Jovani was frantically trying to get at the scissors in her pocket. Charlotte was kicking and screaming and soon the voice of Charlie emerged. "I'm going to kill you, Mother Fucker!"

Father Jovani ground the ridges of his Timex onto the bridge of Charlotte's nose. Blood began to run, and Charlotte took both hands trying to push him away. The scissors slipped from her robe, and he grabbed them. Lifting his hand above his head he drove them into the side of her neck. Charlotte let out a scream and her body became limp.

Father Jovani's eyes shot open, and he sat up from his recliner. The links of the metal chains that bound him brought him back to reality.

Chapter 63

Porsche, wearing her mask, stepped into the dimly lit room, balancing two Subway sandwiches and drinks with one hand. Sergeant Tim, also masked, rose from his chair. Porsche placed the sandwiches and drinks on the table. Her attention shifted to Borka.

She handed him a drink and sandwich from the table. Borka took the food with trepidation. The memory of his torture still fresh in his mind. He peeled back the Subway paper and took a huge bite. A pronounced exhale escaped him as he then raised the cup, savoring a long sip through the straw. The fizz of his cola offered a fleeting escape from the haunting memories that clung to his consciousness.

Gripping his sandwich and drink, Sergeant Tim strode into the adjacent room, followed by Porsche. As she closed the door, she unmasked herself, Tim followed suit.

"Man, I'm starved," he said, quickly taking a large bite of his sandwich.

"You know," Porsche said. "Something just doesn't seem to add up about the Slovak information,"

"What are you getting at?"

"The Chief told us the news of Slovak's death came straight from Daugherty. Now we know that was a lie."

Porsche unholstered her pistol, the metallic click echoing as she and Sergeant Tim tensed upon hearing the deadbolt of the door turning. Relief washed over them as Carly walked through the door, lessening the tension that had momentarily gripped them.

"Carly," Porsche said, holstering her firearm. "What are you doing here?"

"I just got off the phone with Stacey…Daugherty's dead."

"Dead!" both reacted in unison.

"He was killed in a car accident. I don't have any more details than that. And I still haven't mentioned Slovak to her yet."

"That's just crazy," Porsche remarked. "Are they sure it was an accident and not sabotage or something."

"That's all I was told. Stacey promised to keep me posted if anything further develops."

Carly's attention left Porsche and went to Tim. "Where's he at?"

"Back room," Tim answered, handing Carly a mask.

Entering the rear room, the trio proceeded further. Seeing an additional masked figure come into the room, Borka's anticipation surged, his heart quickened. Carly's attention was drawn to a band-aid concealing a notably swollen pinky finger.

"This is how this is going to work," Porsche asserted with authority. "You're going to text your partner Grego."

"And tell him what?" Borka inquired, hesitantly.

"The Blind Pig. Do you two frequent that often?"

"Not often. We've only been in Dusseldorf for a few days," Borka said.

"So, it wouldn't raise any red flags if you were to request a rendezvous later on this afternoon?"

Borka shook his head. "I don't think so."

Porsche turned towards Carly and Tim, gesturing for them to follow. They entered the adjacent room and swiftly removed their sweaty masks. Porsche took charge, saying, "Let's get everyone staged. We'll execute the same type of abduction. We'll bring him here, to be with this scumbag."

****

As the hours ticked by without a single word from Daugherty, Slovak's unease deepened. The silence fueled his concern, compelling him to take matters into his own hands. Drawing on his network of sources, outside the grasp of *Kolo's* influence, Slovak uncovered the disconcerting truth – a leading figure in American counterintelligence had met an untimely death.

In the absence of Daugherty, the threat of *Kolo* discovering his continued existence vanished. A sense of relief washed over him, presenting a newfound opportunity for a fresh start. Yet, there were lingering matters to attend to – pressing issues that required swift resolution. Slovak needed money and he needed it fast. A wry smile played across his face as he discerned just where he could get it. The prospect of a fresh beginning and the means to address his immediate concerns ignited a renewed sense of determination.

****

Grego opened the door to his hotel room and was surprised to see Slovak standing there. He allowed him to enter without hesitation.

"Your nephew is not here," Grego informed him.

"Any idea when he'll be back?" Slovak inquired, his eyes surveying the room in search of the briefcase containing the twenty grand.

Grego maintained, "You never know with your nephew. If he finds himself a piece of ass, he could be gone for hours."

Slovak chuckled, "Oh, to be young again. Have you any more information that might prove useful for me?"

"I have not, and that's unusual. I usually get an info dump by twelve noon, German time. Nothing came today."

Slovak's eyes caught the briefcase, tucked between the wall and bed. Simultaneously, he observed a shift in Grego's demeanor, a subtle change that did not escape his notice. Adding to the tension, both of them became aware of Grego's gun, resting on the nightstand. The room hung in a charged silence, until Grego lunged for the gun!

He was no match for Slovak.

The two wrestled until Slovak gained the upper hand. He grabbed the gun and delivered a blow, pistol-whipping the old man until he slumped into unconsciousness. Slovak placed his hands around Grego's neck, squeezing it in a frenzy, until Grego moved no longer. He lifted himself, and straightened his clothes, before grabbing the briefcase, leaving Grego bleeding out from his head wounds.

****

Emilia Klein, Borka's lady friend, hesitated at the hotel door, noticing it was slightly ajar. As she pushed it open, the shocking reality of the scene unfolded before her. Blood was splattered across the walls, and an elderly man lay lifeless, his head resting in a pool of red.

In her frantic escape from the scene, Emilia grappled with the decision to involve the authorities. Aware of the way they scrutinized her, she feared potential harassment and even the possibility of being implicated. Nevertheless, she steeled herself, reaching into her coat to dial the police.

Earlier in the day, Borka sent the text, persuading Grego to meet him at The Blind Pig by 6:00 pm. As David and Bo patiently waited in ambush by the dumpster, their anticipation turned to surprise when the unmistakable blue and red flashers of the authorities suddenly illuminated the area near the hotel. They watched as armed police rushed into the building.

"Could that be something to do with our boy?" Bo asked.

"Wow, I don't know."

"Should I go take a look?"

"I wouldn't if I were you, David suggested. "If Slovak is there, he may recognize you. Plus, you don't speak German. Porsche needs to get over there to listen and learn.

"Good point. I'll text her now," Bo agreed.

Chapter 64

Agent Canter and Officer Wells glanced up from their workstations as Special Agent Gideon walked through the door.

"You got a minute, Canter?"

"Sure do."

Gideon handed Agent Canter an iPad and said, "Take a look at these."

Stacey tapped the thumbnails of various pictures. They were of an apartment or some type of living space. Her gaze then went to Gideon.

"Look familiar?" Gideon asked.

Stacey's forehead creased. "They do, but I can't place it."

"It's that apartment of the priest you interviewed."

"Father Jovani??" Stacey asked.

"Yes. He's been missing for a week. Vanished without a trace. These are the pictures of his apartment that the detectives took. They opened a missing persons case.

"I didn't put it together until I saw it on the news. Detroit PD didn't share it with the Bureau because there is no indication, he crossed state lines."

"That's crazy," Stacey said. "I mean what are the chances. Maybe he just needed a vacation?"

"His secretary called the police last Monday morning when she went to the rectory, and he was gone. I don't know if this has anything to do with our case, but I thought I would let you know."

Stacey walked to Aleister's workstation. She placed the iPad in the middle of it, pulled out a chair and sat next to him.

"I'll leave you two alone to scrutinize those and see if anything comes up," Agent Gideon said walking out the door.

The two hovered over the iPad. Stacey tapped the first thumbnail and the picture enlarged.

"Looks like a picture of his bedroom," Stacey said, then pointed to the open closet. "Let me zoom in on this."

Stacey took her index finger and thumb and enlarged the pic. She then focused on the open closet door.

"Look. There's a suitcase. Can we assume he didn't go on a spur of the moment vacation?"

Aleister nodded. "Maybe, but he may have more than one suitcase. I'm sure with all his duties he would have told his secretary if he was planning a trip.

Didn't you tell me during your interview his demeanor changed once you showed him the pictures from the Carlson farm?"

"Yeah. I did. I felt once he looked at those pictures, he knew more than he was saying. It was kinda strange. His body language definitely changed. He seemed a little nervous and tried to change the subject."

Stacey closed the thumbnail and tapped another. It was a picture of the refrigerator. Milk, eggs, and orange juice were next to an open container of mini-Cokes. Five Bud Lights were pushed into a far corner sitting next to a bottle of Riesling. What looked like dinner from the evening before was covered in plastic wrap. Besides various condiments, nothing much more was in the fridge.

"I think if he was planning a trip for a week or so he wouldn't have saved leftovers from dinner. He probably would have tossed them out."

Stacey nodded and closed the thumbnail, opening another. The shot was of the front room where she and Father Jovani had their discussion about the pendent and the Carlson photos.

"This is where we talked… me and Father Jovani," Stacey said. Moving around the room. "There's a coffee table with some books and a pen. Looks like a wordsearch."

"What's that in the corner?" Aleister asked as he pointed to the screen.

"I think it's a water and food dish for a dog," Stacey said as the corner of the room came into focus. "Yep, that's what it is. I do remember him having a dog. It was a cute little thing. Sat right next to him on the couch when we were talking."

"No food or water. The bowls are empty," Aleister said. "If the priest was going on some kind of vacation surely, he would get someone to come and feed the dog. I wonder if the dog was there when the police arrived."

"I'm going to get in touch with the lead detective on this and see if they have anything. Did Gideon give us a name?"

"Not that I know of," Aleister said leaning back in his chair.

Stacey pushed herself away from the table and stood. "I'm going to get a name and contact info from Gideon."

****

Charlie had convinced Charlotte that it would only be a matter of time before that Agent Canter would come poking around. He had agreed not to kill Father Jovani right away if she would agree to let Charlie handle things as he saw fit.

"Why are you so paranoid?" Charlotte asked Charlie.

"Because that agent in the news briefs was at St. Mary's."

"Maybe it was just a coincidence…Maybe she just wanted to join the church."

"Oh, bullshit, Charlotte!!" Charlie snapped. "With all the churches in the area, you just think she wanted to join St. Mary's."

"Stop swearing!!" Charlotte retorted. "You promised the family you'd watch your language around us."

"Whatever," Charlie said rolling his eyes.

Charlie walked to Pug's terrarium and tapped on the glass wall with his index finger. Pugs lifted his head and sniffed the air, thinking food was on the way. Charlie scooped him up and sat down in the folding chair sitting next to the terrarium. He brought the rodent to eye level.

"What do you think, Pal?" Charlie asked.

Pug's thoughts entered Charlie's mind. "I think the Jazzman should ax the son of a bitch!"

"Me, too. But Charlotte won't hear of it. At least not yet."

"Fuck her," Pugs snapped. "Who's the boss? You or your punk-ass sister."

Charlie began to squeeze Pugs; the rodent began to squirm.

"I told you don't talk about her like that. She's my sister and we have been through a lot together."

"Fine," Pugs said into Charlie's mind. "Could you loosen your grip? Don't want to bite you again."

Charlie loosened his grip and Pugs relaxed.

"I'm worried that agent is going to come snooping around. I told Charlotte that."

"Then you need some sort of distraction. Something that throws suspicion off Charlotte and on to someone else."

"Like what?"

"I don't know…You're the Jazzman…You're brilliant…You'll figure it out."

Charlie lowered Pugs onto his lap and stroked him gently. He stared into space until a thought crossed his mind. He smiled slightly as he kissed Pugs on the nose and dropped him back into his glass prison.

"Thanks for the advice, Pal. It's time for the Jazzman to get creative."

****

Judith pulled into the lot of Old Saint Mary's and parked. She sat there, engine idling, staring at her Saint Christopher medal hanging from the rearview mirror.

Where are you, Lorenzo???

Judith loved her parking spot. She was flabbergasted when unbeknownst to her, Father Jovani had it painted…RECTORY SECRETARY PARKING ONLY. She felt special and she owed it all to him. Since his disappearance, Judith struggled with her mornings.

No longer were there butterflies every time she walked down the hall to his apartment. She missed him. She missed Buddy's yapping at the door when she would greet him. But, most of all, she missed Father's Jovani's warm touch.

Judith pushed the button to her Buick Regal and the engine quieted. She preferred keys, but the newer models did not have them. She grabbed the canvas tote bag that had both her purse and sack lunch. She inhaled deeply and exhaled slowly, then opened the door and started her day.

****

Agent Canter heard the snapping of the flags and looked up as she walked past the cluster of flagpoles on her way to the Detroit Public Safety Headquarters. It was a huge building that housed both Detroit PD and the fire department. This was not her first time in the complex. She showed her ID and confirmed her appointment before heading to the large lobby sign.

Detective William Hearst. Fourth floor Suite G, she read, before heading for the elevator. This was the contact, given to her from Gideon.

Detective Hearst looked up from his desk as Agent Canter knocked on his door. A small smile played on his lips as he rose from his chair to welcome her.

"Agent Canter, I presume?" he greeted, extending his hand for a shake. "Please, have a seat," he gestured toward a chair positioned in front of his desk.

Stacey lowered into the chair and waited for Hearst to seat himself behind the desk. He placed his hands on top of his desk, interlocking his fingers. "I'm all yours," he said.

"I'm investigating a serial killer case. Are you aware?"

"Oh, yes. I've seen you on TV."

"There seems to be a potential connection with a missing person case you're involved in – Father Jovani. Agent Gideon said you received a strange phone call."

Nodding, Hearst began. "I got this phone call and when I answered it, this female voice said, and I quote 'When it comes to Father Jovani… The secretary knows more than she is letting on.'"

"The *secretary?*" Agent Canter asked, a little surprised. "Did you trace the call?"

"No. Whoever made that call used a burner phone with a blocked number. The secretary's name is Judith Kratz. She was the one who first noticed Father Jovani missing. She called us and that's how the investigation started. I don't have much more than that. It looks like the guy fell off the face of the earth. Maybe you want to have a talk with the secretary."

"She's a little bit of an odd duck. I interviewed her when we first opened the investigation. Maybe you could follow up especially since we got that phone call. Not sure it will lead to anything but it's worth following up."

"You don't know how much I appreciate the lead," Canter said, before standing. "It might not be anything, but it's worth a shot. I'm sure Agent Gideon will keep you posted with any further developments."

"I'm sure she will," Hearst said, as he stood and walked Agent Canter out the door.

Chapter 65

Sergeant Tim and Porsche occupied the neighboring room within the confines of the black site. They engaged in a hushed conversation.

"I'm almost positive the dead person is Borka's partner," Porsche shared. "At least that's what I could tell. The cops were pretty much tight lipped about it."

"That would explain, why he never left for the rendezvous at The Blind Pig."

"Exactly," Porsche agreed.

"Maybe we can leverage him to get to Slovak?" Tim suggested.

"We'll find out. Let's go talk to our boy," Porsche said, donning her mask over her face.

Borka straightened his back as the two entered the room. His blood pressure surged, and his heart palpitations quickened, as he watched Porsche remove the wire-cutting-pilers from her jacket pocket, placing them on the nightstand.

"Your colleague, Mr. Szabo, is dead at the hands of your uncle. If you don't want the same fate, you're going to help us," Porsche said, her voice, cold, death-like.

"Grego?" Borka questioned. "Why would my uncle kill him? He was his source."

"That's what you are gonna tell me," Porsche said. "If not, your uncle can kiss your ass goodbye, as well."

Borka huffed, suppressing a half-hearted chuckle before saying, "You might as well kill me now. My uncle doesn't give a rat's ass what happens to me."

A heavy silence fell over the room. Porsche slowly crept to the nightstand and picked up the pliers. She placed her free hand atop Borka's and raised the pliers into the air.

"Have you forgotten my warning? For every falsehood you say, you sacrifice a nail." Porshe lowered the pliers and seized hold of a nail. Borka pleaded one more time.

"For the love of God! I am not lying! I thought he was dead!"

"What do you mean, you thought he was dead"? Porsche asked firmly.

"Word had spread within our organization that he died of Covid. When he showed up, I was as surprised as anyone."

Porsche stopped, motioned with a nod for Tim to join her in the adjoining room. She tossed the pliers on the nightstand and left. Borka let out a long exhale and slumped back into his chair.

Tim and Porsche entered the room, shedding their masks and tossing them onto an empty chair. Porsche shut the door, then turned to Tim.

"I think the dumb son of a bitch is telling the truth."

Tim nodded, "I'm getting that feeling too."

"It's gotta be the CIA. Who else has the ability to go to this extreme to fake someone's death?"

"But why?" Tim asked.

"I don't know. They must have needed him for something. That's how they work."

"So, what's next?"

"Slovak must feel like he's invisible," Porsche said. "Everyone thinks he's dead. Why don't you head back to your hotel. I'll get back in touch with you there."

"What about him?" Tim questioned, motioning with a nod to Borka.

"I'll handle it. No need for you to come back."

As Sergeant Tim departed, he understood exactly what Porsche was about to do. He had done it in Iraq when loose ends needed to be tied up. He never delegated that to anyone. Porsche walked to her backpack resting on a chair and removed a thin ply garbage bag, along with plastic zip ties. She wasn't wearing her mask when she walked back into the room.

****

David and Carly found themselves isolated in the quiet confines of the Dusseldorf apartment. The revelation of Slovak's survival and continued presence prompted a strategic decision.

They needed to separate. Bo and Mrs. Fletcher would seek refuge at Helga's residence. Sergeant Tim would remain solo, staying at the hotel he had checked into.

Meanwhile, Porsche would continue to live with her grandparents. There could be no red flags. At this point Slovak was unaware they were on to him. As far as the four of them were concerned, they held the upper hand.

Carly placed the cup of coffee on the table beside David before settling onto the couch beside him, cradling her own cup in her hands.

"The silver lining with all this, is the chance for me to finally get my revenge," Carly spat out to David. "He may be alive, but it won't be for long!"

"I understand why you want revenge, Carly, but it doesn't always bring closure. I learned that the hard way myself, with what I did to those boys. It didn't ease the pain of losing Penny."

An odd look washed across Carly's face. "You don't think Slovak should live, do ya!?"

"Oh, hell no!" David emphasized. "He's got to be dealt with permanently, or you will never be safe. It's personal to him now."

David set his coffee mug on the table and did the same with Carly's before grasping her hands. He looked deep into her eyes.

"This is personal for me too, Carly. As long as I can take a breath, I will never let anything happen to you."

Carly leaned in, her lips meeting David's in a tender kiss. Their kiss lingered, a silent agreement passing between them as they savored the warmth of each other's presence, reluctant to part.

"I had a talk with Bo," Carly confided, as she gently pulled away. "He has feelings for Helga. It's as though they're fighting their own *Slovak* called addiction. We decided he should pursue those feelings."

"Does that mean... um, does that mean a possibility between you and me?"

David's words hung in the air as Carly stood up from the couch, alerted by the oven timer's shrill beep.

"I tossed in a couple frozen dinners," she said, walking toward the kitchen. "You haven't eaten all day."

"Thanks," David muttered, his response laden with unspoken implications.

****

Seated in the opulent five-star restaurant, Slovak savored each sip of his cocktail, a smug satisfaction settling over him. As he pondered his next move, thoughts swirled about where he might establish his new base once his current task was completed.

Aware of the dwindling twenty grand he had stolen from Grego, he recognized the urgency of securing an income, particularly given his plan for an extravagant lifestyle.

The notion of seeking employment with another organization briefly crossed his mind, only to be dismissed. Slovak understood all too well the swift dissemination of information among underworld circles.

Any association with a rival outfit would inevitably lead to *Kolo's* discovery that he was alive, prompting a vengeful, retaliatory death. Absolutely not. He refused to let that scenario unfold. His intention was clear. Conclude his dealings with Carly, then disappear without leaving any evidence behind.

Chapter 66

The light in the room flicked on and Father Jovani jumped. As his eyes adjusted, his heart leapt. Standing in front of him wearing jeans, tennis shoes, and a hoodie was Charlie. On his side, a hand axe hung from his belt. On a paper plate, he had a bologna sandwich with mustard, a handful of chips and a yellow one-inch tin container with a half dozen baby aspirins in it. He handed the plate to Father Jovani, then removed a Pepsi from his middle hoodie pocket.

"Charlotte wanted me to give this to you."

Father Jovani said nothing as he brought his shackled hands to his mouth and took a bite of his sandwich, then washed it down with Pepsi.

Charlie walked to the corner of the room and grabbed a folding chair that was leaning against the wall. He took it back to the recliner, unfolded it, then sat just far enough out of Father Jovani's reach. He stared at him, his eyes shark-like.

"What am I going to do with you?" Charlie said, his voice low and menacing.

Father's gaze never left Charlie. He couldn't help but notice an uncanny likeness to Charlotte.

"So, I finally get to meet you. I didn't realize you and Charlotte were twins."

"We are much more than twins."

The sleeves of Charlie's hoodie were pulled up to his forearms. Father Jovani noticed the scar across Charlie's left wrist. It was the same scar he and Charlotte had many conversations about.

Father Jovani took a hand full of chips and shoved them into his mouth. He wasn't sure how to proceed. He had ministered individuals who had different personality states. Certain abrupt and unexpected triggers set them off and they became violent. He knew he had to remain calm and act nonchalant. Anxiety by either party was a known trigger.

"Is Charlotte okay? Any chance I can speak with her?"

"That's why I'm here. I want to lay down some ground rules. If I had my way, I would treat you like those other bitches and given you the axe a long time ago. Charlotte won't let me. She's the one keeping you alive."

The revelation of Charlie being the axe killer tied his stomach in knots, and his heart quaked. He snapped open the tin container and removed a baby aspirin, swallowing it with a sip of his Pepsi, aware of his sweaty palms.

"I see you went through my pockets and found my aspirin. Had a couple of stents put in last year and the doc said take one a day to keep the blood flowing. Tell your big sister I appreciate it."

"Little sister," Charlie snapped. "She's my little sister and I have taken care of her my entire life."

"Yes, little sister. Sorry," Father Jovani quickly recovered. "I'm glad you're listening to your little sister."

He lifted his hand and touched the wound at the back of his head. His temples throbbed.

"I take it that your grandfather is the one who did this to me."

"Yep. He's whipped my ass more than once with that cane. You went down with one crack."

"How'd I get here? Am I in a basement?"

"Me and Charlotte dragged your ass down. Or should I say we rolled you down."

"I see," Father Jovani said, as his jaw muscles strained to keep him from grinding his teeth. "What are the ground rules?"

"First. Don't play with Charlotte's emotions. If you try to get her to help you, I will find out. I find out everything eventually."

"I can live with that."

Charlie smiled. "Did you say that on purpose, or did it just come out that way?"

"On purpose, Charlie. I'm known for being witty. I'll do whatever you and your little sister want me to do. I'm prepared to meet the Lord, but not just yet. Can we talk about you? I heard a lot about you from Charlotte," he said, hiding any deception in his voice.

"Shut up, Priest! I'm tired of your babbling! Why the hell would I want to talk to you?!!"

"Because you're a celebrity, Charlie," Father Jovani quickly answered. "You are *The Jazzman*. Isn't that what the authorities are calling you? The Jazzman."

Charlie fought a smile. He was pleased that Father Jovani knew of him.

"Have you documented your journey?" Father Jovani asked. "People want to know what makes you tick. Just like *Jack the Ripper* or *Son of Sam*. People are fascinated with you. They want to read about what made you do it.

"I can help you with that. I'm not only a priest, but I am also a writer. It's a hobby of mine that I have been doing for years. Some people say I am pretty good."

Father Jovani's pulse was racing as he was thinking of anything that could buy him some time. He breathed slowly, waiting for Charlie's reaction.

Charlie stood up from the chair, folded it, and placed it back into the corner. He returned and removed a key from his jean pocket and unlocked the leg shackles bolted to the floor. He pulled out his axe and stepped back.

"Go use the bathroom," he said, motioning with his axe to the far side of the basement. "If you try anything, Charlotte will understand why I did what I had to do."

Father Jovani stood up from the recliner and stretched his arms.

"Thank you, Charlie," he said. "Think about your legacy. I can help you with that."

Charlie motioned with the axe and Father Jovani turned and walked toward the bathroom. He stopped midstride when he heard Charlie say, "I'll think about it."

Father Jovani smiled slightly and kept walking.

****

Agent Canter stepped into the rectory office of Old Saint Mary's Catholic Church, greeted by the sight of a woman peering up from her desk who appeared to be in her mid-forties.

"May I help you?" she said pleasantly.

"Hi, yes. I am Agent Canter with the FBI. Could I speak to a Judith Kratz?"

A concerned look crossed over the woman's face.

"I'm Judith."

"Is there somewhere where we can talk? I just have a few questions."

"Is this about Father Jovani?" Judith asked, rising from her chair.

"It is," Agent Canter said.

Judith guided Agent Canter to a modest office, where they settled into chairs positioned opposite each other.

"I've already provided the police with all the information I have," Judith stated firmly.

"I am aware that you spoke with the police. But I was wondering, is there any new information you may have learned as to his whereabouts?"

"No." Judith said hesitantly.

"You sure?" Stacey asked again.

"I'm sure."

"You know Detective Hearst?"

"I do. He's the lead detective trying to find Father Jovani."

"Yes. That's right. I am just going to cut to the chase. Detective Hearst received an anonymous phone call a couple of days ago. A female left a message that said, and I quote, 'When it comes to Father Jovani, the secretary knows more than she is letting on.'"

Judith began to rub her neck as the expression on her face changed. "There must be some mistake."

"Are you sure, Judith?" Agent Canter pressed. "If you are purposely withholding information, you could be charged with obstructing an investigation."

Judith squirmed in her seat and fidgeted with her skirt.

"I need some water. Can I get you some water?"

"I'm fine," Agent Canter calmly said. "Come clean with me, Ms. Kratz."

Judith took a deep breath and exhaled slowly.

"I'll be right back," she said standing up from her chair and walking out of the door to the office across the hall.

Agent Canter watched as Judith walked to a desk. She bent down and opened the lower file drawer and lifted out her purse. She returned and sat back down setting the purse in the middle of her lap. Judith reached in and handed Agent Canter a letter.

"I got this two days ago addressed to me in the parish mail."

Stacey looked at Judith, waiting to hear what the letter had to do with the case.

"I hoped I never would have to tell the police about this," Judith began, "but it appears I now have no choice.

"Father Jovani and I met ten years ago at the *Cathedral Church of St Paul*. It just happened to the two of us."

"What do you mean it just happened?" Canter asked.

"The two of us. We fell in love. I followed him here and became the church secretary. We would work late hours and have dinner together. Lorenzo is an amazing cook. Neither of us had children and Lorenzo's family is in Minnesota. We bonded. We were trying to find a way to see if we could marry. Looks like he got cold feet. I mean this came out of nowhere. I wish he would have talked with me. This makes no sense."

Stacey opened the letter.

Dear Judith,

I wish I had a better way to say this. I have much to tell you and I feel this is the best way to share my feelings. First and foremost, I do love you. I love you more than you could ever know. This love I have for you is equal to the love I have for the church and the Holy Father.

The last few years I have spent with you have been the happiest times of my life. You have been there for me. You have been my sounding board and confidant when it came to my questioning some of the teachings of the church. Most of all, you have been there through my dark periods with PTSD. Surprising me with Buddy as my comfort dog was the sweetest thing anyone could have done.

My years in the Army were both wonderful and tragic. I felt so good doing the Lord's work, ministering to the troops during their time of need. I thought I would be a lifer and then I got wounded and everything changed. I questioned my resolve, and I questioned God.

You got me through it all and I will never forget that. This letter is not intended to end things. I have a lot on my mind, and I needed some time away. I need time away from the church and the responsibilities that go along with it. Please understand that this has nothing to do with you. It has everything to do with me.

God Bless.

Love, Lorenzo

Stacey looked from the letter at Judith. She noticed her eyes had reddened, and she was struggling to hold back tears.

"I'm sorry, but I am going to have to give this letter to Detective Hearst."

"Go ahead," Judith said. "If it helps find Lorenzo, that will be all the better."

Agent Canter placed her hand on Judith's shoulder.

"At least you know he's all right. It sounds like he just needs some time away to sort his feelings out. I hope it will all work out for you."

Chapter 67

Carly and Bo were well aware of the danger as they drove around the city of Dusseldorf. There was no choice, they had to keep up the appearance that life was getting back to normal, with the fabrication of the demise of Slovak.

Porsche continued to rely on support from her network within the German intelligence agency, though it was constrained by the fact that her contacts held lower-ranking positions. The information they shared was strictly off the books and not officially sanctioned.

Bo unloaded the card tables from the trunk of his car, while Carly and Porsche retrieved her artwork from the back seat. Carly had secured a small spot at the art festival to showcase and sell her pen and ink drawings. Meanwhile, David and Sergeant Tim positioned themselves discreetly nearby, keeping a watchful eye on the art stand.

Slovak traveled the streets with a sense of confidence. Thanks to the CIA, his new identity allowed him pure anonymity to blend in with the international community. He pondered what he would do after he eliminated Carly and anyone who might stand in his way. He envisioned a future where his forged credentials would grant him unrestricted access to any corner of the free world. He followed the waitress to his table on the balcony overlooking Carly's art stand as he eagerly plotted his next move.

****

Before unhooking his seatbelt and maneuvering back onto the winding road, Daughtery composed one last text. It was a heartfelt plea to his wife, Linda Laurice, seeking her forgiveness.

He explained that he knew it was her who leaked the sensitive information and tied it to him. He didn't blame her, he blamed himself and stated that the best way for her life and their child to continue was if he was gone.

He also desperately requested her assistance. Daughtery entrusted Linda Laurice with crucial information about Slovak's whereabouts and the intricate web of deception surrounding his identity. He implored her to relay this information to Sergeant Tim, whose name triggered recognition in Linda Laurice's mind. It was his last-ditch effort at redemption.

Sergeant Tim's attention was drawn to his phone as he heard it chime with a message from an unfamiliar number. Confused, he opened it to find an anonymous sender relaying information that puzzled him. The information provided indicated that Alexsander Slovak had undergone a significant identity overhaul, adopting the persona of the recently deceased Samuel William Bently, an American citizen. All official documents, including passport, social security card, and driver's license bore the new identity.

It was disclosed that Slovak had traveled alongside Carly from the United States to Germany, prompting ongoing surveillance of her ever since. The message concluded with a cryptic directive, offering a web address and password for accessing additional intel. Further details and updates were promised to be disseminated through that channel.

Sergeant Tim summoned the group to Helga's home. He wanted secure internet access and was not sure if Bo and Carley's apartment was compromised. The five sat around Helga's laptop as Tim typed in the web address. He handed Carly his phone so she could read the complex password, making sure to type it correctly. He knew that at many of these clandestine dark sites, you get one shot at entering the password and if incorrect, the site will self-implode.

The room fell into a hushed silence as the screen revealed a layout devoid of any graphics, except for one lone send button. It simply looked like an internal memo brief. Against the dark gray backdrop, the white text stood out in stark contrast. As Tim read the text out loud, the rest of the group followed along silently.

It seemed that Daugherty manipulated Slovak into playing the role of a *Useful Idiot*. While Slovak was under sedation, battling the simulated case of Covid, an Implantable Medical Device (IMD) laced with cyanide was placed into his nasal passage, similar to that of nasal stents. The choice of the nasal cavity as the location for this weapon was strategic due to cyanide's rapid impact on respiratory function, resulting in immediate death.

Daugherty harbored no intentions of allowing Slovak to live once the name of the leaker was divulged. Slovak's fate would be sealed with a mere tap of the send button.

Tim turned to the group. No one spoke a word until he broke the silence.

"What the hell! We're a click away from ending that bastard!"

"Let's do it now," Bo said impatiently.

With casual ease, Carly forwarded the text message with the complex password to her phone, before deleting the text from Tim's phone and handing it back to him.

"I say we wait," Carly proposed as she looked at her watch. "This is something we definitely should discuss with Stacey. It's 9:00 pm here, so it 3:00 am there. Let's wait and go over this with Stacey in the morning tomorrow."

Porsche nodded. "I agree with Carly. Agent Canter isn't even aware that Slovak is still alive. Carly is going to have a hell of a lot of explaining to do."

Carly shook her head slowly. "Won't be the first time," she remarked.

****

Special Agent Gideon strode into the office, drawing the attention of both Stacey and Aleister. She shut the door behind her and gestured for the two to join her at the table.

"You're not going to believe this," Gideon said, as the two sat down and scooted in their chairs. She held the letter from Father Jovani and the letter left by the Jazzman killer. Certain words from both letters were highlighted in yellow.

"I just got this from forensics," Gideon said. "They have a young tech there that just made a name for herself."

Stacey and Aleister brought the letters closer into view. "What are we looking at?" Stacey asked.

"There were no fingerprints on the letter from Father Jovani," Gideon said. "Totally clean like it was prepared with gloves. A new hire fresh out of school remembered the letter she reviewed from the Jazzman. It was her first document and it stuck with her. She remembered some of the letters were faint and worn. We just lucked out with her connecting it to the Jovani's letter."

"I knew it," Aleister said excitedly. "That letter from Jovani just didn't add up. Getting the burner phone so we couldn't track the phone call made to Detective Hearst. Mailing the letter to the secretary instead of just leaving it on her desk before he left made no sense."

Agent Gideon nodded. She then pointed to the highlighted areas of the documents and explained.

"The uppercase M and T are distinct. You can see where they are worn. The same typewriter used in the Jazzman letter found at the Detroit library was also used to write the letter from Father Jovani."

"Damn," Agent Canter said just above a whisper. "So, my hunch was right. Father Jovani might have known more then what he was letting on when I first interviewed him at his apartment."

"It looks that way," Agent Gideon said. "Our killer could attend Old Saint Mary's. It narrows down the pool of suspects and is the best lead we've had in this case."

We need to get a directory of the parishioners at that church," Aleister said.

"We just can't go and get one," Stacey warned. "If our killer does go to that church, we can't let on what we suspect and ruin our investigation. I think we should have one of our agents go undercover and join the church. This way we could get a directory and not raise any suspicion."

"Do they even give out directories these days?" Gideon asked. "You know with all the privacy issues and such."

"Good point," Stacey said. "We'll just have to see. Worst case scenario, we get a warrant. I noticed that there were security cameras at the church when I interviewed Ms. Kratz. I'd like to get my hands on that footage. I say we just get the warrant and serve it on Ms. Kratz. We will let her know that this is part of the investigation and that she can't share that information with anyone. I think she will keep her mouth shut."

"I like it," Gideon said. "I'll get the warrant issued and think of a plan to serve it on Ms. Kratz without raising suspicion."

A look crossed over Gideon's face. "Do you still think he's alive? The priest that is."

"I'm not sure," Stacey replied with a shrug. "If he is, he's going to have one hell of a story to tell."

****

The aroma of freshly brewed coffee wafted through the air as Charlotte, Grandma, and Grandpa sat at the wooden table in the kitchen.

"Isn't there another way?" Charlotte pleaded then stood up from the kitchen table and turned her back to the two of them.

"Sit down here, Charlotte," her grandma demanded. "You got us into this mess. This has to be done."

Charlotte turned and reluctantly sat back at the table. Her grandfather used a rolling pin to crush sedatives between pieces of wax paper. He then used a razor blade to lift the small chunks onto a plate where he began to cut them into a fine powder.

Grandma nervously fiddled with the roll of duct tape that was sitting on a white folded kitchen garbage bag. A tray with potatoes, sausage, toast, and coffee sat in front of Charlotte.

Charlotte's grandfather reached over and took the coffee mug from the tray and sat it in front of him. He lifted the saucer of crushed Ambien and scraped it into the coffee, stirring with his finger until none of the white powder could be seen.

"He's not going to feel a thing," her grandma assured her. "He'll eat a good meal and drink his coffee. When he falls asleep, I'll place the bag over his head and tape it up. It will be over in a matter of minutes."

Grandma stood from the table and lifted the tray.

"Get your brother and have him go with Grandpa to the woods. You need to finish digging the final resting spot. He will be ready by the time you get back. After a prolonged pause, Charlotte stood up from the table and went to get Charlie.

****

The creak of the stairway caught Father Jovani's attention. He was surprised to see Grandma holding a tray walk into the room. He had only met her a couple of times. His memory was hazy the first few days of his incarceration.

He was sure it was she who showed Charlotte how to take care of his head wound. There was something about her that he liked. Grandma sat the tray on the table next to him and removed the keys from her robe pocket. She showed them to him before dropping them in his lap.

"There's been enough killing going on," Grandma said. "You got about forty-five minutes before Charlie and his grandpa return."

Father Jovani sat up in the recliner and took hold of the keys. His brow stitched together as he unlocked his wrists, never taking his eyes off her. He leaned over and unlocked his leg shackles, then stood.

"There's one thing you need to do for me," Grandma said, as she lifted the tray and hurled it into the air covering her and Father Jovani with food and drink.

"You need to beat me up and give me a few bruises before you go. It better look real because if it doesn't, that grave they went to dig for you, will end up being mine."

****

Special Agent Kelly McKeown walked through the doors of Old Saint Mary's and sat near the back of the church for Wednesday morning mass. She scanned the pews for anyone who could be a suspect and felt some disappointment because there were barely 20 people there, and most of them were aged or looked too weak to overpower anyone.

The mass lasted less than an hour and McKeown waited until the service had ended to approach Father McNally.

She entered the line of parishioners who were leaving the church and saying some last words to the priest. When the last parishioner had finished, Agent McKeown approached.

"Father," she said.

Father McNally turned. "How may I help you?"

"I'm new to this area and would like to join the church. Can you lead me in the right direction?"

"Of course. I am headed to the rectory myself. I'm not sure if the secretary is in but we can check. This is not my church; I'm helping out for a while. I believe the secretary's name is Ms. Kratz. She would be the one to have the paperwork."

Agent McKeown offered her hand, "I'm Kelly McKeown."

"Nice to meet someone with good Irish roots. I am Father McNally. Let me guess you're from the province of Connacht in Northwestern Ireland."

"You'd have to ask my husband; my maiden name is Davies."

"Oh, British, are you? I won't hold that against you," Father McNally said with a smile. "I'm an amateur genealogist. I love researching family names from a historical hierarchy. Please walk with me. I'll take you to Ms. Kratz."

Judith looked up from her workstation when they entered the rectory office. Father McNally took a quick glance at the nameplate sitting on her desk.

"Ms. Kratz… this is Mrs. McKeown. She would like to join the church. Could you give her the proper paperwork? I am heading back to Sacred Heart. If you need anything, I will have my phone with me."

Father McNally lifted his arm and the two shook hands. "Again, it was a pleasure meeting you. Hope to see you again sometime. God bless."

"Thank you," Agent McKeown said. "The pleasure was mine."

"Please have a seat," Ms. Kratz said as she walked to a three-drawer file cabinet and slid out the top drawer. She thumbed through the various forms and removed two. She then grabbed a clipboard that was sitting on top of the cabinet. A pen dangled from a small chain attached to the board.

"If you would like to volunteer, Mrs. McKeown, or work with our youth services, I will need to see your license and we will have to do a background check," Ms. Kratz said.

"May I shut the door?" Agent McKeown asked.

"Sure," Ms. Kratz said with a puzzled look.

Agent McKeown shut the door and returned. She fished from her purse her FBI credentials and warrant. As she handed them to Ms. Kratz, she said, "I am Special Agent Kelly McKeown. I am part of a team investigating the disappearance of Father Jovani."

Surprised, Ms. Kratz said, "I've told the police everything I know."

"I know you have. I came here undercover so not to raise any suspicion. We don't want anyone in the congregation to think we are doing more investigating. By law, you may not tell anyone the things that are stated in that warrant or who I am or why I'm here."

Ms. Kratz scooted in her chair and read the warrant.

She looked up and asked, "Do you think someone at the church had something to do with Lorenzo's disappearance?"

"Since this is an active investigation, I can't share anything about the case with you."

Ms. Kratz took a deep breath and nodded.

"We have a database. The only person with a directory was Father Jovani. We discontinued the directories years ago for privacy reasons. He was old school and wanted quick access to the parishioners. He didn't want to look people up in the database. I'm getting really worried about Father Jovani. Can you tell me if he's okay? This is just so surreal!"

"Again, I can't discuss an ongoing case with you. The database will be perfect. Are the background checks part of that database?"

"Yes."

"Perfect," Agent McKeown said. "You can also supply me with the surveillance tape?"

"Yes. It only goes back I think thirty days. I will get you what I can. When do you need this by?" Ms. Kratz asked.

Agent McKeown stood from her chair and went and opened the office door.

"I have nowhere else to be," she said returning. "I'll wait while you gather the items the warrant is requesting."

Chapter 69

Awakened at 12:00 am in the Dusseldorf apartment, David rose from the couch and made his way to the bathroom. As he passed Carly's closed door, he noticed a faint sliver of light seeping out from underneath. Pausing, he rapped lightly on the door. Silence greeted him.

"Carly?" he called out, growing increasingly worried. With no reply, concern etched across his face. David turned the doorknob and pushed the door open. His heart plummeted as he scanned the empty room----Carly was nowhere to be found!

David rushed to the window, yanking the drape aside, only to find the car gone. Panic surged through him as he hurried to the bedroom, hastily throwing on his shirt. Snatching his phone, he immediately called Porsche.

****

Carly waited in her car, positioned down the street from Helga's residence. Her eyes tracked Bo's departure from the house, and as soon as he settled into the passenger seat, she asked, "Did you do it?"

Bo nodded. "I did."

Carly persisted, her tone probing. "So, this Rambo guy, he was the one who you interacted with, trying to leave witness protection?"

Bo paused before answering, ashamed for blowing their cover. "I'm sorry Carly, I hope you can forgive me."

Carly's hand reached out, gently grasping Bo's arm as a gesture of comfort and solidarity.

"None of this has been easy for any of us," she reminded him softly. "And let's not forget, I'm the one who brought this upon you, not the other way around."

Bo nodded, saying nothing.

"So, you think Rambo will give the information to Slovak?"

"Pretty sure he will. I emphasized the urgency of leaving Germany. Told him we were outed and hiding in the cellar of the Alte Steinhaus bakery."

"Good," Carly agreed.

"I imagine Slovak manipulated his nephew into giving him the information to communicate with Rambo. Big bucks talk and according to Borka, Slovak was dishing out big bucks."

"The bakery is only closed for the weekend. If Slovak doesn't show, we'll just access the website and kill the bastard."

"That's our ace in the hole," Bo assured her. "His ass is cooked, either way."

Carly and Bo selected the Alte Steinhaus bakery as the place for their trap. With the keys still in Carly's possession, they saw it as an ideal location to confront Slovak. The dry storage in *the belly of the beast*, as Carly called it, was the perfect place to dampen screams or gunfire. They felt they were in control with Slovak being absolutely clueless as to what awaited him. They would take no chances, realizing he was a formidable foe.

The decision to deceive Slovak carried deep significance for both of them. For Carly, it symbolized the culmination of her burning desire for retribution following the killings of her father, brother, and Ahmed. For Bo, it embodied the need to confront the individual accountable for his abduction and subsequent torture. Slovak's demise would serve as redemption for them both.

****

The knock at the door so late at night heightened Seargent Tim's senses. Based on instinct, he retrieved his firearm from the nightstand. Glancing through the peephole, he recognized Porsche and David, and promptly swung the door open.

"What the hell's going on!?" Tim asked, his eyes darting towards the clock. "It's four in the morning, for God's sake!"

"Carly's vanished," David blurted out, his voice strained with urgency. "I woke up at midnight, and she's nowhere to be found!"

"Bo's gone, too," Porsche revealed. "Carly's mom called and told me."

"Damn! Where the hell could they have gone?" Tim asked.

"David thinks they went for Slovak," Porsche said. "Something about Carly wanting retribution."

Sergeant Tim directed his attention to David. "Did she confide in you?" he asked.

"Not exactly," David responded. "We discussed seeking retribution, and I attempted to tell her that it doesn't always provide the closure one seeks."

"Let's go to the website and terminate that bastard before Carly and Bo get hurt?" Tim exclaimed.

Porsche nodded, placing her purse on the bed before retrieving Tim's laptop from the couch and handing it to him.

"Let me grab my phone," Tim said, reaching for it on the nightstand and tapping the screen. Porsche observed Tim's expression shifting.

"What's the matter?" Porsche asked, her concern evident.

Tim glanced up from his phone, his furrowed brow revealing his dismay. "The text from Daughtery. It's gone!"

"What do you mean it's gone?" David inquired, stepping closer to peer over Tim's shoulder.

"It's gone," Tim muttered, more to himself than to the others. "It's gotta be Carly. I had it yesterday when she read me the passcode from my phone. Could she have deleted it?"

Chapter 70

Grandma lay on the basement floor. Her lip was bleeding and beginning to swell. She could taste the coppery, salty flavor of her own blood. Her right eye was puffy, and a laceration was visible across her cheekbone. The nightstand lay broken amongst splattered food and coffee. Grandma closed her eyes when she heard Grandpa yell her name.

"Jess...where are you?"

Charlie and Grandpa stood in the kitchen. Traces of dirt and mud were on both their shoes and hands. He yelled her name a second time.

"She must still be in the basement," Grandpa assumed. "Go see if the priest is dead."

Charlie adjusted the axe hanging from his waistbelt. He opened the basement door and tromped noisily down the stairs.

"Grandpa!!" Charlie hollered from the bottom of the stairs.

"Grandma's on the floor," he called up to Grandpa. "And *he's* gone! That fucking priest is gone!"

Charlie raced to Grandma's side and knelt beside her. He grabbed her cheeks and turned her head towards him.

"Grandma! Grandma! What happened? Where's the priest?"

Guttural moans left Grandma's throat as she barely opened her eyes.

"He tricked me. When I came down the stairs, I thought he was sleeping, and I let down my guard. Before I knew it, the tray of food went flying, and he overpowered me."

Charlie heard footsteps coming down the stairs and Grandpa quickly appeared and stood beside Charlie.

"Father Jovani is gone! That son-of-a-bitch is gone!" Charlie said. "I gotta see if I can find him."

"Dammit," Grandpa lashed out. "And do what?!!"

"Stop him from going to the cops!" Charlie said in reply. "He couldn't have gotten far. Leave the priest to me."

Charlie flew up the stairs two steps at a time and into the kitchen.

****

Charlie bolted out the front door, not stopping to close it behind him. His eyes searched the cement walks on both sides of the street hoping to see some sign of the priest.

He zipped up his jacket to conceal the hand axe and hurried down the street. He thought he saw someone's head ducking down in one garage and ran to it. He looked through a window in a side door. It was empty.

He hustled back to the front in time to see a large black dog charging down the sidewalk, dragging his owner behind him. The owner took one look at Charlie and guided the dog across the street.

"Hey," Charlie yelled as he crossed and approached the man.

The man held up a blue plastic bag.

"I told you it wasn't me. I don't let my dog poop on a neighbor's lawn without picking it up."

"Did you see a man about 50 years old, a bit taller than me, wearing baggy pants going down the street?"

The man frowned as he looked Charlie up and down. "Well, that's a switch. Last time I saw you, you looked like you were ready to kill me thinking my dog pooped on your lawn."

Charlie ignored what his neighbor said.

"Did you see anyone looking like that?" he repeated.

"I saw a man limping if that's who you mean. He was trying to run but wasn't going very fast. Is something wrong? Do you want me to call the cops?" he said reaching in his pocket and pulling out his cell phone.

"No!" Charlie said louder than he should have, startling the man.

"Thank you, but please don't. My uncle has early onset dementia and I think if the police got involved it would only scare him."

"That dementia is bad stuff. My mother suffered with it. The guy I saw was on Cobble. He was heading toward Tescot and went into the Burger King."

Charlie darted away without saying another word. He ran down Cobble and headed to the Burger King. The sirens of two police cars came up from behind. Charlie stopped in his tracks. He watched as both police cars turned into the Burger King parking lot.

Chapter 71

Carly parked a couple of blocks away from The Alte Steinhaus bakery. It was a quiet Saturday morning, the streets devoid of any activity as they made their way towards their destination.

With a backpack slung over her shoulder, she opened the door, casting one last glance to ensure they weren't being trailed. They hoped Slovak would fall for their plan; they would maintain the appearance of frightened sheep, barricading themselves in the basement with the door securely locked.

Carly removed a small penlight from her coat pocket and clicked it on. It would be enough light to get them down the hall and into the kitchen.

"You gonna call my phone?" Carly asked.

Bo nodded and dialed. She answered it then placed it back in her coat pocket, leaving her phone turned on.

Carly pointed to a coat rack holding various aprons, next to a windowsill.

"Put your phone on that windowsill, behind the aprons. We'll hear if anyone walks through that door."

The creaking floors of the old bakery echoed with each step as Carly and Bo proceeded toward the kitchen. Once there, Carly opened the dry storage cellar door and turned on the lone light just inside the door.

"I've always hated going down here," Carly confessed. "Gives me the creeps every time."

"Leave the door cracked just enough," Bo said. "It will lure Slovak into heading down."

Carly didn't have to wait long before she heard the sounds of the bakery's front door being tampered with.

Her heart raced as she stood behind the cooler, listening to the intruder making his way inside. Slovak cautiously advanced into the bakery, weapon in hand, but seemingly unprepared for any resistance. Upon noticing a faint glow coming from the cellar door, he approached it with caution and pushed it open.

Slovak stood in the kitchen, straining to hear any sound emanating from the cellar below. Silence greeted him, but as he took a cautious step forward, his eyes caught sight of the telltale signs of a recently removed banister and flaked paint chips on the steps. Every fiber of his being screamed a warning of a trap. Instinctively, he recoiled from the door, his mind racing with alarm.

Carly emerged from the shadows, her sudden appearance catching him off guard. With a forceful shove to his back, she propelled him forward, sending him tumbling down the steep staircase. At the bottom, Bo was waiting, swift to act. He kicked Slovak's weapon away, securing him at gunpoint. Carly flew down the stairs and immediately removed duct tape from her backpack.

"Get up, you worthless piece of shit," Carly ordered.

Slovak slowly rose to his feet, his arms raised in surrender. Without notice, Carly slapped him across his face, causing his lower lip to bleed. Slovak, unfazed by the pain, dabbed at the blood with the cuff of his shirt, a crooked grin playing on his lips.

"You are your father's daughter," he said.

Carly gave him another blow and as she went to strike him again, Bo intervened, firmly catching her arm.

"Stay focused, Carly. Stick to the plan."

Carly motioned to a five-gallon bucket, resting up against a wooden pillar used to support the weight of the bakery's structure.

"Go sit on that bucket and put your hands behind your back and around that pillar," she ordered.

Slovak made his way to the bucket and settled onto it, positioning his hands behind his back and wrapping them around the pillar. Carly wasted no time, dropping to her knees and securing his wrists with tape, all with Bo maintaining a watch over him with his gun. Once finished, Carly stood before Slovak, meeting his eyes as he looked up at her.

"Why did you kill my brother? He was only eight years old."

The cellar was engulfed in silence, tension thickening the air until Slovak finally spoke.

"He was collateral damage…wasn't supposed to die," he said, no remorse in his tone.

From the duffel bag, Carly retrieved what appeared to be brass knuckles, slipping them onto her hand and concealing them beneath a leather glove. Without hesitation, she unleashed a swift blow to

Slovak's cheek. Slovak's chin fell to his neck. Carly yanked his head up by his hair and continued.

"Dr. Hayes, Ahmed, my father. You're intertwined with their deaths. Why? Just for power and wealth?" Carly's accusation hung heavy in the air.

Slovak's throat tightened as he struggled to swallow. His face contorted, swelling and in pain. "You fail to understand," he managed to rasp out.

"What don't I understand?" Carly demanded, her voice sharp with anger.

"I'm driven by a cause, just like your father," Slovak replied, his voice strained.

Carly scoffed, her disdain evident. "You could never be like my father. He was a true hero, defending our country with honor."

Slovak looked up from the bucket. His right eye was black, almost closed.

"Many of my people think I'm a hero."

"Hero my ass! You're nothing but a two-bit thug! No more, no less."

Carly's attention then shifted to Bo. "He's all yours."

Bo approached Slovak, closing the distance between them. He crouched down, ensuring eye contact with him. With a pointed finger, Bo traced the scar on his face… "Remember giving me this scar?"

Slovak gave a silent nod.

Bo lifted a switchblade, holding it inches from Slovak's eyes. With a subtle push of the button, the blade sprung into view, gleaming in the dim light. Bo pressed the blade against Slovak's cheek, prompting Slovak to shut his eyes tightly.

"How did you find us?" Bo pressed. "Who within the CIA did you work for?"

Slovak hesitated at first, waiting for the impending pain that was sure to come, then continued.

"Daughtery was my handler. Not sure how far up the chain it went. There was a leak in the CIA, and he was trying to plug it. He's dead now, so I guess it does not matter."

There was a long pause before Slovak felt the knife leave his face and Bo cutting the tape that bound his wrists. His expression was a mix of confusion and apprehension as he brought his arms forward.

"You're not going to kill me?" Slovak questioned.

Carly stepped forward; her gun trained on him. "There's no need to kill a dead man walking," she declared coldly.

"I don't understand?" Slovak said.

Carly sneered at Slovak. "I hit your face, and your cheeks are swollen. Your lips are split and bruised. The one place I didn't hit you was your nose."

A confused look washed across Slovak's face, as he gently touched his swollen cheeks.

"When you were under sedation, a cyanide filled medical implant was inserted into your nasal cavity and we have the detonation code," Carly revealed with a smirk, holding up her phone.

Slovak remained silent.

"You don't think the CIA was going to let you live now, do ya?" Bo said. "We're going to let you walk from the bakery and kill you on the street. Carly didn't want the Chef to find your smelly, decaying ass when he gets in on Monday. Now put your fucking hands in front of you."

Slovak presented his wrists where Bo promptly zipped tied them. Bo made his way up the steps and stood at the top of the stairwell, waiting for the two of them. Carly lifted her phone, making sure Slovak saw her screen.

"I have the website brought up, and I have entered the detonation code. All I have to do is tap submit and your life is over. Now move," Carly ordered, motioning with her gun, for Slovak to ascend up the stairs. The three walked down the narrow hallway to the door.

"Don't forget your phone," Carly reminded Bo.

With their weapons concealed, Bo led the two down the three concrete steps of the bakery, he turned and cut the zip tie from Slovak's wrists. Suddenly, without warning, Slovak lunged, wrestling the knife from Bo, and swiftly turning, he found his mark in Carly's abdomen. Carly released a shrill scream and fell to her knees.

In the chaos, Slovak lunged once more, his blade driving deep into the flesh of Bo's neck. Slovak raised the knife again, poised to strike another blow but within a split-second, Carly unleashed a torrent of gunfire. Her shots tore through Slovak's back. As he staggered away, Carly tapped the submit button and mumbled, "Rot in Hell, you motherfucker." She watched as Slovak collapsed fifteen feet away.

Carly crawled to where Bo lay, his once vibrant eyes now graying.

"Don't you leave me, Bo Harris," she implored, as she dialed 112, Germany's lifeline in the face of emergencies.

With every ounce of strength, Carly pressed her hands against the gushing wound on Bo's neck, desperately trying to stop the bleeding. As his vision began to fade, a faint whisper escaped from Bo's lips... "I always loved you, Carly Fletcher."

****

David, Tim, and Porsche opted to divide their efforts, believing it would speed up their search for Carly and Bo. As Porsche rounded the corner onto Alpine Street, she stopped at the sight of the pandemonium unfolding outside the Alte Steinhaus bakery.

As the authorities worked to keep the curious onlookers at a distance, Porsche's attention was drawn to the sight of two ambulances racing away, their lights flashing and sirens wailing. Hastily parking her car, she dashed towards the police line, desperate to glean any information about the unfolding events.

Her heart pounded as she reached the scene, her eyes widening in horror at the sight of the blood-stained sidewalk. Frozen in shock, she couldn't tear her eyes away, her expression etched with disbelief. Amidst the chaos, she spotted what appeared to be a covered body nearby.

"Have they been taken to University Hospital?" a voice from the crowd called out, but the authorities remained silent, disregarding answering the question. Porsche quickly turned and ran to her car, knowing she had to get to that hospital.

Porsche rose from the bench sitting outside the nurse's station as soon as she spotted Mrs. Fletcher, Tim, and David entering the hospital. Mrs. Farris rushed towards her, enveloping her in a tight embrace.

"Oh my God! How's Carly?" Mrs. Farris's voice quivered.

Porsche's expression tensed as she relayed the information.

"She's in surgery," reflecting the gravity of the situation. "They're not giving me much detail; they say I'm not family."

"And Bo?"

Porsche's eyes welled up; she could barely speak. "He's gone," she mutters.

"That son of a bitch," Sergeant Tim spewed.

Porsche looked at Tim. "I think Slovak's dead! From what I can tell, there was a body at the crime scene. It was covered with a blanket. It's gotta be Slovak. Somehow, they must have met up with him."

Chapter 72

Charlie kept watch through the nicotine-stained blinds of the picture window in the front room. He expected the wailing of sirens, the approach of police cars, and sharpshooters in SWAT gear jumping out of vans and rushing toward the house. Hotboxing cigarette after cigarette, he perched nervously on a kitchen stool with his rifle resting across his knees.

Grandpa left his post at the back door, passed Grandma still sitting at the kitchen table, and went into the room where Charlie was stationed.

"No one is coming, Charlie," Grandpa said straight-faced as he leaned his rifle against the wall in the corner of the room. "Are you sure that priest went into Burger King?"

"The neighbor said he went into the Burger King," Charlie answered. "I was there when the cop cars showed up. I just put two and two together."

Grandpa reached down to the sill and fished a cigarette out of Charlie's pack. He lifted his lighter from his front pocket, lit it, and took a deep drag. Through a thick cloud of exhaled smoke, Grandpa spoke.

"This doesn't make any sense. Even if he didn't run into that restaurant, he's got to be somewhere talking to the cops. It's been over three hours so where the hell are they and the whole squad that comes with them?"

"They're coming," Charlie said as he slid off the stool and engaged the safety on his rifle. "I can feel it in my bones. They *are* coming."

"Oh, they're coming alright," Grandpa told him. "We just don't know when or why they're not here. I think I will head over to that Burger King and get some lunch. See if I can find out why the cops were there and what the fuss was all about. In the meantime, I want you to start packing."

"Packing!" Charlie said surprised. "Where the hell am I going?"

Grandpa said nothing, taking the last drag of his cigarette and butting it in the ashtray.

"Grandpa," Charlie said more forcefully. "*Where* am I going?"

"We'll discuss it when I get back," Grandpa told Charlie as he grabbed his cane from the wooden umbrella stand and headed out the door. Grandpa stopped midstride and turned back around. "Pack it all, Charlie. It's all got to go."

****

Stacey had been waiting for this day. It was just past noon, and she was driving to the gym. She would later get her nails done and hair highlighted. Days off lately had been few and far between. She was to pick up Chinese food-- egg rolls, chicken lo mein, and pepper steak, -- along with a bottle of wine. A dinner with Aleister was later that night. Her phone rang and she saw it was him.

A naughty smiled formed on her face. She brought the phone close to her lips and sang in a low soft voice.

"Feel the music playing soft and low,

You and me and the lights down low…

 With nothin' on but the ra-di-o."

She stopped singing and waited. She heard Aleister inhale.

"Stacey, they found him!!"

"Found him? You mean Father Jovani??"

"Yes! He's being transported to Detroit Receiving. That's all I have; I am heading there now."

Stacey's eyes went to the clock in her car.

 "It's a little after 1:00. I should be able to get there in about 40 minutes."

"I'll wait for you in the lobby."

"See you there," she said. "Be sure that you wait for me."

Aleister was sitting in the lobby of Detroit Receiving talking with a uniformed police officer when Stacey spotted him. She was in baggy sweatpants, a tank top with a sports bra, and her hair was tied in a loose ponytail pushed through a baseball cap. A purse with a long strap hung from her shoulder.

"Sorry for the way I look," she said, as she sat down next to them. "I was on my way to the gym."

"You look great no matter what you're wearing," Aleister said approving her style. "Thanks for meeting us on your day off. This is

Officer Guswiler. He is the officer who interviewed the manager of the Burger King where Father Jovani was found."

"Burger King?" Stacey questioned.

Officer Guswiler nodded. "Yes. The paramedics shocked him back to life. He was flatlining by the time I got there."

Stacey looked puzzled. "Shocked him back to life? What are we talking about?"

"Father Jovani ran into a Burger King in Madison Heights," Aleister said. He turned to Officer Guswiler. "Tell her what you told me about your interview with the manager."

"Sure," Guswiler said. "According to the manager this guy came in. We now know it was that missing priest, Father Jovani. The guy claimed he was a priest and that he was being held captive by this crazy family. Said he was chained in a basement. I guess he grabbed his chest and collapsed before he said more. The manager said he was acting crazy like he was on PCP. They called 911 and started CPR."

"Damn," was all Stacey could mumble.

"Officer Wells told me you two are working that serial killer case," Guswiler said. "You think this has something to do with that?"

"It might," Canter said. "But keep that between us."

"So, you've set up twenty-four-hour security for Father Jovani?" Aleister asked.

"Yes. There's a cop outside his room as we speak. We'll keep an eye on him."

Stacey stood followed by Guswiler and Wells.

"Let's go talk to the doctor in charge," she said to Aleister. "See if there is any way we might be able to talk with Father Jovani."

****

As Grandpa turned into the parking lot, the back wheel of his black truck clipped the corner of the curb. He cursed as his tires hit the concrete jostling him around. The Burger King lot was packed as he cruised the lot looking for cops. Seeing none, he continued into the handicap spot closest to the door and parked.

He placed his pistol into the waistband of his jeans and made sure his sweatshirt concealed it before grabbing his cane and pushing open the door. He would make a show of it by hobbling into the restaurant and standing in line.

He brushed back his long shaggy hair and took his place behind a short pudgy woman wearing an orange and black baseball jersey. She fidgeted in line, and he heard her complain under her breath.

"Come on.... hire more people. I don't have all day."

She turned around and looked at Grandpa.

"They had some kind of emergency here a couple hours ago," she grumbled. "Maybe they sent people home, and now, we gotta pay for it."

"I heard cops were here earlier this morning?" Grandpa said to her. "Do you know anything about it?"

The woman raised her eyebrows. "Not much. I just saw the police cars and an ambulance in the parking lot. I live down the street."

A teenager wearing a badge with the name Debbie shouted from behind the counter for the next in line and the woman hurried to place her order.

Grandpa shuffled with the rest of the customers as the line slowly moved.

Grandpa finally stood at the counter, and he placed his order.

"I will have a Number 1 meal with a large Coke. No ice."

"For here or to go?"

"Here. Could you have someone deliver it to the table?" Grandpa said smiling and lifting his cane to show the cashier.

"Of course. Where will you be sitting?"

Grandpa nodded to the far corner. "I'll be sitting at that table."

Grandpa settled himself at the table and looked around the dining room. He listened to conversations close to him hoping to hear anything about what happened earlier that involved the police.

A young woman looking to be in her twenties wearing a uniform slightly different from the others walked up to Grandpa's table carrying a tray of food. She looked at the slip of paper resting on the tray and said, "Number 1 meal, large Coke, no ice."

Grandpa looked up from the table and smiled, "That would be me, my Dear."

"Hey, did anyone ever tell you that you look like Willie Nelson?" the woman said.

Grandpa laughed good naturedly.

"You mean the "On the Road Again" guy?" he answered. "Yeah, I've been told I look like him and a lot of other old guys!"

Grandpa exuded charm and affability, a trait he had since he was very young.

The dayshift manager laughed out loud and set the tray on the table. "Enjoy your meal."

"Before you leave," Grandpa quickly said "can you tell me what all the fuss was about this morning. I heard sirens and saw the cops here. Did someone try to rob the place?"

"Oh, no," the manager said. "Looks like one of our customers may have suffered a heart attack. The paramedics got here in a heartbeat and loaded him onto an ambulance. No pun intended with the heartbeat comment."

"I knew what you meant," Grandpa said. "So did the guy die?"

"I think he did but then they shocked him back to life with one of those paddle things. He was unconscious when they loaded him into the ambulance. Hope he pulls through."

"Oh, me, too," Grandpa said, popping a French-fry into his mouth.

****

Agent Canter and Officer Wells held up their credentials and showed the police officer keeping guard outside Father Jovani's ICU room. The drapes were drawn but they could see movement behind the curtains. A door opened and a woman walked out carrying a clip board and wearing a name tag, Dr. Karen Pradha.

"Excuse me," Agent Canter said holding up her ID. "Can I ask you some questions about Father Jovani?"

Dr. Pradha stopped.

"Is there a chance that we could speak with Father Jovani?"

"Father Jovani passed away about a half hour ago," Dr Pradha said. She brought the clipboard to her eyes. "Time of death, 3:22 pm."

Stacey noticed Aleister shake his head. "Son-of-a-bitch," he mumbled.

"And what was his cause of death?" Agent Canter asked.

"Looks like myocardial infarction. All signs point to a heart attack. We will know more when an autopsy is performed."

"You're doing an autopsy?"

"Yes. There was other trauma to the body. His right arm was quite swollen and bruised. Consistent with being struck. Wouldn't be surprised if it was fractured. His wrists and ankles had abrasions on them consistent with being restrained in some fashion. There was also a laceration on the back of his head, consistent with being struck."

"Thank you, Dr. Pradha," Agent Canter said. "I appreciate you answering my questions. Can we get a copy of the autopsy?"

"Of course."

Stacey took a deep breath and turned to Aleister as Dr. Pradha turned and left. "This is getting more bizarre as the case goes on."

"I know," Aleister said. "God, I would have loved to interview him. He *knew* who our serial killer was."

"He did. Let's get back to the office and see what Agent McKeown has for us. We at least have a location where Father Jovani was being held. He had to have been somewhere in that subdivision, close to that Burger King in Madison Heights."

****

With the death of Father Jovani, things were moving fast. Stacey entered the office to find Agent McKeown and Officer Wells leaning over a plat map of the area where the Burger King was located. She had briefed Agent Gideon before meeting back in the office.

A one-mile square of the adjacent subdivision was outlined in black. A seventy-five-page database of the parishioners from Old Saint Mary's was sitting next to the map. The names were arranged in alphabetical order and listed by last names.

"What do we have?" Agent Canter asked, taking a place beside Aleister.

"We traced a mile square of the area with the Burger King being in the center. If the day manager is correct, Father Jovani was held captive somewhere within this square mile," Aleister replied.

Special Agent McKeown held up the seventy-five-page database the secretary from Old Saint Mary's had run off for her. "Somewhere in these pages could be the name and address of our killer. We figured we would divide this up into thirds and each take a section and find who lives in Madison Heights."

"Why don't we just call Ms. Kratz and ask her to type in Madison Heights into a descriptor and run it through the database," Stacey asked. "Save us a lot of time."

"We called," Aleister said. "A substitute secretary answered and said Ms. Krantz had an emergency and left. The substitute did not have access to the database. How much you want to bet that Ms. Kratz just found out about Father Jovani's death?"

Stacey shook her head. "I can't keep from feeling bad for that woman. She had plans with him. One way or another, they were going to build a life together. Now that's all gone."

Agent Canter grabbed a third of the database and walked to her workstation. Agent McKeown and Officer Wells did the same.

"Let's start scouring the names and addresses," she said. "Our needle has to be somewhere in this haystack."

Chapter 73

The University Hospital in Dusseldorf lay silent under the dim glow of the overhead lights. At 3:45 am, only a skeletal crew lingered in the expansive corridors of the surgical floor. Tim, exhausted from the day's endeavors, had fallen asleep in a cushioned chair, his coat crumpled beneath his head as a makeshift pillow.

David and Porsche had ventured off to the vending machines, as the cafeteria remained closed. Mrs. Farris noticed a man, gray around the temples and wearing scrubs walk into the waiting room. She immediately stood from the chair.

"Are you Mrs. Winters?" inquired the surgeon, his footsteps echoing softly as he approached her.

"Yes, I am," replied Carly's mother, her voice tinged with urgency. "Please, tell me she's alright."

The surgeon nodded, and a feeling of relief washed over Carly's mother. "She lost a lot of blood," he said, "but I feel she will make a full recovery."

Overtaken by emotion, Mrs. Fletcher leaned in and hugged the surgeon just as David and Porsche returned to the waiting room.

"What's going on?" Porsche inquired.

"Fantastic news!" Mrs. Fletcher exclaimed enthusiastically, jolting Tim from his slumber. He sprang to his feet, donning his coat as he joined the surgeon in addressing the group.

"Can we go see her?" Porsche asked.

"Not just yet," the surgeon said. "She's sedated and is sleeping comfortably. Why don't you go home and get some rest. You all look like you could use it. We will keep you posted and let you know when she's ready for visitors."

With that, the surgeon departed, leaving the group in a moment of relief and anticipation.

"Thank God for that wonderful news," David said, straightening the brim of his ballcap. "Do you think she knows about Bo?"

"I don't know," Mrs. Fletcher replied, her face still showing the anguish of losing Bo.

"How did Helga take it?" Porsche addressed Sergeant Tim.

Tim combed his hand through his hair, shaking his head. "Not well. The last few days have been such a whirlwind for her. I think she is just basically in shock." His attention then went to Carly's mom.

"I've got all your things, Mrs. Fletcher. Helga sends her condolences."

"Thank you, Tim," Mrs. Fletcher replied.

Porsche hoisted her purse, slinging it over her shoulder from where it rested on a nearby chair.

"I suppose I should just get this over with," she remarked. "Stacey's going to have a meltdown when she hears the news."

Chapter 74

Grandpa knew it was only a matter of time before Agent Canter and Officer Wells put the dots together and all dots led to Charlotte. The old man was thorough and meticulous, traits in his mind his granddaughter didn't possess.

He knew very soon the world would come to know Charlotte Spatchler. Grieving families would want to know why, and zealous prosecutors would want to make a name for themselves.

****

"I really don't want to leave," Charlotte pleaded, sitting at the kitchen table with her grandma. "Charlie doesn't want to go either. Please don't make us leave."

"I got no choice and neither do you," Grandma said firmly. "Once your grandpa makes up his mind there is nothing to change it. Plus, you knew this could happen. Once that priest showed up everything changed."

Grandpa entered the kitchen and Charlotte and Grandma stopped talking. He looked at both of them as he sat down.

"I could hear you two talking. Get me a beer and sit back down. I want to go over the plan."

Charlotte pushed herself up from the table and went to the fridge. She knelt down and reached deep inside removing three cans of Miller Lite. She returned to the table, handing them a beer and placing one in front of her place at the table. She turned her head and faced her grandpa.

"I really don't want to leave."

Grandpa said nothing as he cracked opened the beer and took a long slug. He set the can back on the table and muffled a burp. "You don't have a choice, Charlotte. It won't be forever."

Charlotte's demeanor changed. Her eyes squinted and her forehead creased. She cracked the beer and took a belt, then slammed the can back to the table.

"Where am I going to live, Old Man?" Charlie asked, setting his can aside, readying for battle.

"Take it easy, Charlie," Grandpa said. "Remember when I left for a week when that priest first showed up."

"Grandma said you were gone taking care of business."

"The business I was taking care of was setting up a safehouse for us if the time ever came that we would have to leave. That time has come, Charlie. I figured if we didn't die in a shootout with the cops, we would need to hide out until things calmed down."

"Us?" Charlie said surprised. "So, you and Grandma are coming?"

"Not Grandma. Just me and you. Grandma has done nothing wrong except for marrying me. She hasn't done anything that they could put her in jail for. She barely even talked with that priest until just before he escaped."

Grandpa eyeballed her suspiciously as Grandma lifted the beer to her mouth. "Still don't know how he got the better of you when he was all chained up."

Grandma shook her head. "I went over it a thousand times!!," she snapped. "He just outsmarted me. I let my guard down because he was a priest."

"I taught you better than that and you know it!!"

"Quit bickering! It doesn't matter anymore," Charlie cut in. "Jovani is gone, and we just have to deal with it. So, where are we going?"

"You'll know once we get there."

****

Cumberland Kentucky the sign read as Charlie looked over at his grandfather who was driving the truck.

"Are *we* going to Cumberland?" Charlie groaned.

"We *have* to go there," Grandpa said. "There is no other choice."

"Why Cumberland? I hate that place."

Grandpa ignored Charlie, keeping his focus on the paved road they were on and the hills edging its side, covered with pines, shrubs, along with white oaks and maple trees.

He turned off the main blacktop street and headed down a dirt road. Dust stirred behind them as they drove the peaks and valleys of the heavily wooded hills. They turned down a two track which led to a log cabin and parked.

Piles of cut firewood were neatly stacked along one side of the cabin. A fishing boat sat on a trailer and was backed up next to a pole barn.

A gray-haired woman, her hair in rollers, walked out onto the porch followed by a man wearing bib overalls and a pale-blue shirt. Charlie kept his composure and said nothing as he left the truck and adjusted the axe that was concealed under his baggie hoodie.

"Teresa, you're looking well," Grandpa said with his usual charming flair.

Teresa lowered her head and squinted through her glasses to see him better.

"Hello brother, cut the crap," the old woman said, turning her back on him and going back into the cabin.

"Don't mind her, Uncle Al," a man in bib overalls said as he approached the two. "That's the way she acts when she is happy to see someone!"

His stare went to Charlie, and he held out his hand. "You must be Charlie."

"Charlie," Grandpa said. "This is your cousin, Walter. Walter Spatchler."

Charlie forced a smile and shook Walter's hand. Walter then turned and embraced his Uncle Al. "Let's get you guys inside."

Walter led the way inside the cabin. His shoes made the wooden steps leading up to the porch creak under his weight. He held the door open for Charlie to go in first and then he secretly gave Grandpa a look and a flicker of a nod that said that everything was set and was going to work out.

Grandpa let Charlie enter Teresa's home first. Charlie took note of the normal things that would be found in a cabin. Pots and cast-iron pans hung from hooks in the kitchen and white plates and cups were neatly stacked in the cupboards.

An old stainless-steel toaster sat on the counter alongside a scuffed wooden cutting board and a Mason jar half filled with bacon grease. He took notice of a knife block with black handled knives stored within it.

Aunt Teresa was pouring hot water into a coffee cup in the kitchen.

"Anyone else want some coffee? I only have instant."

"I'm coffee-ed out," Grandpa answered. Charlie never said a word.

Teresa then joined them in the family room walking to an oversized burgundy recliner with a basketful of skeins of yarn next to it. Walter sat down in a wooden rocking chair across from a worn out black and red plaid couch.

"Have a seat," Walter said pointing to the couch.

Grandpa lowered himself onto the couch followed by Charlie.

"So, what's it been Teresa—twenty some years? Grandpa asked.

"Somewhere around there. You high-tailed it out of here once you killed Billy."

"I killed Billy?! Dear Sister, you forget. You're the one that poisoned him. I simply supplied the means."

The atmosphere was heavy with tension, silence hung in the air before Walter continued.

"So, Uncle, you removed the VIN number on your truck?"

Grandpa nodded. "All that will be left to do is to dump the truck once you drop us off. With no truck there will be no way the cops can link you to us. They would charge you with aiding and abetting."

"So, I'm dropping you off by the trail that leads up the hills through the thick brush and driving to the old quarry pit. Ma will be there to drive me back. No one is going to find that pit. I barely could, and I grew up in these parts. I'll take the truck to the top and drive it off the cliff. That pit has at least thirty feet of water in it. No one's ever going to find your truck."

Grandpa stood followed by Charlie. "Well, then. Let's get this party started," he said tossing his nephew Walter the keys.

Chapter 75

Mrs. Fletcher was the first to notice Carly stirring from sedation. Swiftly, she rose from her chair and approached Carly's bedside, sitting, and gently clasping her hand. David joined Carly's mother, standing by her side.

"Darling, it's me," Mrs. Fletcher murmured softly, her touch tender as she caressed Carly's arm.

Carly's head swayed from side to side, her eyes struggling to find clarity in her surroundings. Abruptly, she shifted her legs and attempted to rise.

"Bo," she murmured urgently, "We need to help Bo. Slovak..."

Mrs. Fletcher applied gentle pressure to Carly's shoulders, preventing her from getting up. She looked up at David, her eyes pleading for help.

"Carly," David spoke softly, drawing nearer to her. "You need to take it easy. You've just had surgery."

Carly's body gradually relaxed as the weight of David's words sank in, the reality of her situation dawning upon her.

"I know he's gone," Carly disclosed softly, tears trickling down her cheeks. "I understand why I'm here. It was Slovak. He stabbed me and... and killed Bo, before I shot him."

"It's over, Carly," David said gently, as Mrs. Fletcher stood up, allowing David to take her place beside Carly. "How did you get Slovak to meet with you?"

"We ambushed him, lying in wait. We lured him to the bakery cellar. He thought we were hiding there, scared and off guard, waiting to leave the country."

"So, you and Bo had all this planned from the beginning?"

"As soon as Porsche shared that picture of Slovak, we decided we wanted to handle him our way."

Carly became quiet, staring at the ceiling. An awkward stillness filling the room.

"Carly, what are you thinking?" David broke the silence.

"Does Helga know?" Carly asked, her voice tinged with concern.

"Yes. Sarge informed her before he left for Australia."

A small grin formed on Carly face. "He went back to Isla. They're going to be a family."

David nodded. "They sure are. He couldn't wait to get back to her. Once he found out you were going to be fine, he was out of here."

"How long have I been here?" Carly asked, her voice filled with uncertainty.

"About three days. They just brought you out of the ICU. You're gonna make a full recovery," David reassured her.

"Has Porsche spoken with Stacey? She's not going to be happy with me!"

"She has. I guess she was really pissed at first, but Porsche said she has since come around. She would be here right now, if it wasn't for that case she's working on."

"What about Bo? How's he getting back?"

"Stacey made all the arrangements. Bo's body is being flown to the states tomorrow. His next of kin has been notified."

Carly took a deep breath, the weight of the situation settling up on her.

"That bastard has caused so much pain. I'm glad he's dead, and I am glad I was the one who killed him."

David clasped Carly's hand, his eyes carrying an unspoken message that stirred curiosity within her.

"David, what's on your mind? I can sense there's something you want to share," Carly inquired.

"Umm... that kiss. Umm... Did that kiss mean something to you?" David hesitated, his words hanging in the air.

Without a word, Carly reached up, drawing David closer, and they shared another kiss. As they parted, their eyes met. "Yes, Mr. Farris, that kiss meant something to me."

Feeling the weight of the moment, Mrs. Fletcher gracefully excused herself. "I'm going to leave you two alone. I'll be in the cafeteria."

"So, where do we go from here?" Carly asked.

"You and your mom could come back with me. I was thinking, I could help my dad finish remodeling the farmhouse. I thought your mom could have Penny's room and I would add another room for me and you."

"Wow, Mr. Farris. You have this all figured out."

"We wouldn't live with my parents forever. It would just be until we figure out how all this will work."

"And your parents are fine with it?"

"Haven't shared my plan with them. But with everything that went down, I'm sure they'll be fine with it."

David sought affirmation in Carly's eyes, searching for any hint of agreement.

"Well, Carly, what do you think?"

A gentle smile graced Carly's lips as she reached up, her hand finding its place behind David's neck, drawing him closer.

"Let me demonstrate," she whispered softly before their lips met in a tender kiss, expressing more than words ever could.

Chapter 76

Old Saint Mary's had a little over 600 registered families from throughout metro Detroit. Twenty-eight of them lived in Madison Heights. Four of them lived within a five-mile radius of the Burger King. One parishioner stood out from all others. A Ms. Charlotte Spatchler.

The registered address of the house that she listed was three blocks from the Burger King. Agent Canter immediately put her name into the FBI national database search and got a hit.

"She has a record, and it has been sealed from the public under juvenile protection," Stacey said as her eyes traveled up and down the computer screen.

"Let's see what our girl did in her early years."

Agent Canter began to read from the screen. She paraphrased for Agent McKeown and Officer Wells.

"Wow! There's a laundry list here. She was one messed up kid. Both mother and father committed suicide when she was two. She was in and out of foster care until she went to live with an aunt in Kentucky. According to the report, a man by the name of Rick Saggot was molesting her. She was sent to a psych hospital for setting him on fire. She was a preteen when she did it.

"The report states that she has borderline personality disorder brought on by post-traumatic stress. The disorder will get worse if left untreated. This is accompanied by anxiety and obsessive-compulsive disorder and often times violent behavior."

"Well, we know she can be violent," Agent McKeown added. "She set a guy on fire."

Stacey nodded and continued. "Her treatment lasted a year and looking at the list of medication she was on must have made her a zombie. There is a note by one of her therapists stating that she found an evil side to Charlotte's personality. As if she had a split personality to cope with what was going on in her life. The report ends saying there is no known defined cure for her condition, but long-term treatment may help combine her personalities into one."

"Has she lived at that address since she left the hospital?" Aleister asked.

"No," Stacey said as she continued to read the report. "It says here she was in and out of foster care in her early teens once she was released from the hospital. Kept being sent back from the families she was being fostered by because of violent behavior.

"She eventually ended up with her grandparents where she lives to this day. That's the address she gave the church when she became a member."

Aleister stood from the table and walked to a three-drawer filing cabinet. He thumbed through the files before removing one. He laid it on the table and removed the pictures from the Carlson farm.

"Is there a picture of our girl?" he asked.

"There is," Stacey said, as she enlarged the picture and focused in. "She looks pretty young."

Agent McKeown and Officer Wells went and stood behind Stacey's computer screen. Aleister placed the clearest of the grainy pictures of the suspect next to the picture on the screen.

"I can't tell," Aleister said. "It could be her but can't be sure."

Furrows formed on Stacey's forehead as she zoomed in on the t-shirt Charlotte was wearing. A picture of Duke Ellington was on the front and emblazoned under it in all red letters were the words…IT'S ALL ABOUT THE JAZZ!!

****

Grandma heard the doorbell ring and pushed herself up from the kitchen table. Her eye was now purple with a slight shade of green. She placed the pencil in the seam of the crossword puzzle book, then shuffled to the door.

Even before she looked out the peephole, she knew it was the law.

Officer Wells and Agent Canter stood at the top of the stoop. She cracked the door slightly before showing her face.

"Yeah," Grandma said.

Agent Canter removed her ID from the side pocket of her jacket and placed it in front of Grandma's eyes.

"I'm FBI Agent Stacey Canter, and this is Officer Wells. We'd like to speak with a Ms. Charlotte Spatchler. Is she available?"

"She ain't here," Grandma said abruptly trying to close the door. Agent Canter pushed her foot up against it. Grandma paused and looked down at Cantor's foot and back up again. She turned and walked back into the kitchen leaving the door open for the two to enter.

Aleister drew his gun and walked in first. Stacey drew hers and followed behind. Neither said a word as they walked through the hall to where Grandma sat at the table.

"You don't mind if we take a look around?" Aleister said when he entered the kitchen. "We have a warrant."

"Suit yourself," Grandma said as she picked up the pencil to continue her crossword puzzle.

Wells placed his gun back in his holster and stepped behind grandma. He grabbed his cuffs from the side of his belt and asked her to put her hands behind her back. Grandma dropped the pencil onto the table and shook her head as she placed her hands behind her.

"What?? Am I under arrest?" Grandma crowed in a gruff smoker's voice. "I told you she ain't here!"

"We are going to check the house and we want you staying right here. This is as much for your protection as it is ours," Aleister said, gently placing the cuffs around Grandma's skinny wrists.

"Are those too tight?" he asked. Grandma said nothing and simply ignored him.

"Mrs. Spatchler," Agent Canter began, never holstering her gun. "Where is your husband?"

"He ain't here either. And my name ain't Spatchler. It's Klenke. Couldn't stand that last name. Kept my own. Always reminded me of a kitchen utensil." Stacey's gaze went to Aleister where she saw him fighting a smile.

"Ms. Klenke, can you tell us where your husband and Charlotte are?" Agent Canter once again asked.

"No, I can't. I woke up this morning and they was gone. Maybe he went out for a paper or doughnuts. What's this all about anyway?"

"I think you know, Ms. Klenke," Aleister said. "Any surprises we should be aware of when we search the house?"

"Nope. The only surprises in this house are you two pains in my ass!"

Stacey looked to Aleister. "How about I'll check the upstairs and you keep Ms. Klenke company."

"Sure, you don't want to check this out together."

"Both of us climbing the steps. Too easy of a target."

"Good point! Keep your guard up."

Agent Canter carefully walked up the steps of the old house. The steps creaked as she made it to the top. She stood and waited, both hands on her gun. From the top of the stairs, she noticed three separate rooms. Stacey walked slowly down the hallway.

She saw that two of the rooms had doors open. They were void of any furniture or bedding. The third room had the door closed and Stacey could hear movement coming from inside.

"FBI, Charlotte," Agent Canter announced, standing to the side of the door, and tapping the door with her gun. She could still hear movement coming from the room.

"Charlotte. I am Agent Stacey Canter with the FBI. If you don't answer the door, I'm coming in."

Still there was no response. Agent Canter gripped the doorknob and turned, pushing the door open while at the same time pulling herself back away from the door. Ever so slightly she looked into the room. It was then she noticed a guinea pig running on his wheel.

The room was empty but for a glass terrarium sitting on top of a chest of drawers. Pugs spun wildly as Agent Canter approached the dresser. She slid out a drawer and then another. There was not a single article of clothing in any of them. The mattress had been stripped and the only thing that could be seen were faded urine stains.

Agent Canter made her way down the stairs and back into the kitchen. As she entered, Grandma launched into conversation.

"I told you they ain't here. Can you take these goddam cuffs off? They're hurting my arms."

The old lady squirmed in her chair. Aleister could see she was in pain from her arms being behind her back. He lowered himself to the chair and removed the cuffs. He then asked, "Where's Charlotte?"

Grandma rubbed and kneaded her shoulder once the cuffs were removed.

"I told you I don't know. She moved out a few weeks ago and we haven't heard from her since. Do you mind if I have a smoke?"

"Go ahead," Stacey said.

Grandma grabbed the pack of Kool menthols sitting on the table and tapped a cigarette out. She lifted it to her mouth before a coughing spell took over. Placing her hand to her mouth, she struggled to catch her breath. Aleister grabbed a glass sitting next to the sink and filled it with tap water. He then sat it in front of her.

Grandma's hand trembled as she lifted the glass to her mouth and swallowed. She set the glass back on the table, then picked up the lighter and lit her cigarette. Her cheeks hollowed as she sucked in a deep drag before releasing a thick cloud of smoke.

"Ms. Klenke," Agent Canter began, "Whose bedroom is it with the guinea pig?"

Grandma did not answer right away. She sat there, hotboxing her smoke, unfocused staring off into space. "Charlotte's," she finally said. "She left me her guinea pig to keep me company."

"You said you woke up this morning and the two were gone. But, a minute ago you said she moved out a few weeks ago. Which story is true?"

"I'm old, I get confused. You figure it out."

"There is not one piece of clothing in that room and the bedding is off the mattress. Whoever cleaned up that room doesn't look like they are coming back any time soon. Did Charlotte move away? I really don't want to take you in, but I may not have a choice."

Aleister noticed the door to the basement. "Is that the cellar?"

Grandma nodded. "Ain't nobody down there."

Officer Wells opened the door and looked down the steps of the dark basement. He felt for a light switch. Finding none, he turned back to Grandma. "Where's the switch?"

With her chin she pointed to a switch on the sidewall of the door. "It's the furthest one on the left."

"How about you stay here with Ms. Klenke while I take a quick peek," Aleister said.

"We'll be here waiting for you," Stacey replied.

Aleister drew his gun and slowly descended the steps of the Michigan cellar. The basement was dingy and musty smelling. He looked from side to side as he announced his presence.

"Charlotte, this is Officer Wells. We need to talk. Come out with your hands in the air."

Hearing nothing, he made it to the bottom of the stairs and began to search. As he entered what looked like a bedroom, he noticed two eye hooks drilled and anchored into the cement floor. The room was empty but for a folding chair and recliner. Aleister walked from the room to what appeared to be some type of woodshop.

There was a door in the far corner. He slowly walked towards it, gun raised in the air and stood next to it. He reached down and turned the handle before jumping out of view. As he peeked into the door the only thing he saw was light seeping through the seams of an old coal chute.

"ALL CLEAR!" Aleister announced as he climbed back up the stairs.

Chapter 77

A steady drone of voices flowed through the FBI press conference room in the McNamara Federal Building in downtown Detroit. Photographers hoisting cameras wandered throughout the room, filming clusters of reporters waiting anxiously for the latest update on the Jazzman investigation and details about Father Jovani, the kidnapped priest.

The conference was slated to start at 10:00 a.m. and it was well past that. The din of conversations in the room abruptly stopped when a group of government officials emerged from the side of the stage. A woman in a suit took a place behind the podium while the rest of the group formed a row behind her across the stage.

The speaker looked directly at the reporters seated in front of her.

"I want to thank all of you who came here today. I am FBI Special Agent Margaret Gideon, the head of investigation on the Jazzman case. Behind me are Detroit Police Chief Thomas Porter, Assisting Attorney General Robert Matthews, and FBI lead investigator Stacey Cantor whom many of you already know. We are here to give the latest details regarding this case, and we will take questions afterwards.

"On June 14, 2022, a man entered a Burger King in Madison Heights asking for help. He claimed that he had been held prisoner in the basement of a nearby home. He was transported to Detroit Receiving Hospital, but he died before giving us any statement regarding his time in captivity.

"Through our investigation, we identified the home he was in as the Spatchler residence and the kidnapped man as Father Lorenzo Jovani. We know the Spatchler family resided in the home in the city of Madison Heights. Living in the home were A.C. Spatchler, his wife, Jessica Klenke and Charlotte Spatchler. Charlotte is the granddaughter of A.C. Spatchler and his wife.

"The grandmother is currently under medical supervision. Charlotte and the grandfather are missing. We hope that through this press conference, the public can guide us to their location.

Gideon looked back at Stacey. "I will now turn this over to Agent Stacey Cantor. She will update you on other details we have now."

Gideon stepped back and nodded to Stacey to come forward.

Stacey replaced Gideon at the podium, but before starting, she scanned the audience. She recognized many faces, but the one she recognized the most was Aleister. Through his eyes, she gained a boost in confidence.

She reached into her suit jacket and removed a folded piece of paper. She unfolded it and laid it out on the podium before addressing all the reporters.

"For the past year and a half our state, as well as other surrounding states, has witnessed a series of killings and attempted killings that we believe are related. The victims of these crimes were women. At each crime scene, the deceased women were dressed in flapper type dresses along with headbands, hats, and shoes typical of the 1920's era. The perpetrator of these crimes calls himself the Jazzman.

"Though we do not specifically know who this person is, we believe that these two people are valuable to our investigation."

Stacey turned and referenced the photos.

"I would like you to pay close attention to these pictures," she said, indicating the enlarged photos on easels by the podium.

"This is Charlotte Renee Spatchler. She is a 27-year-old white female. We believe she is accompanied by her grandfather Allen Carl Spatchler. He is also known to go by the initials A.C."

Her attention then focused on the camera people. "Could the cameras get a closeup of the two please?

She pointed to Charlotte's picture first.

"We believe Charlotte Spatchler at times passes herself off as a man. Jeans, hoodie, tennis shoes, hair pulled back into a ponytail."

"Next, Allen Spatchler, her grandfather. He is approximately 57 years of age, has long gray braids, and often walks with a cane. He has a distinct birth mark on the side of his neck best described as an irregular splotch of red. Through our investigation we have learned they have family ties in Kentucky. It's possible they may have crossed state lines.

"Both of these persons of interest may have changed their appearance. If you see them, do not approach them. They could be armed and dangerous.

"Please contact your local police or call the 1-800 number listed under the pictures of each suspect. That is all the information I can release at this time."

Chapter 78

The three sat squeezed shoulder to shoulder in the pickup truck as Walter drove deep into the Appalachian Mountains. Grandpa was familiar with the area. He had made his living there.

Gone were the copper stills and coils hidden in the hollows next to the shack. The dirt roads had turned to two tracks and the two tracks led to an overgrown path. It was hot and humid when they left the air conditioning of the truck.

"Wow!!! It's going to be a hot one," Walter said, wiping his forehead with the back of his hand. He reached into the bed of the truck and handed Charlie and Grandpa their backpacks.

"I stocked enough food and supplies at the shack to last about three months. You remember how to get in there?" Walter asked Grandpa.

Grandpa smiled slightly. "You forget, Walter. I used to rule this area. Nobody knows it better than me."

The three of them stood by the tailgate of the truck. Grandpa looked at Charlie.

"We got a couple of hours to get where we're going. I want to get settled in before nightfall. You don't want to be wandering *these* woods at night."

Charlie looked at Grandpa expecting some kind of explanation.

"I never saw anything myself, but there were always lots of stories of strange goings on. Bluish lights that appeared suddenly... flashing, flickering, and burning holes in the grass. Some said it was UFO's; others said it was the government taking soil samples looking for oil."

Walter nodded his head having heard that story since he was young. Charlie, however, looked doubtful.

"Is that supposed to scare me?" he said. "If there were lights flashing, I'd be one of the first ones running to see what it was."

Grandpa ignored Charlie, pursed his lips, and rested an arm on the tailgate of the truck.

"One time your cousin was sent to get some red-eye from an old moonshiner on the hill. His daddy sent him. Emmet was taking a short cut through an old graveyard to get there. Nuthin' happened on the way in, but coming back, he saw something on a horse galloping 'cross the graves. Never went back!"

"Sounds like Emmet got into some of that red-eye himself," Charlie scoffed. "Probably ate some magic mushrooms, too!"

Walter laughed.

Grandpa lifted his backpack by a strap and brought it to his shoulder. He stuck his hand through the other strap and jerked the backpack up on to his back. Charlie did the same.

"Get rid of that truck," Grandpa told Walter before walking to him and locking his arms around him in a tight hug.

"I'll see you in about three months when you bring in more supplies," he said.

"You boys take care," Walter said before climbing back into the truck and cranking on the air.

****

The path that snaked through the forest of Cumberland Kentucky had become overgrown; it was a tough journey in. They waded through shallow streams that meandered through the bright green vegetation. The saplings of the sugar maples and white ash were fully leafed and made it almost impossible to walk.

Grandpa stopped, lowered his backpack to the ground and removed a canteen of water. He tilted his head and took a long drink. The water was still as icy cold as the mountain stream it had come from. He handed the canteen to Charlie who also took a long drink. Grandpa noticed the sun was just above the trees and soon would set. He looked puzzled staring at the horizon.

"We are fucking lost, aren't we?" Charlie said, studying Grandpa's face.

"No, give me a minute," Grandpa said scanning the terrain.

"There," he pointed to cut branches forming a faint trail through the woods.

"Follow the trail. We're probably a half mile from the shack."

Charlie began to follow the cut branches as he plowed through the bush. His grandfather remained where he had stopped.

"Are you coming?" Charlie asked stopping and turning around looking for him.

He saw Grandpa fumbling with the zipper of his pants and his hand reaching inside.

"Nature's calling… got to take a whiz," Grandpa said. "Keep on going… I'll catch up in a minute."

Grandpa watched as Charlie turned and pushed on forward. He cringed when he saw him vanish from the path.

The pit trap worked as well as it did years ago when law enforcement was trying to shut down A.C.'s father's still. The beauty of a pit trap was that it doubled as a grave. Gone were the punji sticks that made the trap so lethal. He could never end her life that way.

Grandpa walked cautiously to the pit he and Walter had secretly dug six weeks earlier. Gripping the strap of his backpack, he peered over the edge.

Charlie stared up at him. Flat on his back, arms splayed out to both sides, and out of breath.

Grandpa stepped back and knelt down, unzipping his backpack. He removed an eight-by-eight-foot plastic tarp and four wooden stakes. Grabbing ahold of it, he fluffed it in the air like a bed sheet before laying it over the pit.

"Grandpa? What the fuck is going on??" Charlie could barely speak, now standing up in the pit.

Grandpa said nothing and quickly removed the hammer from his backpack. He pounded a stake into three corners of the tarp, leaving one corner of the pit exposed. He knelt next to the pit and looked down to the bottom. The hand axe came flying out, barely missing his head.

"You fucking cocksucker!!" Charlie shouted. "I should have split your head with the axe when you were filling the canteen."

Grandpa dragged his backpack close to him and removed the balloon filled with 10 grams of potassium cyanide along with the pint mason jar half filled with sulfuric acid. He continued to talk as he prepared to mix the two chemicals together.

"When the gas starts forming, you'll want to take deep breaths. Don't fight it and try to hold your breath. A couple of deep breaths and you'll fall asleep.

"I always knew this day would come. It kills me to do this, but it's got to be done."

A soft voice rose from the pit. "Grandpa, I understand."

Grandpa no longer looked down into the pit. He knew the length of twine needed to dangle the jar just out of reach. He opened the pint of sulfuric acid and dropped the balloon in.

He quickly replaced the lid with the one he had drilled holes through. Grandpa lowered the jar into the pit and tied it off. He then pounded the last stake through the corner of the tarp, trapping the gas, then walked away.

By the time Grandpa returned with the first wheelbarrow of dirt, Charlotte and Charlie were gone. He removed the stakes from the corners of the tarp and let it drop in. He then tossed in the hand axe which landed very near the center, close to where the body lay.

It would be hours before he could fill the pit, and this time, he didn't have his nephew Walter to lend a hand. Adjusting the headlamp securely, he steeled himself for the long task ahead and carried on.

****

Stacey turned the key to her communal mailbox and grabbed her mail. As she scanned each piece one at a time, she saw various letters of different sizes along with flyers with pictures of burgers and pizza and sales for garage doors and new gutters.

One piece of mail caught her attention. She noticed the red letters of FIRST-CLASS MAIL on a cream-colored envelope and looked at the return address. She strolled back to her condo and into the kitchen where she took a knife and slid it through the envelope opening it. A smile formed on her face as she read.

Ms. Carly Lynn Fletcher and Mr. David Nathan Farris request the honor of your presence at their marriage, Saturday, the twenty-seventh of August 2022 at four o'clock at
  Christ Church, Livingston, Michigan.

Stacey secured the invitation on the fridge with a magnet. She stared at the elegant script and reflected on it. The upcoming wedding would be a chance to reconnect with Carly and David and celebrate the love that had kept them together through the most terrible of times. She would not pass up the opportunity for this reunion with the person who meant the world to her. The one she called her "little sister."

In her thoughts, Stacey imagined the warmth of their hugs, the catching up they would have, and the dancing to the band. This time, no one or nothing would be there to stop it.

About the Author

James T. Byrnes was born in Detroit Michigan. He enlisted in the Marine Corp in 1977. He graduated from Oakland University in 1984 and taught for 30 years. He and his wife have two sons, a daughter-in-law and three grandchildren. Burying The Shadow is his second novel.

www.byrnesgroup.net
Facebook.com/JamesByrnes
jamesbyrnes@byrnesgroup.net

Book Club Discussion Questions can be downloaded at
www.byrnesgroup.net